Praise for the Previous Volumes of
Nebula Awards Showcase

"Would serve well as a one-volume text for a course in contemporary science fiction."
—*The New York Review of Science Fiction*

"Reading all of *Nebula Awards Showcase 2002* is a way of reading a bunch of good stories. It is also a very good way to explore the writing of tomorrow." —John Clute, SciFi.com

"Conveys a sense of the vitality and excitement that have characterized the field's internal dialogues and debate over the last few years. One of the most entertaining Nebula volumes in years." —*Locus*

"The vast majority of the stories included are simply wonderful, and absolutely deserve recognition. . . . Bottom line: This year's *Nebula Showcase* actually succeeds in showcasing a great variety of truly good work. Read it now."
—InterGalactic Medicine Show

"The annual *Nebula Awards Showcase* anthologies always have something interesting to offer up. . . . There are plenty of solid, entertaining pieces in this anthology." —*Subterranean*

continued . . .

NEBULA AWARDS®

SHOWCASE

2010

THE YEAR'S BEST SF AND FANTASY

Selected by the Science Fiction and
Fantasy Writers of America®

EDITED BY

Bill Fawcett

A ROC BOOK

ROC
Published by New American Library,
a division of Penguin Group (USA) Inc.,
375 Hudson Street, New York, New York 10014, USA
Penguin Group (Canada), 90 Eglinton Avenue East, Suite 700, Toronto,
Ontario M4P 2Y3, Canada (a division of Pearson Penguin Canada Inc.)
Penguin Books Ltd., 80 Strand, London WC2R 0RL, England
Penguin Ireland, 25 St. Stephen's Green, Dublin 2,
Ireland (a division of Penguin Books Ltd.)
Penguin Group (Australia), 250 Camberwell Road, Camberwell,
Victoria 3124, Australia (a division of Pearson Australia Group Pty. Ltd.)
Penguin Books India Pvt. Ltd., 11 Community Centre,
Panchsheel Park, New Delhi - 110 017, India
Penguin Group (NZ), 67 Apollo Drive, Rosedale, North Shore 0632,
New Zealand (a division of Pearson New Zealand Ltd.)
Penguin Books (South Africa) (Pty.) Ltd., 24 Sturdee Avenue,
Rosebank, Johannesburg 2196, South Africa

Penguin Books Ltd., Registered Offices:
80 Strand, London WC2R 0RL, England

First published by Roc, an imprint of New American Library,
a division of Penguin Group (USA) Inc.

First Printing, April 2010
1 3 5 7 9 10 8 6 4 2

Copyright © Science Fiction and Fantasy Writers of America, 2010
Additional author copyrights and permissions can be found on pages 419–20.
All rights reserved

 REGISTERED TRADEMARK—MARCA REGISTRADA

Set in Bembo
Designed by Elke Sigal

Printed in the United States of America

CONTENTS

CONTENTS

NEBULA
AWARDS®
SHOWCASE

2010

BILL FAWCETT

Welcome.

Putting together the Nebula Award anthology is an activity that has been rather thought-provoking. Looking at the amazing list of past, and reading the current, winners has made me think back to a life spent reading and working with Science Fiction and Fantasy. A personal history that begins as a very young boy under a shade tree struggling to learn to read with *Tom Swift* books and growing up following and then creating in what has become a media-conquering genre. You can't turn on the television without finding a ghost, alien, or advanced technology on the screen, and those are the reality shows. Science Fiction has sure come a long way.

In this Nebula Awards anthology we take a look at the long and starlit road. Included among the stories of this anthology are a number of articles in which we take a look back at the evolution of Science Fiction writing, mostly as seen on a very personal level, over the last century. Each of these articles covers a decade or era in the history of SF.

Fortunately many of them are written by the very authors who wrote and shaped the genre during that time. So, among them you will find the esteemed and prolific Robert Silverberg telling you about the fifties and Lynn Abbey explaining the explosion of shared-world anthologies in the eighties.

This collection also has the privilege of including along with all four Nebula Award–winning works an excerpt from the Andre

Norton Award winner's novel, the amazingly creative Joss Whedon's acceptance speech for the Bradbury Award, and more SF insights from the three esteemed winners of the Solstice Award that is now given for Service to the Science Fiction community. Finally, we feature at the end a short story by Grand Master Harry Harrison that is introduced by TOR publisher Tom Doherty.

A few themes stand out when you look at the field of Science Fiction as a whole. Subject always to exceptions that are numerous because that is the nature of SF itself, to be the exception and outside the box, the unexpected and the new. But over time one thing has begun to stand out to me when reading, sitting on a panel at a SF convention, or even just chatting with a few other writers and fans by e-mail.

After half a century in the field I have come to a startling conclusion that explains not only the still growing and continuing popularity of what we read and write, but why so many of the people who do one or both are someone you want to meet at a convention. We Science Fiction writers and readers are optimists. Yep, positively Pollyanna-like, even the darkest of us, even Harlan Ellison. This is the case whether you write fantasy or more traditional Science Fiction. Why, simply put, Science Fiction assumes there will be a future.

From the books of Jules Verne to *WALL-E* mankind survives, reaches the stars, and prevails, or at least survives and will prevail in the sequel. We all assume that man will travel someday to the stars. Some of us even work towards that with NASA or other organizations, but we all start with the idea that the human race will prevail, will not blunder and fall into darkness (at least not permanently), and will eventually reach some higher destiny. That is optimism, that is the positive attitude that underlies *Star Trek, Stargate, Star Wars*, and the other mass media successes. It is part of their appeal. Even in the darkest tale of Science Fiction futures always end with hope. One of the first and darkest SF disaster novels, Wells' *The Time Machine,* ends with the new mankind beginning to progress again with the Morlocks defeated.

There was, in the sixties, a group of post-holocaust novels, mostly set after a massive atomic war. That is a scenario that is about as dark as you can conjure up. One that was very real, and still is, for those of us who were taught to "duck and cover" in grade school. Among them you find novels set after the holocaust such as *A Canticle for Leibowitz* and *A Boy and His Dog* and again everything has gone wrong and nuclear war just about destroyed civilization, but mankind survives and begins once more to triumph. *On the Beach* is the exception here, and it really is about the human spirit prevailing even in the face of total doom. In the backstory for *Star Trek* you have the Vulcans landing not long after Earth has suffered a nuclear disaster so traumatic that it changed the world views of the survivors in very positive ways. Even those very dark *Mad Max* movies always end with us being told the race survived and has begun again to move forward. Optimism. We SF types are by genre and nature optimists. Individually we can be occasionally cantankerous, feel the same day-to-day pressures as mundane, and many of us are fairly sure the publishing industry is doomed. But still we write about the future from the assumption that there will be a future. And an interesting future at that. Shared optimism is part of why SF readers and writers are fun to be with, interesting, and our gatherings are so famously open and welcoming.

So welcome to the Nebula Awards Showcase, my fellow optimists. Join us where mankind has a long and interesting future, where human nature can overcome demons and dark spells, and we even have a few laughs along the way.

SFWA is a nonprofit organization of professional writers of science fiction, fantasy, and related genres. Founded in 1965 by Damon Knight, the organization now includes over 1500 speculative authors, artists, editors, and allied professionals. SFWA presents the prestigious Nebula Awards, assists members in legal disputes with publishers, and hosts the well-known Writer Beware Web site. SFWA administers a number of benevolent funds, including the Emergency Medical Fund, the Legal Fund, and a Literacy Fund intended to encourage genre reading and literacy in general. Online discussion forums, member directories, and private convention suites help its members keep in touch with each other and stay abreast of new developments in the field.

Since 1965, the Nebula Awards have been presented yearly for the best works of science fiction or fantasy published in the United States. The winners are chosen by a vote of the active members of SFWA; awards are made in the categories of novel, novella, novelette, short story, and script. The award itself was originally designed by Judy Blish. Over the years additional awards are now presented at the Nebula Awards ceremony honoring those who have contributed to science fiction and fantasy in other ways. These include such awards as Grand Master, Solstice, and Author Emeritus. The winning shorter fiction is published annually in volumes like this, the *Nebula Awards Showcase*.

NOVELS

Little Brother | Cory Doctorow Tor Books, *April 2008*

Powers | Ursula K. Le Guin Harcourt, Inc., *September 2008*

Cauldron | Jack McDevitt Ace Books, *November 2007*

Brasyl | Ian McDonald Pyr, *May 2007*

Superpowers | David J. Schwartz Three Rivers Press, *June 2008*

NOVELLAS

The Spacetime Pool | Catherine Asaro *Analog Science Fiction and Fact, March 2008*

Dark Heaven | Gregory Benford *Alien Crimes*, ed. Mike Resnick, Science Fiction Book Club, *January 2007*

Dangerous Space | Kelley Eskridge *Dangerous Space*, Aqueduct Press, *June 2007*

The Political Prisoner | Charles Coleman Finlay *Magazine of Fantasy and Science Fiction, August 2008*

The Duke in His Castle | Vera Nazarian Norilana Books, *June 2008*

NOVELETTES

"If Angels Fight" | Richard Bowes *Magazine of Fantasy and Science Fiction, February 2008*

"The Ray-Gun: A Love Story" | James Alan Gardner *Asimov's Science Fiction, February 2008*

"Dark Rooms" | Lisa Goldstein *Asimov's Science Fiction*, *October/November 2007*

"Pride and Prometheus" | John Kessel *Magazine of Fantasy and Science Fiction, January 2008*

"Night Wind" | Mary Rosenblum *Lace and Blade*, ed. Deborah J. Ross, Norilana Books, *February 2008*

"Baby Doll" | Johanna Sinisalo Translated from the Finnish by David Hackston *The SFWA European Hall of Fame*, ed. James Morrow & Kathryn Morrow, Tor Books, *June 2007*

"Kaleidoscope" | K. D. Wentworth *Magazine of Fantasy and Science Fiction, May 2007*

SHORT STORIES

"The Button Bin" | Mike Allen *Helix: A Speculative Fiction Quarterly*, *October 2007*

"The Dreaming Wind" | Jeffrey Ford *The Coyote Road: Trickster Tales*, ed. Ellen Datlow and Terri Windling, Viking Press, *July 2007*

"Trophy Wives" | Nina Kiriki Hoffman *Fellowship Fantastic*, ed. Martin H. Greenberg and Kerrie Hughes, DAW Books, *January 2008*

"26 Monkeys, Also the Abyss" | Kij Johnson *Asimov's Science Fiction, July 2008*

"The Tomb Wife" | Gwyneth Jones *Magazine of Fantasy and Science Fiction, August 2007*

"Don't Stop" | James Patrick Kelly *Asimov's Science Fiction, June 2007*

"Mars: A Traveler's Guide" | Ruth Nestvold *Magazine of Fantasy and Science Fiction, January 2008*

SCRIPTS

The Dark Knight | Jonathan Nolan, Christopher Nolan, David S. Goyer Warner Bros., *July 2008*

WALL-E | Andrew Stanton, Jim Reardon Original story

by Andrew Stanton, Pete Docter Walt Disney, *June 2008*

The Shrine | Brad Wright Stargate Atlantis, *August 2008*

THE ANDRE NORTON AWARD

Graceling | Kristin Cashore Harcourt, *October 2008*

Lamplighter | D.M. Cornish Monster Blood Tattoo, Book 2 Putnam Juvenile, *May 2008*

Savvy | Ingrid Law Dial, *May 2008*

The Adoration of Jenna Fox | Mary E. Pearson Henry Holt and Company, *April 2008*

Flora's Dare: How a Girl of Spirit Gambles All to Expand Her Vocabulary, Confront a Bouncing Boy Terror, and Try to Save Califa from a Shaky Doom (Despite Being Confined to Her Room) | Ysabeau S. Wilce Harcourt, *September 2008*

BEST NOVEL

Powers by Ursula K. Le Guin

BEST NOVELLA

The Spacetime Pool by Catherine Asaro

BEST NOVELETTE

"Pride and Prometheus" by John Kessel

BEST SHORT STORY

"Trophy Wives" by Nina Kiriki Hoffman

BEST SCRIPT

WALL-E Screenplay by Andrew Stanton, Jim Reardon,
Original story by Andrew Stanton, Pete Docter

ANDRE NORTON AWARD

*Flora's Dare: How a Girl of Spirit Gambles All to
Expand Her Vocabulary, Confront a Bouncing Boy Terror, and Try
to Save Califa from a Shaky Doom (Despite Being Confined
to Her Room)* by Ysabeau S. Wilce

ALGIS BUDRYS   SOLSTICE AWARD

M. J. ENGH   AUTHOR EMERITA

MARTY GREENBERG   SOLSTICE AWARD

HARRY HARRISON   DAMON KNIGHT
MEMORIAL GRAND MASTER

JOSS WHEDON   RAY BRADBURY AWARD

KATE WILHELM   SOLSTICE AWARD

EARLY SF IN THE PULP MAGAZINES

ROBERT WEINBERG

The pulp magazine was the invention of publisher Frank A. Munsey, who, in 1896, reasoned that readers were more interested in the content of a magazine than the quality of paper it was printed on. In December 1896, Munsey dropped the price of his all-fiction magazine, *Argosy*, from a quarter to a dime and changed the paper stock from glossy white finish to cheap wood pulp. Almost immediately, circulation doubled, and by 1905 had soared from selling 40,000 copies a month to ten times that number.

Argosy published a variety of popular fiction, ranging from short stories to complete novels to multipart serials. Adventure fiction of all types was the main thrust of the magazine, and there were no rules regarding content. So Frank Aubrey's novel, *A Queen of Atlantis*, appeared in *Argosy* for February through August 1899 and William Wallace Cook contributed "A Round Trip to the Year 2000" in the July through November 1903 issues. And there was more science fiction, much more, to follow.

In American publishing, success breeds competition. Thus it was with the pulp magazines. By 1910, Munsey was publishing a second magazine, *Munsey's,* modestly named after himself, and had announced a third, a weekly fiction magazine, titled *The All-Story*. Other publishers had their own cheap "wood-pulp paper" fiction magazines, soon nicknamed "pulps." *Adventure* began in 1910, and it was quickly followed by *Detective Story Magazine*. Pulps began to diversify in content and by 1930, more than a hundred different titles crowded the newsstands, with a combined circulation of over 50,000,000 copies.

Editor of *The All-Story* magazine was Bob Davis, who had worked for the Munsey chain for years. Davis understood the appeal of good science fiction, having bought George Allan England's *Darkness and Dawn* trilogy in 1908. The three novels told of a modern couple who fell into suspended animation; their awakening hundreds of years later in a long-abandoned New York City; and their search for civilization. The series was immensely popular and was reprinted complete in one thick hardcover soon after serialization. But even Davis couldn't predict the incredible success of his next science fiction discovery.

The serial, published in *The All-Story* from February to July 1912, was titled "Under the Moons of Mars," and the author, under a pen name, was Edgar Rice Burroughs. The story told of ex-soldier John Carter, who was magically transported to the planet Mars, where he discovered an ancient, dying civilization; barbaric green men with four arms; and a beautiful princess name Dejah Thoris. Fortunately, John Carter was one of Earth's greatest swordsmen.

Carter and "Mars" was a tremendous hit and the Age of the Scientific Romance was born. A year later, Burroughs cemented his place as the world's most popular pulp author with the publication of *Tarzan of the Apes* complete in the October 1912 issue of *The All-Story* magazine. For the next quarter-century, much of science fiction consisted of vividly imagined adventure stories taking place on far worlds or among lost civilizations with noble heroes conquering savage hordes and winning beautiful princesses. It was all quite entertaining but not very deep.

Notable pioneers of the scientific romance included Ray Cummings, Ralph Milne Farley, and Abraham Merritt. Cummings' first story, "The Girl in the Golden Atom," popularized the concept of atoms resembling miniature solar systems and advanced civilizations living on electrons. A prolific author, Cummings moved effortlessly from the Munsey pulps to the early science fiction magazines.

Ralph Milne Farley wrote a series of immensely popular novels featuring Myles Cabot, *The Radio Man*. A scientist sent via "radio waves" to the planet Venus, Cabot battled giant intelligent ants and rescued the inevitable beautiful princess. In the 1930s, Farley wrote *The Radio Flyers* and *The Radio Gunrunners*, although neither novel took place on Venus or involved Myles Cabot.

Abraham Merritt was perhaps the only writer of fantastic fiction whose popularity rivaled that of Edgar Rice Burroughs. Merritt wrote lost-race novels filled with exotic crumbling civilizations and near-magical super science. His heroines were not only beautiful but sensual, a remarkable achievement in otherwise prudish pulp magazines. A master of purple prose, Merritt created some of the most memorable villains in the pulps, ranging from Nimir, a gigantic stone face that dripped tears of gold, to Khalk'ru, an octopoid monster-god from another dimension that fed on human souls. Except for two short stories, all of Merritt's fiction appeared in the Munsey pulps.

Along with Frank A. Munsey and Edgar Rice Burroughs, a third figure important to the development of pulp science fiction was Hugo Gernsback. An immigrant from Luxembourg, Gernsback started the world's first mail-order business selling radio parts. By 1908, his catalog had evolved into the first real magazine about electronics and radio, *Modern Electrics*. In 1911, Gernsback serialized his magnum opus, a science fiction novel, *Ralph 124C41+,* in *Modern Electrics*. In the story, Gernsback made numerous predictions about future inventions, including a description and diagram of radar, a quarter-century before its actual appearance. In 1913, Gernsback began publishing *Electrical Experimenter* magazine, which in 1920 evolved into *Science & Invention*. The magazine ran one science fiction story per issue, with art done by Frank R. Paul, an architectural artist discovered some

years earlier by Gernsback. The August 1923 issue of *Science &
Invention* was dubbed "the scientifiction issue" and featured sev-
eral science fiction short stories and serials, along with a space-
suited man on the cover. The issue served as a trial balloon for
Amazing Stories, the first all science fiction magazine, which
Gernsback launched in April 1926.

The new magazine was a major success even though during
its first two years Gernsback filled the issues mostly with reprints
of stories by H. G. Wells and Jules Verne. Slowly, ever slowly,
Amazing began to print new material. However, it wasn't till
his magazine published "The Skylark of Space" by E. E. Smith,
Ph.D., that *Amazing* reached for the stars.

Dr. Smith wrote "space operas" filled with smart heroes,
beautiful heroines, evil villains, and lots of spaceships. More important, Smith's stories soared to distant planets, far outside the
solar system. He was the author credited with opening the universe for science fiction.

The success of *Amazing* led to competition. Clayton Magazines began publishing *Astounding Stories* in January 1930 and
attracted top authors with their word rate of two cents a word,
three or four times better than what Gernsback offered. When
Gernsback lost control of *Amazing Stories* in 1929, he immediately started two other SF pulps, *Air Wonder Stories* and *Science
Wonder Stories*. Notable authors working for the early SF pulps
included John W. Campbell Jr., Nat Schachner, John Taine, and
Murray Leinster. All survived to contribute to the onrushing
"Golden Age" of SF. Unfortunately, Stanley Weinbaum did not.

Weinbaum's first story, "A Martian Odyssey," was published
in *Wonder Stories* for July 1934. The story, which told of a trek
across the surface of Mars by a human astronaut accompanied by
Tweel, an intelligent ostrichlike Martian, was written with style,
grace, and humor. The aliens encountered on Mars were truly
alien, and Tweel was a believable but definitely nonhuman character. Weinbaum was hailed as the first science fiction writer to
write literate, intelligent science fiction. For the next two years,

Weinbaum stories, each as good as the one before, poured from the writer's typewriter in Milwaukee and into the pages of *Wonder Stories* and *Astounding Stories*. And then there was nothing.

Stanley Weinbaum died in surgery on December 14, 1935.

Childhood days were over. It was time for science fiction to grow up.

THE SPACETIME POOL

CATHERINE ASARO

This is the second time Catherine Asaro has won a Nebula Award. The first was for her novel *Quantum Rose*. A
dancer, Harvard Ph.D., and endlessly creative, Catherine
combines physics and just about everything else in her
many books and stories. She is always testing the boundaries in her writing and her winning novella, *The Spacetime Pool*, is no exception.

I
APPALACHIA

The hiker vanished.

Janelle peered at the distant hill. She could have sworn
a person had appeared there—and disappeared just as fast.
Perhaps it was a trick of the wind. The rhododendron bushes
on the hillside where she sat undulated in the breezes like a dark
ocean frothed with purple flowers, and a hum of cicadas filled the
air. The Great Smoky Mountains rose in the distance, green and
gray against a late afternoon sky as blue as a cerulean glaze.

She shifted her weight uneasily, wondering if she should have
come out here alone. Her hair blew across her face in a swirl that
reminded her of yellow corn in the fields back home. The breeze
whispered against her arms and rippled the summer dress she had
worn instead of sensible hiking clothes. Right now she probably
resembled some forest creature more than a new college graduate.

She smiled at the image that conjured up: Janelle the wild-woman stalking into math class, strewing leaves and equations. Then her disquiet returned, like a hawk gliding in the sky, circling a rabbit, ready to plunge.

"Oh, stop," she muttered, annoyed at herself. She pulled her hair out of her face. Birds wheeled above the figure on the next ridge—

Someone *was* there. She strained to see better. A man was standing on that hill with his back to her. As she rose to her feet, he turned in her direction.

Then he compressed into a line and vanished.

Whoa. Janelle squinted at the hill. She must have mistaken whatever she had seen. She had no wish to share her solitude, but curiosity tugged at her. She hiked up the hill, headed back to the trail, uncertain whether to investigate the vanished fellow or return to her car. Although it would take thirty minutes to reach the parking lot, she should probably go back; the afternoon had cooled as it aged, and her flimsy dress couldn't stave off the chill. Seeking an escape from her hectic life, she had left her cell phone and purse in the car, taking nothing more than her keys.

The leafy canopy of an old growth forest arched above her. Wood chips crackled under her feet, and a red squirrel skittered up the trunk of a basswood. Stretching out her arms, she turned in a circle, her eyes closed. Sweet blazes, she loved these mountains. Laughing, she opened her eyes. Life was good. She had finished her math degree at MIT just a few days ago, and it felt great.

Like a shift in a sea current, her mood changed. She had no one to share her happiness. It had been two years since her father's assassination in Spain. Her mother and brother had unexpectedly joined him for lunch that day, and the explosion that destroyed his car had taken them as well, her entire family. Even now, the pain felt raw.

Janelle inhaled deeply. She would survive this moment, as she had all the others, until the grief became bearable.

"Janelle?" a voice asked.

What the . . . ? She whirled around.

A man stood several paces away. He resembled the figure from the hill, though she hadn't seen him well enough to be sure this was the same person. She stepped back. He had only said her name, but given that they had never met, that was plenty to make her nervous.

His presence did nothing to allay her unease. He was too tall, maybe six foot six, with a muscular physique that reminded her of her vulnerability. His clothing was strange. She had nothing against unconventional self-expression, but in some subtle way, this went beyond that. The blue of his shirt vibrated in the shadowed forest, as vivid as an ocean where sunlight slanted through the water. His black pants were tucked into black boots. Silver links set with abalone gleamed on his shirt cuffs and in the silver chain around his neck. Well-trimmed hair brushed his shoulders, glossy and black. It wasn't the length that surprised her, but the gray at the temples. Although obviously hale and fit, he seemed rather old to adopt such styles. Then again, just because she knew no one his age who made such fashion statements, that didn't mean it never happened.

What compelled her the most, though, was his face. His high cheekbones and strong nose, and the dark brows arching above his gray eyes, made her think of a senator in the Roman Empire. He projected a sense of contained force.

Then she saw what hung from his belt. Ah, hell. *Dagger* was too tame a word. The sheath for the knife stretched as long as her forearm.

"I didn't mean to startle you." His gravelly voice had an unfamiliar accent, harsh and throaty. "You are Janelle Aulair, aren't you?"

She stood poised to run. "Why do you want to know?"

"I was sent to look for you."

With relief, she realized what must have happened. Ben, the grocer in town, had sent him to check on her. Ben always worried when she came up here alone. The last time he had sent his sister and brother-in-law, and they had startled her the same way.

"Have we met?" she asked. "At Ben's?" She thought she would remember someone so striking, but maybe not.

"Never," he said. Then he added, "Destiny requires your presence," as if that explained something.

Destiny indeed. She should get back to her car. He hadn't threatened her, but if that changed, she could surely outrun someone his age. She stepped to the side—

"No, wait!" he said, lunging forward.

Startled, she jumped away—

Darkness enveloped Janelle, muffled and cold. Muted voices echoed, calling, fading. Then the light brightened. She stumbled on the sand and barely caught her balance.

Sand?

She looked up—and froze.

II
THE RIEMANN GATE

A white beach stretched around her, dazzling in the bright day. Waves crashed a few yards away, and their swells glinted in the slanting rays from the Sun, which was low in the sky. The ocean stretched to the horizon, wide, blue, and endless.

"What the blazes?" Janelle spun around—in time to see the man appear out of thin air.

He came out of nothing, taking a long, slow step. His progress was slowed to a surreal speed, and his body flickered as if he were a projection of light. It *couldn't* be real. He had to be doing this with mirrors. Either that, or she had overworked herself in school more than she realized, and her mind was lodging a protest by wigging out.

The man solidified. For a moment he just stood, focusing on her. He seemed as disoriented as she felt. The large tendons in his neck corded under the chain he wore, and the Sun caught gleams from the abalone. The metal looked like real silver. The contrast of his powerful build and the jewelry unsettled her; no one she knew wore such items, let alone a man this daunting. It wasn't right or wrong, just eerily different.

"Are you all right?" he asked.

What a question. Her heart rate had ratcheted up and her head was swimming. "Is this a movie set?" If he had equipment to create this illusion, she should have seen it, but she grasped at the possibility like a swimmer clutching at driftwood in the ocean.

"A moving set? No." He rested his hand on the hilt of his knife and scanned the area. "Did anyone see you?"

She glanced at the knife, then at his face. "I don't want trouble."

"Nor do I." He stepped toward her. "We shouldn't stay here."

She stepped back. "Why? Where is this? What happened to the mountains?"

He spoke carefully, as if she were breakable and his words were hammers. "They are elsewhere." He indicated a line of straggly trees up the beach, where the sand met a sparse forest. "We must go. We will be safer if we aren't in plain view."

"Safer from what?" She wasn't going anywhere with him.

"Raiders." He scanned the beach, poised as if he were ready to fight. Wind blew his hair back from his face, accenting his prominent nose and strong chin. His profile looked like it belonged on a coin. "We must leave before they come."

"I'll just go home," she said.

He turned toward her and she was acutely aware of his height. Large men rattled her. They lived in another dimension, one where you could use the top of bookcases and see over the heads of a crowd. They loomed, and he was doing it much too well.

"I'm not sure you can," he said. "This last time, I barely made it through before the gate closed."

"What gate?" Sweat was gathering on her palms. "Who *are* you?"

"You may call me Dominick."

"What do you want with me, Dominick?"

"You are part of a prophecy," he said, as if that were a perfectly reasonable statement. "Before my brother or I was born, it was foretold that whichever of us married you would kill the other."

Marriage and murder. Right. She should have listened to Ben and not gone hiking alone. "Don't play with me." Her voice cracked on the last word.

His strong features softened unexpectedly. "I am sorry. I didn't really expect the gate to open."

"My friends are waiting for me." She was talking too fast. "If I don't show up, they'll phone the police." In truth, no one expected her for days. But he didn't know that. She hoped.

"I don't know what is phone," he said. "But we *must* go." He strode forward.

As Janelle whirled to run, the sand shifted under her feet and she tripped. Dominick easily caught her. Twisting in his grip, she raked his arm with her fingernails, and the two of them nearly fell into the sand. He ended up swinging her in a circle with one arm around her waist. He wrapped the other arm around her torso, pinning her while he bent over to hold her in place. He felt as if he were built from iron. She struggled, and he tightened his hold.

"Janelle, listen." He spoke urgently. "I won't hurt you. But if we stay here, we could be killed. Outlaws have been raiding homesteads in this area. You're a beautiful woman. If they find you with no defense except me, you would be in far worse trouble than you think I might cause you. And I would be dead."

She didn't want to listen. But she had to do something. What if he was telling the truth? What if he *wasn't*? If she made the wrong choice, could one or both of them end up dead?

"Janelle?" he asked.

She took a deep breath. "All right." For now.

He released her, then grasped her upper arm and set off for the trees. She had to run to keep up with his long-legged stride. So much for her assumption that age would slow him down; he could easily outrun her. His large hand engulfed her arm. His grip could have bruised, but he didn't let it. The contrast between the contained violence of his personality and his careful touch confused her.

The fine-grained sand showed little trace of their progress. They soon reached the forest and strode under its sparse cover. He kept up the grueling pace as they plunged into the deepening woods, until a stitch burned in her side.

Dominick angled through a tangle of bushes into a denser knot of trees. As they pushed through the bushes, he used his knife to cut away branches. The thicker foliage screened them from view, but it wasn't until they reached the center of the glade that he slowed down. He motioned her toward a boulder that jutted up to about waist height. Sitting on another, he planted his boots on the ground, braced his palms on his knees, and heaved in large breaths. Janelle stayed on her feet, too nervous to sit as she struggled to catch her wind.

"We can rest here," he said as his breathing settled.

She rubbed her arms, feeling cold despite the heat. It was much warmer than in the Smoky Mountains, and she didn't want to dwell on the implications of that fact. "I don't understand how you know me."

"Only through the prophecy." He watched her as if she were the apparition rather than this entire place. "I didn't really expect to find you."

"How do you know I'm the right person?"

"You look like the vision in the Jade Pool. It's near a mountain lodge where my father took his seeress." Sarcasm edged his voice. "Apparently she made better predictions when she was alone with him in secluded retreats."

From his tone, she suspected he had been painfully aware in his childhood of his father's involvement with his "seeress." Choosing tact, she said only, "What did she predict?"

"Just days before my mother gave birth for the first time, she showed my father a vision of you. She said Maximillian and I would be his oldest sons, that whichever of us married you would kill the other, and that if either of us tried to kill you, that brother would die."

"That's horrible."

Dryly he said, "My parents weren't delighted with it." He studied her face. "The scribes copied your image from the pool. But you are much younger than the woman in those portraits."

"I doubt they were pictures of me."

"It's more than appearance," he said. "The gate was supposed to bring me to you. It took me three tries to get it right, but it did work. And the seeress knew your name. Janelle Aulair."

"You could have looked me up on the Internet."

"What is the Internet?"

Like he didn't know. Maybe next he would try to sell her swampland in Florida. "It's not important. Just tell me how to get back home."

He dropped his hand to his belt and set his palm over a disk. It differed from the abalone circles; this one had a metallic sheen. He stared at the ground, his gaze unfocused.

"Dominick?" she asked.

He looked up at her. "The gate doesn't open."

She pushed back her growing fear. "That's convenient."

"It's true." He ran his fingers over the disk. "Do you feel anything?"

"Nothing."

"I'm trying to create the gate where you're standing."

She didn't know what to think. "How did you learn to use it?"

"One of the monks told me."

Right. Monks, too. "How did he find out?"

"I don't know."

"A description has to be somewhere. Books, files, storage."

He seemed oddly bewildered. "You mean a library?"

"Yes!" If they had web service there, she could email someone for help.

"I have one at my home," he said.

The last place she wanted to go was his house. "A public library would be better."

"I don't know what that is."

She couldn't believe him. That he sounded sane made none of this more plausible. "And you have no idea how this gate works?" she challenged.

His gaze flashed. "Of course I do. It's a branch. From here to your mountains."

"A tree, you mean?"

"No. A branch cut to another page. Your universe is one sheet, mine is another."

She gaped at him. "Do you mean a *Riemann sheet*? A branch cut from one Riemann sheet to another?"

"That's right." He hesitated. "You know these words?"

She laughed unsteadily. "It's nonsense. Not the sheets, I mean, but they're just mathematical constructs! They don't actually exist. You can't physically go *through* a branch cut any more than you could step into a square root sign."

He was watching her with an expression that mirrored how she had felt when he told her about his prophecy. "I have no idea what you're talking about."

"Complex variable analysis." She felt as if she were in a play where she only knew part of the script. "A branch cut is like a slit in a sheet of paper. It opens onto another sheet. I suppose you could say the sheets are alternate universes. But they aren't real."

"They seem quite real," he said. "When you went through the gate, it threw off my calibration. I had set it to come out at my camp." More to himself than to her, he added, "I hadn't actually expected to *leave* the camp."

"Tell you what," Janelle said. "How about you and your brother find wives here? I'll just drop out of the picture." She thought of what he had said about his father. "Unless you're already married. Because if you're pulling this bit looking for some fun on the side, forget it."

"Neither Maximillian nor I is wed. I have had concubines, though not in some years."

"Concubines!"

He grinned. "You don't like that?"

Just like a guy, to be pleased because he thought she was jealous. "Oh, cut the sexist crap."

He had the audacity to look intrigued. "What does 'sexist' mean? Is it to do with love-making?"

"No. It means I should go back to Tennessee."

His voice softened. "This world would be much poorer, to lose such beauty as yours."

"Don't." For some reason, it angered her that he actually sounded sincere with that line. Or maybe the anger masked her fear. Right now, he could do whatever he wanted with her.

"Max wouldn't give you a choice." He was no longer smiling. "If not for the prophecy that we would die if we killed you, he would probably execute you on sight."

An unwelcome memory jumped into her mind: she had learned about the deaths of her family from the media. Someone with too much ambition or too little compassion had leaked the story, sensationalizing it as an "execution." Janelle had been visiting a girlfriend in Virginia during a school break, and the news had gone public even as government officials scrambled to find her.

Dominick spoke quietly. "Your face looks like a dark cloud passed over it."

She shook her head, unable to answer.

"I do regret all this." He stood up and lifted his hand, inviting her to leave the glade. "Are you rested enough to go on? Let me at least bring you to my home, as my honored guest."

Janelle didn't want to be his guest. But she was beginning to absorb that this might be real, and she doubted staying in the glade would help her escape.

The Sun was setting when they emerged from the screen of bushes. The world had darkened and blurred, as if they saw it through old glass on the seashore, brown and rounded by tumbling waves.

Dominick set off along a faint path scattered with leaves. They had only gone a few yards, though, when he turned to her and paused, listening. Then he spoke in an urgent whisper. *"Run."*

She took one look at his face—and broke into a sprint.

III
THE TRANSFORM PALACE

Janelle raced through the woods, and Dominick's boots thudded behind her. Then she tripped on a jutting rock, and he plowed into her. Holding on to her, he lurched past a tangle of wild berry bushes and fell behind a large boulder and the bushes. He twisted in midair and landed on his back, cushioning their fall so she came down on top of him. Her breath went out in a rush. It happened so fast, she had no time even to tense up.

For one second, he held her in a viselike embrace. Then he sat up fast, rolling her off his body and onto her stomach. She pushed up on her hands, but when he laid his palm on her back, she stopped with her head raised. He crouched next to her, his knife drawn, his head tilted as if he were listening to the distant waves. Her surge of adrenaline sharpened her hearing, and she caught the shushing of hooves on sand. Dominick raised his dagger in a single sure motion, the blade glinting in the last rays of the Sun.

Hooves stamped nearby. Janelle stayed silent, though surely they could hear the thud of her heart. Voices spoke in a patois of heavily accented English sprinkled with unfamiliar words. Straining to understand, she recognized they were talking about the "two on the beach," that they would finish off the man and take the girl. When she heard what they wanted to do with her, bile rose in her throat.

The voices moved away, until she heard only waves on the beach. Dominick spoke under his breath, no words she recognized, what sounded like an oath. She breathed out, aware of her rigid posture.

"I think we can go," he said in a low voice.

A reaction was setting in as Janelle comprehended she might truly be stranded in this violent place with no anchor except this stranger. "I can't," she whispered.

"It will work out." Despite his rough voice, he had a kind tone. "Come with me, Janelle. I will do well by you."

Get a grip, she told herself, and climbed to her feet. "I'm all right."

Standing with her, he inclined his head. He lifted his hand as if to touch her face, but when she tensed, he lowered his arm.

They set off again, and the ocean's mumble receded as they went deeper among the trees. The woods thickened into a heavy forest, and tufts of wild grass stuck up in the soil. Dusk came like a great beast, one barely noticed until it spread its wings, darkening every copse and glade. Luminescent bottle flies hummed among the trees.

Dominick drew her to a stop. Holding his fingers to his mouth, he gave a whistle that rose and fell in an eerie tune. A bird answered his call.

"Hai," a low voice said.

Janelle started. A man had appeared under a nearby tree. He wore leather armor and a dagger similar to Dominick's, but without the silver or abalone. He also had an "extra" that made her mouth go dry, a monstrous broadsword strapped across his back with its hilt sticking above his shoulders.

Dominick spoke in the same dialect used by the men who wanted to kill him. It sounded like "Hava moon strake camp," but she thought he meant, "Have the men strike camp." Although she didn't understand the other man's response, she saw the deference in his bow. The man glanced at her with curiosity, then withdrew into the trees and vanished as silently as he had come.

She and Dominick continued on, and although she saw no one else, she didn't think they were alone anymore. They soon entered a clearing of trampled grass. Several tents stood on the far side, and men moved in the trees beyond, soldiers it looked like, in leather armor. Most were tending animals. Their mounts resembled horses, but with tufts for tails. Each had two horns, one on either side of its head, with the tips pointing inward. Some of the men wore helmets with similar horns. The scene had a dreamlike quality, all in the dusk, with mist curling around the animals. But the cooling air on her arms and legs and the pungent smell of wet grass were all too real.

The men greeted Dominick with respect. Although Janelle had trouble deciphering their words, she understood their intent. They were preparing to leave.

And she was going with them.

Fog muffled the night. Janelle sat in front of Dominick on one of the two-horned animals, which he called a biaquine. Starlight, his mount, had a silver coat with stiff hair. He changed the animal's saddle to a tasseled blanket woven in heavy red and white yarn so Janelle could more easily sit with him. A few scouts went on ahead, but the rest of the men stayed together, with extra biaquines to carry the tents and other supplies.

Fear and curiosity warred within Janelle. She had agreed to go with Dominick because she saw no other viable choices, at least not where she stayed alive and healthy. But she didn't trust him.

They passed through veils of mist, climbing into the mountains. Her muscles ached from the unfamiliar ride. Moonlight lightened the fog, and she strove to keep track of landmarks that loomed out of the night: a gnarled tree with two trunks or a weathered statue of an elderly man in a niche of rock. Her ties to home were growing tenuous, unable to compete with the reality of this impossible place.

Dominick put his arms around her waist, so she didn't fall off the biaquine. At first she sat ramrod straight. Gradually, though, Starlight's rocking gait lulled her. Nor did Dominick act in any way to make her uncomfortable. She had forgotten how comforting it felt just to be held. Her mother had always been effusive with affection, and although her father had been less demonstrative, he had never let them doubt his love. She had grown up secure in those close-knit ties. One instant of violence had shattered everything. Drowning in grief, she had withdrawn from human contact; in the past two years she had barely touched another person.

Dominick had a strange request. He wanted a curl of her hair. When she agreed, he pulled out his dagger. She stiffened, her gaze riveted on the long blade as it glittered in the moonlight, but he only cut off a small tendril. He gave it to one of his riders, who carefully placed the strands in a packet of cloth. Then the man took off up the trail, galloping ahead of their party.

"What'll he do with it?" Janelle asked.

"My monks will examine it," Dominick said. "To see if you are who I think."

"How can they know from a lock of hair?"

"They have . . . spells."

"Spells?"

"Well," he amended, "so they say."

From his tone, she suspected he didn't believe it any more than she did. She just hoped his monks didn't decide her hair had demonic properties.

Exhaustion was catching up to her, but she feared to rest, dreading what she might find when she awoke. She had rarely slept enough during school, often studying late into the night. It paid off; she earned high marks, even the top grade in Mathematical Methods of Physics. Now her simple pleasure in a job well done seemed forlorn.

An owl hooted, its call muted by the fog. Janelle shuddered.

"Are you cold?" Dominick asked.

"I was thinking of home."

Regret softened the hard edges of his voice. "I am sorry about this." After a pause, he added, "But I would be lying if I denied I am glad you are here. I never really believed this would happen."

"Prophecies aren't real." She watched the biaquines plodding ahead of them on the trail. "A rational explanation has to exist."

"Truthfully?" he said. "I don't think the seeress made that prediction. It was Gregor, a monk from the monastery. He is the one who can read the Jade Pool." His voice tightened. "Father's soothsayer had never even been there before. She stayed at the palace."

"Palace?"

"Where my brother is."

"Does he work there?"

He gave a bitter laugh. "You could say that."

"What does he do?"

"He is the Emperor of Othman."

Good Lord. What had she landed in? "You're the brother of an emperor?"

"Yes." He said it simply, just verifying a fact. "He was born first."

If neither he nor his brother had married, that suggested neither had legitimate offspring. "Does that mean you're his heir?"

"For now. Until he sires one."

"Sweet blazes," she murmured. "I've never heard of Othman."

He swept out his hand as if to show her all of the land. "The provinces stretch from the snow fields in the far north to the great gulf in the south. Maximillian rules it, and I govern the Atlantic Province under him."

"The entire continent?" It sounded like Canada and North America.

"Only the eastern half. Britain has the rest." In a voice that sounded deceptively soft, he added, "For now."

A chill went through her. "And later?"

"That depends on what happens with Max."

From his tone, she suspected that if he ever became emperor, he would kick out the British and absorb their territories. What a strange history for the colonial revolution.

"Your brother is afraid you're after his throne," she said.

"Supposedly, whichever of us marries you will rule Othman."

"This is crazy. I have nothing to do with either of you."

"Not according to the seer."

Or the politicians, more likely. "Dominick, surely you see this so-called prophecy is a trick, one guaranteed to set you and your brother against each other. It's bunk."

"Bunk?"

"Lies. Moonshine."

"Moonshine." Wryly he added, "An apt image."

Janelle had used the word on instinct, and now she regretted it. It evoked sweetly faded memories of her southern childhood: grits, biscuits and gravy, and bluegrass music. Her family had later moved to Washington, D.C. and then Europe, but the girl who loved country ham and the unique twang of a steel guitar was still inside of her. Her memories glimmered of the golden hills she had wandered during late summer days, spinning the enchanted dreams of youth. She couldn't let herself think she might never again see them.

"I would agree it is 'moonshine,'" Dominick was saying, "except everything else in the prophecy has come true. It foretold the birth of eight children to my parents. Max and I have six siblings, and they fit every detail predicted." His breath condensed in the air, spuming past her. "Gregor gave my father a sealed letter, to be opened after Father's death. Father died of pneumonia ten years ago, three days after his sixtieth birthday. After the funeral, Maximillian opened the letter."

"What did it say?"

He answered quietly. "That my father would die of pneumonia three days after his sixtieth birthday."

She shivered. "That's eerie."

"Indeed."

"You and Maximillian can never trust each other."

"True. Not that I would trust him anyway."

"Why not?"

"He craves power."

She suspected that applied to Dominick as well. "Why are you so certain it's me in that prophecy? You've only seen drawings of an older woman."

"We will verify your signature."

"You've never seen me write, I'm sure."

"Not writing. It's hard to explain."

"Try."

He paused for a moment. "Your signature is inside your body. It has forty-six characters, half each from your father and mother. You can't see it, I think because it is too small." He nuzzled the top of her head. "It determines everything about you, from the color of your eyes to whether you are a man or a woman."

The touch of his lips on her hair startled Janelle. It was a simple gesture, but that just made it more intimate, as if they took such affections for granted. Attractive he might be, but he was too threatening. She started to tell him to stop, then froze as she realized what else he had said. The "signature" sounded like DNA. Based on what she had seen, she wouldn't have expected his people to know genetics at the molecular level needed to identify a person. Then she gave a frayed laugh. She didn't believe they understood DNA, but she accepted gates to other universes?

He lifted his head and spoke stiffly. "What is funny?"

Belatedly, she realized how her reaction must have sounded. "Dominick, I wasn't laughing at—" She foundered at the word "kiss," which felt much too awkward, and wasn't exactly what he had done, anyway. So she told another truth. "I'm tired. Nervous." Softly, she added, "Don't push."

He let out a breath. "It is my fault you were ill prepared. I wasn't ready, either. I had never before used the gate."

"You must have studied it." How else could he have found her?

He shook his head, or at least his hair rustled; seated in front of him, she couldn't see his face.

"I just use the tools Gregor gave me," he said.

"The disk on your belt."

"Yes. Except it no longer does anything."

"Maybe I can get it to work."

She expected him to refuse. Instead, he took his arm away from her waist, and she heard a click. Then he pressed a metal plate into her hand. It had a diameter the size of her palm and felt cool on her skin. No marks embellished its polished surface.

"How does it operate?" she asked.

"I rub it. Supposedly my finger ridges activate the spells."

Spells indeed. If his fingerprints operated the mechanism, it wouldn't work for her. When she rubbed the disk, nothing happened. "Should I touch it in any pattern?"

"Not that I know of."

"You said before that you calibrated it."

"Actually, Gregor did. He's secretive. He tells me nothing." Wryly he added, "I don't think he understands it, either." He guided Starlight around an outcropping, and the biaquine snorted as if to protest the inconvenience.

"What you said about 'sheets' earlier," Dominick said. "What did you mean?"

Janelle handed him back the disk. "It's kind of abstruse."

"Does that mean you don't know?"

"No," she growled. It was a fair question, though. "Imagine one Riemann sheet as my universe. It has a phase."

"Like the Moon."

"Not that." She paused, thinking. "Do you have clocks here?"

"Well, yes. Certainly."

"Twenty-four hours a day? Twelve and twelve again?"

"Of course."

It relieved her to have that much in common with him. "Think of the phase as time. Say it goes from midnight to noon in my universe." She almost said "like hands on an old-fashioned clock," but then realized analog timepieces might be the norm here.

"And my world is the second clock?" Dominick asked. "Time goes from noon to midnight here?"

"Yes!" It gratified her that he understood so fast.

"The time here and where I found you was the same."

"I know. I don't mean my world and yours are literally related by a twelve-hour difference. Just that they're in some way out of phase with each other, like three in the morning is different than three in the afternoon, even though they're called the same thing."

He was quiet for a while. Then he said, "So the branch cut to your universe is located at a certain phase. It's like saying the gate opens only at a certain time."

"That would be my guess."

"To go around this metaphorical clock and return to the branch cut must take longer than twelve hours. The disk never worked before."

"How long have you been trying?"

"About forty years. Since I was very small."

Forty! That wasn't what she wanted to hear. "Every *day*?"

"Well, no." He sounded embarrassed. "I should. Max does more than I do, and we've both tried more as we've grown older, with the pressure to settle this matter and produce heirs." He hesitated. "It just all seems so fanciful." Then he added, "Seemed."

She agreed. At least if he didn't always check, he could have missed the gate. She hoped that was why he hadn't found her before this. Or she could be wrong about the whole thing. "I need to read about the theory."

"Such studies are for monks." He sounded surprised.

Janelle had no objection to being considered monkish if it would get her home. What she lacked in savvy about this world she could make up for in her ability to solve problems. "Do you have books about the gates?"

"In my library."

"Maybe I can learn to make one." Or find a more logical explanation for all this.

"If it pleases you to look, you may."

She wondered if reading would be a problem. "But Dominick."

He bent his head, bringing his lips next to her ear. His breath tickled the sensitive skin there. "Hmmm?"

"Oh." She forgot what she had been about to say. His scent surrounded her, a combination of saffron, thyme, and sweat. She was suddenly conscious of how close they were sitting on the biaquine.

He spoke against her ear. "I like your hair. You look like a forest sprite." He brushed his lips across her cheek.

"Stop." She was almost stuttering.

He exhaled. But he lifted his head and straightened up. The night air cooled her cheek.

"What did you want to ask me?" he asked, more formally.

"Your speech." She wasn't certain what unsettled her more,

his kiss or that she had liked it. But he was going too fast. "When you speak to your men, you don't use English."

"Yes, I do."

"What do you call what we're speaking?"

"Erst. No one uses it anymore." His voice lightened. "As a youth I complained greatly about having to learn a dead language. I'm glad now I did."

"It's not dead to me." She hoped.

"Then I'm gratified I know it."

"Tell me something," she said. "Why didn't you expect to find me?"

"I guess I assumed that if you existed, it would lead naturally to your coming here. I didn't think it would happen by mistake, *only* because I looked for you."

She rubbed her eyes. "Talk about a self-fulfilling prophecy."

"Apparently so. We will have to marry as soon as possible."

"*What?*" He had just taken "too fast" to "light speed."

"My brother." Dominick paused as Starlight picked his way across a gully that cut across the trail. "If he finds out what happened, he will come to get you."

Janelle's head ached. "Let me see if I have this straight. If you and I marry, you become emperor and he dies. If I marry him, he stays emperor and *you* die. If either of you kills me, he dies."

"Unfortunately, yes."

"If no one marries me, do things stay as they are now?"

"I think so."

"The answer is simple, then. I go home."

"And after that?" he asked. "My men know about you. So will the monks who check your hair. If you are who I believe, how long before Max finds out? If you go home, he might find you someday. I did." Then he added, "That assumes you can go back."

"I have to believe it's possible."

"I understand. But as long you are here, I will risk neither my life nor yours."

Janelle wondered why she couldn't have normal problems, like fixing the plumbing or finding a job. "If we marry, won't your brother die?"

"I don't want his death."

"But you want his title."

"I would be a better emperor."

"Why?"

"Maximillian is brutal man."

"What makes you any different?"

He gave a terse laugh. "I can think of no one else who would dare ask me such a thing."

Well, tough. "It's a fair question. You two are brothers."

"Your questions are too personal."

She let out an exasperated breath. "You say we have to marry so you stay alive and I don't get brutalized. That's pretty personal."

Silence.

Janelle bit back her impatience. She knew too little about Dominick to judge when to push and when to bide her time. But push she would, if that was what it took to find her way home.

They rode for a while with only the thud of hooves on the trail to break the silence. But eventually he did answer. "My father raised my brother. He ignored me because I wasn't his heir. I spent my childhood with my mother. I had her love. Maximillian had whippings." Tension corded his muscles, and his hold tightened, though she didn't think he realized it. "Father intended to 'shape' Max into a man like himself. He succeeded. Max is exactly like him." Anger honed his voice. "My mother is dead. I couldn't protect her. But I won't let my brother do the same to you."

His words had so many painful implications, she hardly knew what to say. She spoke softly. "I'm sorry."

He clenched the reins so hard, his knuckles whitened. "Max

and I were close as boys. He has hardened over the years. I mourn the loss of the brother I loved, but I hate what he has become."

"It must be difficult for you both."

"You are generous, to offer sympathy to those who put you in this situation."

She had no answer for that.

"Janelle." He spoke thoughtfully. "Make a bargain with me."

"How do you mean?" she asked, wary.

"Marry me, and I will do what I can to help you return home. If you get back, who is to say the marriage exists in that universe? You can resume your life without me."

Given her lack of options, he could have demanded she do what he wanted. It mattered that he asked her consent and offered his help. But she knew too little about him. So far he had acted with honor, and a kindness incongruous with his obvious capacity for violence, but she had no guarantee that would continue. Nor did she doubt his offer came with strings; he wasn't talking about a marriage in name only. Her face heated. Yes, she found him attractive. But that wasn't enough. She needed to know him better. To trust him.

"I'm not ready," she said.

"We don't have the luxury of time. This is the best way I know to protect us both."

What to do? Given how little she knew about life here, going it alone didn't seem particularly bright. After a moment, she said, "All right. I accept your bargain."

It wasn't until his rigid hold eased that she realized how much he had stiffened. He said only, "Good," which relieved her. She wasn't ready for any heart-to-heart talks with the fiancé she had just acquired.

They rode higher into the mountains, and the fog thinned until they were traveling under a sky brilliant with stars, far more than she saw in the city of Cambridge where she lived. The day's warmth had fled. When Janelle shivered, Dominick reached to the bags he had slung over the flanks of his biaquine. He folded a sheepskin around her shoulders, with the fleecy side against her skin.

"Thank you," she murmured.

As they rode, Janelle mulled over his words. She couldn't fathom why she would figure in anyone's "prophecy." Her only talents were writing proofs and solving equations. She smiled wryly. Maybe she could subdue the nefarious Maximillian with Bessel functions.

Up ahead, peaks rose out of the fog, dark against the sky. Then she realized it was a cascade of onion-bulb towers, each topped by a spire. Dominick's party approached a cliff that stood about ten feet high—no, not a cliff, a great wall that curved away in either direction, topped by crenellations.

Eerie whistles broke the night's quiet as the biaquines gathered before the wall, stamping and snorting. A gate swung outward, huge and dark, groaning. Torchlight flickered beyond, where men were cranking giant wheels wound with rope as thick as their burly arms. Past the gate lay courtyards, and past them, a huge building surrounded by smaller structures. The layout resembled a European castle, but the architecture evoked the palaces of Moorish Andalusia that Janelle had visited when her family lived in Spain. Icy moonlight edged it all, turning the spires, domes, and delicate arches into frozen lace.

As much as the scene enthralled Janelle, it also bewildered her. Who had settled this land? Dominick's men spoke a dialect of English, but their names sounded Mediterranean, Arabic, or Near Eastern, with English more rarely in the mix. That described their appearance, too. Maybe the Ottoman Empire had spread farther across Europe in this universe. If East and West had blended more, the mix of colonists who settled the New World here could have been different than in her world.

They rode to a courtyard in front of the palace. An im-

mense horseshoe arch framed the entrance of the building like
the keyhole for a giant antique key. Its sides rose in pillars, and
at the top, an onion-shaped arch curved out and back around to
a point. Mosaics tiled the pillars and glistened like silver in the
moonlight.

As their party dismounted, stable-hands swirled around
them. The biaquines were taller than most horses, but Dominick
swung off with little effort. He reached up, offering his arms
to Janelle. She hesitated, staring at his harsh features, which
were blurred by moonlight and the hint of mist in the air. Then
she pulled her leg over and slid down. She ached everywhere.
He eased her to the ground, his hold solid after the swaying gait
of the biaquine.

The sheepskin had fallen off, and she shivered. Dominick
pulled her close, under a jacket he had donned earlier. It was fur
lined, not as warm as the skin, but soft and thick against her
arms. For just a moment, she gave in to her fatigue and buried
her face against his shirt as if that would hide her from his
world.

When she looked up again, Dominick brushed her hair back
from her face, and calluses on his palm scraped her cheek. She
wondered how he had developed them—and then remembered
the swords his men wore.

"Welcome to my home," he murmured. Then he bent his
head.

Janelle knew what he intended, but she froze, unable to believe he would go through with it. When he kissed her, his lips
felt as full as they looked, a sensual contrast to his harsh power.
She tensed, but before she could respond, someone behind them
coughed.

Dominick raised his head, letting go of her, and she turned
around, relieved by the interruption. A lanky man was coming
down the steps of the palace, his attempt not to stare at her all
the more obvious for its lack of success. He stopped next to

them and spoke with Dominick. Although Janelle couldn't catch all of their words, it sounded as if the man was reporting another raid. Dominick and his men had been out searching for the outlaws, intent on stopping the harassment of his people.

Dominick turned to Janelle. "I will see you later." He took off his jacket and wrapped it around her shoulders. His smile was crooked, almost boyish. "It looks much better on you than on me."

"Thank you," she said, uncertain how to act with him.

He climbed the steps with the other man, leaving her with two guards. She noted how easily Dominick assumed authority. He listened carefully and asked questions. When he gave orders, he did it with confidence and tact. She had seen those same qualities in the strongest leaders she had met while her father was the American Ambassador to Spain.

Bracketed by guards, she went up the steps, through a foyer, and into a hall gleaming in the light of torches carried by Dominick's men. Janelle's breath caught. Soaring arches filled the immense hall, row after row of them, a forest of pillars in perfect lines. Tessellated mosaics in gold, blue, and green curved around columns and patterned the vaulted ceiling. In each V-shape where the arches met, a stained-glass window glowed with gem colors, showing scenes similar to those of Catholic churches in Spain. It was like an exquisite blending of Moorish art with the styles of a European cathedral.

A group of men met Dominick just inside the entrance. Janelle's guards drew her to a stop. She just waited, too tired to deal with her confusion over what had happened with him in the courtyard. It had to be past two in the morning.

People came and went. It wasn't long before three women appeared, walking through the arches from deeper within the palace. Silk wrapped them from neck to ankle, glistening in the smoky torchlight, crimson and saffron, shot through with gold threads. Their shimmering dark hair fell to their waists.

The trio stopped in front of Janelle. The oldest woman, a

matron with silver hair, spoke in melodic phrases that almost sounded like English, but that went by too fast to catch.

"I'm sorry." Janelle's voice rasped with fatigue. "I don't understand."

The woman tried more slowly. "Come with us." She didn't smile. "To someplace you can wash. And sleep."

Relief washed over Janelle. "Thank you."

The woman just barely inclined her head, stiff and cool.

As Janelle set off with them, accompanied by her guards, she glanced back at Dominick. He remained deep in conversation with his men, and she wasn't certain he knew she had left.

The older woman spoke curtly. "His Highness has important matters to attend."

Janelle nodded, not wanting to interrupt his conference. They went down a "corridor" of arches, one of many in the hall, walkways delineated by columns instead of walls. It was dizzying, all that geometrical beauty gleaming in the torchlight.

The older woman was watching her face. "This hall is why Prince Dominick-Michael's home is called the Palaces of Arches."

"It's glorious," Janelle said. "Is this the Hall of Arches?"

"No. The Fourier Hall."

"Fourier?" She blinked. "Like the mathematician?"

The woman gave a sharp wave of her hand. "It has always been called this. That is all I know."

Janelle didn't push. Having lived as the child of a diplomat for so many years had taught her a great deal about dealing with cultures other than her own, and she could tell her interactions here were on shaky ground. She had discovered early on that if she wasn't certain how her words would be received, it was often better to say nothing.

She couldn't stop staring at the arches, though. What an exquisite challenge, to portray those graceful repeating patterns as a periodic function. Their Fourier transform would be a work of art. An unsteady urge to laugh hit her, followed by the desire to sit down and put her head in her hands. Such a strange thought, that she could capture in mathematics the essence of a dream palace that couldn't exist.

The women's slippered feet padded on the tiled floor, and Janelle's tennis shoes squeaked. At the back of the hall, they passed under a huge arch built from gold-veined marble rather than the wood used in the Fourier Hall. A true corridor lay beyond, with stone walls tiled in star mosaics. Its size dwarfed their party, and other halls intersected it at oddly sharp angles. The pillars at corners where the halls met were carved to portray men with great broadswords or women in elegantly draped robes holding long-stemmed flowers. It spoke to the European influence here that the designs included human statues, which weren't seen in Moorish architecture.

Janelle tried to keep track of their route through the maze of halls, but exhaustion dulled her mind. She was lost by the time they stopped at an oaken door. The guards stayed outside while the women took her into a small room. Plush rugs covered the floor, and mosaics with pink tulips and swirling green stems graced the lower half of the walls. Something odd about the stems tugged at her mind, but she was too tired to puzzle it out. In one corner, a white table supported a blue vase with real flowers. Blue velvet bedcovers lay in another corner, on a thicker pile of rugs, with pillows heaped there like a tumble of rose and jade clouds.

"It's beautiful," Janelle said. "Thank you."

No one answered. They led her across the room and under an archway. In the chamber beyond, a small, sunken pool steamed, and a lamp glowed dimly in a seashell claw on the wall.

The older woman finally spoke. "We can help you bathe."

Janelle's face heated. "It's kind of you to offer. But I can manage."

"Then we will leave you to rest." She was so aloof, she could have been a hundred miles away. The trio bowed and gracefully exited the chamber. A moment later, the outer door creaked on its hinges.

Janelle hoped she hadn't just committed some social blunder. Unsure what she would find, she returned to the bedroom. An oil lamp hung on a scrolled hook by the entrance. It gave less light than the torches, which was probably why the women hadn't carried it, but Janelle preferred the lamp, which neither smoked nor sputtered. To her relief, the door had a lock on this side and opened when she tried it. One of her guards stood a short distance down the hall, severe in his leather armor. Light from a wall sconce glinted on the hilt of the broadsword strapped across on his back.

"Hello," Janelle said.

He turned with a start. Then he said what sounded like, "My greetings, Lady."

"Isn't that sword heavy?" she asked.

He seemed bemused by her attention. "Not for me."

"Oh. Good." She wasn't sure why she asked, but she felt the need to connect to people, to make this less strange. "Good night."

His craggy face softened. "Good night."

Janelle closed the door and sagged against the wall. She could think of many reasons Dominick might post a guard: to keep her in, as a courtesy, or because she wasn't safe even in his home. For all its extraordinary beauty, his world had a starkness that kept her off balance.

Ill at ease, she explored her suite. In the bathing room, an elegantly carved bench stood against one wall, with a jade-green towel, a silver brush inlaid with mother-of-pearl from abalone, two soaps carved like tulips, and a crimson silk robe. It was all gorgeous, everything handmade. The suite, however, had only the one exit. They had closed her in well.

No one said you couldn't leave, she reminded herself. More than anything, she wanted to clean up. She carried the soaps to the pool, an oval filled with scented water, but then she hesitated. The idea of undressing made her feel vulnerable. The grimy scrapes on her arms and legs decided her; she quickly peeled off her clothes, shivering as the cold air chilled her bare skin. Then she slid into the heated pool.

Warmth seeped blissfully into her body as she lay back. Silence filled the room, a contrast to the muted city roar she had lived with these last years, at MIT. No sirens or engines interrupted the quiet, none of the constant hum that rumbled even in the deepest hours of an urban night. She was immersed in a great ocean of quietude.

Her thoughts drifted to Dominick's gate. A branch cut? They came from complex numbers. She could write such a number as $z = e^{(i\phi)}$, where ϕ was called the phase angle. Varying the phase from $\phi = 0$ to $\phi = 2\pi$ was like going around an analog clock from 12 to 12. Just as 12 was the same at the start and finish, so 0 and 2π were the same. However, if she divided ϕ by 2, then $z = e^{(i\phi/2)}$. Now the phase was $\phi/2$. As ϕ went from 0 to 2π the phase only changed to π. The angle ϕ had to go around a second time before $\phi/2$ returned to its starting value of 2π. But the same ϕ couldn't have two different values of z. To avoid that contradiction, z slipped through a branch cut to a second sheet for the second cycle ϕ. Just as 3 a.m. and 3 p.m. were different times, so ϕ on each sheet was considered different. Her world was one "clock" and Dominick's was another.

That suggested some sort of phase here had to go through a full cycle before Dominick's gate reopened. Her twelve-hour model was only an analogy; she had no idea how long she would have to wait before the actual gate reopened. Days? Months? *Years?*

Nor was that her only problem. Suppose she divided ϕ by 3. The phase would be $\phi/3$. It meant she would need three "clocks." Three universes. Divide ϕ by 4, and she needed four. Many sheets could exist. If she went through a gate, she could end up on yet some other "clock"—some other universe—instead of her own.

Janelle groaned. Her head hurt, and the water had cooled. Putting away her thoughts, she soaped her body and washed her hair. Then she climbed out and dried off with the luxuriant towel. She reached for her wrinkled sundress, but then paused. The robe was far nicer and scented with perfume, certainly more pleasant than her gritty clothes. She slipped on the robe, and the sensuous glide of silk against her bare skin stirred her thoughts of Dominick. She tried to smile at her reflection in the pool. "Hey, Aulair, you look hot." But her voice shook like the ripples flowing over the water.

She padded barefoot into the other room. She was so tired she could barely stand, but she felt too exposed to sleep. The bed consisted of no more than layers of rugs covered by velvet. She sat on it in the corner, with the wall at her back, facing the door as she drew pillows around her. It wasn't until they crumpled in her grip that she realized how tightly she had clenched them.

Her eyelids drooped, and she forced them up. She wouldn't sleep. The lamp swung on its hook, moving shadows on the walls, back and forth, back and forth . . .

The scrape of wood against stone roused Janelle. She lifted her head, disoriented. She had slid down and was lying amid the pillows. The lamp had burned low, leaving the room swathed in velvety shadows.

The scrape came again. She thought she said, *Who is it?* but no words came out.

The door swung inward, moving slowly. Dominick stood in the archway, filling it with his height and his presence. The dim light turned his shirt a darker blue and glinted on the hilt of his sheathed dagger. The way he loomed, his face harsh and starkly intense, evoked the specter of conquerors who swept across continents, laying waste to their enemies.

"Hello." Janelle barely managed the word. Such a quiet greeting for so dramatic a man.

"May I come in?" he asked.

She appreciated that he asked, given that he could have done whatever he wanted. "Yes," she said.

He entered, and the room seemed to shrink. He closed the door, then came over and knelt on the other side of the bed. His shirt was open at the neck, revealing a tuft of chest hair, black and curly.

"Have you slept?" he asked.

"A little." She wondered how the rest of his chest looked.

He watched her watching him, and his lips curved upward. The shadows eased the hard edges of his face. Sitting on the bed, he tugged off one of his boots.

Janelle froze. Now he was taking off the other boot. He set it next to the first and started to undo his shirt.

"Wait." Her cheeks flamed. If she hadn't been so groggy, she would have realized sooner what she might be agreeing to when she invited him into her room.

Dominick paused. "No?"

"I can't. I mean—that is—"

He waited. Then he asked, "Do you want me to leave?"

"I don't want to be alone. But I don't—" She stuttered to a halt, feeling like an idiot.

"It's all right." He slid across the rugs and stretched out on his side facing her, with his head propped up on one hand. He took up the entire length of the bed. She could see why he might like sleeping on the floor; his legs were too long for a mattress.

"My monks checked your hair," he said. "You are Janelle Aulair."

She flushed, unsettled to have him so near. "Well, I knew that."

He trailed his finger along her hip, sliding up the robe, which suddenly seemed too short. "This is pretty."

She put his hand back on the bedspread. Maybe she should

ask him to leave. But she dreaded being alone. He continued to watch her, his head tilted to the side as if she were a puzzle.

"You must have more names than Dominick," she said, flustered.

"Indeed I do. Dominick-Michael Alexander Constantine."

Now *that* was a moniker. "Those names are famous in my universe." She was talking too fast again. "Like Alexander the Great."

"The Great." His gaze turned sleepy, as if he were a satisfied cat. "Tell me more."

"He conquered Persia—" She stopped as he tugged the sash of her robe. His knuckles brushed her inner thigh.

"Don't," Janelle said.

He traced his finger along her cheek. "Do I offend you so much?"

"Sweet heaven, no."

"Good." His voice was like whiskey, dark and potent. "Otherwise, this would be a rather uneventful wedding night."

Whoa. "You have the wedding night before the wedding?"

"If the bride and groom agree, yes."

"What if they don't agree?"

"I thought you did."

There was that. "If you stay tonight, are we, uh, married?"

He watched her face. "If agreement is reached, and the bride receives rings from the groom, then yes. But public ceremonies are traditional and expected, especially for the royal family."

"Oh." She hesitated. "Does that happen tomorrow?"

"In the morning. Is that all right?"

After a moment, she said, "Yes. It's just so strange."

"For me, also." He stroked his knuckles along her thigh. "But not unwelcome."

"Dominick . . ."

He rubbed the hem of her robe between his thumb and finger. "This cloth is beautiful on you." Putting his finger under her chin, he tilted up her face. He kissed her deeply, and she tensed, wanting him both to stop and to keep going. Her only experience with seduction was on the level of sending out for pizza and Cokes; she was so far out of her depth here, she was drowning.

When she didn't protest, he pulled her closer and eased the robe off her shoulders. When he slid his palm over her breast, his calluses scraped her nipple, and she tingled in places he wasn't touching her. Then he drew back, his face unexpectedly tender.

"Women are so small," he said. "Look at this." He put the heel of his hand at the bottom of her rib cage. His palm stretched up her torso and his fingers closed around her breast. "I can hold so much of you, but you couldn't even cover my ribs."

His ribs. Clever, sexy man. Of course she looked at his chest where he had unfastened his shirt. A mat of hair curled over his muscles. She laid her palm against his abdomen, feeling the springy hair, the hard muscles. Very nice. But very intimidating, too.

"You smell like flowers," he said. Laying her on her back, he stretched out on top of her, easing his hips between her thighs. Then he reached for the waistband of his trousers.

"Wait!" Janelle said. He didn't seem to have any speed between *pause* and *fast forward*.

He lifted his head, his eyes glossy with arousal. "Wait?"

"No more." She felt like a fool, but she had just discovered she couldn't go this far with someone she barely knew, even if he would be her husband tomorrow.

He brushed his lips across hers. "I won't hurt you."

"Dominick, I—no. No more."

Frustration crept into his voice. "You tease me."

"I don't mean to. I just—I can't."

He lifted his head to look at her. "First your behavior says yes. Then no. Then yes. Then no. Which is it?"

"I'm not ready."

He lay there, propped up on his hands, and she knew they

both realized the truth. He could do whatever he wanted and she couldn't stop him. She lay still, meeting his gaze.

Dominick groaned and rolled off her, onto his back. Then he threw his arm over his eyes and inhaled deeply. He stayed there, silent and still, except for the rise and fall of his chest.

Gradually his breathing slowed. Finally he lowered his arm and turned his head to her. "You are an unusual woman."

That was tactful. Better than *Make up your damn mind*. She wanted to hold him, to feel safe, but she wasn't safe with him. Although she didn't think he meant to force her, he would get angry if he thought she was deliberately leading him on, and she could end up with more than she bargained for. She could also, she realized, end up pregnant.

Dominick studied her with that close focus of his. "I don't mean to pressure you." He smiled ruefully. "But you're so lovely, Janelle. Difficult to resist."

Her face heated. "You do sweet-talk a girl." The southern drawl she had lost after her family moved to Washington often slipped back into her voice when she was nervous.

"It may be 'sweet-talk.' But I mean what I say." He took off only his shirt, nothing more. Then he slid down the velvet cover and drew it over them both. Settling on his back, he pulled her into his arms. She closed her eyes, relieved, letting her head rest in the hollow where his arm met his shoulder.

"Dream well," he murmured.

"You too."

Dominick soon fell asleep, his eyes twitching under his lids. As she drifted into slumber, she wondered if he dreamed of the towns and countryside that would someday fall to his army. He could be gentle with her, but she had no doubt he was capable of conquering a continent.

Would he wrack his world with the ambition that led men to create empires—at immense human cost?

IV
THE SHATTERED HALL

Birdsong awoke Janelle. She lay in a pleasant haze, listening to the dawn.

Then she remembered.

Her eyes snapped open. It was real. She was still in the palace. Early morning light filtered through high window slits she hadn't seen last night. The room otherwise looked as she remembered, beautiful and spare. And empty. Dominick had gone.

She rubbed her eyes. Yesterday she had been a new graduate with good prospects; today she had nothing but the unknown. She thought of Rupert Quarterstaff, the lawyer who dealt with her inheritance. Two years ago, when she had been paralyzed by grief, Rupert had stepped her through the estate settlement with a solicitude that went beyond his professional duties. He expected to see her in a few days. What would he do when she didn't show? It would be a mess.

Janelle sat up, rubbing her eyes. She couldn't stay here as the plaything of a warlord who wanted to conquer half of North America. She needed a library. *Someone* had invented Dominick's gate. Pushing off the covers, she shivered in the cold air. She went into the other room and bathed, then dried off with a towel someone had left while she slept. Her clothes from yesterday were gone.

As Janelle searched for something to wear, she kept noticing the walls. Something strange . . . ? Stepping closer, she peered at the mosaics. Wavelike curves intertwined in the tulip designs. She hadn't seen them clearly last night because they were the same color as the swirling stems. The curves weren't just wavelike, they *were* sinusoids: diffraction patterns, harmonics, or quantum wave functions, beautiful and elegant. They were too accurate for coincidence; someone had understood them well enough to reproduce the curves. It was another piece of the puzzle, along with the Fourier Hall and Riemann gate.

Deep in thought, she returned to the bedroom. Someone had come in while she bathed; her robe was gone, and the bed had been remade, with fresh rugs and a jade-green bedspread. As she toweled her hair, she surveyed the empty room. She couldn't dress without clothes.

When the doorknob turned, she jumped. She barely had time to wrap herself in the towel before the door opened. The three women from last night stood there, each holding a large box decorated with abalone and opals.

"Uh . . . good morning," Janelle said, clutching the towel around her body.

Her greeting seemed to be the signal they expected. They bowed and entered the room. The older woman took an ornate key off a hook under the lamp and handed it to a soldier outside. He closed the door, and a loud click came from the lock.

Janelle watched them uneasily. "Why did he lock us in?"

"For privacy." The older woman spoke in the same slow voice she had used last night. "I am Farimah." She introduced the younger women as Silvia and Danae.

Janelle was becoming accustomed to the dialect and understood better this morning. It reminded her of times she had spent with the families of dignitaries who visited her father, how she had striven to learn their language. To her, such new words were gems strung together to create sparkling necklaces of meaning.

"What can I do for you?" she asked, awkward in her towel.

Danae offered her box. "It's for your wedding."

Janelle felt the tickling in her throat that came when she was nervous. "Oh. Yes."

"The ceremony will take place immediately," Farimah said. "His Highness has had word that the Emperor's army gathers in the south. Prince Dominick-Michael and his men must leave today to discover what Maximillian plans."

Well, that was romantic; her groom intended to spend his honeymoon spying on his brother. It would give her time to adjust, though, and to learn about the gate.

"We can wait for the ceremony until he returns," Janelle offered.

"He wishes otherwise." Farimah's voice had a definite edge.

"Here, Lady Janelle." Danae opened her box and revealed a treasure, gold hoops and rings, all inset with mother-of-pearl.

"They're stunning," Janelle said. "But I don't wear jewelry."

Farimah stiffened. "Generations of Constantine brides have worn these with pride. You consider yourself above them?"

"No. No, I didn't mean that." Mortified, she tried to repair her faux pas. "I just don't want to presume."

Farimah gave her a look that said plainly, *You do.* But she only said, "His Highness wishes you to have them."

"It's kind of Dominick," Janelle said.

Farimah jerked up her hand as if to strike her. Then she took a deep breath and lowered her arm. Her voice was ice. "You will refer to His Highness as Prince Dominick-Michael."

Janelle wondered if she could say anything right. "I'm sorry. He told me to call him Dominick."

"Ai," Silvia murmured. She glanced at Farimah with sympathy. To Janelle, she said, "Farimah did not know."

Before Janelle could further cram her foot down her throat and tickle her tonsils with her toes, Danae intervened by fastening a luminous torque around her neck.

"These jewels will help ensure your safety," Danae said.

Janelle tensed. "My safety from what?"

Silvia clipped a bracelet around Janelle's wrist. "The heirlooms indicate you are wife to the emperor's brother. With so much unrest in the provinces, a woman needs more protection than in normal times."

Janelle liked what she was hearing less and less. Running her fingers over the necklace, she realized it was a delicate version of the heavy chain Dominick wore. The bracelet had the same pattern as the abalone in his shirt cuffs.

While Farimah put a belled chain around each of Janelle's

ankles, Silvia took out a blue velvet cloth with gold highlights. Then she waited. Janelle blinked at her.

Farimah sighed as she rose to her feet. "It would be easier to dress you without the towel."

"Oh." Embarrassed, Janelle let the cloth drop to the floor.

"Goodness," Silvia said, as if Janelle had achieved an impressive feat instead of just standing there naked and feeling like an idiot.

"No wonder he wants to marry you so fast," Farimah muttered. "Men see only one thing."

Silvia put the velvet cloth around Janelle's hips. The skirt fit low on her pelvis, showing too much of her abdomen. The hem almost reached her knees, but a slit went up the left side to her hip.

Janelle flushed. "I can't wear this."

"Why?" Farimah asked. "It appears to fit."

"It shows too much skin."

Danae laughed good-naturedly. "What is a wedding for, but to entice the groom?"

"Come now," Farimah said. She knelt by her box and withdrew a girdle designed from beaten coins, with a border of little gold bells. Janelle squinted while they fastened it around her hips. Heavy and snug, the girdle fit over the skirt and sparkled with sapphires and mother-of-pearl. It jangled when she moved. Then Silvia brought out a bra made from silver coins, with loops of abalone and opal beads.

Enough is enough, Janelle thought. "I *can't* wear that."

Silvia considered the halter and then Janelle. "You are right. It is too small."

"I didn't mean my breasts," Janelle muttered. No one listened. Silvia went to the door and knocked. As the guard outside opened it a sliver, Silvia blocked his view of the room. A child squeezed past her, a girl of about three with black curls and a sweet face.

Silvia glanced back at Janelle, her gaze malicious, then slipped outside and closed the door. Janelle stiffened, wondering what she had done to evoke Silvia's hostility.

The child ran to Farimah. "Fami!"

The elderly woman laughed and reached for her. Then she froze, her gaze darting to Janelle. Panic surged over her face.

Puzzled, Janelle gave the child a friendly smile. "Hello."

The girl hid her face in Farimah's skirts.

Farimah lifted the child into her arms, her attention riveted on Janelle. "My apology." She sounded terrified. "I didn't realize she had followed me here."

"It's all right," Janelle said. Both Farimah and Danae had gone deathly pale. *Why?* "She is welcome to stay."

"Thank you." Farimah spoke stiffly.

"She's charming," Janelle said. "What's her name?"

"Selena. Like her mother."

"You seem to know her well."

"She is my granddaughter." Farimah took a breath. "I also care for her siblings. Her mother died in childbirth."

"I'm sorry," Janelle murmured.

The girl was watching her with big, dark eyes that somehow looked familiar. "You mama now?" she asked.

Mama? *Mama?* Ah, hell. Janelle stared at Farimah. "She is Dominick's child?"

Farimah answered tightly. "Yes."

Life grew messier by the moment. "How many does he have?"

"Five." Farimah was as taut as a coil. "The oldest is twelve."

Janelle wondered when he had planned to tell her. "Are they all your daughter's children?"

"Of course!" Anger flashed in her gaze. "After Selena came into his life, His Highness had no other women."

Janelle rubbed her neck, trying to ease her aching muscles. Selena hardly sounded like a concubine, if Dominick had lived monogamously with her for so many years, raising a family. Had some stupid prophecy kept them from marrying? No wonder Farimah resented her.

Farimah's fear also made sense now. Janelle spoke quietly. "Your grandchildren are welcome in my household."

Farimah just nodded, her posture rigid. But her frozen look thawed a bit. She took the girl to the door and gave her into the keeping of someone outside.

Silvia returned then, watching them with an avid gaze. Janelle wanted to sock her. Silvia could have kept the girl outside and protected Farimah from that heart-stopping moment when the grandmother realized *she* would have to tell Janelle about the children. What had Silvia hoped to achieve? It didn't take a genius to see women had little power here. It created a dynamic foreign to Janelle, an unstated enmity and maneuvering for sexual power. Silvia was a beauty, with glossy black hair and a voluptuous figure. Had she hoped for Dominick's favor? Maybe she believed discord between his new wife and the mother of his former favorite could work to her advantage.

Janelle had no interest in such machinations. Compared to this place, her world was so enlightened it glowed in the dark. She didn't think women here would be burning their bras anytime soon. Given the halter Silvia was holding, they would have to *melt* the damn things.

At least this one fit better than the last, though "fit" was a generous description. It held her breasts in a scanty gold mesh with a few jewels in strategic places and more of those bells fringing the bottom. Her groom would certainly have no trouble finding her, given all the noise she would make in this outfit.

"This is the most appallingly prehistoric contraption I have ever seen," Janelle muttered.

Her companions regarded her politely. She didn't think they had understood what she said. Frustrated, she added, "Why are guards outside of my door?"

Danae answered obliquely. "As far as we know, Emperor Maximillian has no idea you are here."

"And if he did?" Janelle asked.

"I would never speak ill of the emperor," Farimah said, "to suggest he might brutalize you out of spite for Prince Dominick-Michael."

Janelle was starting to feel queasy. "Are all women here treated this way?"

"Those with value are protected," Silvia told her.

"I'm afraid to ask what 'value' means."

"I should think it is obvious," Farimah said. "Beauty. Youth. Fertility. Good birth. Gentle nature. Intelligence. You obviously have the first two. Maybe a few of the others." She shrugged. "So if you lack the last, it does not matter."

Ouch. Janelle barely managed to hold back her retort.

They ignored her protests and inflicted makeup on her next. Silvia brushed her hair, working until she had dried and fluffed up the curls. Then they took her into the bathing chamber, where a long mirror hung on the wall. Her reflection stopped her cold. She glistened in gold and sea colors. Her eyes looked larger and greener than normal, and her hair floated around her shoulders like a gold cloud. Even her bangs curled in traitorous perfection. She had to admit, the effect was impressive—and in that it became seductive. They turned her into a woman of mystery and beauty, and it tempted her to believe it increased her worth. That wasn't a path she wanted to go down, one where her intelligence and character had less value than her body or fleeting youth.

"That isn't me," Janelle said.

"It will please Prince Dominick-Michael," Silvia answered with strained patience. "That is the purpose, is it not?"

"What about pleasing his bride?" Janelle asked.

Farimah threw up her hands. "You are *marrying* him."

"Only because of a prophecy."

"Yes." Farimah's voice quieted.

They left her then, so she could "prepare" for the ceremony. She had no clue what that entailed, but she suspected she was supposed to think of ways to entice the groom. She smiled wryly. Maybe she should entertain herself by deriving equations for the sinusoids on the walls. That ought to stir up Dominick's libido.

She stepped up on the bench in the bathroom to look out the window—at a spectacular panorama. Mountains towered on both sides, east and west. In the south, before her, they dropped to a mesa several miles distant, where mounted riders moved in chesslike patterns. Dominick's army? It had thousands of men. She hoped that qualified as a large military, one comparable to the emperor's, if Dominick's brother was as bad as everyone implied. Then again, maybe Maximillian was a saint and Dominick just coveted his throne, as disenfranchised brothers had since time immemorial.

Wood grated in the other room. Janelle returned to the bedroom and found a group of strangers waiting for her. Six older women stood in the front, their carriage and jewels surely marking them as noblewomen. Blue silk wraps covered them from neck to ankle, making Janelle even more self-conscious about her skimpy attire. Behind them, an array of servants carried platters of food.

They offered her the feast and waited while she ate. Everyone declined her invitation to join in, but no one seemed offended by the thought. The meal was delicious, though odd, with Janelle standing up, surrounded by silent people, sampling foods and wine. Strong wine. Well, good. Right now, a few shots of whiskey would have done nicely.

When she finished, they took her outside. Twelve warriors waited in the corridor, hulking in armor, with what looked like ceremonial broadswords on their backs, the gilded hilts inlaid with jewels. While the servants took off with the platters, the noblewomen and soldiers escorted Janelle the other way. She went in a daze. She wanted to believe this was a delirium; maybe a car had hit her and she was lying in a hospital. But it felt all too real.

Up ahead, shouts echoed in the halls. It seemed out of place with the reserve of the people here. Apparently she wasn't the only one who thought so; her escorts were slowing down. Those broadswords weren't ceremonial after all, for the men drew the weapons, and the honed blades glittered.

Crashes sounded in the distance. More shouts came, and the halls vibrated with a great pounding. The guards split their group into two, half of the warriors taking the noblewomen one way and the others hurrying Janelle into a side corridor. They ran hard, with drilled precision, while all around them the rumble intensified.

A rangy soldier kept pace with Janelle. "We will go to tunnels under the palace," he said. "They exit into the mountains."

She nodded, rationing her breath.

The rumble surged into a roar—and raiders thundered out of a cross-hall, all astride biaquines. The man in front brought his mount to an abrupt halt, and it reared, its hooves smashing the pillar of an arch that framed the corridor. Dominick's men skidded to a stop, but momentum carried the groups together. Biaquine screams rent the air, and metal rang as swords flashed. Janelle had about as much military knowledge as a toadstool, but it took no expert to see Dominick's men were outnumbered and in trouble. She couldn't understand how outlaws had broken into such a well-defended fortress.

The rangy soldier pulled her into a side hall, and they ran hard down the corridor. The bells on her clothes chimed as if announcing their location. Only a few lamps lit the area. Despite the dim light, her guard took the turns with confidence, always choosing hallways too narrow for a biaquine.

Until they hit a dead end.

"Ah, no!" Janelle stopped, heaving in air. They were *trapped*.

"Don't worry." Her guard stepped into a wall recess and pushed the tiles in what looked like a combination.

"What happened back there?" she asked.

"I cannot say. I saw no symbols I recognized on those men." He leaned into the wall and it slid inward, revealing a tunnel. Taking a lamp off a hook in the recess, he motioned her forward.

She entered the passage. "Do you think they came to stop the wedding?"

"I doubt it." He shut the door, closing out the distant clamor. As they headed along the path, he added, "Emperor Maximillian is the person with the most reason to stop it, and those weren't his men. Nor would he raid his brother's home. Even if he were willing to commit such an atrocity, too much chance exists that in the heat of the attack, you would be killed despite his orders. He wouldn't risk it."

Janelle blanched. His answer had an obvious corollary: whoever *was* raiding the palace had no qualms about killing her or anyone else.

They followed an ancient tunnel. Cracks cut through the walls, and lichen encrusted them in eerie patterns. It wouldn't have surprised her to see a wraith coalesce in the recesses where shadows pooled. The damp air smelled musty, and the stone chilled her bare feet. She shivered, wishing she had more clothes.

Then it hit Janelle: not all those marks on the walls were cracks. Wave functions oscillated down here, too, engraved in the stone.

She indicated the patterns. "What are those designs?"

"Artwork," her guard answered. "They're all over the palace." He looked apologetic. "These tunnels aren't kept up well because so few people use them. The levels above are in better repair."

"Ah. I see." In truth, she didn't see at all. The designs looked ancient, which didn't make sense to her.

A murmur of flowing water came from ahead. The path widened into an open area, and a crude rail blocked the way, with walkways curving to either side. She went to the rail and looked down into a well about ten feet across. It plunged into darkness. She toed a pebble over the edge, and a good five seconds passed before she heard a faint splash.

"I'm glad that wasn't one of us," she said. "Pushed by an invader."

The warrior spoke gruffly. "It is a cruel business, this life." He motioned to the walkway on the right. "This should take us to another set of tunnels."

They followed the path—and neither of them saw the break until almost too late. Janelle had already stepped forward when the lamplight revealed the ground had collapsed into the well. She jerked back and stumbled into the guard. Grasping her shoulder with a steadying hand, he held her until she caught her balance.

She stared bleakly at the fissure. It was too large to jump, and the rail that bordered the well was broken. Although two sheets of wood lay across the gap, neither looked solid. Whatever bridge they had once belonged to had fallen into neglect.

Her guard squinted at the boards. "Maybe we can go another way."

They tried the left side, but the fissure extended through that path as well. The tunnel contained nothing they could use to repair the bridge, and the rail around the well consisted of sections too short to bridge the gap.

The chill seeped into Janelle, and the clink of her clothes seemed muted in the damp air. She pried off the bracelets and anklets and hid them in a crack to retrieve later—if she survived to tell anyone. She couldn't remove the girdle because it held on her skirt, but at least she didn't jangle as much.

The guard knelt to examine the boards. "I think they can hold you. Perhaps me, but I can't be sure." He looked up at her. "If we go back, you could be killed. Or captured, which could be worse."

"What will happen to you?" she asked.

His gaze never wavered. "I serve Prince Dominick-Michael."

Janelle understood what he didn't say. "To get to me, they would have to kill you."

His face gentled. "Do not look so dismayed. In battle, death is always possible."

Please, God, not today. She knelt next to him. "Can we wait here?"

"I think it unwise. People know of these tunnels." He indicated the shadows beyond the break. "The passages that way will let you escape the palace. You must not be caught. The rest is secondary."

"Your life isn't secondary to me."

His face gentled. "I thank you. But it is my honor to serve Prince Dominick-Michael." He handed her the lamp. "You try first, in case the bridge won't hold me."

"But if you can't cross, you won't have any light."

His grin flashed. "That will make it harder for our enemies to find me, eh?"

It amazed her that he could joke at such a time. She managed a smile for him. "I hope so." She took a deep breath, then turned and stepped onto the bridge. She walked forward, her hand clenched on the lamp, and the span bent under her weight.

Halfway over, one of the boards snapped.

Janelle flailed, dropping the lamp, and it plummeted into the well. As she fell to her knees on the remaining board, darkness closed around her. A splash took away the last hint of light.

"Lady Janelle?" Her guard's voice was rough with concern.

"Here." In a louder voice, she said, "I'm here."

"Blessed Almighty! Are you all right?"

"Almost." She inched forward on her hands and knees. "I'm not to the other side yet."

"You can make it." He sounded as if he was trying to convince himself as much as her.

From your lips to God's ear. She moved another inch and her knuckles hit the jagged, broken edge of the path. Even as relief surged over her, the remaining board creaked. In the same instant that she threw herself forward, the board snapped and dropped out from under her. Her torso landed flat on the path, but her legs hung into the fissure. She scrabbled at the ground, frantic as rocks fragmented under her and clattered away.

With a heave, Janelle hauled herself onto the path and sprawled on her stomach. She groaned as the girdle jabbed her skin.

"Lady!" the guard called.

"I'm here." The pound of her heart felt like storm waves. "The boards fell. You'll have to stay there."

"Ah." He sounded subdued. "You must go on alone, then."

She stood up slowly and swayed, dizzy. When her head cleared, she said, "Will you tell me your name?" She didn't want to leave without even knowing his identity.

"I am Kadar." He paused. "If I do not see you again—I would like to say—" He stopped.

"Yes?" Janelle asked.

"We have heard how you were pulled into our land," he said. "Given all that has happened, you could have hated us and denied our prince. Instead, you treat us with grace. I am just a soldier. I have no great knowledge of other places. But it seems to me that you are a gift to His Highness."

Good Lord. Janelle had thought she mostly stepped on people's toes. She could have done better if she hadn't been so bewildered. But she hadn't thought in terms of hostility. She valued the chance to learn other cultures. Her parents had left her with the treasured memory of how they honored the depth and range of the world's peoples. It didn't make her willing to tolerate mistreatment; she had a temper and had always reacted strongly against cruelty or injustice. But according to their ways, Dominick and his people had treated her well.

She spoke quietly. "Thank you, Kadar."

He became all business then, describing the tunnels ahead. Then he said, "The prince has a hunting lodge in the forest. The last passage will let you out near there. I'll meet you at the lodge."

She rubbed the goose bumps on her arms. "Don't you get killed."

His voice lightened. "I shall endeavor not to. Farewell for now."

"Good-bye." Janelle set off, keeping her right palm on the wall for guidance. No light softened the darkness; she couldn't even see her other hand in front of her face. She went with care, probing each step with her foot before she put down her weight, lest she stumble into another chasm. But she didn't dare take too long; she had no idea who else knew about these tunnels or would discover them.

Her palm hit stone. A dead end. Alarm surged through her, but she pushed it down and searched the surface. She did indeed find tiles, as Kadar had described, and she pushed them in the sequence he had given her. When she leaned into the wall, it slid inward with a creaking protest and swung aside. She ventured into the suffocating darkness.

It felt as if she walked for hours. Then she noticed a change; the air had warmed. A scent of pine wafted around her, a welcome change from the stench of musty stone. Even more encouraging, she could see her hand. Up ahead, light sifted through a crevice shaded by fir trees. She was free!

Voices drifted to her from outside.

Janelle stopped and swore silently. The speakers were in front of the opening. She could decipher enough to determine they were sentries for the raiders. Demoralized, she quietly retreated back along the tunnel.

Boots clanked at the exit.

Damn! That had to be the sentries. It was all she could do to keep from running and start her wretched clothes jangling.

After an eon, she reached the place where she had opened the secret door. The sentries were closer. A man swore and another laughed. She slipped past the door, then grabbed its edges and pulled hard. It swung closed with a screech of stone on stone. She barely managed to snatch away her hands before it crashed into place.

A shout came from the other side, muffled by the stone. Then a heavy object slammed the door.

Janelle stumbled forward, raising her hands in the dark. If she retraced her steps, she would end up trapped at the fissure. Kadar had said another path led off from this junction; a true dead end would make the secret entrance too obvious. And indeed, she found a passage that slanted sharply to the right. She followed it, wanting to run but afraid to take the risk. Darkness weighed on her, smothering and dank. She imagined specters at every step, terrors crouched low or clinging to the walls, waiting for her to dislodge them.

Wings brushed her face, and furry bodies. Janelle pressed her fist against her mouth to stop her scream. Then she sagged against the wall and folded her arms across her body while she shook.

Bats. It's only bats. She stretched out her arms and forced herself to go on. Distant crashes rumbled as the sentries beat at the door. No way back existed, only forward into the dark.

Suddenly her palms hit wood: another dead end. She searched the wall, sliding her hands frantically over the rough, splintered surface. Nothing. *Nothing.*

Then she found it, a latch up high. She had to stand on her toes to reach it. As her fingertips scraped several gears, a tiny window creaked open. She peered out—and gratitude flooded over her. The Fourier Hall lay beyond the door.

With light filtering in the window, she managed a better search and found the aged gears that locked the door. They crumbled under her touch, as did the lock. She inched the door open and slipped out into the hall of arches. Walking softly through the forest of pillars, she headed for the palace entry. The great double doors were open, revealing an overcast day outside. Freedom.

Hooves clattered behind her.

Janelle whirled around—and barely ducked in time to evade

a bareheaded rider leaning down in his saddle to grab her. His biaquine pounded past her under the tall arches.

Janelle sprinted for the entrance, and the rider came around in front of her. As he reined in his mount, it sidestepped toward her. She fled the other way, back through the arches, and tiles shattered behind her as the man pursued. When she swerved into another row of arches, a splintering crack sounded, followed by an oath. Glancing back, she saw an arch collapsing around the rider as his biaquine tried to turn in too confined an area. She kept running.

More shouts rang through the air, and hooves pounded the floor. Riders were pouring into the hall from deeper within the palace and thundering down the columned aisles.

"No!" Janelle skidded to a stop as they came toward her. She reversed direction, but the outlaw chasing her blocked her escape. Desperate, she swung around—to face a second biaquine. It snorted in the confined area, looming above her, its breath hot against her face. Stumbling back, she looked up—and up. She couldn't see the eyes and nose of the man who sat astride the animal; a cougar helmet hid his upper face. But she saw his mouth. The bastard was *laughing*. He urged his mount closer, backing Janelle up against the biaquine of the bareheaded raider behind her.

Chaos filled the hall. Someone screamed, a cry of terror that abruptly broke off. An outlaw goaded his biaquine to rear and its forelegs pawed the air, smashing a pillar and raining broken tiles over the floor. Farther down the hall, another pillar fell in a cloud of dust, and the battle boiled over its remains. The raiders were deliberately ruining the hall, and Janelle could have wept for the destruction of such beauty.

The two outlaws caged her between their mounts. Laughing, the bareheaded man planted his boot between her shoulder blades and shoved her hard into the helmeted man's animal.

"Asshole!" she yelled. The helmeted man grabbed for her,

and she socked his arm. Behind her, the other outlaw grabbed a handful of her hair and pulled back her head until she was looking up at him. Exhilaration flushed his face. His yell rang through the clamor, and she thought either he was mad with battle lust or just plain crazy.

Janelle twisted free, but the effort sent her lurching into the other biaquine. It danced to the side and reared, rising far, far too high. Its hooves smashed a column, showering debris. Gasping, shielding her head, she staggered back, too terrified by the enraged animal even to cry out. As it came down, it knocked her over, and she fell to the floor, landing hard on her hands and knees. When it reared again, a scream wrenched out of Janelle.

Scrambling to her feet, she dodged the frenzied animal. The bareheaded outlaw grabbed her, and this time she didn't fight when he hefted her upward. Better to be caught up there than trampled down here. His saddle was narrow enough that he could throw her stomach-down in front of it, her legs hanging down one side of his biaquine and her torso on the other, with the edge of the saddle jutting into her side. He pulled up her skirt and slapped her behind, and she cussed loudly at him. He didn't try to hold her down, though, and she managed to struggle up until she was astride the animal. She nearly fell in the process, but she kept her seat by clinging to the biaquine.

Calls rang through the mayhem, and dust clogged Janelle's nose. The raider kept one arm around her, clenching his reins while he snapped a whip against his mount's flank. She recognized Dominick's men among the warriors. The outlaws far outnumbered them, and most were no longer fighting, they were trashing the incomparable Fourier Hall.

Then she saw Dominick.

Towering in leather armor, he rode a massive dark animal. He held his sword high, his face harsh with rage. When he shouted, the marauders surged away from him, toward the palace entrance. The first wave reached the entry and flooded out, and Janelle's captor galloped after them.

In the courtyard outside, the clamor lessened, muted by the open space. Almost no one remained to oppose the invaders. Ahead of them, two men on biaquines were forcing along a limping warrior. With a jolt, Janelle recognized the injured man as one of her guards from this morning. His sword arm hung useless at his side, and blood pumped from a wound in his shoulder.

One of the outlaws raised his sword above the bleeding man. In horrified disbelief, Janelle saw the blade descend, flashing in the chill sunlight. She jerked around so she couldn't see, but nothing could shut out the thud of impact or the hideous gurgle that followed.

"Oh, God," she whispered. She prayed it had happened fast enough to spare him pain. She thought of Kadar and her skin felt clammy. Nausea surged over her.

Her captor galloped with the other men across earthen courtyards toward the huge wall that should have protected the palace. Yells broke out behind them. Looking around, Janelle saw a party of ten men on biaquines racing toward their group.

The outlaws reined in their mounts with sprays of dirt and wheeled to face the palace. The sight chilled her; several hundred raiders confronted the small party of defenders. They would massacre ten adversaries.

Then she saw Dominick—with the *outlaws*. He sat on his huge dark biaquine at the front of the formation, his gaze intent on the ten men from the palace. The defenders slowed as they came closer, near enough for her to see who led them.

Dominick?

Janelle blinked, looking from Dominick with the raiders to Dominick with the defenders. The Dominick in the small party rode Starlight, the big silver biaquine from yesterday. He wore only trousers and a shirt, with a sword on his back as if he had grabbed it when he was too rushed to don his armor.

His party stopped a short distance from the outlaws. Everyone remained silent, watching while Dominick on the dark biaquine cantered out to meet Dominick on the silver biaquine. Janelle understood then. Dominick and his brother were identical twins.

"It's Emperor Maximillian," she said.

"You'd best be silent," her captor answered.

She couldn't fathom how Maximillian could do this to his brother. No wonder the guards had opened the gate. They wouldn't leave the emperor's party milling about outside. They had probably welcomed him, never knowing they were inviting raiders into their midst.

Had Maximillian come to stop the wedding? Supposedly he didn't know. That could mean he also didn't know his men had caught her. Dominick was probably too far away to see her among several hundred riders, particularly since she wasn't the only woman they had taken. But even from here, she could see the fury on his face.

The brothers met in the stretch of dirt between their groups. Their voices carried to Janelle.

"To what purpose?" Dominick was demanding. "Do you take joy in killing? Hurting innocent people? Destroying beauty?"

Maximillian lifted his hand, and one of his men rode forward with a rough leather bag that bulged. At the emperor's signal, the man opened the bag and dumped its contents. Something large fell to the ground and rolled toward Dominick.

A bloody head.

"No," Janelle whispered.

Frozen silence followed the gruesome offering. Then Maximillian said, "Think on this, brother. Next time you send a spy to my army, my response won't be so gentle." His voice hardened. "You were lucky today. We could have killed your servants and burnt your home to the ground."

Dominick bit out his words. "You've spied on me for years."

Maximillian lifted the reins. "If I ordered an attack now, who would stop me? The major portion of your army has been practicing maneuvers. Even riding hard, they won't be here for fifteen minutes. Be wise, Dominick. Fight me and I will retaliate. Is that what you want? No! Leave this land. Go across the sea. Anywhere." He regarded his brother steadily. "Because if you stay, someday I will have to take your life."

Then the emperor turned and cantered toward his men.

Dominick reached over his shoulder for his sword. Janelle felt her captor go for his own weapon, and all around her, other raiders were doing the same. When Maximillian saw his men drawing steel, he reined in his biaquine. But he didn't turn to Dominick. He sat in his saddle as if daring his brother to charge and kill him from behind.

Dominick let go of his sword and lowered his arm.

"No!" A woman cried out from within the raiding party. "Prince Dom—" Her voice cut off.

Dominick scanned the riders, his strained expression clear even at this distance. Janelle doubted he could tell who shouted; even from within the group, Janelle couldn't locate her. The raiders had taken at least fifteen women, probably more. If she called to warn him that his bride was among the captives, she would also be warning his brother.

Then she thought of a way to let him know without revealing herself. She was apparently one of the few people he let use his single name. "Dominick!" she shouted. "Here—"

The raider clamped his hand over her mouth. *"Quiet."*

Janelle clawed at his hand, and he pinned her arms to her sides. Although Dominick looked in their direction, she didn't think he saw her. She struggled to free herself.

"If you make trouble," her captor said, "it will anger the emperor. If he becomes angry, he will retaliate against his brother. And you. He knows this palace. He gave it to Prince Dominick-Michael. He could destroy everyone here. Is that what you want?"

She went still, then shook her head.

Dominick was watching his brother. "Max."

The emperor brought his biaquine around to face him. "We will let the women go when we finish with them."

"This isn't done," Dominick said. "You went too far."

"You have my warning," Maximillian told him. "I give it for our mother's sake, in her memory. But it is the last I will give you."

With that, the emperor wheeled around and set off at a gallop. His men went with him, stirring up a great cloud of dust, pounding out the great gate and away from the palace of shattered arches.

V
MAXIMILLIAN

The raiders followed a trail that switch-backed across the face of a cliff. They rode on the edge of the world, a sheer wall of stone to their left and an abyss of astonishingly clear air to the right, with endless, verdant mountains far below. The line of biaquines clung to the cliff like a fragile string that could snap anytime.

Janelle saw why Dominick had avoided this route. The path was barely wide enough for one biaquine, with nothing to catch anyone who stepped off the trail. It was also obvious why Maximillian used it; the trail offered a faster path to the flatlands, insurance against Dominick's pursuit when his army arrived to defend their liege.

She shivered as her reaction to the raid set in. She had never witnessed anyone die before, let alone in such violence. Even with so little knowledge of Othman, she could tell Dominick wasn't ready to take on Maximillian. The ramifications went much further than a violent argument between brothers. Would the people here tolerate a challenge to their emperor? She didn't doubt Dominick would come for the women of his household, but she had no idea how far he would go to rescue them or what he would do when he discovered she was gone.

They kept a grueling pace, and around noon they reached a meadow at the foot of the mountain. The grasses and wildflowers had been trampled earlier, probably by the passage of this same party. Cliffs rose starkly behind them, and hilly fields stretched to the south, swirled by yellow and blue blossoms.

The emperor finally called a halt. With a sigh, Janelle's captor reined in his mount. He slid his arms around her waist and leaned against her. "Maybe we can get to know each other better now, little bride. You were wanting a man tonight, eh?"

She pulled away from him. "Don't touch me."

He yanked back her head and pressed his lips and teeth against her neck. But when she twisted away, he didn't wrestle her back. Instead he froze—and released her as if she had a plague. No one paid them any heed; the other men were dismounting, checking biaquines, taking out trail rations. An older man with a gray beard rode through the group, stopping to confer with various people.

Still behind her on the biaquine, Janelle's captor spoke sharply. "What is your name?"

"Salima." She even managed to keep the tremor out of her voice.

"You're lying."

She had no chance to answer, for the bearded man had reached them. "How goes it, Aker?" he asked her captor.

"Fair enough," Aker said, his voice cautious.

The other man indicated Janelle. "You can have a few minutes with her. But be ready to ride when the call comes. Maximillian wants to leave the women here, so they don't slow us down."

Aker answered in an oddly subdued voice. "I think His Highness will want to take this one."

Ah, hell. Janelle spoke fast, grabbing her thought from before, doing her best to use their dialect. "I'm sick. I'll give a killing fever to anyone who touches me."

The bearded man cocked an eyebrow. "You don't look sick to me." His gaze traveled slowly over her. "Far from it."

"I'm in the early stages. The most contagious time."

He snorted. "Which is why you were married today, eh?"

"She's fine," Aker said with a laugh. "You should have seen her in the palace. She can scream like a banshee."

Screw you, Janelle thought.

"I will tell the emperor of your offer," the bearded man told him. Then he continued on to a cluster of other riders.

Aker dismounted and helped Janelle down, but he otherwise went out of his way to avoid touching her. She didn't know whether to be relieved or even more afraid.

The bearded man soon reappeared on foot—accompanied by Maximillian. Janelle's pulse lurched. The emperor could have been Dominick; he had the same eyes, the same strong features, the same height. But unlike Dominick, who warmed with his gaze, Maximillian's stare was ice. He appraised her as if she were an object for sale.

The emperor glanced at the bearded man. "You didn't exaggerate. She's lovely. Exotic, with that yellow hair. Yes, we will keep the bride." He nodded to Aker. "I will remember your generosity."

"Your Highness." Aker sounded strained. "Look at her jewels."

Puzzlement creased Maximillian's face. He pushed Janelle's hair over her shoulder to see her necklace better. For a long moment he stared at it. When he spoke, his voice was too quiet, like the calm in the center of a storm. "Are you my brother's wife?"

Janelle met his gaze. "Yes." She prayed he didn't find out they had never finished the ceremony.

"It *cannot* be. Dominick would never risk his own death to marry some pretty tidbit." He took her chin and turned her face to the side. "My God, you do look like her. But you're too young." His voice hardened. "From where do you come?"

"Cambridge." She had no idea if it existed here. "Near Boston."

"Boston? Where is that?"

"Dominick called it 'another sheet.'"

His posture went rigid. "And your name is Salima?"

She didn't see any point in lying now. "No. It's Janelle."

"Hai," Aker murmured.

Maximillian swore. "That's impossible."

The bearded man spoke. "If she is the one, Your Highness, you have her now instead of your brother."

Maximillian answered with barely controlled fury. "One day earlier. *One day*, and I would have been in time." He reached toward Janelle. When she backed away, Aker stepped behind her and grasped her upper arms, holding her in place.

The emperor grabbed strands of Janelle's hair and yanked them out, making her gasp at the stab of pain. He thrust the tendrils at the bearded man. "Ride to the palace. *Fast*. Have her signature checked. And tell Major Artos to prepare the army. Dominick will soon realize she is gone, if he hasn't already."

Maximillian turned back to Janelle. "You," he said grimly, "will come with me."

The emperor's company rode hard during the day, with stops only to change and rest the biaquines. They continued into the night, lighting their way with torches. Maximillian had Janelle sit in front of him on his biaquine. At least he changed his saddle to an animal skin with fleece against her legs. Smells saturated her senses: leather, sweat, musky animals. Maximillian's armor jabbed her back and his thighs pressed against her hips. Her chafed skin burned.

"You know Dominick has five children," Maximillian said when they slowed to rest the horses. "He loved their mother. He hasn't touched another woman since. If it wasn't for that god-forsaken prophecy, he wouldn't touch you, either."

If he expected to get a rise out of her, he would be disappointed. When she didn't respond, he spoke tightly. "Dominick will be uncle to your children. Not father."

She made herself stop gritting her teeth. "How noble of you, to rape your brother's wife."

He leaned near her ear. "You will regret that."

It no longer surprised her that his men had inflicted such cruelty at the palace. A leader's personality was reflected in those who followed him. Yet she also saw Dominick in the emperor; they moved alike, gestured alike, spoke alike. Maximillian led his men with the same natural authority and intelligence, and he obviously had their respect. Both he and Dominick exuded an ingrained arrogance, though in Dominick it was softened by a sense of humor that suggested he took himself less seriously than his brother.

Sometime after the Moon began its descent, an officer rode up alongside them, a husky man with well-kept armor. "A messenger has arrived, Your Highness, from the scouts you left to watch the palace."

Maximillian didn't look surprised. "Has Dominick come, then?"

"I cannot say. Shall I bring the messenger?"

"Immediately."

As the rider fell back, Janelle's mood lifted like a tentative bird uncertain whether or not to take flight. Although it seemed unlikely Dominick had already gathered sufficient forces to come after Maximillian, she could hope.

The officer soon reappeared, accompanied by a red-haired man on a biaquine. Janelle could better tell the difference now between Maximillian's soldiers and the outlaws he had hired to augment his company. This man had the scuffed armor worn by the raiders.

"What is your message?" Maximillian asked.

"It's the bride." The redheaded man nodded toward Janelle. "The wedding never took place."

Janelle silently swore.

Behind her, Maximillian tensed. "She has his jewels."

"They reversed the ceremonies," the man said. "He gave her the jewels this morning."

Maximillian took Janelle's shoulders and turned her until she could look up at him. "Then you are not yet his."

She met his gaze. "Dominick and I are married."

"My messenger says otherwise." He glanced at his officer. "Go get Brother Anthony."

"But you must have a proper ceremony," the officer protested. "One fit for an emperor. That takes time."

"And give Dominick time to rescue her?" Maximillian said. "I think not. Get Anthony. *Now.*"

Brother Anthony turned out to be another warrior. He rode with Maximillian, and the emperor's aides surrounded them, all on biaquines. The torches cast stark shadows, leaving the faces of the riders half in darkness and half lit by wavering orange light. Anthony wore an unadorned cross, but Janelle couldn't tell if he was a monk, a priest, or a cleric that didn't exist in her universe. She just wished she were somewhere else. Anywhere. Like on the Moon.

Fleeing the specter of Dominick's pursuit, Maximillian didn't even stop for his own wedding. He let them slow enough so Anthony could speak, and then they held the ceremony on the run, as the army rumbled across the plains.

"Each day the Sun rises," Anthony droned. "Each night the Moon graces the sky in one of its myriad phases, during the ices of winter and the droughts of summer. In the joy of spring or the fertility of autumn, so shall you cleave to each other." He glanced at the emperor. "Maximillian Titus Constantine, do you accept this woman, Janelle Aulair, as your wife?"

"Yes," Maximillian said.

"No," Janelle said.

"No one asked you," Maximillian told her.

"The hell with this," she said. "I'm married to Dominick."

Anthony cleared his throat awkwardly. He produced a scroll and handed it to Maximillian. "I've already signed it."

Alarm surged in Janelle. "That's *it*?"

"It is done," Maximillian said. "You are Empress of Othman." His voice cut like steel. "And you will learn to respect me, wife, or you will find out just how thoroughly that title can be a curse."

VI
THE FIRE PALACE

The stars glittered as soulless witnesses to the passage of the army. Here in the plains, the night never cooled; even hours past midnight, the air felt like a steam bath. Lines of riders bearing torches wound across the land in rivers of fire.

Janelle dozed, leaning against Maximillian. When she opened her eyes, bleary and confused, the sky had turned crimson. Silhouetted against the horizon, a palace dominated the view. It dwarfed Dominick's home. The central onion dome was surrounded by smaller domes that clustered like great water droplets, gold-plated and glistening. Bridges arched from tower to tower, glowing in the dawn as if they were flames. The palace shimmered in the morning's fire.

"Do you like it?" Maximillian asked.

"It's spectacular," she admitted.

"It is my home." He sounded tired but satisfied. "And now yours."

The stairway wound around the tower, circling a central shaft of air. Janelle could see over the railing all the way to the bottom, many stories below. They climbed single-file: two guards, Janelle, Maximillian, and two more guards. She could barely walk, she hurt so much from the ride. Only the unwelcome prospect of being carried kept her from collapsing. Maximillian was a foreboding presence at her back, threatening in his silence and unstated intent.

At least he had no time for her now. The moment they arrived, people had sought to see him: officers, clerks, servants, aides. His advisors were at the bottom of the tower, sorting out what needed to be done, but he obviously had to return to his duties.

Their climb ended at a landing with a heavy wooden door. One of the guards lifted its iron bar and pulled the handle. With a creak of protest, the door swung ponderously open.

They took Janelle into a circular stone cell with a high ceiling and four small windows, one each looking north, south, east, and west. A wheel across the chamber was wound with a thick chain, which then snaked up the wall and across the domed ceiling to its highest point, held in place by iron rings. From the top of the dome, it hung halfway to the ground. A pair of leather shackles dangled from its end.

Two guards went to the wheel, and one tapped a combination into some mechanism there. Leaning their weight into their work, they cranked out the chain. It rattled up along the wall, pulled by its own weight as the shackles descended. A stench of oil permeated the air. The guards let the chain down to Janelle's height and locked it in place. Another guard pushed her forward, and she stumbled into the shackles, which swung away, then came back and thwacked her shoulder. The entire time, Maximillian watched with an avid gaze.

While Maximillian watched, two guards came up on either side of Janelle, towering over her. They stank like sweat and biaquines. They lifted her arms, and they tightened their hold when she tried to pull away. Then they shackled her wrists above her head.

"Why?" she asked Maximillian. "I've done nothing to you."

"Nothing?" he said, incredulous. "You've torn apart my life and destroyed my bond with my brother. That prophecy has brought us nothing but endless grief."

"That may be true. But I have nothing to do with it."

"Of course you do. You *are* it."

"I'm here *only* because Dominick looked for me. If Gregor had never said anything, you would have never known I existed." She suspected Maximillian and Dominick would have been antagonists anyway; they were too much alike, two conquerors in a land that had space only for one.

"You would have come anyway," he said. "When you were seventy."

Janelle doubted it. By that time, he and Dominick would be close to ninety, if they lived that long. Age added a great deal to a person, maybe the serenity of a long life or a cynicism steeped in discord, but whatever happened, surely they wouldn't still be locked in this duel of fates half a century from now. Far more likely, Gregor or the "seeress" had misread whatever evoked this miserable prophecy.

The guards at the wheel cranked out the chain, and the shackles rose until they pulled Janelle's arms tight over her head. She had so far hidden her distress, but as the chain continued to rise, lifting her into the air, it was too much. She groaned, and a tear ran down her face. When they finally locked the chain in place, she hung painfully by her wrists in the center of the cell.

Maximillian came over and stood eye-to-eye with her. "My brother thought he could take my title and my life. He will pay for that." He lifted his riding quirt in front of her. "I shall send him this. Soaked with your blood."

She wanted to spit at him. "I don't care how great your title. What you're doing is sick."

Janelle expected him to deny it. But he only said, "A man in my position can never show weakness." Fatigue saturated his voice, revealing far more pain than he probably realized. "For our entire lives, Dominick and I have been pitted against each other. He must learn I will never tolerate his betrayals. It is true, you will pay the price. But that is the way of life."

She regarded him steadily. "He would never do this."

He answered bitterly. "Dominick and his 'moral imperatives.'

It is easy for him to preach when he has never had to serve as emperor. He grew up flawed by a mother's softness, and now he presumes to suggest I lack a conscience. But inside, he is just like me."

"If he chooses compassion over cruelty, so can you."

"You confuse weakness with compassion."

Her anger sparked. "Brutality is easy. It takes no strength."

A muscle twitched under his eye, and his voice hardened. "I will see you tonight." He went to a small table by the door and set down his whip so she would be staring at it. Then he regarded her with an unyielding gaze. "While you are waiting, my empress, it would behoove you to think long and hard about how you speak to me."

Sweat gathered on Janelle's forehead. She was having trouble breathing, and her wrists burned from supporting her weight. "You can't leave me like this."

"Why not?"

"I'll suffocate." She strove to keep the fear out of her voice. "If I die, so do you, according to the prophecy."

He raised an eyebrow, but he didn't refute her statement.

"At least give me the combination to release that wheel with the chain." She suspected he would refuse even if he thought she had a good point, to assert his control, but he might let a guard bring her down if he could do it in the guise of denying her request. After all, the guards already knew the combination. And the emperor would want her in good enough shape for whatever he intended later.

Maximillian didn't take the bait, though. Instead he smiled with condescension. "You couldn't figure out the combination even if I gave you the key."

She scowled at him. "Why not?"

"You may be well apportioned in certain aspects." He looked over her body, while her face heated. Then he said, "But I hardly imagine abstract thought is one of them."

She had to make a conscious effort to hold back the retort that hovered on her lips. His attitude gave her another idea, though. If he thought she was stupid, he might respond just to taunt her.

"As long as this key doesn't involve math," she said, trying to look blank.

"What, you don't like numbers?"

She grimaced with distaste. "They don't like me."

"Very well." His laugh grated. "The combination that releases the chain is the same as the number of terminal zeros in 4089 factorial."

What the blazes? She understood what he meant, but it astounded her that he offered such a game of number theory. It wasn't something most people knew even in her own universe.

"You do know what a factorial is?" he said.

"No," she lied.

"Pity. Not that it would help you. You could never multiply all those numbers together." With that, he motioned to his men. They strode from the cell, and the door slammed shut, the rumble of its closing vibrating through her prison.

Janelle closed her eyes, demoralized. Then she steeled herself. She had to escape. She didn't know what to think about this "key." Of course he thought she couldn't solve the problem; to calculate 4089 factorial she had to multiply the first 4089 natural numbers together. No way could she do it in her head. Except . . . she didn't need the entire number to determine how many zeros it ended in; she needed only to know how many factors of five it contained. Every five, when multiplied by an even number, added a terminal zero. It was simple. She had done such problems in middle school.

Janelle concentrated. Dividing 4089 by 5 gave 817 plus a remainder she discarded. She divided by 5^2, 5^3, 5^4, and 5^5 and added the results. The first time she calculated 1018. So 4089 factorial ended in 1018 zeros—if she hadn't made a mistake. She redid it and got 1019. Again, for 1017. It took six tries to convince herself 1019 was the answer. All that time, the pain in her arms and shoulders worsened.

"Now what?" she muttered. She stared at the table where the whip lay, along with several spiked implements she neither recognized nor wanted to. Flinching, she wondered if she would pass out when Maximillian went to work on her. It would be *hours* until night—

No. It wouldn't be that long. She gritted her teeth. He had left her this way because he wanted her to dwell on it. So she would think about something else. She craned her neck to look around the cell. If she swung like a pendulum, she might reach the walls and catch the chain where it stretched up the stone. From there, she could stretch her leg down to the wheel.

She kicked her legs to start swinging, which worked, but it also made her spin. Her clothes chimed, creating far too much noise. The chain twisted until it could wind no tighter and then unwound, faster and faster. When it finished, it twisted the other way. It was agonizing on her wrists, and bile rose in her throat. As she came to a rest, she closed her eyes and breathed slowly until her nausea receded.

Then she tried again. This time she controlled her swings better. The chain still twisted, but less than before. She finally managed a big enough arc to hook her foot on the chain where it snaked up the wall. She jerked to a stop—and her foot slipped. With a groan of frustration, she swung away, across the chamber.

Janelle slowed to a stop and hung there, breathing hard. She strained to hear if anyone was outside, but no sound penetrated the thick walls. That worked in her favor; she doubted anyone could hear her bells ring, either. The Sun was low in the sky, shining through a window, and she closed her eyes against the glare. She cursed at Maximillian's image in her mind—yet it was the same as the man who had treated her so well the night before. No, it wasn't the same. She would never confuse the cruel lines etched into Maximillian's visage with Dominick's starkly handsome face.

Wetness ran down her arm. Looking up, she saw blood ooze out from under one shackle. *Deal with it,* she thought, and kicked her legs to swing again.

On her fifth try, she caught the chain and wedged her foot between it and the wall so she didn't swing away. Straining, she stretched her other leg to the wheel. Her big toe barely scraped the lock, which consisted of five horizontal levers. She had no idea how the levers corresponded to 1019, if they did at all. For lack of a better idea, she assigned the digits 0 through 9 to the five levers, two for each. Then she pressed out 1019 with her big toe. Each time she pushed a lever, it snapped back up into place.

Nothing.

Gritting her teeth, she reassigned the numbers and tried again. No success. Her third attempt fared no better.

Janelle blew out a gust of air. Holding herself by the chain on the wall eased the strain on her wrists, but her foot ached and her leg was shaking. She scraped the levers with her toe and noticed they tilted backward as well as forward. Maybe that was how they accounted for ten digits. She assigned 0 through 9 to all the positions, forward and backward, and retried the pattern.

Nothing.

Sweat ran into her eyes. Maximillian had probably made up the damn combination. She couldn't quit, though. She switched numbers and pressed the combination—

The lock snapped open.

With a squeal of metal, the wheel jerked and the chain slid up the wall, rattling against the stone. Janelle's foot slipped and she swung into the center of the cell, all the time dropping as the chain played out. Her feet smacked the ground and her arms slammed down in front of her. As she sprawled onto her stomach, the clang of the chain hitting the floor rang through the chamber.

For a moment she lay, stunned. Then she sat up, shaking, praying no one had heard. Euphoria swept over her, followed by an urge to cry, then to laugh. No time to hesitate. She pried at the lock on one shackle, but it didn't budge. With her muscles protesting, she climbed to her feet and limped to the table, dragging the chain. A belt studded with metal spikes lay near the whip. She blanched, hoping she never found out why Maximillian had left it there. She had her own use for it, though. She worked a spike into the shackle, and kept at it until, with a loud snap, the lock clicked open.

As Janelle took off the shackle, blood oozed over her wrist. Ignoring the queasy lurch of her stomach, she went to work on her other wrist. As soon as she was free, she dropped the chain and ran to the closest window. Rising on her toes, she peered through the pane. It looked north, over the plains where Maximillian's forces had camped, thousands of men and biaquines, more even than she had seen in Dominick's army. They must have been coming in all day. If she climbed out on this side, anyone down there could see her.

The east window also faced the army. The south overlooked a garden with a fountain. Two women sat on a bench, chatting and eating fruit. The west window faced another tower, and the palace spread out below in a jumble of yards and crooked alleys. She pressed close to the glass and squinted down at her tower. She was in its dome, which curved out and down from the window to a ledge that circled the widest point of the onion. The ledge didn't look sturdy, but she saw no better options.

The window, however, wouldn't open. Janelle ran to the table and lugged it across the chamber, her sore arms protesting. She swung it hard at the glass, and the pane shattered under the impact, shards flying into the air. She knocked off the jagged pieces with one of the table legs, acutely aware Maximillian might return any moment. Then she set the table under the window and climbed through the opening, careful of the broken glass around the edges. Finally she was outside, sitting on the slanting dome, balanced high above the world. Wind blew back her hair, and for a heart-stopping instant she felt certain it would knock her off her precarious perch and send her plummeting to the ground far below.

Breathe, she thought. She waited until her pulse slowed. Still sitting, she inched down the bulb, using friction from her soles to control her descent. She started to slide anyway, until she feared she would hit the ledge and flip into the air. She dragged her palms on the surface, and it burned her skin, but it slowed her descent. With a jolt, her feet smacked the ledge, and she crouched down, fighting for balance. Her heart was beating so hard, she could feel it pumping.

A breeze clinked the bells on her girdle. She held her breath until they quieted and her pulse calmed. Then she inched along the ledge toward a bridge of scrolled grillwork that arched from this dome to the next. Far below, an alley squeezed between the towers.

After what felt like eons, she reached the bridge and climbed onto it, keeping low behind its grill. Then she crouched down, absorbing that she hadn't fallen to her death. *And now?* She was trapped in a place full of people with no reason to help her and plenty not to. If she reentered the palace, she could be caught. She peered between the scrolled bars of the bridge. The small courtyard below contained no people, only a cart piled with rugs. No ladders descended any wall she could see, but a flimsy trellis with vines and red flowers stretched up the other tower.

Don't look down. She checked the doors at both ends of the span, but neither opened from the outside. Finally she clambered over the bridge above the trellis. Gripping the iron, she lowered herself until she was hanging from the bottom of the grillwork. Her feet scraped the trellis. She concentrated on finding a foothold and tried to ignore the trembling of her aching arms. But she had hung too long in the cell; her arms gave way and she lost her grip.

With a gasp, Janelle fell down the trellis. She managed to grab the framework and yank to a shoulder-wrenching stop. Immediately she thrust her feet between the slats, taking the weight off her arms, and then she clung there, gulping in air as if it were a rarity she might never again experience. But she couldn't stop. Clenching her teeth, she resumed her descent. She closed her eyes, narrowing her world to the lowering of her body inch by inch. She waited for the trellis to break, for someone to discover her, for that shout of recognition—

Her foot touched the ground.

Janelle collapsed against the wall. But she had no time to rest; voices were coming from the alley that curved around the tower. She darted into a recessed doorway and knelt in a deep pool of shadow created by the building.

Two men entered the yard carrying boxes. From their conversation, it sounded like they were taking supplies to the monastery. They loaded the cart promptly, with no fuss, and returned to the palace.

Janelle ran to the cart and climbed in the back. She had no wish to end up at a monastery supported by Maximillian, but this might at least get her out of the palace. Working fast, she hollowed out a cavity under the rugs, then squeezed in and hauled the rugs over her body, arranging them as much like before as she could manage. Several sacks of some goods and a crate poked into her cramped hideaway under the rugs. Weighed down by carpets, buried in the sweltering heat, she waited.

The darkness grew close, and the odor of dyed cloth was smothering. Any moment Maximillian would discover her escape and search the area. If this cart hadn't left by then, she would be in serious trouble. She had been a fool to hide here. She should have snuck into the palace, found some clothes, and pretended to be a servant.

A shout came from the courtyard, and her pulse leapt. Another shout—and with relief, she realized one of the monks was telling the other to hurry up.

The cart jolted into motion. She held her breath, though she knew, logically, they couldn't hear her through piles of rugs. A different voice called out, and the cart stopped while conversation trickled into her hiding place. Did Maximillian know she was gone? *Let it be something else.* Anything. Maybe a sentry had to check their identification.

The rickety cart started again. Its wheels creaked, planks groaned, and the rugs whispered against each other.

After a while, she breathed more easily. She parted the rugs a bit, to make a spy-hole. They were rolling through the encamped army. It seemed to go on forever, soldiers everywhere, with biaquines, oxen, supplies, and the many helpers who tended to the needs of a military force. Gradually the sea of people thinned out. She couldn't see much through the hole, only that they were headed toward the mountains.

Janelle lay still, wrestling with her thoughts. She felt as if she were part of a jigsaw puzzle. A prophecy pulled a mathematician from one universe to another; a gate relied on an abstract concept somehow turned into reality; a fabulous hall was named after a mathematician. Dominick understood abstruse theoretical concepts with little background, and his twin also had an unusual knowledge of math. *Why?* She could see the pieces, but not the overall picture.

Her stomach growled, a reminder she had eaten nothing since last night, when Maximillian shared his trail rations. Taking care to be quiet, she checked the goods crammed tight around her, several sacks and a crate. The sacks held grain. It tasted awful, and she disliked taking supplies from monks, but she liked the prospect of starving even less.

Then she hit gold. Or, more accurately, wine; the crate held ten bottles. It took a while to dig out the cork in one, but she managed. She drank in gulps, soothing her parched throat. By the time she finished half the bottle, she felt amazingly content. She had escaped Max the Nightmare, and she could almost forget she had no refuge.

The pain in her wrists was harder to ignore, and she feared the lacerations would become infected. Then it hit her: she had an antiseptic. Shifting her weight, she poured wine over the cuts. It stung like the blazes, but she was so tipsy it dulled the pain. She opened a second bottle as a reward for her efforts, and soon after she started it, she fell asleep.

Fire licked her wrists. Flames, heat, burning, burning, *burning* . . .

Janelle opened her eyes, passing from sleep to waking without the usual moment of pleasant nothing. The agony in her wrists made that impossible. Tears wet her cheeks. Her spy-hole revealed that night folded over the land with only a flickering glow to light the way, probably from a lamp near the driver.

With clumsy hands, she cleaned the cuts on her wrists again. Then she ripped strips of cloth off one of the sacks and bandaged her wounds as well as she could manage. She drank more wine to ease the pain. Eventually she dozed, floating in a sea of flame.

Birdsong woke her. Bleary-eyed and hungover, she peered through her hole and saw dawn lightening the world. The pain had receded, and she dozed more easily this time. Around noon, she roused enough to change her bandages. Dried blood caked the cloth, but the scabs were clean, without infection.

Sometime in the afternoon, the cart rattled up to a building of dark red stone that could be the monastery. Square towers rose at its corners. Voices rumbled nearby, and she glimpsed two men walking from the cart to the building.

With caution, she widened her spy-hole. The cart stood in a yard paved with stones and mud. Mountains rose behind the building, sharp in the sky, rough-hewn sentinels not yet softened by erosion. Moving stiffly from her cramped sleep, she squeezed out of the cart and eased down by its large wheel. Her head swam, but even as she sagged against the side, voices came from the left side of the building.

She took off in a limping run, and dodged onto a narrow path between the right wall of the monastery and a muddy hillside. Her vision blurred, but she kept going, holding her bells against her body and praying no one heard the infernal clinking of those she couldn't reach.

Janelle wasn't sure what to do. She could ask for sanctuary, but she questioned whether anyone would honor that request. She doubted they wanted to provoke Maximillian, particularly in the matter of this odious prophecy.

She came out behind the monastery. The roughly mortared wall in the back had two entrances, each a wooden door with iron braces. The first opened on a storeroom stacked with crates, which didn't bode well if the monks were about to unload the cart. She went back outside and ran to the second door. It opened into a foyer, with a staircase to the right. After easing the door closed, she limped up the stairs. At the landing, they turned right, and sunlight slanted through a round window high on the outer wall. She looked out onto a walled quadrangle in the center of the building, a yard open to the sky. The three men crossing it didn't fit her image of monks; instead of robes, they wore trousers, work boots, and simple shirts.

She continued up to another landing, this one with a door. When she leaned against the portal, she heard nothing. She edged it open, and a long hall stretched before her. She limped to the first door and listened; voices rumbled in the room beyond. At the next one, silence greeted her. Holding her breath, she opened the door.

A library. An *empty* library

Janelle slipped inside and locked the door with a large key she found on a hook inside. Then she took stock of her refuge. A table occupied the center of the room, old and exquisitely carved with vines. But what compelled her were the *books*. They filled shelves on every wall. The only open space was a panel across the room, where a cushioned banquette stood below a window. She hurried to the window and looked out. The quadrangle lay below, empty now except for vegetable plots and apple trees.

With a sigh, she sank onto the bench. The worn look of this place suggested either the monks had forgone material wealth or else they had poor support. She fingered the coins on her girdle. Would it backfire if she offered them payment to send for Dominick? With all the gems and precious metals she was wearing, she might have some bargaining power. Then again, Maximillian would probably reward anyone who returned his wife, and she doubted her bangles had much value compared to his wealth. Nor were her jewels likely to tempt people if they feared helping her would earn them the type of punishment the emperor had threatened her with in the tower.

Janelle raked her hand through her hair. She needed to know more about this world. She went to a shelf and pulled out a book at random. The text had an odd title: *Elektron Motion: Antique Editions, Monografs of Rekord. Elektronik form: Albambra Graphiks.*

The date was 1546 A.D.

She squinted at the cover. If dates were the same here as in her world, this book was centuries old. Elektronik form? From *1546 A.D.*? The title implied it was a collector's monograph, an "antique" created from an electronic publication. Given everything she had seen, that level of technology five hundred years ago made as much sense as cave men with cell phones.

Then again, these people could step between universes.

She flipped through the book. A preserving finish protected its pages. Reading wasn't as difficult as she expected, despite the odd spellings; physics was physics regardless of language. The first chapter dealt with electronics and the second with an electron gas. A chapter on electrochemistry followed, then one on quantized energy levels of an atom. Unlike texts in her world, which treated the topics as different subjects, here they were lumped into one text on "elektron motion."

She replaced the book and took another. Even older than the last, from 1489 A.D., it discussed heat flow. Although the models differed from those in her world, they gave the same results: heat came from molecular motion and was a form of energy.

Eager now, she pulled out a fat tome titled *Dynamical Analysis.* The first half focused on her specialty, differential equations, and the rest applied their solutions to problems in classical motion and semiclassical models of molecular behavior. Other books followed the same form, opening with chapters on theory, followed by applications. A book on genetics described how biaquines had been bioengineered from horses for strength, speed, and the ability to fight.

Then she found a treatise on tensor analysis.

By themselves, tensors were just arrays of numbers. Nothing unusual. But they appeared extensively in certain sciences, including general relativity. Einstein's bailiwick. Einstein had believed it was impossible to travel faster than light, a result that would limit the ability of humans to leave the solar system. This theory closely resembled his work, with one difference—its author assumed faster-than-light travel existed. A chill ran through Janelle. This read like a historical text, one written *after* the advent of such travel.

She began a methodical search then. And she found what she sought. Titled, simply, *Advanced Formulations,* it covered wormholes, space warps, and complex speeds that circumvented the singularity at light speed. One chapter presented resolutions to the paradoxes for superluminal travel, including a discussion of alternate spaces and times. It proposed a "Riemann screen" that could offer views of those other continuums. Then she understood; the "Jade Pool" of the prophecy was a viewing portal into alternate universes.

The final chapter detailed the design of a starship drive.

Janelle sat at the table, surrounded by books, too stunned to read any more. If this record was accurate, these people had achieved interstellar travel *five centuries ago.* What the blazes had happened since then?

Footsteps sounded outside.

Janelle froze. A door opened nearby, then closed. She glanced around quickly, but saw nowhere to hide. As the doorknob to the library turned, she jumped to her feet, and her clothes jangled.

The footsteps receded.

Janelle went to the door and leaned against it, straining to hear what was happening outside.

More footsteps.

She backed up until the table stopped her retreat. A key clinked in the lock. *No.* To have come this far, to have made this incredible discovery, only to be caught—*no, not now.*

The door opened.

VII
PROPHESIER

A slender man stood in the archway. Wrinkles surrounded his eyes, and he wore his gray hair long, in a queue. His clothes were simple, brown trousers and an unadorned gray shirt. For a long moment he stared at Janelle. Then he stepped inside and closed the door.

"This is an odd place for a bride," he said.

She folded her arms over her skimpy clothing. "I need to contact my husband."

"I've seen that girdle," he said coldly. "The emperor's aunt wore it at her wedding. So will the bride of the emperor's brother."

"Yes, I'm Prince Dominick-Michael's wife." In truth, she had no idea who she was married to, but she wasn't about to tell him that. "I need to send him a message."

He spoke dryly. "My apology if this is too blunt—but why are you in a monastery, alone, on your wedding day?"

"It's not my wedding day."

"Why else would you dress that way?"

"The wedding already took place."

"Who hurt your wrists?"

Startled, she covered one of the bandages with her hand. "I must go to Dominick."

He lifted his chin. "This monastery serves the emperor. We will send for him."

"No! You can't do that."

"We are loyal servants to Maximillian." He made no attempt to hide his suspicion. "If his brother needs to be contacted, the emperor will do so."

"I can offer you a reward." Inspiration came to her. "One worth far more to you than jewels or gold." She indicated the books on the table. "I can tell you what these mean. It could improve your lives beyond imagining." Whether she could actually do that was debatable, but she had no doubt she could offer him more than he had now, if the level of understanding she had seen accurately portrayed how little the people here retained of their ancient knowledge.

"That is hard to believe," the monk said.

"But true."

His voice hardened. "Prince Dominick-Michael would never marry any woman except the one from the prophecy. And Lady Janelle, the emperor would do anything to prevent that marriage."

She stiffened. "You seem to have decided who I am. You have me at a disadvantage."

"I am Gregor."

Her anger surged. "*You* made that ghastly prophecy." She waved at the library. "You figured out enough here to look across space and time, right? But you don't really understand it, do you? Otherwise, you could have told them more, like how it works."

Anger tightened his expression. "I have spent my entire life studying these books. I understand them better than anyone else alive."

She plunged ahead, ad-libbing. "That's why I'm the prophecy." For all she knew, it was true. It was no stranger than anything else that had happened. "I was sent to you, Brother Gregor. Would you like to know more? Give me sanctuary and I'll tell you."

"You think I would betray Othman in my own lust for knowledge?"

"A love of knowledge is a gift, not an undesirable lust."

He scowled at her. "You talk a great deal."

"Think what you could learn. You're a brilliant scholar; you must be, to have tamed space and time." She didn't know him, but if he understood even a small part of these books with no formal training, it could be true. "I can help unlock these mysteries for you."

"You speak *blasphemy*." He cut the air with a sharp wave of his hand. "Such study is for men, and only those who dedicate their lives to the monastery, forgoing riches, prestige, *and* women."

"A lot of these books have female authors."

He glared at her. "That may be. But living women aren't allowed in here." His gaze traveled over her body, and he made a visible effort to pull his attention back to her face. "You will not seduce me into betraying the emperor."

"What betrayal?" She clenched her fists, ignoring the pain in her wrists. "You think it's all right for Maximillian to kidnap his brother's wife, but heaven forbid she should protect herself?"

"I don't claim Maximillian is a gentle man." He stepped back to the door and pulled a cord hanging there. "But he is my master and I am sworn to obey his word and law."

Janelle swallowed. "What does the cord do?" When he didn't answer, her anger surged. "Was it a game, pitting Maximillian and Dominick against each other from the day of their birth?"

"No." Fatigue showed on his lined face. "It threatens all I value. The well-being of Othman."

"And you think that depends on me going to Maximillian?"

"He is the emperor." Gregor pulled himself up straighter. "It is my moral duty to act in his best interest."

She made an incredulous noise. "How can you talk about moral duty when you intend to send me to be raped and tortured by a monster?"

"I hardly think you are fit to pass judgment on an emperor."

"Why not? I know brutality when I see it."

Gregor shifted his weight. "How he treats you and how he rules Othman are different matters."

"Like hell."

"At your age and with your female attractions—" He cleared his throat. "You don't have what it takes to make such judgments."

"I may be young," she said, "but that doesn't mean my brain doesn't work. And what does you finding me sexually attractive have to do with my ability to think?"

His face turned a deep red. "You twist my words."

"No, I don't." Frustrated, she said, "You make it sound as if I'm evil because I don't want to go back to a man who plans to thrash me until my blood soaks his whip, after which he's going to send it to my husband."

"I have to do what I believe is right. I cannot sacrifice higher principles for your welfare."

She regarded him steadily. "I question the validity of your principles."

His face turned red. "If my principles weren't *valid*, it wouldn't have mattered to me whether or not you had reason to remain in your cold, soulless universe. You had no one there. Nothing to stop you from leaving."

"What?" Janelle whispered. He couldn't mean what she thought.

His voice quieted. "I saw them die. The nobleman in Andalusia. His lady. Their son." Softly, he added, "Your family. I'm sorry."

The air seemed to rush out of the room. At first she could say no more than, "He wasn't a nobleman." Then she inhaled deeply. "They were making bridges among different peoples. They *died* for it. How can you call that soulless?"

He shook his head. "Right or wrong, they left you alone."

Footsteps sounded in the hall. Four men entered the room, all dressed like Gregor. Turning to them, he indicated Janelle. "We have a guest. We must send word to the emperor."

The monks gave Janelle a cloth she could use as a shawl to cover herself, though she suspected they did it more for their own peace of mind than for her. They locked her in a high corner room, provided water and a basin, and brought her fruit, cheeses, and a carafe of wine. Then they left her alone.

As demoralized as she felt, she was ravenous. She wolfed down the food, then washed up and searched her cell. Shaped like a piece of pie, it measured five paces by three at the wide end. The walls were whitewashed plaster. A bench stood against the outer wall, and above it, light trickled in a window slit. Swirls on the cloudy glass reminded her of the Mandelbrot fractal. Had Dominick's ancestors learned chaos theory? *What secrets were locked in that library?*

She was still reeling from what Gregor had told her. He saw her family die. It was apparently part of what convinced him she was destined to come here. She knew he couldn't have affected what happened through the Riemann screen, that he might not have even seen their actual deaths, only that horrific news clip of the car exploding. But nothing would stop the pain that flooded her.

Janelle rapped the walls; she prodded, scraped, pushed, and yanked anything she could reach. She pounded the window, trying to break the glass, even knowing she couldn't wriggle out the narrow opening. It offered a view of the yard that fronted the monastery—and so she saw when the riders left, galloping down the same trail the cart had taken up here. She thought of Maximillian, and bile rose in her throat.

Eventually, she sank onto the floor in one corner and pulled her knees to her chest. Laying her head on her knees, she closed her eyes and gave in to her exhaustion.

Janelle awoke with sunlight slanting across her face. A clamor outside had roused her: men calling, biaquines trumpeting, boots stamping. Muzzy with sleep, she climbed onto the bench and peered out the window. Warriors filled the slice of the yard she could see, men in armor on biaquines.

And Maximillian.

Her panic flared. He strode across her field of view, his black armor absorbing the sunlight, his dark hair whipping around his face.

"No!" She scraped at the window, trying to dig out the glass. Only a sliver of stone crumbled under her assault. She kept going, frantic, knowing it would take hours to dislodge the window, that she wouldn't fit through the opening anyway. But she couldn't quit. She remembered the shackles, the whip and spiked belt, and the ugly hunger in Maximillian's gaze.

A key turned in the lock.

Janelle spun around. Jumping off the bench, she pulled the shawl around her body, as if that could shield her.

The door opened, revealing Gregor. Maximillian towered in the shadows behind him, the hilt of his sword jutting above his shoulder.

Gregor stared at her, his face unreadable. He stepped aside and bowed deeply to the emperor. Then he left, his footfalls receding down the hall. Maximillian remained, his unsmiling gaze fixed on Janelle. With a slow tread, he walked into the cell—

And it wasn't him.

"Dominick!" Janelle flung herself across the room, and he caught her in an embrace. She wrapped her arms around him and laid her head on his chest, closing her eyes while tears squeezed out under her lids.

"Ai," he murmured, stroking her hair. "I wasn't sure what to expect. I feared hatred."

"I don't hate you." Her voice caught. "I hate what you've done to my life."

He drew back to look at her. Then he touched her bandaged wrists. "I swear my brother will never hurt you again. *Never.*"

She felt dizzy with the release of fear. "Gregor told me he was sending for Maximillian."

"Whatever you said convinced him to seek me instead. His men found my army en route to Max's palace." Unexpectedly, he laughed. "You have sorely traumatized our Brother Gregor. He informs me that you are a most disturbing woman. He says he does not envy my marital state."

She managed a smile. "Trauma builds character."

"So it does." His amusement faded. "I will leave my Sixth Regiment here. You and I can ride home with the rest of my army."

From what Janelle had gathered, only twenty men lived at the monastery, scholars rather than warriors. "Do you really need so many to counter a few monks?"

"Not counter. Protect. In summoning me, they have risked Maximillian's wrath." He held out his hand. "Come with me, Janelle."

She took his hand.

VIII
THE KEY

The library in Dominick's palace awed Janelle. She wandered through room after room with bookcases built into the walls from the floor to the vaulted ceiling. Sliding ladders gave access to the upper shelves. Engravings in the wood curved in vine motifs, and marble panels bore quotes from scholars she didn't recognize. Gold and burgundy brocade upholstered the arm-chairs. Tall lamps stood in the corners, flickering with flames behind their stained-glass shades. Most of all, books filled the rooms, embossed, gilt-edged, gleaming everywhere in the golden light.

Janelle's bodyguards stayed back, giving her a semblance of privacy. She had barely spoken to Dominick during the ride here from the monastery today. She needed time to sort out her thoughts. Nor did she know what to say; they had so little in common, and she felt far out of her league with him. Yet he stayed on her mind. It was more than the physical attraction; he also intrigued and compelled her. But she wasn't ready for this man who would be emperor.

Perhaps he understood. He hadn't insisted on accompanying her here. He had to know she was avoiding him; what happy bride immediately sought out a library upon arriving at her new home? Then again, most brides hadn't just discovered such a momentous trove of knowledge. Although Dominick seemed puzzled by her excitement, he didn't resist her pursuit of the knowledge.

Judged from the most modern scrolls in this library, the year here corresponded to that in her universe. However, just as in Gregor's library, the science collection had no recent books. The tomes were centuries old, the most recent dated 1557 A.D. A layer of dust covered them. She found no history of science, no explanation of how these people had once possessed such great knowledge and now had so little.

In fact, she found few histories of any kind, though she searched for an hour. Several works described the reign of Dominick's family, but they didn't go back to the sixteenth cen-tury. Although it was harder to read the historical accounts, they clearly focused on wars and politics, what the authors considered great deeds of the Constantines. Yet she found many hints that his ancestors had also distinguished themselves in scholarly pursuits, showing that same gift for abstract thought she had seen in Dominick and Maximillian.

One section of the library dealt with architecture, including books about the Palace of Arches. Nothing explained the Fourier Hall, but a few studies mentioned a "key" to that great room. She eventually found a description in a book on ancient military codes, of all places. Settling into an armchair, she pored over the text, puzzling out the words. The arches of that gorgeous hall formed a code. Their Fourier transform was a key. But to *what*?

Janelle sat back, thinking. In two dimensions, the transform would probably be a peak with rippled tails; in three dimensions, it might resemble the diffraction pattern for a circular aperture. The locations of the central peak would specify a time. For what? The text seemed to describe a portal, not the gate that had brought her here but something for a much bigger event.

She went to a desk and rummaged in its drawers until she found an inkbottle, quill, and parchment. It took her a while to figure out how to use the quill, but finally she set to work, trying to derive the Fourier transform of the arches. She couldn't do it exactly; that would require a computer. But the book gave drawings and measurements for the hall, and she could model the arches as the sum of a few squared sine waves.

As she ground away at the equations, the lamp behind the desk burned low. The transform had the shape she expected, with a large peak at the number 2057. Why 2057? She thought it represented a time. Perhaps it meant 2057 years in the future or that many years since something had happened. Or the year 2057.

A chill went through her. In 2057, she would be seventy-one, about the age of the woman in the prophecy. This *couldn't* connect to her—for that implied she would still be here in fifty years.

Dismayed, she went on another search—and hit gold: a modern account of the Jade Pool. The "jade-hued surface" had to be a Riemann screen. The author considered it an enigmatic artifact of mythical proportions and presented equations for it as if they were runes of a spell. Janelle could appreciate what Gregor had achieved, if he had unraveled practical knowledge from such fanciful treatments.

The book also discussed Riemann gates, which turned out to be a more complicated application of the screen. She didn't understand the technology, but she worked through the equations. No matter how many times she tried to find a mistake in her work, she derived the same result: the gate didn't depend on two sheets—it involved *hundreds*. Dominick had managed to go back and forth to her universe because he used the same gate, but it was closed now, and the entire cycle would have to complete before it reopened. That would take centuries, maybe even millennia.

She stared at the parchment with its blotted ink. Then she folded her arms on the desk and put her head on her forearms.

Sometime later, a man said, "Janelle?" A hand rested on her arm.

She lifted her head to find Dominick watching her. He had pulled a stool up to the desk and was sitting next to her.

"What happened?" he asked.

She shook her head, too disheartened to answer.

"Tell me," he said softly.

"I don't think I can go home." The words burned inside her. "If you hadn't opened the gate when you did, you could never have found me. I would have been long dead before the cycle returned to my universe."

"You are telling me the prophecy created itself? That if Gregor had never said anything, you wouldn't be here?"

She could only say, "Yes."

He answered in a low voice. "Then I am doubly sorry."

"Something happens in fifty years," she said unevenly. "When I'm the age of the woman Gregor saw in the pool. Another gate is going to open. A big one. During those few months, your people may be able to do something incredible."

He seemed bewildered. "What something?"

"I don't know." She hesitated. "Maybe your ancestors didn't strand you forever. Maybe you can find them." She laid her palm against his chest. "Your family had the gifts to understand once."

A strange look came into his eyes. "There is a saying." He spoke in an unfamiliar language.

"What does it mean?"

"Roughly translated: Constantines are the key to the future."

She stared at him. "Who else besides you and the monks has a library like this, with the ancient books?"

"Just Maximillian."

"My God," she whispered. "It's *you*. Your family. *You're* the key. The Fourier Hall is a clue, or a remnant, like the waveforms on the walls, but you're the guardians of the knowledge. It's probably why your family ended up ruling Othman." She motioned at the library. "Everything you've lost is still here. The ability to unlock it is *in* you, in your genes, your minds. If you can find it." She felt as if she were breaking. "But why me? How could you reach across universes for someone to help you do this?"

He spoke in a subdued voice. "Gregor said the pool showed many futures. My father wanted the one that maximized his empire. I always assumed it depended on who ruled, Max or me, and that you came into it because you brought power into our family, probably through an alliance." Quietly he said, "Maybe it is much larger than this battle between brothers. Perhaps it is something only you can do."

A tear slid down her face. "At what price to me?"

"Ai, Janelle." He put his arms around her shoulders and drew her to him. "I don't know how to take you home. But if you let me, I will give you a home here worth having."

She laid her head against him and fought back her tears.

Dominick's suite was far different than the chamber where Janelle had spent her first night in the palace. It was five times the size. Low black-lacquered tables stood around the room, surrounded by big cushions instead of chairs. Rich tapestries in gold, red, and green hung on the walls. The rugs he used for a bed filled one corner, tumbled with velvet pillows. Braziers burned in other corners, and oil lamps flickered in wall sconces, shedding a dim golden light. It all had a barbaric elegance.

Janelle sat with Dominick on his bed, leaning against the wall. They had come here from the library, and now he held her. She fitted to his side, unable to talk, her thoughts edged with pain.

After a while, she said, "It is hard to believe you are brothers."

He answered in a low voice. "Do not see me with blinders. What Max does and believes—it is in me also. I had a different life, and it taught me other ways. Had brutality molded me instead, I would be just like him."

"Will you go to war?"

"He is my brother, despite everything." He sounded tired. "But I will not desert my home and people to go 'across the sea,' as he says I must. If that means we must fight, so be it."

She understood. Six of his officers had died in the raid on the palace. He could rebuild the hall, but nothing would bring back those men. At least Kadar, the guard who had helped her in the tunnels, had survived. He had been injured, but he was recovering.

"Gregor told me about your family," Dominick said. "I'm sorry."

She couldn't talk about it. So she said only, "My father was an ambassador. Do you have them here?"

"Yes. It is a position of honor, usually held by a nobleman."

He rubbed his hand along her upper arm. "The people of Othman have a history of strife with the Andalusian Empire. We descend from their colonies, but we gained our independence centuries ago."

Andalusia. Southern Spain. "The empire doesn't exist in my universe. But Spain is a nation. I lived there for years."

He didn't seem surprised. "It is no wonder the prophecy predicted you would affect our balance of power. Your background suits you well to the throne."

Dryly she said, "I don't think your brother was interested in my background."

The corded muscles in his arm tensed. "Max will never be satisfied until he takes you from me or kills us both." Grimly he added, "He will succeed with neither."

"He says he and I are married."

Ire sparked in his voice. "He cannot marry my wife."

"His spy told him you and I never wed."

"I gave you the jewels. And we consummated the marriage. So we are wed."

"Uh, Dominick." She lifted her head. "We didn't consummate it."

"I stayed the night. As far as anyone knows, we did." He cleared his throat. "Unless you plan to say otherwise."

She smiled. "I won't."

He looked relieved. "Good."

"I met your daughter. She's charming."

His tone gentled. "Yes. All my children are."

"I'm sorry . . . about their mother."

"Ah, well." He sounded muted. "It has been years."

He fell silent after that, and she regretted bringing up the memories. After a while, she said, "What happened to your people five hundred years ago? Was there a war? A catastrophe?"

"I don't think so." For one of the few times since she had met him, he sounded uncertain. "Some of the people just left."

"To where?"

Dominick pointed upward. "There. Somewhere." He pushed his hand through his hair. "I have more education than most because my mother insisted Max and I study history, language, astronomy, and mathematics when we were boys, as much as anyone could teach us. But it barely touches what is in my library. Why did our ancestors desert this world and never come back?" He shook his head. "We have lost that knowledge. They took so much with them. Legend says they left us behind deliberately. Some claim a political rift existed between those who went and those who stayed. Others say we remained of our own free will, as guardians of Earth, and that those who left cannot return because they became lost between worlds, even universes." Softly he said, "Perhaps it is both. But it's been half a millennium. Our memories are faded."

It was heartbreaking to think of the human race fractured that way. "Maybe they'll return someday."

"You will search for answers?"

She nodded, gratified he didn't object. "Gladly."

"You say I have some small talent for scholarly pursuits." He sounded bemused.

"More than small, I think."

"I haven't the interest, though." His smile flashed. "But ah, Janelle, our children will be brilliant."

It hurt to realize her children would never know her world. Yet it was true; if they inherited their parents' ability for abstract thought, and learned to use it, they might truly reach for the stars. She would teach them what she knew. But most of all, she would love them, as her parents had loved her.

He was watching her face. "Together, you and I can achieve much."

"I hope so." Her voice caught. "We will make a good place." Somehow.

"Aye," Dominick murmured. "We will."

Janelle didn't know if she would ever understand this complicated man, but she wanted to try. She knew life here wouldn't be easy. It was a violent world, harsh and unyielding, and Maximillian would always be there. Yet it also had an incredible beauty. If she could never go home, she could at least have her work in the library, a family to love, and dreams of the day when humanity might soar beyond the bounds of Earth.

A bittersweet peace settled over her. This wasn't a life she would have chosen. But it might hold joy, even astonishing events, and for that, she could look forward to the future.

DAVID DRAKE

'm defining the Golden Age of SF as July 1939 through 1945. At the time there were few SF hardcovers and no paperbacks; the field was almost entirely a matter of stories in pulp magazines.

You can argue about the ending date, but the beginning is easy: A. E. van Vogt's first story, "Black Destroyer," appeared in the July 1939 issue of *Astounding*; Robert Heinlein's first story, "Lifeline," would appear in the next issue; and *Astounding* was fully under the direction of John W. Campbell (earlier issues used a good deal of material purchased by his predecessor).

In my view, Golden Age SF is the SF bought by Campbell for *Astounding* (and its fantasy companion, *Unknown/Unknown Worlds*) during his great initial period as editor.

Modern SF was largely defined by the stories written for *Astounding* during this period by Heinlein (above all), van Vogt, L. Sprague de Camp, L. Ron Hubbard, the team of Henry Kuttner and C. L. Moore, and Isaac Asimov (who also had an early story in the July 1939 *Astounding*).

Two other major writers worked in this period: Murray Leinster, who had started writing important SF in 1919, and Ray Bradbury, whose best contemporary work appeared in *Weird Tales*. Neither man can be described as "a Campbell writer," though Leinster did major work for *Astounding*.

There's a tendency to believe nowadays that stories which appeared in other magazines during the Golden Age had been rejected by Campbell. There certainly were magazines assembled from rejects, paying salvage rates for their material, but that doesn't mean they were unsuccessful or ignored at the time. In 1940, issues of Fred Pohl's *Astonishing* outsold Campbell's *Astounding* by seventy thousand copies to fifty thousand, though Pohl paid roughly half Campbell's word rates.

But many of the SF magazines of the time were simply different from *Astounding*, not necessarily better or worse. Ray Palmer's Ziff–Davis publications *Amazing* and *Fantastic Adventures* were the bestselling SF magazines of all time, selling 180,000 copies per issue. Their market appears to have been unsophisticated but not juvenile: sex and violence were strong, consistent themes. Though their stories had a great deal of action, they were often as plotless as literary fiction.

Standard's *Thrilling Wonder Stories* and *Startling Stories* (and, for that matter, *Captain Future*) did tend to be juvenile. Not stupid, not badly written, but likely to appeal to an audience younger than that of *Astounding*. Kuttner and Moore did about as much good work for *Standard* as they did for *Astounding,* and when Bradbury came into his own (after my period), the *Standard* magazines were his natural habitat.

Finally, *Planet Stories* was a frankly adventure market. Unlike the Ziff–Davis magazines, stories in *Planet* did have plots. They were likely to involve lost Martian cities and exotic princesses, but they had beginnings, middles, and ends.

SF cover art in the Golden Age is very well known—but here it's the magazines other than *Astounding* that are either famous or notorious, depending on your point of view. This is the period of bug-eyed monsters and girls wearing brass bras or transparent spacesuits over swimsuits. These garish cover paintings were intended to be noticed on newsstands.

There are modern collectors who appreciate these covers as art, but there are many others who consider them sexist, juvenile embarrassments. Exactly the same attitudes appear in the letter columns of the magazines themselves, argued with passion on both sides.

The contents of the magazines, however (with the limited exceptions of the Ziff–Davis magazines), don't reflect the implications of the covers. Some pulps were explicitly sadistic and violent, but not the Golden Age SF mags. The readers knew that, but a layman scanning a newsstand might honestly have lumped *Thrilling Wonder Stories* in with *Terror Tales*.

Astounding was the one magazine in the field in which the arguments for decorous, respectable covers won over exploitation and sales. *Astounding*'s covers were often extremely accomplished art, but they were determinedly sedate even when the story being illustrated would honestly lend itself to a more active development. For example, the March 1943 cover shows people rising through water in a transparent elevator shaft. This is indeed an illustration of Kuttner and Moore's *Clash by Night*, but that novelette also includes battles between giant warships on the storm-tossed, monster-ridden seas of Venus.

Campbell, who from the moment he took over the magazine tried to get rid of the name *Astounding* (he finally succeeded in 1960), was also trying to keep his covers respectable. Battles and monsters weren't respectable, even if they appeared in the stories themselves. (*Unknown Worlds* had even gone to basically typographic covers before paper shortages killed the magazine.)

There's a final factor about the Golden Age that is often overlooked: it almost precisely overlaps World War II. Not only did this affect the contents of stories (there are more Nazi spies and heroic allied castaways than you might expect), it affected the writers. By 1944, Heinlein, de Camp, Hubbard, and Asimov were either in or employed by the Navy, and artists were doing war work also.

Stories were written not by who was best but by who was left. That doesn't mean there was no good work—Leinster's *First Contact* comes from 1945, and Kuttner and Moore were at their very peak—but some commentators have made a case for ending the Golden Age in November 1943, when *Astounding* shrank to digest size.

Our present-day vision of the Golden Age of SF is in many ways a creation of post-war editors who mined the period for fat hardcover anthologies. Those editors focused on *Astounding*, and rightly so. But the magazines of the day were remarkably diverse—and remarkably interesting, in their widely different ways. It was a time when there was SF for everybody, not just a narrow group . . . and personally, I wish that situation held true today.

POWERS

URSULA K. LE GUIN

This year's Nebula Award–winning novel is *Powers* by Ursula K. Le Guin. There is a quandary in commenting on just how wonderful Ms. Le Guin's novels are. When I really want to say a book has really well-developed and fascinating characters and a deep rich environment, I normally comment that it is like a Le Guin novel. This *IS* a Le Guin novel, or rather an excerpt from it, which rather says it all. From her *Earthsea* and *The Hainish Cycles* to *Powers* she simply sets the standard for wonderfully crafted tales set in amazing places.

EIGHT

Four of them were around me before I saw one of them. I was barely awake. I had sat up, on the open hillside by the dead fire, alone. They were around me, without movement, out of the grass, out of the dim grey air of early dawn. I looked from one to the next and sat still.

They were armed, not like soldiers but with short bows and long knives. Two carried five-foot staffs. They looked grim.

One of them finally spoke in a soft, hoarse voice, almost a whisper. "Fire out?"

I nodded.

He went and kicked at the few half-burnt sticks left, trampled them carefully, felt them with his hands. I got up to help him bury the cold cinders.

"Come on then," he said. I bundled up my blanket and the last scraps of dried meat to carry. I wore the cape of rabbit and squirrel skins for warmth.

"Stinks," said one of the men.

"Reeks," said another. "Bad as old Cuga."

"He brought me here," I said.

"Cuga?"

"You was with him?"

"All summer."

One stared, one spat, one shrugged; the fourth, the one who had spoken first, motioned with his head and led us down the long hill towards the forest.

I knelt to drink from the stream at the foot of the hill. The hoarse-voiced leader nudged me with his staff while I was still drinking thirstily. "That's enough, you'll be pissing all day," he said. I scrambled up and followed them across the stream and under the dark eaves of the trees.

He led us all the way. We moved hastily through the woods, often at a trot, until mid-morning, when we stopped in a small clearing. It smelled of stale blood. A pack of vultures flapped up heavily on great black wings from some remnants of guts and skulls. The carcasses of three deer had been butchered and hung, glittering with flies, high from a tree limb. The men brought them down and divided and roped them so each of us could carry a load of meat, and we set off again, but now at an easier pace. I was tormented with thirst and by the flies that kept swarming around us and our burdens. The load I carried was not well balanced, and my feet, sore from the long walk yesterday, blistered in my old shoes. The trail we followed was very slight and winding, seldom visible more than a few paces ahead among the big, dark trees, and often made difficult by tree roots. When we came at last to a stream crossing I went right down again on hands and knees to drink.

The leader turned back to stir me up, saying, "Come on! You can drink when we get there!" But one of the other men was down with his face in the water too, and looked up to say, "Ah, let him drink, Brigin." The leader said nothing then, but waited for us.

The water bathed my feet with wonderful coolness as we waded across the stream, but then as we went on the blisters grew worse, my wet shoes rubbing them, and I was hobbling with pain by the time we came to the forest camp. We cast down our burdens of venison in an open shed, and I could stand up straight at last and look around.

If I'd come there from where I used to live, it wouldn't have looked like anything at all—a few low huts, a few men, in a meadow where alders grew by a small stream, dark forest all around. But I came there from the lonesome wilderness. The sight of the buildings was strange and impressive to me, and the presence of other people even stranger and more frightening.

Nobody paid any attention to me. I got up my courage and went to the stream under the alders, drank my fill at last, then took off my shoes and put my raw, burning, bloody feet in the water. It was warm in the meadow, the autumn sun still pouring into it. Presently I took off my clothes and got into the water entirely. I washed myself, then I washed my clothes as well as I could. They had been white. White clothing is worn by a girl in her betrothal ceremony, and by the dead, and by those who go to bury the dead. There was no telling what color my clothes had been. They were brown and grey, rag-color. I did not think about their whiteness. I laid them on the grass to dry and got back in the stream and put my head underwater to wash my hair. When I came up I couldn't see, for my hair hung down over my eyes, it had grown so long. It was filthy and matted and I washed it again and again. When I came up from the last dip and scrubbing, a man was sitting beside my clothes on the stream bank, watching me.

"It's an improvement," he said.

He was the one who'd told the leader to let me drink.

He was short and brown, with high, ruddy cheekbones and narrow, dark eyes; his hair was cut short to his head. He had an accent, a way of talking that came from somewhere else.

I came up out of the water, dried myself as well as I could with the old brown blanket, and pulled on my wet tunic, seeking modesty, though there seemed to be only men around, and also seeking warmth. The sun had left the clearing though the sky was still bright. I shivered. But I didn't want to put the filthy fur cape on my hard-won cleanness.

"Hey," he said, "hang on." He went off and came back with a tunic and some kind of garment I did not recognize. "They're dry, anyhow," he said, handing them to me.

I shucked off my limp wet tunic and put on the one he gave me. It was brown linen, much worn, soft, long-sleeved. It felt warm and pleasant on my skin. I held up the other piece of clothing he had brought. It was black and made of some heavy, dense material; it must be a cape, I thought. I tried to put it on over my shoulders. I could not get it to fit.

The man watched me for a little while and then he lay back on the stream bank and began to laugh. He laughed till his eyes disappeared entirely and his face turned dark red. He curled up over his knees and laughed till you could tell it hurt him, and though it wasn't a noisy laugh, some men heard and came over and looked at him and looked at me, and some of them began laughing too.

"Oh," he said at last, wiping his eyes and sitting up. "Oh. That did me good. That's a kilt, young'un. You wear it—" and he began to laugh again, and doubled up, and wheezed, and finally said, "You wear it on the other end."

I looked at the thing, and saw it had a waistband, like trousers.

"I'll do without," I said. "If you don't mind."

"No," he said, wheezing. "I don't mind. Give it back, then."

"Why would the kid want one of your fool skirts, Chamry?"

one of the onlookers said. "Here, kid, I'll get you something decent." He came back with a pair of breeches that fit me well enough, though loosely. When I had them on he said, "Keep 'em, they're too tight for my belly. So you came in with Brigin and them today? Joining up, are you? What'll we call you?"

"Gavir Arca," I said.

The man who had given me the kilt said, "That's your name."

I looked at him, not understanding.

"Do you want to use it?" he asked.

I had done so little thinking for so long, my mind would not move quickly at all; it needed a lot of time. I said at last, "Gav."

"Gav it is," said the man who had given me the kilt. "I'm Chamry Bern of Bernmant, and I use my name, for I'm so far from where I came that no one can track me by name or fame or any game."

"He's from where the men wear skirts and the women piss standing," said one of the onlookers, and got some laughter from the others.

"Lowlanders," said Chamry Bern, of them, not to them. "They know no better. Come on, you, Gav. You'd better take the oath, if that's what you came for, and get your share of dinner. I saw you carrying in your share of it and more."

The god Luck is deaf in one ear, they say, the ear we pray to; he can't hear our prayers. What he hears, what he listens to, nobody knows. Denios the poet said he hears the wheels of the stars' great chariots turning on the roads of heaven. I know that while I was sunk far beneath any thought of prayer, with no hope, no trust in anything, no desire, Luck was always with me. I lived, though I took no care to survive. I came to no harm among strangers. I carried money and was not robbed. When I was alone and on the verge of death, an old mad hermit beat me back to life. And now Luck had sent me to these men, and one of them was Chamry Bern.

Chamry went and whacked on a crowbar hung from a post

of the largest hut. The signal brought men to gather around the porch of the hut. "Newcomer," he said. "Gav is his name. He says he's been living with Cuga the Ogre, which would explain the smell that came with him. And after a bath in our river he seeks to join our company. Right, Gav?"

I nodded. I was intimidated by being the center of what seemed to me a great crowd of men—twenty or more—all looking me over. Most of them were young and had a trim, fit, hard look, like Brigin, the man who'd led me here, though there were several grey or bald heads and a couple of slack bellies.

"Do you know who we are?" one of the bald heads demanded.

I took a deep breath. "Are you the Barnavites?"

That caused some scowling and some laughter. "Some of us used to be," the man said, "maybe. And what do you know of Barna's lot, boy?"

I was younger than they were, but I didn't like being called kid and boy all the time. It put my back up.

"I heard stories. That they lived in the forest as free men, neither masters or slaves, sharing fairly all they had."

"Well put," said Chamry. "All in a nutshell." Several men looked pleased and nodded.

"Well enough, well enough," the bald man said, keeping up his dignity. Another man came up close to me; he looked very much like Brigin, and as I learned later they were brothers. His face was hard and handsome, his eyes clear and cold. He looked me over. "If you live with us you'll learn what fair sharing means," he said. "It means what we do, you do. It's one for all with us. If you think you can do whatever you like, you won't last here. If you don't share, you don't eat. If you're careless and bring danger on us, you're dead. We have rules. You'll take an oath to live with us and keep our rules. And if you break that oath, we'll hunt you down surer than any slave taker."

Their faces were grim; they all nodded at what he said.

"You think you can keep that oath?"

"I can try," I said.

"Try's not good enough."

"I'll keep your oath," I said, my temper roused by his bullying.

"We'll see," he said, turning away. "Get the stuff, Modla."

The bald man and Brigin brought out of the hut a knife, a clay bowl, a deer antler, and some meal. I will not tell the ceremony, for those who go through it are sworn to secrecy, nor can I tell the words of the oath I took. They all swore that oath again with me. The rites and the oath-speaking brought them all together in fellow feeling, and when all was done and spoken several of them came to pound my back and tell me I'd borne the initiation well, and was a brave fellow, and welcome among them.

Chamry Bern had come forward as my sponsor, and a young man called Venne as my hunting mate. They sat on either side of me at the celebration that followed. Meat had already been roasting on spits, but they added more to make a feast of it, and night had fallen by the time we sat to eat—on the ground, or on stumps and crude stools, around the red, dancing fires. I had no knife. Venne took me in to a chest of weapons and told me to choose one. I took a light, keen blade in a leather sheath. With it I cut myself a chunk out of a sizzling, dripping, blackened, sweet-smelling haunch and sat down with it and ate like a starved animal. Somebody brought me a metal cup and poured something into it—beer or mead—sour and somewhat foamy. The men laughed louder as they drank, and shouted, and laughed again. My heart warmed to their good fellowship—the friendship of the Forest Brothers. For that was the name they called themselves, and had given me, since I was one of them.

All around the firelit clearing was the night forest, utter darkness under the trees, high leaf crowns grey in the starlight for miles and miles.

If Chamry Bern hadn't taken a liking to me and if Venne hadn't taken me as his hunting partner I would have had a worse time of it that fall and winter than I did. As it was, I was often at the limit of my endurance. I'd lived wild with Cuga, but he'd looked after me, sheltered me, fed me, and that was in summer, too, when it's easy to live wild. Here my city softness, my lack of physical strength, my ignorance of the skills of survival, were nearly the death of me. Brigin and his brother Eter and several other men had been farm slaves, used to a hard life, tough, fearless, and resourceful, and to them I was a dead loss, a burden. Other men in the group, town-bred, had some patience with my wretched incompetence, and gave and taught me what I needed to get by. As with Cuga, my knack at fishing gave me a way to show I could try at least to be useful. I showed no promise at all in hunting, though Venne took me with him conscientiously and tried to train me with the short bow and in all the silent skills of the hunter.

Venne was twenty or so; at fifteen he had run away from a vicious master in a town of the region of Casicar, and made his way to the forest—for everybody in Casicar, he said, knew about the Forest Brothers, and all the slaves dreamed of joining them. He enjoyed the life in the woods, seemed fully at home in it, and was one of the best hunters of our band; but I soon learned that he was restless. He didn't get on with Brigin and Eter. "Playing the masters," he said drily. And after a while, "And they won't have women with us . . . Well, Barna's men have women, right? I think of joining them."

"Think again," said Chamry, sewing a soft upper to a shoe sole; he was our tanner and cobbler, and made pretty good shoes and sandals for us of elk hide. "You'll be running back to us begging us to save you. You think Brigin's bossy? Never was a man could match a woman for giving orders. Men are by nature slaves to women, and women are by nature the masters of men. Hello woman, goodbye freedom!"

"Maybe," Venne said. "But there's other things comes with her."

They were good friends, and included me in their friendship and their conversation. Many of the men of the band seemed to have little use for language, using a grunt or a gesture, or sitting stolid and mute as animals. The silence of the slave had gone so deep in them they could not break it. Chamry on the other hand was a man of words; he loved to talk and listen and tell stories, rhyming and chiming them in a kind of half-poetry, and was ready to discuss anything with anybody.

I soon knew his history, or as much of it as he saw fit to tell, and as near or far from the truth as suited him. He came from the Uplands, he said, a region far north and east of the City States. I'd never heard of it and asked him if it was farther than Urdile, and he said yes, far beyond Urdile, beyond even Bendraman. I knew the name of Bendraman only from the ancient tale *Chamhan*.

"The Uplands are beyond the beyond," he said, "north of the moon and east of the dawn. A desolation of hill and bog and rock and cliff, and rising over it all a huge vast mountain with a beard of clouds, the Carrantages. Nobody deserves to live in the Uplands but sheep. It's starving land, freezing land, winter forever, a gleam of sunlight once a year. It's all cut up into little small domains, farms they'd call them here and poor sorry farms at that, but in the Uplands they're domains, and each has a master, the brantor, and each brantor has an evil power in him. Witches they are, every one. How'd you like that for a master? A man who could move his hand and say a word and turn you inside out with your guts on the ground and your eyes staring into the inside of your brain? Or a man who could look at you and you'd never think a thought of your own again, but only what he put into your head?"

He liked to go on about these awful powers, the gifts he called them, of the Upland witches, his tales growing ever taller. I asked him once, if he'd had a master, what his master's power was. That silenced him for a minute. He looked at me with his bright narrow eyes. "You wouldn't think it much of a power, maybe," he said. "Nothing to see. He could weaken the bones in a body. It took a while. But if he cast his power on you, in a month you'd be weak and weary, in half a year your legs would bend under you like grass, in a year you'd be dead. You don't want to cross a man who could do that. Oh, you lowlanders think you know what it is to have a master! In the Uplands we don't even say slave. The brantor's people, we say. He may be kin to half of 'em, his servants, his serfs—his people. But they're more slaves to him than ever the slave of the worst master down here!"

"I don't know about that," said Venne. "A whip and a couple of big dogs can do about as well as a spell of magic to destroy a man." Venne bore terrible scars on his legs and back and scalp, and one ear had been half torn off his head.

"No, no, it's the fear," Chamry said. "It's the awful fear. You didn't fear the men that beat you and the dogs that bit you, once you'd run clear away from 'em, did you? But I tell you, I ran a hundred miles away from the Uplands and my master, and still I cringed when I felt his thought turn on me. And I felt it! The strength went out of my legs and arms. I couldn't hold my back up straight. His power was on me! All I could do was go on, go on, go on, till there was mountains and rivers and miles between me and his hand and eye and cruel power. When I crossed the great river, the Trond, I grew stronger. When I crossed the second great river, the Sally, I was safe at last. The power can cross a wide water once but not twice. So a wise woman told me. But I crossed yet another to be sure! I'll never go back north, never. You don't know what it is to be a slave, you lowlanders!"

Yet Chamry talked often of the Uplands and the farm where he had been born, and all through his railing at it as a poor, unhappy, wretched place I heard his yearning homesickness. He made of it a vivid picture in my mind, the great barren moorlands and cloudy peaks, the bogs from which at dawn a thousand wild white cranes would rise at once, the stone-walled, slate-roofed farm huddled under the bare curve of a brown hill. As he told about it, I could see it almost as clearly as if I remembered it myself.

And that put me in mind of my own power, or whatever it was, of remembering what was yet to happen. I remembered that I had had such a power, once. But when I thought about that, I began to remember places I didn't want to remember. Memories made my body hunch up in pain and my mind go blank in fear. I pushed them away, turned away from them. Remembering would kill me. Forgetting kept me alive.

The Forest Brothers were all men who had escaped, run away from something unendurable. They were like me. They had no past. Learning how to get through this rough life, how to endure never being dry or warm or clean, to eat only half-raw, half-burnt venison, I might have gone on with them as I had with Cuga, not thinking beyond the present hour and what was around me. And much of the time I did.

But there were times when winter storms kept us in our drafty, smoky cabins, and Chamry, Venne, and some of the other men gathered to talk in the half dark by the smouldering hearth, and then I began to hear their stories of where they came from, how they'd lived, the masters they'd escaped from, their memories of suffering and of pleasure.

Sometimes into my thoughts would come a clear image of a place: a big room full of women and children; a fountain in a city square; a sunny courtyard surrounded by arches, under which women sat spinning . . . When I saw such a place I gave it no name, and my mind turned away from it hastily. I never joined the others' talk about the world outside the forest, and did not like to hear it.

Late one afternoon the six or seven tired, dirty, hungry men around the crude hearth in our cabin had run out of anything to talk about. We all sat in a dumb discouragement. It had been raining a cold hard rain almost ceaselessly for four days and nights. Under the cloud that pressed down on the dark forest trees it seemed night all day long. Fog and darkness tangled in the wet, heavy boughs. To go out to get logs for the fire from the dwindling woodpile was to be wet through at once, and indeed some of us went out naked, since skin dries quicker than cloth and leather. One of our mates, Bulec, had a wretched cough that shook him about like a rat in a dog's mouth. Even Chamry had run out of jokes and tall tales. In that cold, dreary place I was thinking of summer, of the heat and light of summer on the open hills, somewhere. And a cadence came into my mind, a beat, and the words with it, and without any intention I said the words aloud.

> *As in the dark of winter night*
> *The eyes seek dawn,*
> *As in the bonds of bitter cold*
> *The heart craves sun,*
> *So blinded and so bound, the soul*
> *Cries out to thee:*
> *Be our light, our fire, our life,*
> *Liberty!*

"Ah," Chamry said out of a silence that followed the words, "I've heard that. Heard it sung. There's a tune to it."

I sought the tune, and little by little it came to me, with the sound of the beautiful voice that had sung it. I have no singing voice, but I sang it.

"That's fine," Venne said softly.

Bulec coughed and said, "Speak some more such."

"Do that," Chamry said.

I looked into my mind for more remembered words to speak to them. Nothing came for a while. What I found at last was a line of writing. I read it: "'Wearing the white of mourning, the maiden mounted the high steps . . .'" I said it aloud, and in a moment the line led me on to the next, and that to the next. So

I told them the part of Garro's poem in which the prophetess Yurno confronts the enemy hero Rurec. Standing on the walls of Sentas, a girl in mourning, Yurno calls down to the man who killed her warrior father. She tells Rurec how he will die: "Beware of the hills of Trebs," she says, "for you will be ambushed in the hills. You will run away and hide in the bushes, but they will kill you as you try to crawl away without being seen. They will drag your naked body to the town and display it, sprawled facedown, so all can see that the wounds are in your back. Your corpse will not be burned with prayers to the Ancestors as befits a hero, but buried where they bury slaves and dogs." Enraged at her prophecy, Rurec shouts, "And this is how *you* will die, lying sorceress!" and hurls his heavy lance at her. All see it pass through her body just below the breast and fly out, trailing blood, behind her—but she stands on the battlement in her white robes, unharmed. Her brother, the warrior Alira, picks up the lance and hands it up to her, and she tosses it down to Rurec, not hurling it, but end over end, lightly, contemptuously. "When you're running away and hiding, you'll want this," she says, "great hero of Pagadi."

As I spoke the words of the poem, in that cold smoky hut in the half-dark with the noise of the rain loud on the low roof, I saw them written in some pupil's laboured handwriting in the copybook I held as I stood in the schoolroom in Arcamand. "Read the passage, Gavir," my teacher said, and I read the words aloud.

A silence followed.

"Eh, that's a fool," Bacoc said, "thro'n a lance at a witch, don't he know, can't kill a witch but with fire!"

Bacoc was a man of fifty by the look of him, though it's hard to tell the age of men who have lived their life half-starved and under the whip; maybe he was thirty.

"That's a good bit of story," Chamry said. "There's more? Is there a name to it?"

I said, "It's called *The Siege and Fall of Sentas*. There's more."

"Let's have it," said Chamry, and the others all agreed.

For a time I could not recall the opening lines of the poem; then, as if I had the old copybook in my hand, there they were and I spoke them—

To the councils and senate of Sentas they came, the envoys in armour,
With their swords in their hands, arrogant, striding into the chamber
Where the lords of the city sat to give judgment . . .

It was night, true night, when I finished saying the first book of the poem. Our fire had burned down to embers on the rough hearth, but nobody in the circle of men had moved to build it up; nobody had moved at all for an hour.

"They're going to lose that city of theirs," Bulec said in the dark, in the soft drumming of the rain.

"They should be able to hold out. The others come too far from home. Like Casicar did, trying to take Etra last year," said Taffa. It was the most I'd ever heard him say. Venne had told me Taffa had been not a slave but a freeman of a small city-state, conscripted into their army; during a battle he had escaped and made his way to the forest. Sad-faced and aloof, he seldom said anything, but now he was arguing almost volubly: "Stretched out their forces too far, see, Pagadi has, attacking. If they don't take the town by assault quick, they'll starve come winter."

And they all got into the discussion, all talking exactly as if the siege of Sentas was taking place right now, right here. As if we were living in Sentas.

Of them all Chamry was the only one who understood that what I had told them was "a poem," a thing made by a maker, a work of art, part history of long ago, part invention. It was, to them, an event; it was happening as they heard it. They wanted it to go on happening. If I'd been able to, they'd have kept me telling it to them night and day. But after my voice gave out that first evening, I lay in my wooden bunk thinking about what had been given back to me: the power of words. I had time then to think and to plan how and when to use that power—how to go on with the poem, to keep them from exhausting both it and me. I ended by telling it for an hour or two every night, after we ate, for the winter nights were endless and something to make them pass was welcome to all.

Word got about, and within a night or two most of the men of the band were crowded into our hut for "telling the war," and for the long passionate discussions and arguments about tactics and motives and morals that followed.

There were times I couldn't fully recall the lines as Garro wrote them, but the story was clear in my mind, so I filled in these gaps with tags of the poetry and my own narrative, until I came again to a passage that I had by memory or could "see" written, and could fall back into the harsh rhythm of the lines. My companions didn't seem to notice the difference between my prose and Garro's poetry. They listened closest when I was speaking the poetry—but those were also often the most vivid passages of action and suffering.

When we came again in the course of the tale to the passage I'd recited first, Yurno's prophecy from the battlements, Bacoc caught his breath; and when Rurec "in a fury uplifts his heavy lance," Bacoc cried out, "Don't throw it, man! It's no good!" The others shouted at him to pipe down, but he was indignant: "Don't he know it's no good? He thro'n it before!"

I was at first merely bemused by my own capacity to recall the poetry and their capacity to listen to it. They didn't say much to me about it, but it made a difference in the way I was treated, my standing among them. I had something they wanted, and they respected me for that. Since I gave it freely, their respect was ungrudging. "Hey, haven't you got a fatter rib than that for the kid? He's got to work tonight, telling the war . . ."

But every up's a down, as Chamry said. Brigin and his brother and the men closest to them, their cabin mates, looked in at one time or another on the recital, listened a while standing near the doorway, then left in silence. They said nothing to me, but I heard from others that they said men who listened to fools' tales were worse fools than those who told them. And Brigin said that a man willing to hear a boy yammer booktalk half the night was no fit Forest Brother.

Booktalk! Why did Brigin say it in that contemptuous tone? There were no books in the forest. There had been no books in Brigin's life. Why did he sneer at them?

Any of these men might well be jealous of a knowledge that had been jealously kept from them. A farm slave who tried to learn to read could have his eyes put out or be whipped to death. Books were dangerous, and a slave had every excuse to fear them. But fear is one thing, contempt another.

I resented their sneers as mean-spirited, for I couldn't see anything unworthy of manhood in the tale I was telling. How was a tale of warfare and heroism weakening the men who listened to it so hungrily every night? Didn't it draw us together in real brotherhood, when after the telling we listened to one another argue the rights and wrongs of the generals' tactics and the warriors' exploits? To sit stupid, mute, night after night under the rain like cattle, bored to mindlessness—was that what made us men?

Eter said something one morning, knowing he was within my hearing, about great idle fools listening to a boy tell lies. I was fed up. I was about to confront him with what I've just said, when my wrist was caught in an iron grip and a deft foot nearly tripped me.

I broke free and shouted, "What d'you think you're doing?" to Chamry Bern, who apologised for his clumsiness while renewing his grip on my wrist. "Oh keep your trap shut, Gav!" he whispered desperately, hauling me away from the group of men around Eter. "Don't you see he's baiting you?"

"He's insulting all of us!"

"And who's to stop him? You?"

Chamry had got me around behind the woodpiles now, away

from the others, and seeing I was now arguing with him, not challenging Eter, he let go my wrist.

"But why—Why—?"

"Why don't they love you for having a power they don't have?"

I didn't know what to say.

"And they've got the hard hand, you know, though you've got the soft voice. Oh, Gav. Don't be smarter than your masters. It costs."

In his face now was the sadness I had seen in the face of every one of these men, the mark of the harrow. They had all started with very little, and lost most of that.

"They're not my masters," I said furiously. "We're free men here!"

"Well," Chamry said, "in some ways."

NINE

Eter and Brigin, if they resented my sudden popularity, must have seen that any attempt to break up the evening gathering might rouse real opposition. They contented themselves with sneers at me, and at Chamry and Venne as my mates, but let the other men alone. So I and my fierce audience went on through all *The Siege and Fall of Sentas,* as the dark winter slowly turned towards spring. We came to the end of it just about the time of the equinox.

It was hard for some of the men to comprehend that it was over, and why it had to be over. Sentas had fallen, the walls and the great gates were torn down, the citadel burnt to the ground, the men of the city slaughtered, the women and children taken as slaves, and the hero Rurec had set off triumphant with his army and loot to Pagadi—and so, what happened next?

"Is he going to go by the hills of Trebs now?" Bacoc wanted to know. "After what the witch said?"

"Sure enough he'll go by Trebs, if not this day then another," said Chamry. "A man can't keep from going where the seer's eye saw him go."

"Well, why don't Gav tell it, then?"

"The story stops at the fall of the city, Bacoc," I said.

"What—like they all died? But it's only some of 'em dead!"

Chamry tried to explain the nature of a story to him, but he remained dissatisfied; and they were all melancholy. "Ah, it's going to be dull!" said Taffa. "I'll miss that sword fighting. It's a horrible thing when you're in it, but it's grand to hear about."

Chamry grinned. "You could say that of most things in life, maybe."

"Are there more tales like that, Gav?" somebody asked.

"There are a lot of tales," I said, cautiously. I wasn't eager to start another epic. I felt myself becoming the prisoner of my audience.

"You could tell the one we had all right over," said one man, and several agreed enthusiastically.

"Next winter," I said. "When the nights are long again."

They treated my verdict as if it were a priest's rule of ritual, accepting it without dispute.

But Bulec said wistfully, "I wish there was short tales for the short nights." He had listened to the epic with almost painful attention, muffling his cough as well as he could; to the battle scenes he preferred the descriptions of the rooms in the palaces, the touching domestic passages, the love story of Alira and Ruoco. I liked Bulec, and it was painful to see him, a young man, getting sicker and weaker day by day even as the weather brightened and grew warm. I couldn't withstand his plea.

"Oh, there's some short tales," I said. "I'll tell you one." And I thought first to say *The Bridge on the Nisas,* but I could not. Those words, though they were clear in my mind, bore some weight in them that I could not lift. I could not speak them.

So I put myself in the schoolroom in my mind, and opened

a copybook, and there was one of Hodis Baderi's fables, "The Man Who Ate the Moon." I told it to them word for word.

They listened as intently as ever. The fable got a mixed reception. Some of them laughed and shouted, "Ah, that's the best yet! That beats all!"—but others thought it silly stuff, "foolery," Taffa said.

"Ah, but there's a lesson in it," said Chamry, who had listened to the tale with delight. They got to arguing whether the man who ate the moon was a liar or not. They never asked me to settle or even enter these discussions. I was, as it were, their book. I provided the text. Judgment on the text was up to them. I heard as keen moral arguments from them as I was ever to hear from learned men.

After that they often got a fable or a poem out of me in the evening, but their demand was not so urgent now that we no longer had to cower in our huts from the rain and could live outdoors and be active. Hunting and snaring and fishing went on apace, for we'd lived very thin at the end of winter and beginning of spring. We craved not only meat but the wild onions and other herbs that some of the men knew how to find in the forest. I always missed the grain porridge that had been much of our diet in the city, but there was nothing like that here.

"I heard the Forest Brothers stole grain from rich farmers," I said once to Chamry, as we grubbed for wild horseradish.

"They do, those who can," he said.

"Who's that?"

"Barna's lot, up north there."

The name rang strangely in my head, bringing around it a whole set of fleeting images of young men talking in a crowded, warm dormitory, the face of an old priest . . . but I ignored such images. Words were what I could remember safely.

"So there really is a man called Barna?"

"Oh, yes. Though you needn't mention him around Brigin."

I wheedled for more, and Chamry never could resist telling

a story. So I found that, as I had suspected, our band was a splinter from a larger group, with which they weren't on good terms. Barna was the chief of that group. Eter and Brigin had rebelled against his leadership and brought a few men here to the southern part of the forest—the most remote from any settlements and so the safest for runaway slaves, but also the poorest in resources except, as Chamry said, cattle with antlers.

"Up there, they bag the real thing," he said. "Fat bullocks. Sheep! Ah! what wouldn't I give to taste mutton! I hate sheep from the pit of my heart, wily, woolly, wicked brutes. But when one of 'em lies down and turns into roast mutton, I could swallow him whole."

"Do Barna's men raise the cattle and sheep?"

"Mostly they let other folk do that for them. And then pick out a few choice ones. There's those who'd call it thieving, but that's too delicate and legal a word. Tithing, we called it. We tithed the farmers' flocks."

"So you lived there, with Barna's band?"

"A while. Lived well, too." Chamry sat back on his haunches and looked at me. "That's where you should be, you know. Not here, with this lot of hard rocks and knotheads." He knocked the dirt off a horseradish root, wiped it on his shirt, and bit into it. "You and Venne. You should be off. He'll be welcome for his hunting, you for your golden tongue . . ." He chewed raw horseradish a while, wincing and his eyes watering. "All your tongue will do here is talk you into trouble."

"Would you come with us?"

He spat out fibre and wiped his mouth. "By the Stone, but that's hot! I don't know. I came away with Brigin and them because they were my mates. And I was restless . . . I don't know."

He was a restless man. It wasn't hard for Venne and me to coax him into coming with us, when we made up our minds to go. And we did that soon.

Brigin and Eter, feeling dissatisfaction among us, tried to repress it with ever harsher demands and commands. Eter told

Bulec, who was deathly ill by now, that if he didn't go out hunting for meat for the camp pot, he'd get nothing to eat from it. Eter may have just been bullying, or may have believed his threat would work; some men who live hard and in good health can't believe sickness or weakness is anything but laziness, a sham. At any rate Bulec was scared or shamed into insisting that a hunting party take him along. He got a little way out of camp with them and collapsed, vomiting blood. When they carried him back, Venne confronted Eter, shouting that he'd killed Bulec like any slave driver. Venne rushed off in his distress and rage. He found me fishing at a pool up the stream. "We were going to find Bulec a place he could sit down and wait for us, soon as we got clear away from camp, but he couldn't even walk that far. He's dying. I can't stay here, Gav. I can't take their orders! They think they're masters and us their slaves. I want to kill that damned Eter! I've got to get out."

"Let's talk to Chamry," I said. We did; he counselled at first that we wait, but when he saw how dangerous Venne's anger was, he agreed to go that night.

We ate with the others. Nobody talked. Bulec lay fighting for breath in one of the cabins. I could still hear the slow, gasping drag of his breath in the darkness before dawn when Venne, Chamry, and I stole out of camp with what little we considered ours by right: the clothes we wore, a blanket apiece, our knives, Venne's bow and arrows, my fishing hooks and rabbit snares, Chamry's cobbler's toolkit, and a packet of smoked meat.

It was a couple of months after the equinox, late May, perhaps; a sweet dark night, a slow misty dawn, a morning of birdsong. It was good to be going free, leaving the rivalries and brutalities of the camp behind. I walked all day lightly, lighthearted, wondering why we'd borne Eter and Brigin's bullying so long. But at evening, as we sat fireless, lying low in case they pursued us, my heart went down low too. I kept thinking of Bulec, and of others: Taffa, who, being a deserter, had also deserted the wife and children he loved and could never go back to them; Bacoc, the simple heart, who didn't even know the name of the village where he'd been born a slave—"the village" was all he knew . . . They had been kind to me. And we had sworn a vow together.

"What's the trouble, Gav?" said Chamry.

"I feel like I'm running out on them," I said.

"They could run, too, if they liked," Venne said, so promptly that I knew he'd been thinking along the same lines, justifying our desertion to himself.

"Bulec can't," I said.

"He's gone farther than we've gone, by now," Chamry said. "Never fret for him. He's home . . . You're too loyal, Gav, it's a fault in you. Don't look back. Touch and go, it's best."

That seemed strange to me; what did he mean? I never looked back. I had nothing to be loyal to, nothing to hold on to. I went where my luck took me. I was like a wisp of cloth twisting and drifting in a river.

Next day we came to a part of the great forest I'd never been to. We were outside our territory from here on. The trees were evergreens, fir and hemlock. They made impenetrable walls and mazes of their fallen trunks and the young trees that sprouted out of them. We had to travel along the streambeds, and that was hard going, scrambling through water, over rocks, and around rapids, in the half darkness of the huge trees overhead. Chamry kept saying we'd be out of it soon, and we did come out of it at last late on the second day, following a stream up to its spring on an open, grassy hillside. As we sat luxuriating in the soft grass and the clear twilight, a line of deer came walking past not twenty feet away downhill; they glanced at us unconcerned and walked on quietly, one after the other, flicking their big ears to and fro. Venne quietly took up his bow and fitted an arrow. There was no sound but the twang of the bowstring, like the sound of a big beetle's wings. The last deer in line started, went down on its knees, and then lay down, all in that peaceful silence. The others never turned, but walked on into the woods.

"Ah, why'd I do that," Venne said. "Now we've got to clean it."

But that was soon done, and we were glad to have fresh meat that night and for the next day. As we sat, well fed, by the coals of our fire, Chamry said, "If this was the Uplands I'd have said you called those deer."

"Called 'em?"

"It's a gift—calling animals to come. A brantor goes out hunting, well, he takes a caller with him, if he hasn't the gift himself. Boar, or elk, or deer, whatever they're after, they'll come to the caller."

"I can't do that,"Venne said after a while in his low voice. "But I can see how it might be. If I know the land, I know pretty much, most times, where the deer are. As they know where I am. And if they're afraid, I'll never see them. But if they're not afraid, they'll come. They show themselves—'Here I am, you wanted me.' They give themselves. A man who doesn't know that has no business hunting. He's only a butcher."

We went on for two days more through rolling, open woods before we came to a good-sized stream. "Across that is Barna's country," said Chamry. "And we'd best stay on the path and make noise, let them know we're here, lest they think we're sneaking in to spy." So we came crashing into Barna's lands like a herd of wild pigs, as Venne said. We came on a path and followed it, still talking loudly. Soon enough there was a shout to halt and hold still. We did that. Two men came striding down the path to meet us. One was tall and thin, one was short and broad-bellied.

"Do you know where you are?" said the short one, false-jovial, not quite menacing. The tall one held his crossbow loaded, though not aimed.

"In the Heart of the Forest," said Chamry. "Seeking a welcome, Toma. You don't remember me?"

"Well, by the Destroyer! The bad penny always turns up!" Toma came forward to take Chamry by one shoulder and shake him back and forth with aggressive welcome. "You Upland rat," he said. "You vermin. Crawled off at night you did, with Brigin and that lot. What did you want to go with them for?"

"It was a mistake, Toma," said Chamry, getting his footing so Toma could go on shaking him. "Call it a mistake and forgive it, eh?"

"Why not? Won't be the last thing I forgive you, Chamry Bern." He let him go at last. "What have you brought with you there? Baby rats, are they?"

"All I took away with me was those pigheads Brigin and his brother," Chamry said, "and what I'm bringing back with me is two pearls, pearls set in gold for the ears of Barna. Venne, here, who can drop a deer at a thousand paces, and Gav, here, who can tell tales and poetry to make you weep one moment and laugh the next. Take us into the Heart of the Forest, Toma!"

So we went on a mile or so through the forest of oak and alder, and came to that strange place.

The Heart of the Forest was a town, with kitchen gardens and barns and byres and corrals outside the palisade walls, and inside them houses and halls, streets and squares—all of wood. Towns and cities were built of stone and brick, I thought; only barns for cattle and huts for slaves were built of wood. But this was a city of wood. It was swarming with people, men, and women too, and children—everywhere, in the gardens, in the streets. I looked at the women and children with wonder. I looked at the cross-beamed, gable-roofed houses with awe. I looked at the broad central square full of people and stopped, scared. Venne was walking right next to me, pressed up against my shoulder for courage. "I never saw nothing like this, Gav," he said hoarsely. We followed as close behind Chamry as two little kids behind the she-goat.

Chamry himself was looking about with some amazement. "It wasn't half this size when I left," he said. "Look how they've built!"

"You're in luck," said Toma, our fat guide. "There's himself."

Coming across the square towards us was a big, bearded man. Very tall, broad-chested, ample in girth, with dark reddish curly hair and a beard that covered all his cheeks and chin and chest, with large, clear eyes, and a singularly upright, buoyant walk, as if he were borne up a little above the ground—as soon as you saw him you knew he was, as Toma said, himself. He was looking at us with a pleasant, keen curiosity.

"Barna!" Chamry said. "Will you have me back, if I bring you a couple of choice recruits?" Chamry did not quite reverence Barna, but his posture was respectful, despite his jaunty tone. "I'm Chamry Bern of Bernmant, who made the mistake of going off south a few years back."

"The Uplander," Barna said, and smiled. He had a broad white smile that flashed in his beard, and a magnificently deep voice. "Oh, you're welcome back for yourself, man. We're free to come and free to go here!" He took Chamry's hand and shook it. "And the lads?"

Chamry introduced us, with a few words about our talents. Barna patted Venne's shoulder and told him a hunter was always welcome in the Heart of the Forest; at me he looked intently for a minute, and said, "Come see me later today, Gav, if you will. Toma, you'll find them quarters? Good, good, good! Welcome to freedom, lads!" And he strode on, a head taller than anyone else.

Chamry was beaming. "By the Stone!" he said. "Never a hard word, but welcome back and all's forgiven! That's a great man, with a great heart in him!"

We found lodgings in a barracks that seemed luxurious after our ill-built, smoky huts in the forest camp, and ate at the commons, which was open all day to all comers. There Chamry got his heart's desire: they'd roasted a couple of sheep, and he ate roast mutton till his eyes gleamed with satisfaction above his cheeks shining with mutton fat. After that he took me to Barna's house, which loomed over the central square, but did not go in with me. "I won't press my luck," he said. "He asked you to come, not me. Sing him that song of yours, 'Liberty,' eh? That'll win him."

So I went in, trying to act as if I wasn't daunted, and said to the people that Barna had asked me to come. They were all men, but I heard women's voices farther in the house. That sound, the sound of women's voices in other rooms of a great house, made my mind stir strangely. I wanted to stop and listen. There was a voice I wanted to hear.

But I had to follow the men who took me to a hall with a big hearth, though there was no fire in it now. There Barna was sitting in a chair big enough for him, a regular throne, talking and laughing with both men and women. The women wore beautiful clothes, of such colors as I had not seen for months and months except in a flower or the dawn sky. You will laugh, but it was the colors I stared at, not the women. Some of the men were well-dressed, too, and it was pleasant to see men clean, in handsome clothing, talking and laughing aloud. It was familiar.

"Come here, lad," said Barna in his deep, grand voice. "Gav, is it? Are you from Casicar, Gav, or Asion?"

Now, in Brigin's camp you never asked a man where he was from. Among runaway slaves, deserters and wanted thieves, the question wasn't well received. Chamry was the only one of us who often talked freely about where he'd run from, and that was because he was so far away from it. Not long ago we'd heard of raids into the forest, slave takers looking for runaways. For all of us it was better to have no past at all, which just suited me. I was so taken aback by Barna's question that I answered it stiffly and uneasily, sounding even to myself as if I were lying. "I'm from Etra."

"Etra, is it? Well, I know a city man when I see one. I was born in Asion myself, a slave son of slaves. As you see, I've brought the city into the forest. What's the good of freedom if you're poor, hungry, dirty and cold? That's no freedom worth having! If a man wants to live by the bow or by the work of his hands, let him take his choice, but here in our realm no man will live in slavery or in want. That's the beginning and the end of the Law of Barna. Right?" he asked the people around him, laughing, and they shouted back, "Right!"

The energy and goodwill of the man, his pure enjoyment in being, were irresistible. He embraced us all in his warmth and strength. He was keen, too; his clear eyes saw quick and deep. He looked at me and said, "You were a house slave, and pretty well treated, right? So was I. What were you trained to do in the great house for your masters?"

"I was educated to teach the children of the house." I spoke slowly. It was like reading a story in my mind. I was talking about somebody else.

Barna leaned forward, intensely interested. "Educated!" he said. "Writing, reading—all such?"

"Yes."

"Chamry said you were a singer?"

"A speaker," I said.

"A speaker. What do you speak?"

"Anything I've read," I said, not as a boast, but because it was true.

"What have you read?"

"The historians, the philosophers, the poets."

"A learned man. By the Deaf One! A learned man! A scholar! Lord Luck has sent me the man I wanted, the man I lacked!" Barna stared at me with amazed delight, then got up from his huge chair, came to me, and took me into a bear-hug. My face was mashed into his curling beard. He squeezed the breath out of me, then held me out at arm's length.

"You will live here," he said. "Right? Give him a room, Diero! And tonight, will you speak for us tonight? Will you say us a piece of your learning, Gav-dí the Scholar? Eh?"

I said I would.

"There's no books for you here," he said almost anxiously, still holding me by the shoulders. "Everything else a man might need we have, but books—books aren't what most of my men would bring here with them, they're ignorant letterless louts, and books are very heavy matters—" He laughed, throwing back his head. "Ah, but now, from now on, we'll remedy that. We'll see to it. Tonight, then!"

He let me go. A woman in delicate black and violet robes took me by the hand and led me off. I thought her old, over forty surely, and she had a grave face, and did not smile; but her manner and her voice were gentle, and her dress beautiful, and it was amazing how differently she moved, and walked, and spoke, from how men did. She took me to a loft room, apologising for its being upstairs and small. I stammered something about staying with my mates in the barracks. She said, "You can live there, of course, if you wish, but Barna hopes you will honor his house." I was unable to disappoint this elegant, fragile person. It seemed everybody was taking my learning very much on trust, but I couldn't say that.

She left me in the little loft room. It had a small, square window, a bed with a mattress and bedding, a table and chair, an oil-lamp. It looked like heaven to me. I did go back to the barracks, but Chamry and Venne had both gone out. I told a man who was lounging on his bunk there to tell them that I'd be staying at Barna's house. He looked at me at first disbelieving, then with a knowing smirk.

"Living high, eh?" he said.

I put what little gear I had with Chamry's, for I wouldn't need fish hooks or my filthy old blanket; but I wore my sheathed knife on my belt, having seen that most men here did. I went back to Barna's house. I could look at it better now that I was not so overawed. Its façade on the central square was wide and high, with mighty beams and deep gables; it was built of wood, and there was no glass in the small-paned windows, but it was an impressive house.

I sat on the bed in my room—my own room!—and let bewildered excitement flood through me. I was very nervous about reciting to this genial, willful, unpredictable giant and his crowd of people. I felt I must prove myself at once and beyond doubt to be the scholar he wanted me to be. That was a strange thing to be called on to do. Coming out of the silence I'd lived in so long, the silence of the forest, the mute forgetfulness . . . But I had recited all *Sentas* to my companions in the silence, hadn't I? I had called on it, and it came to me. It was mine, it was in me. I remembered all I had learned in the schoolroom with—

I came too near the wall. My mind went numb. Blank, empty.

I lay back and dozed, I think, till the light was growing reddish in the small, deep-framed window. I got up and combed my hair as well as I could with my fingers and tied it back again with an end of fishing line, for it hadn't been cut for a year. That was all I could do to make myself elegant. I went down the stairs and to the great hall, where thirty or forty people were gathered, chattering like a flock of starlings.

I was made welcome, and the grave, sweet-mannered woman in black and violet, Diero, gave me a cup of wine, which I drank thirstily. It made my head spin. I didn't have the courage to keep her from refilling the cup, but I did have the wits not to drink any more. I looked at the cup, thin silver chased with a pattern of olive leaves, as beautiful as anything in . . . as anything I had seen. I wondered if there were silversmiths in the Heart of the Forest, and where the silver came from. Then Barna loomed over me, his grand voice rumbling. He put his arm round my shoulders. He took me in front of the people, called for silence, told his guests he had a treat for them, and nodded at me with a smile.

I wished I had a lyre, as strolling tellers did, to set the tone and mood of their recitation. I had to start off into silence, which is hard. But I had been trained well. Stand straight, Gavir, keep your hands still, bring your voice up from your belly, out from your chest . . .

I spoke them the old poem *The Sea-Farers of Asion*. It had

come into my head tonight because Barna said he was from that city. And I hoped it might suit the company I was in. It is the tale of a ship carrying treasure up the coast from Ansul to Asion. The ship is boarded by pirates, who kill the officers and order the slaves at the oars to row to Sova Island, the pirates' haven. The oarsmen obey, but in the night they plot an uprising, unfasten their chains and kill the pirates. Then they row the ship with all its treasure on to the port of Asion, where the Lords of the City welcome them as heroes and reward them with a share of the treasure and their freedom. The poem has a swing to it like the sea waves, and I saw my audience in their fine clothes following the story with open eyes and mouths, just like my ragged brothers in the smoky hut. I was borne up on the words and on their attention. We were all there in the ship in the great grey sea.

So it ended, and after the little silence that comes then, Barna rose up with a roar—"Set them free! By Sampa the Maker and Destroyer, they set them free! Now there's a tale I like!" He gave me one of his bear-hugs and held me off by the shoulders as his way was, saying, "Though I doubt that it's a true history. Gratitude to a lot of galley slaves? Not likely! Here, I'll tell you a better ending for it, Scholar: They never sailed back to Asion at all, but sailed south, far south, back to Ansul where the money came from, and there they shared it out and lived on it the rest of their lives, free men and rich!—How's that?—But it's good poetry, grand poetry well spoken!" He clapped me on the back and took me around introducing me to the others, men and women, who praised me and spoke kindly. I drank off my wine and my head went round again. It was very pleasant, but at last I was glad to get away, go up to my loft in amazement at all that had happened this long day, fall onto my soft bed, and sleep.

So began my life in the Heart of the Forest and my acquaintance with its founder and presiding spirit. All I could think was that Luck was with me still, and since I didn't know what to ask him for, he'd given me what I needed.

Barna's welcome to me hadn't been just jovial bluster; there was a bit of that in most of what he said and did, but under it was a driving purpose. He had wanted men of learning in his city of the free, and had none.

He took me into his confidence very quickly. Like me, he'd grown up a slave in a great house where the masters and some of the slaves were educated and there were books to be read. More than that, scholars who came to Asion visited and talked with the learned men of the house; poets stayed there, and the philosopher Denneter lived there for a year. All this had fascinated and impressed the boy, and he in turn had impressed his masters and the visitors with his quickness at learning, especially philosophy. Denneter made much of him, wanted to make a disciple of him; he was to be Denneter's student and go travelling with him through the world.

But when he was fifteen, the slaves in the great civic barracks of Asion rebelled. They broke into the armoury of the city guard, used the armoury as a fortress, and killed the guards and others who tried to assault them. They declared themselves free men, demanded that the city recognize them as such, and called on all slaves to join them. Many house slaves did, and for several days Asion was in a state of panic and confusion. A regiment of Asion's army was sent into the city, the armoury was besieged and taken, and the rebels slaughtered. Almost all male slaves were suspect after that. Many were branded to mark them indelibly as unfree. Barna, a boy of fifteen, had escaped branding, but there was no more talk of philosophy and travel. He was drafted to refill the civic barracks, sent to hard labour.

"And so all my education stopped then and there. Not a book have I held in my hands since that day. But I had those few years of learning, and hearing truly wise men talk, and knowing that there's a life of the mind that's far above anything else in the world. And so I knew what was missing here. I could make my city of free men, but what's the good of freedom to the ignorant? What's freedom itself but the power of the mind to learn what it needs and think what it likes? Ah, even if your body's chained, if you have the thoughts of the philosophers and the words of the poets in your head, you can be free of your chains, and walk among the great!"

His praise of learning moved me deeply. I had been living among people so poor that knowledge of anything much beyond their poverty had no meaning to them, and so they judged it useless. I had accepted their judgment, because I had accepted their poverty. There had been a long time when I'd never thought of the words of the makers; and when they came back to me, at Brigin's camp, it seemed a miraculous gift that had nothing to do with my will or intention. Having been so poor, so ignorant myself, I had no heart to say that ignorance cannot judge knowledge.

But here was a man who had proved his intelligence, energy, and courage, raising himself out of poverty and slavery to a kind of kingship, and bringing a whole people with him into independence; and he set knowledge, learning, and poetry above even such achievements. I was ashamed of my weakness, and rejoiced in his strength.

Admiring Barna more as I came to know him, I wanted to be of use to him. But for the time being it seemed all he wanted of me was to be a kind of disciple, going about the city with him and listening to his thoughts—which I was happy to do—and then, in the evening, to recite whatever poetry or tales I wished to his guests and household. I suggested teaching some of his companions to read, but there were no books, he said, to teach from, and though I offered to, he wouldn't let me waste my time writing out copybooks. Books would be looked for and brought here, he said, and men of education would be found to assist me, and then we'd have a regular school, where all could learn who wanted.

Meanwhile some of Barna's people coaxed me to teach them, young women who lived in his house seeking a new entertainment; and with his permission I held a little class in writing and reading for a few of them. Barna laughed at me and the girls. "Don't let 'em fool you, Scholar. They're not after literature! They just want to sit next to a bit of pretty boy-flesh." He and his men companions teased the girls about turning into book-worms, and they soon gave it up. Diero was the only one who came more than a few times.

Diero was a beautiful woman, gracious and gentle. She had been trained from girlhood as a "butterfly woman." The "but-terflies" of Asion—an ancient city famous for its ceremony, its luxury, and its women—were schooled in a science of pleasure far more refined and elaborate than anything known in the City States.

But, as Diero herself told me, reading wasn't one of the arts taught to the "butterflies." She listened with yearning intensity to the poetry I spoke, and had a great, timid curiosity about it. I encouraged her to let me teach her to write her letters and spell out words. She was humble, self-distrustful, but quick to learn, and her pleasure in learning was a pleasure to me. Barna looked on our lessons with genial amusement.

His older companions, all of whom had been with him for years, were very much his men. They had brought from their years of slavery a habit of accepting orders and not competing to lead, which made them easy company. They treated me as a boy, not a rival to them, telling me what I needed to know and occasionally giving me a warning. Barna would give you the coat off his back, they told me, but if he thinks you're poaching his girls, look out! They told me Diero had come with Barna from Asion when he first broke free and had been his mistress for many years. She wasn't that now, but she was the woman of Barna's House, and a man who didn't treat Diero with affection-ate respect wouldn't be welcome there.

Barna explained to me one day as we sat up on the watch-tower of the Heart of the Forest that men and women should be free to love one another with no hypocritical bonds of promised faithfulness to chain them together. That sounded good to me. All I knew of marriage was that it was for the masters, not for my kind, so I'd thought little about it one way or the other. But Barna thought about such things, and came to conclusions, and had them enacted in the Heart of the Forest. He had ideas about children, too, that they should be entirely free, never punished, allowed to run about as they pleased and find out for themselves what best suited them to do. This seemed admirable to me. All his ideas did.

I was a good listener, sometimes putting a question, but mostly content to follow the endless inventions and generous vistas of his mind. As he said, he thought best out loud. He soon claimed me as a necessity to him: "Where's Gav-di? Where's the Scholar? I need to think!"

I lived at Barna's house, but I went to see Chamry often. He had joined the cobblers' guild, where he lived snug and complained of nothing but the scarcity of women and roast mutton. "They've got to send the tithing boys out for roasting mutton!" he said.

Venne had soon found that as a hunter he'd have to spend most of his time away off in the woods just as he'd done for Brigin, since all the game near the Heart of the Forest had long since been hunted out. Hunting was not what fed the town these days. One of the groups of "tithing boys" asked him to come with them as a guard when they found what a good shot he was with the short bow, and he joined them. He first went out on the road with them about a month after we came to the Heart of the Forest.

The tithers or raiders went out from our wooden city to meet drovers and wagons on the roads outside the forest. Their goal was to bring back flocks and herds, loaded wagons, drivers and horses, thus increasing our stock of food, vehicles, animals and men—if the men were willing to join the Brotherhood. If they weren't, Barna told me, they were left blindfolded with their hands tied, to wander in hope the next passerby would untie them. He laughed his mighty laugh when he told me that some of the drivers had been robbed so often by the Forest Brothers that they meekly stuck their hands out to be tied.

There were also the "netmen" who went singly or in pairs into Asion itself, sometimes to bargain in the market for things we needed, but sometimes as thieves to steal from the houses of the rich and the coffers of wealthy shrines. No money was used among us, but the Brotherhood wanted cash to buy things the raiders could not steal—including the goodwill of towns near the forest, and the silence of colluding merchants in the cities. Barna liked to boast that he sat on a fortune that the great merchants of Asion might envy. Where the gold and silver was kept I never knew. Bronze and copper coins were to be had for the asking by anyone going into a town to buy goods.

Barna and his assistants knew who left the Heart of the Forest. Not many did, and only tried and trusted men. As Barna put it, one fool blabbing in an alehouse might bring the army of Asion down on us. The narrow, intricate woodland paths that led to and from the gate were closely guarded and often changed and obliterated, so that the tracks of wagons or herds of cattle couldn't easily lead anyone to the wooden city. I remembered the sentries we had met, the challenge and the loaded crossbow. We all knew that if a trail guard saw anyone going away from the gate without permission, he was not to challenge, but to shoot.

They asked Venne to be a trail guard, but he didn't like the idea of having to shoot a man in the back. Raiding wagon trains or rustling cattle suited him better, and being a raider gave a man great prestige among the Brothers. Barna himself said the raiders and the "justicers" who policed the town were the most valuable members of the community. And every man in the Heart of the Forest should follow his own heart in choosing what he did. So Venne went off cheerily with a band of young men, promising Chamry he'd come back with "a flock of sheep, or failing that, a batch of women."

In fact there weren't many women in the Heart of the Forest, and every one of them was jealously guarded by a man or group of men. Those you saw in the streets and gardens seemed all to be pregnant or dragging a gaggle of infants with them, or else they were mere bowed backs sweeping, spinning, digging, milking, like old women slaves anywhere. There were more young women in Barna's house than anywhere else, the prettiest girls in the town, and the merriest. They dressed in fine clothes the raiders brought in. If they could sing or dance or play the lyre, that was welcome, but they weren't expected to do any work. They were, Barna said, "to be all a woman should be— free, and beautiful, and kind."

He loved to have them about him, and they all flirted and flattered and teased him assiduously. He joked and played with them, but his serious talk was always with men.

As time went on, and he kept me his almost constant companion, I felt the honor and the burden of his trust. I tried to be worthy of it. I continued to recite in the evening in his great hall for all who wanted to hear; and because of that and because Barna had me with him so often, most people treated me with respect, though it was often begrudged or puzzled or patronising, since I was after all still a boy. And some of them saw me, I know, as a kind of learned halfwit. They sensed that there was something lacking in me, that for all the endless words at my command, my knowledge of the world was slight and shallow, like a child's.

I knew that too, but I could not think about it or why it should be so. I turned away from such thoughts, and went about with Barna, following him, needing him. His great fullness of being filled my emptiness.

I wasn't the only one who felt that. Barna was the heart of the Heart of the Forest. His vision, his decision, was always the point of reference for the others, his will was their fulcrum. He didn't maintain this mastery by intimidation but through the superiority of his energy and intelligence and the tremendous generosity of his nature: he was simply there before the others, seeing what must be done and how to do it, drawing them to act with him through his passion, activity, and goodwill. He loved people, loved to be among them, with them, he believed in brotherhood with all his heart and soul.

I knew his dreams by now, for he told them to me as we went about the city, he directing, encouraging, and participating in work, I as his listening shadow.

I couldn't always share his love for the Forest Brothers, and wondered how he could keep any patience at all with some of them. Lodging, food, all the necessities of life were shared as fairly as possible, but it had to be rough justice, and one room will always be bigger than another, one serving of pie will have more raisins than another. The first response of many of the men to any perceived inequity was to accuse another man of hogging, and fight their grudge out with fists or knives. Most of them had been farm or hard-labour slaves, brutalised from childhood, used to getting what little they got by grabbing for it and fighting to keep it. Barna had lived that life too and understood them. He kept the rules very simple and very strict, and his justicers enforced them implacably. But still there were murders now and then, and brawls every night. Our few healers, bonesetters and tooth pullers worked hard. The ale made by our brewery was kept weak at Barna's orders, but men could get drunk on it if they had a weak head or drank all night. And when they weren't drunk and quarrelling they were complaining of unfairness, injustice, or the work they were allotted; they wanted less of it, or to do a different kind of work, or to work with one group of mates not another, and so on endlessly. All these complaints ended up with Barna.

"Men have to learn how to be free," he said to me. "Being a slave is easy. To be a free man you have to use your head, you have to give here and take there, you have to give your orders to yourself. They'll learn, Gav, they'll learn!" But even his large good nature was exasperated by the demands on him to settle petty jealousies, and he could be angered by the backbiting and rivalry of the men closest to him, his justicers and the men of his household—our government, in fact, though they had no titles.

He had no title himself, he was simply Barna.

He chose his men, and they chose others to assist them, always with his approval. Election by popular vote was an idea which he knew little about. I was able to tell him that some of the City States had at one time or another been republics or even democracies, although of course only freeborn men of property had the vote. I remembered what I had read of the state and city of Ansul, far to the south, which was governed by officials elected by the entire people, and had no slavery, until they were themselves enslaved by a warlike people from the eastern deserts. And the great country of Urdile, north of Bendile, did not permit any form of bondage; like Ansul, they considered both men and women to be citizens; and every citizen had the vote, electing governing consuls for two years and senators for six. I could tell Barna of these different policies, and he listened with interest, and added elements from them to his plans for the ultimate government of the Free State in the forest.

Such plans were his favorite topic when he was in his good mood. When the bickering and brawling and backbiting and the innumerable, interminable details of provisioning and guard duty and building and everything else that he took responsibility for wore him out and put him in a darker mood, he talked of revolution—the Uprising.

"In Asion there are three slaves, or four, for every free man. All over Bendile, the men who work the farms are slaves. If they could see who they are—that nothing can be done without them! If they could see how many they are! If they could realise their strength, and hold together! The Armory Rebellion, back twenty-five years ago, was just an outburst. No plan, no real leaders. Weapons, but no decisions. Nowhere to go. They couldn't hold together. What I'm planning here is going to be entirely different. There are two essential elements. First, weapons—the weapons we're stockpiling here, now. We'll be met with violence, and we must be able to meet it with insuperable strength. And then, union. We must act as one. The Uprising must happen everywhere at once. In the city, in the countryside, the towns and villages, the farms. A network of men, in touch with one another, ready, informed, with weapons at hand, each knowing when and how to act—so that when the first torch is lighted the whole country will go up in flames. The fire of freedom! What's that song of yours? 'Be our fire . . . Liberty!'"

His talk of the Uprising disturbed and fascinated me. Without really understanding what was at stake, I liked to hear him make his plans, and would ask him for details. He'd catch fire then and talk with great passion. He said, "You bring me back to my heart, Gav. Trying to keep things running here has been eating me up. I've been looking only at what's to be done next and forgetting why we're doing it. I came here to build a stronghold where men and arms could be gathered, a center from which men would go back, a network of men in the northern City States and Bendile, working to get all the slaves in Asion with us, and in Casicar, and the countryside. To get them ready for the Uprising, so that when it comes there'll be nowhere for the masters to fall back to. They'll bring out their armies, but who will the armies attack—with the masters held hostage in their own houses and farms, and the city itself in the hands of slaves? In every house in the city, the masters will be penned up in the barracks, the way they penned us in when there was threat of war, right?—but now it's the masters locked up while the slaves run the household, as of course they always did, and keep the markets going, and govern the city. In the towns and the countryside, the same thing, the masters locked up tight, the slaves taking over, doing the work they always did, the only difference is they give the orders . . . So the army comes to attack, but if they attack, the first to die will be the hostages, the masters, squealing for mercy, *Don't let them slaughter us! Don't attack, don't attack!* The general thinks, ah, they're nothing but slaves with pitchforks and kitchen knives, they'll run as soon as we move in, and he sends in a troop to take the farm. They're cut to pieces by slaves armed with swords and crossbows, fighting from ambush, trained men fighting on their own ground. They take no prisoners. And they bring out one of the squealing masters, the Father maybe, where the soldiers can see, and say: *You attacked: he dies,* and slice off his head. *Attack again, more of them die.* And this will be going on all over the country—every farm, village, town, and Asion itself—the great Uprising! And it won't end until the masters buy their liberty with every penny they have, and everything they own. Then they can come outside and learn how the common folk live."

He threw his head back and laughed, merrier than I'd seen him in days. "Oh, you do me good, Gav!" he said.

The picture he drew was fantastic yet terribly vivid, compelling my belief. "But how will you reach the farm slaves, the city house slaves?" I asked, trying to sound practical, knowledgeable.

"That's the strategy: exactly. To reach into the houses, into the barracks and the slave villages, send men to talk to them—catch them in our net! Show them what they can do and how to do it. Let them ask questions. Get them to figure it out for themselves, make their own plans—so long as they know they must wait for our signal. It'll take time to do that, to spread the net, set up the plan all through the city and the countryside. And yet it can't be too slow in building, because if it goes on too long, word will leak out, fools will begin to blab, and the masters will get jumpy—*What's all this talk in the barracks? What are they whispering in the kitchen? What's that blacksmith making there?*—And then the great advantage of surprise is lost. Timing is everything."

It was only a tale to me, his Uprising. In his mind it was to take place in the future, a great revenge, a rectification of the past. But in my mind there was no past.

I had nothing left but words—the poems that sang themselves in my head, the stories and histories I could bring before my mind's eye and read. I did not look up from the words to what had been around them. When I looked away from them I was back in the vivid intensity of the moment, now, here, with nothing behind it, no shadows, no memories. The words came when I needed them. They came to me from nowhere. My name was a word. Etra was a word. That was all; they had no meaning, no history. Liberty was a word in a poem. A beautiful word, and beauty was all the meaning it had.

Always sketching out his plans and dreams of the future, Barna never asked me about my past. Instead, one day, he told me about it. He'd been talking about the Uprising, and perhaps I'd answered without much enthusiasm, for my own sense of emptiness sometimes made it hard for me to respond convincingly. He was quick to see such moods.

"You did the right thing, you know, Gav," he said, looking at me with his clear eyes. "I know what you're thinking about. Back there in the city . . . You think, 'What a fool I was! To run off and starve, to live in a forest with ignorant men, to slave harder than I ever did in my master's house! Is that freedom? Wasn't I freer there, talking with learned men, reading the books of the poets, sleeping soft and waking warm? Wasn't I happier there?'—But you weren't. You weren't happy, Gav. You knew it in your heart, and that's why you ran off. The hand of the master was always on you."

He sighed and looked into the fire for a little; it was autumn, a chill in the air. I listened to him as I listened to him tell all his tales, without argument or question.

"I know how it was, Gav. You were a slave in a great house, a rich house, in the city, with kind masters who had you educated. Oh, I know that! And you thought you should be happy, because you had the power to learn, read, teach—become a wise man, a learned man. They let you have that. They allowed it to you. Oh yes! But though you were given the power *to do* certain things, you had no power *over* anyone or anything. That was theirs. The masters. Your owners. And whether you knew it or not, in every bone of your body and fibre of your mind you felt that hand of the master holding you, controlling you, pressing down on you. Any power you had, on those terms, was worthless. Because it was nothing but their power acting through you. Using you . . . They let you pretend it was yours. You filched a bit of freedom, a scrap of liberty, from your masters, and pretended it was yours and was enough to keep you happy. Right? But you were growing into a man. And for a man, Gav, there is no happiness but in his own freedom. His freedom to do what he wills to do. And so your will sought its full liberty. As mine did, long ago."

He reached out and clapped me on the knee. "Don't look so sad," he said, his white grin flashing in his curly beard. "You know you did the right thing! Be glad of it, as I am!"

I tried to tell him that I was glad of it.

He had to go see about affairs, and left me musing by the fire. What he said was true. It was the truth.

But not my truth.

Turning away from his tale, I looked back for the first time in—how long? I looked across the wall I'd built to keep me from remembering. I looked and saw the truth: I had been a slave in a great house, a rich house, in the city, obedient to my masters, owning no freedom but what they allowed me. And I had been happy.

In the house of my slavery I had known a love so dear to me that I could not bear to think about it, because when I lost it, I lost everything.

All my life had been built on trust, and that trust had been betrayed by the Family of Arcamand.

Arcamand: with the name, with the word, everything I had forgotten, had refused to remember, came back and was mine again, and with it all the unspeakable pain I had denied.

I sat there by the fire, turned away from the room, bent over, my hands clenched on my knees. Someone came near and stood near me at the hearth to warm herself: Diero, a gentle presence in a long shawl of fine pale wool.

"Gav," she said very quietly, "what is it?"

I tried to answer her and broke into a sob. I hid my face in my arms and wept aloud.

Diero sat down beside me on the stone hearth seat. She put her arms around me and held me while I cried.

"Tell me, tell me," she said at last.

"My sister. She was my sister," I said.

And that word brought the sobbing again, so hard I could not take breath.

She held me and rocked me a while, until I could lift my head and wipe my nose and face. Then she said again, "Tell me."

"She was always there," I said.

And so one way and another, weeping, in broken sentences and out of order, I told her about Sallo, about our life, about her death.

The wall of forgetting was down. I was able to think, to speak, to remember. I was free. Freedom was unspeakable anguish.

In that first terrible hour I came back again and again to Sallo's death, to how she died, why she died—all the questions I had refused to ask.

"The Mother knew—she had to know about it," I said. "Maybe Torm took Sallo and Ris out of the silk rooms without asking, without permission, it sounds as if that's what he did. But the other women there would know it—they'd go to the Mother and tell her—*Torm-dí took Ris and Sallo off, Mother—they didn't want to go, they were crying—Did you tell him he could take them? Will you send after them?*—And she didn't. She did nothing! Maybe the Father said not to interfere. He always favored Torm. Sallo said that, she said he hated Yaven and favored Torm. But the Mother—she knew—she knew where Torm and Hoby were taking them, to that place, those men, men who used girls like animals, who—She knew that. Ris was a virgin. And the Mother had given Sallo to Yaven herself. And yet she let the other son take her and give her to—How did they kill her? Did she try to fight them? She couldn't have. All those men. They raped her, they tortured her, that's what they wanted girls for, to hear them scream—to torture and kill them, drown them—When Sallo was dead. After I saw her. I saw her dead. The Mother sent for me. She called her 'our sweet Sallo.' She gave me—she gave me money—for my sister—"

A sound came out of my throat then, not a sob but a hoarse howl. Diero held me close. She said nothing.

I was silent at last. I was mortally tired.

"They betrayed our trust," I said.

I felt Diero nod. She sat beside me, her hand on mine.

"That's what it is," she said, almost inaudibly. "Do you keep the trust, or not. To Barna it's all power. But it's not. It's trust."

"They had the power to betray it," I said bitterly.

"Even slaves have that power," she said in her gentle voice.

SCIENCE FICTION IN THE FIFTIES: THE REAL GOLDEN AGE

ROBERT SILVERBERG

Historians of science fiction often speak of the years 1939–42 as "the golden age." But it was more like a false dawn. The real golden age arrived a decade later, and—what is not always true of golden ages—we knew what it was while it was happening.

That earlier golden age was centered entirely in a single magazine, John W. Campbell's *Astounding Science Fiction*, and the war aborted it in midstride. Campbell steered a middle course between the heavy-handed science-oriented stories preferred by the pioneering s-f magazine editors Hugo Gernsback and T. O'Conor Sloane and the cheerfully lowbrow adventure fiction favored by pulp editors Ray Palmer and Mort Weisinger. He wanted smoothly written fiction that seriously explored the future of science and technology for an audience of intelligent adult readers—and in the four years of that first golden age he found an extraordinary array of brilliant new writers (and reenergized some older ones) to give him what he wanted: Robert A. Heinlein, Isaac Asimov, Theodore Sturgeon, A. E. van Vogt, Jack Williamson, Clifford D. Simak, L. Sprague de Camp, and many more.

The decade of the fifties is often thought nowadays to have been a timid, conventional, straitlaced time, a boring and sluggish era that was swept away, thank heaven, by the free-wheeling, permissive, joyous sixties. In some ways, that's true. For science fiction, no. The decade of the fifties, staid as it may have been in matters of clothing, politics, and sexuality, was also a period that saw the first artificial space satellites placed in orbit around the Earth; the beginning of the end of legal racial segregation in the United States; and, in the small world of science fiction, a grand rush of creativity, a torrent of new magazines and new writers bringing new themes and fresh techniques that laid the foundation for the work of the four decades that followed. An exciting time for us, yes: truly a golden age.

The disruptions of the Second World War scattered Campbell's talented crew far and wide. Some, like Asimov, van Vogt, and Simak, managed to provide Campbell with an occasional story during the war years, as did some lesser figures of the first Campbell pantheon who now were reaching literary maturity—Henry Kuttner, Fritz Leiber, Eric Frank Russell. Others—Heinlein, Williamson, de Camp—vanished from science fiction "for the duration," as the phrase went then. They all came back after the war, and with their aid, Campbell attempted, with moderate success, to restore *Astounding*. Somehow, though, the magazine never quite became the dazzling locus of excitement that it had been a decade earlier.

And then, suddenly, the fifties arrived—and with the new decade came a host of new science fiction magazines and a legion of gifted new writers. The result was a spectacular outpouring of stories and novels that swiftly surpassed both in quantity and quality the considerable achievement of the Campbellian golden age.

Many of Campbell's original stars were still in their prime, indeed had much of their best work still ahead. But now there was the new generation of writers, most born between 1915 and 1928. They had been too young to have been major contributors to the prewar *Astounding*, but now they came blossoming into literary maturity all at once. I mean such writers as Jack Vance, James Blish, Poul Anderson, Damon Knight, "William

Tenn," Frederik Pohl, Arthur C. Clarke, C. M. Kornbluth, Ray Bradbury, Alfred Bester, and, a little later, Algis Budrys, Marion Zimmer Bradley, Philip K. Dick, Robert Sheckley, Philip Jose Farmer, Walter M. Miller Jr., James E. Gunn, and others.

Most of these newcomers had learned what they knew about science fiction by reading Campbell's magazine. Nearly all (Bradbury was the major exception) subscribed to Campbell's insistence that even the most speculative of science fiction stories ought to be founded on a clear understanding of real-world science and human psychology and his belief in the importance of employing a lucid, straightforward narrative style.

But most of these new writers did their best work for editors other than Campbell. That was a significant change. In the forties, Campbell was the only market for serious science fiction; those who could not or would not write the relatively sophisticated sort of fiction that Campbell wanted to publish wrote simple, low-pay action-adventure stories for his gaudy-looking pulp-paper competitors, such magazines as *Planet Stories*, *Super Science Stories*, and *Startling Stories*.

As the fifties dawned, two of the pulps, *Startling* and *Thrilling Wonder Stories*, were beginning to welcome science fiction of the more complex Campbellian kind under the editorship of Sam Merwin Jr. But the basic task of most of them still was to supply simple adventure fiction to an audience primarily made up of boys and half-educated young men.

The first harbinger of the new era was *The Magazine of Fantasy*, a dignified-looking magazine in the small "digest-sized" format that *Astounding* had adopted during the war. The first issue, on sale in the autumn of 1949, sold for the premier price of thirty-five cents a copy, ten cents more than *Astounding*, and contained a mixture of new short stories, more fantasy than science fiction, by such people as Theodore Sturgeon and Cleve Cartmill (the latter a minor Campbell writer), and classic reprints by British writers like Oliver Onions, Perceval Landon, and Fitz-James O'Brien, that gave the magazine a genteel, almost Victorian tone. But right at the back of the magazine was an astonishing, explosive science fiction story by the poet Winona McClintock: science fiction, yes, but nothing that John Campbell would ever have published, for it was profoundly anti-scientific in theme, and exceedingly literary in tone. It was closest in manner to the sort of fiction that Ray Bradbury had begun to publish in just about every American magazine from *Weird Tales* to *Harper's*, but never in *Astounding*.

The Magazine of Fantasy, by all appearances, was the sort of quiet little literary quarterly that would find a quiet little audience and expire after two or three issues. But its second issue, though still in the same elegant format, showed a notable transformation. The name of the magazine now was *The Magazine of Fantasy and Science Fiction*, and—though there still were a couple of nineteenth-century reprints—most of the issue was science fiction. Not Campbellian science fiction, to be sure: nothing that explored and even extolled the coming high-tech future. Ray Bradbury himself was on hand, with a tale of hallucinatory spaceflight ("The Exiles"), and two of Campbell's regulars, L. Sprague de Camp and Fletcher Pratt, with a funny little fantasy. Damon Knight and Margaret St. Clair, writers just beginning their careers, contributed stories that, though they fit almost anyone's definition of science fiction, Campbell would surely have rejected for their frivolity and their scientific irrelevance. The whole tone of the magazine was light, playful, experimental.

And yet one of Campbell's own regulars was in charge: Anthony Boucher, the author of a baker's dozen of stories for *Astounding* and its short-lived fantasy companion, *Unknown Worlds*, between 1942 and 1946. He and his coeditor, J. Francis McComas, were familiar with Campbell's objectives and were quite willing to concede the high-tech audience to him, staking out a position for themselves among readers whose orientation lay more in the direction of general literature, fantasy, even detective fiction, but who had a liking for the vivid concepts of science fiction as well.

F&SF, as the magazine came to be known, prospered and grew in the fifties, quickly going from quarterly to bimonthly publication and then to monthly. Its pages were a home for scores of writers new and old who chafed at John Campbell's messianic sense of the function of science and his growing literary dogmatism. Bradbury was a frequent contributor. So was Sturgeon. Alfred Bester, a peripheral figure in the Campbell *Astounding*, produced a group of remarkable short stories in a unique pyrotechnic style. Poul Anderson, a Campbell discovery in 1947 and a regular in his magazine ever since, gave Boucher and McComas dozens of stories that went beyond Campbell's ever-narrowing editorial limits. So did James Blish and C. M. Kornbluth, who had served their apprenticeships in the prewar pulp magazines but whose talents were coming now into their real flowering. And for a multitude of new writers launching what would prove to be spectacular careers—Philip K. Dick, Robert Sheckley, Avram Davidson, Richard Matheson, J. T. McIntosh, and on and on and on—the amiable, sympathetic Boucher-McComas style of editing proved to be so congenial that they rarely if ever offered stories to Campbell at all.

While *F&SF* was hitting its stride in the first months of the new decade, another Campbell protégé was busily readying the first issue of his new science fiction magazine—one intended not to be a genteel literary adjunct to Campbell's *Astounding*, but as its direct and ferociously aggressive competitor. He was Horace L. Gold; his magazine was *Galaxy Science Fiction*, which became the dominant and shaping force of this decade of science fiction as *Astounding* had been for the last one.

Gold, a fiercely opinionated and furiously intelligent man, had begun writing science fiction professionally in his teens, publishing stories even before Campbell's ascent to the editorial chair in 1937, and had worked as an associate editor for a pulp-magazine chain just before the war. He had written some outstanding stories for Campbell in those years too; but then he went off to service, and when he returned it was with serious war-related psychological disabilities from which he was years in recovering.

By 1950, though, Gold was vigorous enough to want to make a head-on attack on Campbell's editorial supremacy: to edit a magazine that would emulate the older editor's visionary futuristic range while at the same time allowing its writers a deeper level of psychological insight than Campbell seemed comfortable with. His intention was to liberate Campbell's best writers from what was now widely felt to be a set of constrictive editorial policies, and to bring in the best of the new writers as well; and to this end he offered his writers a notably higher rate of pay than *Astounding* had been giving them.

The first issue of *Galaxy*, resplendent in a gleaming cover printed on heavy coated stock, was dated October 1950. Its contents page featured five of Campbell's star authors—Clifford D. Simak, Isaac Asimov, Fritz Leiber, Theodore Sturgeon, Fredric Brown—along with the already celebrated newcomers Richard Matheson and Katherine MacLean. The second issue added Damon Knight and Anthony Boucher to the roster; the third, another recent Campbell star, James H. Schmitz. A new Asimov novel was serialized in the fourth issue; the fifth had a long story by Ray Bradbury, "The Fireman," which would be the nucleus of his novel *Fahrenheit 451*. And so it went all year, and for some years thereafter. The level of performance was astonishingly high. Every few months *Galaxy* brought its readers stories and novels destined for classic status: Alfred Bester's *The Demolished Man*, Pohl and Kornbluth's *The Space Merchants* (called "Gravy Planet" in the magazine), Heinlein's *The Puppet Masters*, James Blish's "Surface Tension," Wyman Guin's "Beyond Bedlam," and dozens more. Though the obstreperous Gold was a difficult, well-nigh impossibly demanding editor to work with, he and his magazine generated so much excitement in the first half of the fifties that any writer who thought at all of writing science fiction wanted to write for *Galaxy*.

Nor were *Galaxy* and *F&SF* the only new markets for the myriad of capable new writers. Suddenly it was science fiction time in American magazine publishing. Title after title came into being, until by 1953 there were nearly forty of them, whereas in the past there had never been more than eight or nine at once. The new magazines, some of which survived only two or three issues, included *Other Worlds, Imagination, Fantastic Universe, Vortex, Cosmos, If, Science Fiction Adventures*, and *Space Science Fiction*. Long-established pulp magazines like *Startling Stories, Planet Stories*, and *Thrilling Wonder Stories* upgraded their literary standards and drew outstanding contributions from the likes of Arthur C. Clarke, Jack Vance, Henry Kuttner, Ray Bradbury, and Theodore Sturgeon. A trio of ephemeral pulps that had perished in the wartime paper shortage—*Future Fiction, Science Fiction Stories*, and *Science Fiction Quarterly*—were revived after an eight-year lapse.

It was a heady time, all right. The most active writers of the period—people like Sturgeon, Dick, Sheckley, Anderson, Farmer, Blish, Pohl—were in their twenties and thirties, an age that is usually a writer's most productive period, and with all those magazines eager for copy, there was little risk of rejection. In the earlier days when one editor had ruled the empire and a story he turned down might very well not find a home anywhere else, science fiction was too risky a proposition for a professional writer; but now, with twenty or thirty magazines going at a time, the established writers knew they could sell everything they produced, and most of them worked in a kind of white heat, happily turning out fiction with gloriously profligate productivity and, surprisingly, at a startlingly high level of quality as well.

You will note that so far I have spoken of science fiction entirely as a magazine-centered medium. Until the decade of the fifties, there was essentially no market for science fiction books at all. The paperback revolution had not yet happened; the big

hardcover houses seemed not to know that science fiction existed; and, though some of the great magazine serials of the
earlier Campbell era, novels by Heinlein and Asimov and Leiber
and de Camp, were finding their way occasionally into book
form, the publishers were amateurs, lovers of science fiction who
issued their books in editions of a few thousand copies and distributed them mainly by mail.

All that changed in the fifties. The mighty house of Doubleday began to publish hardcover science-fiction novels steadily,
soon joined by Ballantine Books, an innovative new company
that brought its books out in simultaneous hardcover and paperback editions. The sudden existence of willing publishers was all
the encouragement the new writers needed: and suddenly we
had dozens of splendid novels in print in book form, among
them Arthur Clarke's *Childhood's End*, Ward Moore's *Bring the
Jubilee*, Bradbury's *Fahrenheit 451*, Sturgeon's *More Than Human*,
and Asimov's *Pebble in the Sky*, along with hardcover reprints of
recent magazine serials by Heinlein, Asimov, Leiber, and others.

A golden age, yes. Most of the classic anthologies of science
fiction stories are heavily stocked with fifties stories. Any basic
library of science fiction novels would have to include a solid
nucleus of fifties books. And today's science fiction writers are
deeply indebted to the dominant fifties writers—Bester and
Sturgeon and Dick and Sheckley and Pohl and Blish and the
rest—for the fundamental body of ideas and technique with
which they work today.

I know. I was there—very young, but with my eyes wide
open—and I was savoring it as it happened.

Most of the new writers who made the decade of the fifties
what it was in the history of science fiction were on the scene
already as functional professional writers as the decade opened,
or else were only a year or two away from launching their careers; but there were a few who were still only readers of science
fiction then, and would not see print regularly with their own

stories until middecade. I was one of those; so were Harlan Ellison, and John Brunner. (Our generation was a sparse one.)
Though I was only an onlooker at first, and then just the young-
est and greenest of the new writers of the era, I can testify to
the crackling excitement of the period, the enormous creative
ferment.

I don't think it's mere nostalgia that leads me to the view of
the importance of that era. The stories in this book, surely, support my feeling that the fifties were a time of powerful growth
and evolution in science fiction.

Would that evolution ran in a straight upward line. But, alas,
there are periods of retrogression in every trend. The glories
of the fifties were short-lived. By 1959, nearly all of the magazines that had been begun with such high hopes a few years
before had vanished, the book market had been severely cut
back, and many of the writers central to the decade had had to
turn to other fields of enterprise. As the fifties approached their
end, Campbell and his *Astounding* still labored on, now into the
third decade of his editorship, and despite the inroads of his new
competitors he continued to publish some of the best science
fiction. But his increasing preoccupation with pseudo-scientific
fads had alienated many writers who had previously remained
loyal to him, and the magazine grew steadily weaker all throughout the decade.

For the other surviving magazines, things were no better.
Though the potent new magazines *Galaxy* and *F&SF* were
among those that lasted, their editors did not; Anthony Boucher
had resigned his editorial post in 1958; Horace Gold's continuing
medical problems forced him to step down a year later. Without
those two pivotal figures, and with Campbell increasingly remote
and problematical, the spark seemed to go out of the science-
fiction field, and the fireworks and grand visionary dreams of
1951 and 1952 and 1953 gave way to the dull and gray late-fifties
doldrums of science fiction, a somber period destined to last

seven or eight years. The golden age of the fifties was over. Science fiction fans dreamed of a renaissance to come. And it would eventually arrive, bringing with it another rush of new writers, new literary glories, and a vast new audience whose conflicting preferences would transform the once insular little world of science fiction beyond all recognition.

The Solstice Award is given for exceptional contributions to SF publishing. This year three winners all well deserved this and many other honors for all they have given the field. There are few SF magazine editors, except perhaps the legendary John Campbell, that were as effective and well spoken as Algis Budrys. His insight when working with authors often resulted in amazing stories and novels. We are lucky here to have reprints from a few of his many columns written as an editor and reviewer. Some are forty years old but the advice and analysis are still completely relevant. A few years ago I was celebrating with Martin H. Greenberg the publication of the thousandth anthology his company, Tekno Books, had packaged. That's one thousand books, perhaps twenty thousand short stories that exist or were reprinted because Martin Greenberg helped to make them happen. Marty has been generous enough to share with us how he got started in becoming unquestionably the world's top SF anthologist. Finally, the Solstice Award has been given to Kate Wilhelm. The names of the authors this generous and creative woman has mentored reads like a who's who of science fiction. She has taught, inspired, and guided many of those you enjoy reading today. Along the way she has been a successful mystery author along with writing science fiction works. She has won three Nebulas and a Hugo. Ms. Wilhelm has been generous enough to allow us to reprint one of her stories that combines her writing both mystery and SF styles.

ALGIS BUDRYS

JUNE 1965

As you know, the essential conflict is between comfortable ignorance and pitiless intelligence. But it ramifies, and there are days when a man hardly knows how much of himself is on which side. Complicating the whole thing is this Heaven-sent gift of self-consciousness which distinguishes Man from the major life-forms so that a man may sit behind a machine writing words which are either pro- or anti-machine, realize what he is doing, and sit there blushing. And, being reasonable, we also realize that the truth is almost certainly staked out somewhere between the fortress of reaction spangled with the latest technological gimcrackery, and the shabby haven of the thinking wanderer whose favorite victim is himself.

In that No Man's Land, science fiction writers of both sides meet in dim grapple without friend or foe. And if you think there is poetry in that, friend, then you have your first affair with Truth yet before you.

AUGUST 1965

Read any good books lately?

By and large, the first objective of fiction is to establish contact between the writer and the widest possible audience. Whether he writes to get something out of his system, to communicate something, or simply because there is money in it, the writer hopes in his heart of hearts to strike a response from the whole world. In those terms, the three outstanding writers of our immediate time are Erle Stanley Gardner, Mickey Spillane and Ian Fleming. Probably the most successful writer the English language has ever known is Edgar Rice Burroughs. None of these gentlemen can write his way out of a paper bag, as writing is understood by three main types of literary specialists—teachers of composition, literary critics and the other working professional writers who provide the day-in, day-out reading matter for the fiction audience.

Now, whether the fault is with the understanding, or is in fact with the culprits named in the indictment, it still follows, on the basis of evidence observed over a long period of time, that any writer who attempts what is commonly called good prose, or who attempts a seriously intended comment on the human condition, or tries to plot and characterize with some attention to verisimilitude, is deliberately restricting his audience. This is self-destructive madness.

But madness is the common human condition and we have all learned to live with scores of diametrically opposed compulsions. The word is "compromise," or, if you don't care for those connotations, "balance" or "maturity." Somehow, most of us work it out; almost any day, one can meet working writers who are neither Gardner, Spillane, Fleming, Burroughs nor institutionalized.

Any sign of the commonly understood excellences in a piece of fiction therefore indicates one of two things. Most commonly, it indicates a craftsman consciously doing something difficult, for reasons which are not immediately explicable, are not simply logical, and are the result of some often troublesome growth and change within an intelligent human being. More rarely, it indicates a man doing something he can't help, largely because it has never occurred to him to do anything that is not creative. In other words, an artist. A genius. The craftsman may produce a "better" variation on a given theme than the genius. Neither of them may produce anything anywhere near as "good" as the next genius, or craftsman. That is beside the point. The point is there are three kinds of writers: those who can't do much right except to overwhelmingly satisfy the audience, those who seriously study their trade and may very well have excellent technical justifications for what appear to be mistakes, and those who are a law unto themselves because they are extending the limits of the possible in literature. And since there are compromises in all personalities, almost all writers combine some of these aspects—they are only more or less craftsmen, geniuses and what psychological phenomenology calls *idiots savants.* Furthermore, no writer sells a product which can be definitively test-run against another similar product. He sells a service—a subjective experience—to each individual reader.

Problem: Where is there an objective basis for determining whether a piece of fiction is "bad" or "good"?

OCTOBER 1965

The hardcover science fiction books of today are of course published by the same people who publish the straight fiction and mysteries and westerns—Doubleday, Simon & Schuster and so forth. This wasn't always so; it didn't begin to be so until about the time, fifteen years ago, when this magazine's first issue began a similarly meaningful revolution on the newsstands. In 1950, the biggest names in SF books—almost the only names—were Arkham House, Fantasy Press, F.P.C.I., Gnome Press, Hadley, Prime Press and Shasta. Some of them were on their way out, but these were isolated infirmities; a commercially foolish editorial policy in one instance, the publisher's personal circumstances in another. As a group they were promising, though they were essentially one-man operations started by people who had scraped together a little capital or credit. In some hope of profit, they were in the business of reprinting what each personally considered the best magazine science fiction published to that date.

What they produced was various. It varied from one company's systematic resurrection of every big name undermined by the new techniques of the 1940s *Astounding*, through Hadley's editions of such interesting but idiosyncratic pieces as L. Ron Hubbard's *Final Blackout,* to Arkham House's beautifully made volumes not only of Howard Phillips Lovecraft but of A. E. van Vogt's *Slan* and Ray Bradbury's first and best collection, *Dark Carnival.*

They did most of their business by mail order; their ads were column inches in the prozines, mimeographed pages in the fanzines. But in any largish city you could usually find one bookstore which was not above stocking one copy each for the nut trade, and here and there you could find booksellers who boasted that they specialized in it.

1950 was about the time when book review columns became regular features in the prozines. Before that, reviews, like books, had been occasional pieces. They had run as fillers at the bottoms of pages short on story text, and they were often obviously too thrilled at the thought that anything at all had found its way into boards. By 1950, the volume had not only gotten high enough to justify regular columns, it had gotten high enough to justify a nice cathartic bent of expression when a bad one came in, because the bad ones were in hopeless contrast to the good ones.

God grant that such a luxuriant time will never again come to science fiction book publishing. The great hoard of top-rank material waiting to be put into books was the bittersweet result of persistent neglect. Writers had lived, written and died without ever seeing permanent publication. Most of them were not specially conscious of great deprivation in this area, however— not very many people knew the area existed. It was entirely possible to be a science fiction fan in 1945 and not realize that there had been a Golden Age just before World War II; it was only when these books began coming out that the shape and nature of that work became fully apparent.

I would not want you to think that I believe some cosmic switch had clicked over in 1939 and then back in 1944. Neither is it true that between these arbitrary dates *Astounding Science Fiction* published seventy-two issues of solid immortal literature while none of its competitors did a thing but move in place. What *Astounding* did do, over a period of years, was to develop and, until 1950, keep writers who fairly often wrote a certain broad type of story well. It was a type of story which was better received by articulate science-fiction readers of those days than was any other type of story; those same readers were now ready to buy those same stories again in book form, and it so happened that a good number of people who had never read that kind of science fiction before were able to share their taste.

The ASF "Golden Age" in science fiction had been slightly anticipated by a similar phenomenon in crime fiction, with Dashiell Hammett and Raymond Chandler, among others, emerging from the crumbled pages of *Black Mask*. Apparently something just before the War acted to create pulp writers who were willing to break out of the post–World War I shell of neverland cliches which persisted in the pulps until the middle of the 1930s. It may have been an echo of the same tough attitude toward life that had produced Hemingway and Steinbeck in the "mainstream" somewhat earlier. Crime stories in the new mode had been getting serious book publishing attention all during World War II. Now it was perhaps science fiction's turn. The material was there. The new publishers picked it up and made books of it.

Fantasy Press went back a little farther, to publish the early E. E. Smith and Stanley Weinbaum as well as other forerunners of "modern" science fiction as these same book publishers now proceeded to define it, creating sharp distinctions from the past, and from Flash Gordon, simply by running full notices of previous publication and thus making it clear where the "good"—the most readable—material had come from. Centering their attention exactly on the Campbellian writers were Gnome Press and Shasta; while Shasta brought out Heinlein's Future History series, for example, Gnome was busy doing Asimov's Foundation stories. Arkham House, *Slan* aside, was meanwhile tending toward selections from such fantasy magazines as *Weird Tales* and *Unknown*, which had had little golden ages of their own and which Fantasy Press's program also included. Prime Press did a little of both, including collections by Lester del Rey (. . . *And Some Were Human*) and Theodore Sturgeon (*Without Sorcery*) which split their sources mainly between *Astounding* and *Unknown*, and by George O. Smith (*Venus Equilateral*) which was without peer as an example of ASF wiring-diagram fiction. Shasta brought out the Don A. Stuart stories (*Who Goes There?, Cloak of Aesir*), and Gnome did van Vogt's *The Mixed Men* and Henry Kuttner's Gallegher stories (*Robots Have No Tails*, by "Lewis Padgett").

In other words, in the few years between the end of the war and the earliest 1950s, these various people with their varied resources brought out the books which are still the liver and lights of any permanent collection of good science fiction. Random House had issued its legendary Healy-McComas anthology, *Adventures in Time and Space*, and Crown had brought out Groff Conklin's *A Treasury of Science Fiction*, but Gnome had countered with Martin Greenberg's *Men Against the Stars*, an entry fully qualified to run in that field.

If it hadn't been for the houses listed in Paragraph One of this necessarily breathless history, grown-up science fiction might have taken years to find a permanent place in literature via the library catalogues. With the few exceptions mentioned immediately above, the established major houses hadn't touched anything but Verne and Wells in years, the only significant wartime exceptions being Pocket's original paperback, *The Pocket Book of Science Fiction*, and Viking's *Portable Novels of Science*. Both of these had been edited and one assumes fought into life by Donald Wollheim, who has gone on to do his impressive job of making bricks without straw for Ace paperbacks. He, Healy and McComas, Groff Conklin and a few others might eventually have succeeded by applying unremitting pressure over a long period of time. The little specialist houses, operating out of lofts, bookstores and their owners' basements, cut that time dramatically short. They made the 1950s into boom years . . . from which they themselves would draw little but disaster.

By 1951, these people had accomplished two major things, both suicidal. They had exhausted the supply of easily found, high-quality reprints from the magazines, and they had established the financial value of the SF book market. They had gotten to that point because you can succeed with almost any sensible small venture in publishing as long as you're not doing something the potential major competitors want to do as well. At that point, the first Science Fiction Book Club ad had appeared on the back cover of a prozine. Except for differences of detail, it looked and read exactly like its sister ads for the Detective Book Club, which had been riding the back covers of the crime magazines for years. Merchandising had come to the business of publishing SF books for profit, and the incidence of major company names on new titles had begun to rise sharply.

A major publishing house has, by definition, the equipment needed to be a major publisher—a staff of editorial specialists, a production staff which does nothing all day but buy supplies and services having to do with publishing, and a sales staff which can consist of hundreds of specialists, some of them out on the road calling on bookstore owners they have known for years and others sitting home and writing punchy brochure copy. This is what these people do for a living. They have been trained for it under the impetus of believing that this is all they can do for a living. They are paid to do their one thing at least as well as their opposite numbers at the next major house. With this sort of organization, it is possible to produce a million copies of something that may look and be fractionally better than the work of one busy man working for himself. If you have a hundred such specialists, they can produce, say, ten times as many things to make a million copies of.

Once such a major organization has been put in train, it is committed by the inertia of schedules and capital investment. The sight of a major publishing company winding up to give birth to a new program is so impressive that few of its rivals can restrain themselves from following suit. Once the herd has been set in motion it must, by the nature of the beast, proceed along the line of least resistance for an indefinite period of time, leaving nothing in its wake but a stubble of grasses cropped too short to sustain life.

In the area of wholesale bookselling, the brief contention was thus between the specialists in science fiction and the specialists in publishing. In the area of simple packaging—of producing at a profit a book which appears to be worth the retail customer's money—the contest was only a little longer in the drawing out. It was in fact extended past its natural run by something like a happenstance. The merchandising machinery having gotten turned on, the various sales organizations sponsored by the major publishers immediately needed more product than the publishers themselves were yet able to furnish. So for a little while the small houses were able to supply copies to the book club operations owned more or less by their direct competitors. Thus they acquired a little more money to operate on, at the same time that their choice of production standards was sharply narrowed to the more expensive bands of the book-making spectrum.

What this meant for the retail customers was that more conventional-looking science fiction books in far greater quantities had become available. Shopping for books became considerably more convenient. Book prices were reduced, in several senses; over the short term, there was the benefit of having the specialist houses throw their stocks on the cut-rate market in an effort to get hold of additional working capital or simply to bail out. Over the long term, book prices were reduced (not absolutely, but relative to the still rising cost of production) by the combination of high-volume sales and production economies of which only major publishers are capable.

In fact, the only place the SF book-reading public lost anything tangible at all was one from which the small publishers could not have rescued them, but from which the big publishers could. That was in the paucity of remaining publishable book-length material. The result was that the middle 1950s were bad years for quality, and looked worse by comparison to the immediate past.

The middle 1950s were the years in which we got the "novels" pasted together from series short stories, the "science fiction" by outside writers who had obviously seen a monster movie once, and the unfortunate experiments in hapless antiquarianism reminiscent of that pioneering California company which had staked its all on Ralph Milne Farley.

These were the years in which knowledgeable critics lambasted the major companies day and night. If Gnome Press had been able to bring out Isaac Asimov's *I, Robot*, why in Heaven's name couldn't a giant outfit like Doubleday do better than Nelson Bond's Lancelot Biggs series disguised as a novel? Answer, Doubleday wasn't about to do *I, Robot*—yet. Gnome's excellently manufactured edition, with its flossy Cartier jacket making it look exactly like a big-time book, was still very much on sale. Doubleday would of course get to it in the course of time, but meanwhile there was Max Ehrlich's *The Big Eye*, and that was science fiction too. You could tell by the rocket on the title page.

It wasn't all bad. Gnome's *City*, by Clifford Simak, was the outstanding example of a pasteup that had been begging to be done. Doubleday's *The Martian Chronicles* dates from that time—a beautiful Bradbury collection which owes part of its charm to the loose connecting passages between stories, which may be the fragile vestiges of earlier plans to make a novel. Simon & Schuster did take the bit in its teeth and publish an edition of *Slan*. Grossett & Dunlap came out with a mass-priced edition of Henry Kuttner's *Fury*. Frederick Fell, hitherto known as the promulgator of Oscar J. Friend's *The Kid from Mars*—which is not *quite* as bad as its title—began publishing the Bleiler-Dikty annual "best" collections of magazine stories, which served the function of providing the cinderblock base for Judith Merril to later build bigger and better for Simon & Schuster and Dell. And Twayne, another small but nevertheless full-scale publisher who hoped to ride up among the majors on the strength of this new boom, did something very interesting with its "Triplet" series, fostered by Fletcher Pratt and Dr. John D. Clark.

These were anthologies of three novellas each by three major SF writers, who were given a loose outline of a basic story problem and a detailed description of the solar system in which it was to occur, each writer then going his own way as he saw fit. This was one attempt to create books. With all the will and budget in the world, the science fiction magazines of that time could only supply the best of the new gout of wordage the book publishers now needed as they jockeyed for control of the market. They couldn't supply all of it, by a long shot.

Perforce, the book publishers had to be willing to pay enough for original material so that good writers could be induced to occasionally forgo the magazines as a primary market.

No publisher in the world ever pays more than he has to, but the major publishers have people trained to pay that minimum with checks drawn on impressive banks, and with cheerily mesmerrhetic references to the freemasonry of the arts. In this case the book publishers were not only broadening the primary market for original SF, they were now applying the coup de grace to the little specialists, as well as shaking off the coattail riders in their own ranks.

Twayne was one of the companies which dropped out of the picture, But its program left some significant orphans. Among the ultimate results of Fletcher Pratt's brainchild was James Blish's Hugo-winning *A Case of Conscience*, which ran as a long one-parter in *If* before expanding up to its prize book length. Two other Twayne stories, an Asimov and a Poul Anderson, appeared as serials in *Astounding*. In its own lefthanded way, this was the first major case of important work being fed from a book publisher into the magazines—a complete reversal of the established precedence.

At about this same time, two other interesting things happened.

A publisher of paperback originals got on the stands with his edition of a middling-important novel before it had finished running as a serial in *Astounding*. And Doubleday published Cyril Kornbluth's *Takeoff*, a major novel by a major magazine writer, which had seen no magazine publication at all.

After the inevitable stumbling start, the big book houses were getting their programs into full flight. In every other important field of magazine fiction, most of the long serials had in fact been already under contract as books. That had now become the situation in science fiction, as well, and with various ups and downs, that is the situation today. In all, it took the major houses about five years, from 1950 to 1955, to make it so.

After ten years, this pendulum may now be getting ready to swing back the other way. Too many new "novels" are not former magazine serials—however arrived at—but puffed-up novelettes. Some of them were books all along, cut down for magazine use. But by far the greater percentage are not—they are padded, patched together or published in a design form that makes a lousy forty thousand words stretch across too many pages which are mostly margin and elephantiasical type. They are sometimes written by third-rate writers who are being overpaid in compensation for missing the apprenticeship that magazine work forces on its steady practitioners. These flat souffles are in turn subjected to the attentions of blurb writers and sales promotion directors who describe and package them to be more attractive and rewarding than they really are.

DECEMBER 1965

What sane man would be a writer? Consider that he has to please himself; he may claim he does not care what he writes or how, but he must write to sell, and that elementary need alone operates to shape his choice of word-arrangements. He may claim that he does not care if he sells . . . but you can see where that leads. The writer who doesn't care is the least free of all writers, and often a suffering slave to his own notions of excellence.

Then he has to get past an editor, who is in turn conscious of his publisher. To an at least appropriate degree, and often to a point of paranoia, the three of them are conscious of what they believe the reader wants. In many cases, there is the background influence of the distributor, who is dogmatically sure of what will sell and is often in a position to influence everything from cover design to content. The distributor is in turn marginally conscious of the retailer—the storekeeper in whose power it lies to bury a magazine behind a stack of competitors, or to return a bundle unopened, unsold.

But let us assume that the writer's words, however shaped by conscious and unconscious modifications at all these levels, have been published, sold, and are now held before a reader's eyes.

Can the reader read? What influences in his life have made certain words compellingly significant to him? Never mind the twelve-year-old who has stumbled across his first unabridged dictionary, and the certifiable maniac who underscores the words he likes in the publications he likes; these are the extreme cases. But they are significant; you cannot tell me that an individual sufficiently word-conscious to read for pleasure has not developed a complex tangle of reflexes triggered by words. This tangle is not the same as anyone else's, and therefore no reader reads what the writer has written.

Not only are words an arbitrary code with less than perfect accuracy, so are letters only arbitrary marks on paper. I can read German, for instance—but not in the quasimedieval characters of the 1930s. Some groups of letters are difficult for people to read accurately—if your name is Bulger, Swensen, Poul Anderson, Frederik Pohl, Fredric Brown or Frederic Wakeman, or if you are quite accustomed to receiving mail addressed to Algis Burdys, you know exactly what I mean. If you have a name that ends in "s," or if you will observe home-made signs selling tomatoes or chili-and-beans, you will quickly note what can be done with a possessive apostrophe in reckless hands. People have certain pre-dispositions when deciphering the code we call language—in fact, we mis-call it, for in this case we are discussing literation— one of the more infuriating of which is an apparently universal tendency to call one very clangorous SF novel *"Rouge Moon."* (A man who wanted me to hire him once devoted three single-spaced pages to telling me what a great book that was, and not once in some twenty detailed references to its title and specific scenes therein did he even accidentally tumble to the fact the the publisher had called it *Rogue Moon.* Yet he wanted the job very badly.)

And then, poor chap, the writer has gotten his work out into print, and at least some of his readers—as frail, as tangled inside—are critics. Critics think they know everything that went on in the writer's mind, and where he did not say what he intended to say. They correct his arrangements for him before he even makes them, and then they write essays about them.

I, fortunately, am a book *reviewer.* I only know all about editing, publishing, book production, distribution and the difference between making and missing the distributor's tie (not an item of accessory apparel, in this case). I would not dream of telling you what goes on in the mind of any specific writer. I have some understanding of what goes on in my own mind, of course, when I am being a writer, and would be remiss if I did not ascribe my habits and prejudices to the people whose books I review. All this I write down, and send off to my editor, who marks it up and sends it to his printer, who hands it to his composing room foreman, etc., etc., and after a while you get it, complete with occasional typographical errors and idiosyncratic editing, and you understand it, don't you?

JUNE 1966

As you know, the problem with life is that nobody understands the situation. Nonetheless, we have to get through it as best we can. If there is a scheme to it all, it is sufficiently complex and covers sufficient spacetime so that only God could account for it. It is one of the primary purposes of commercial entertainment— and of art—to compensate us for the fact that none of us are God. It is the function of a statue to capture some small slice of something that we say is real, and hold it frozen for us to walk around and look until we are satisfied that we understand it. It is the function of a commercial novel, of the sort to which most science fiction novels belong, to provide what Murray Leinster long ago called a "pocket universe." In this universe, the rules rapidly become comprehensible, or an assurance is quickly given that the rules will become comprehensible. There is a protagonist—a hero, or a fascinating villain, who becomes the reader's particular property, and whose movements, troubles and triumphs become the reader's own. In this way and for some little space of time, the reader inhabits a comprehensible world, and escapes from the real one.

This escape into an organized delusion—if you will, a systematic lie—is distinguishable from psychosis only by the fact that you can walk into a store and buy a package of it, the package having been provided by someone who deals in this service. As you know, psychosis is frowned upon, whereas reading is normally acceptable. Thus commerce does confer a certain absolution on us all.

Some kinds of books are automatically more popular than others, just as some individual books are more popular than others of their same kind. This means, apparently, that there are fashions in psychosis, just as there are degrees to which individual books please their readers—that is to say, provide a delusional system yummier than someone else's delusional system. It might even be possible to psychoanalyze a particular period of human history by running one's finger down a list of the bestsellers. Thus, simple statistics and grubby pennies and dimes lay us all upon the psychiatrist's couch. Never doubt that some day some earnest Ph.D. candidate will do all this for us; hopefully, not in my time or yours.

MAY 1969

As you know, this field functioned without criticism for many years. There was no systematic effort to apply standards to science fiction as a literature. In the earliest days of magazine SF, a story was good or bad in exact relationship to the durability of its scientific rationale, which served as the silent valet on which all the shirtings of prose, characterization and plot were flung.

A little later in our history, the story did begin to be measured against certain purely literary criteria; exactly the same criteria as those applied to the stories in the westerns, crime yarns, confession, sports and air war stories published in the companion magazines belonging to the same pulp chains that included one or two SF titles. The same people who edited *Planet*, for example, also worked on *Sheena, Queen of the Jungle*. And John W. Campbell, Jr., sat in on the plotting conferences for *Doc Savage*. (The last time the subject was raised JWC still had two absolutely perfect murder methods stored up in the back of his mind, should Street & Smith ever revive the Man of Bronze, and JWC ever revive Street & Smith.)

Anyway, all of this was in the period that ended with the extinction of the Golden Age. The demise of The Happy Time coincides with the appearance of book review and critical columns in the magazines, and with the constitution of various conferences, schools, movements and Mafias intended to direct the course of this field in a proper manner and with a respectable goal in sight.

It's only a coincidence, I'm sure. (Actually, I don't think it's a coincidence at all. But to explain why I also don't think there's an obvious cause-effect relationship, I'd have to explain why I think the cause is the thing commonly mistaken for the effect, especially by Sam Moskowitz, and then Sam would write me another letter.)

Okay. For the past ten years, anyway, it has been literally impossible to draw SF breath without being tested for systolic and diastolic rationale-pressure. Two things have been assured every individual who has any sort of statement in this racket, and each of those two things is a fanatical audience, one pro, and the other con. (I'm waiting for my shy followers to make themselves known, by the way. We could use a show of enthusiasm, gang— the other guys arrived on the scene some time ago.)

All this *is* leading up to something. I have four books here I want to talk about, and at least three of them are intended to push some standard. At least three. I do think I should be spinning in my grave.

Actually, the reason three of them definitely push something is that no publisher who's *au courant* (that's French for "Be sure and run in a direction where you won't stub your toe and say *au!*") (Either that or German for a sort of misadventure with a cow) will let you put together an anthology for him unless it has A Higher Reason than simply containing good stories. Thank God, a sufficiently clever and conscientious editor can put together a book which contains both rationale and good reading. It just doesn't happen very often, is all. It is easier to be clever than it is to be conscientious.

MARCH 1970

As many of you will know, science fiction is unique in commercial literature because of the nature of some of its readers. These readers, who are organized into various kinds of clubs, including a large body of individuals who declare affiliation with nothing smaller than SF itself, are collectively called "fans." Unlike Mets fans, James Bond fans, Baker Street Irregulars, Burroughs Bibliophiles or Conan's own Hyborean Legion, these people are not primarily aficionados of a particular character—although some of them, as noted, do subsume that narrower sort of loyalty within their larger concern.

That larger concern is what makes the crucial difference. The institution of fandom ensures that at any given time, in all corners of the English-speaking world and in significant additional precincts, there will be several thousand energetic individuals who care deeply, in detail, continuously—and with positive effect—about the ultimate destiny, good and progress of science fiction.

Because they are organized—via these various clubs and national and international bodies whose regional meetings and annual conventions provide additional social links—they are in a position to lend the field a certain dignity, via awards like the Hugo and its collateral publicity. (Among such awards, the Hugo for excellence is unique. The crime field's Edgar, the western's Silver Spur and motion pictures' Oscar, like the Science Fiction Writers of America's Nebula, are all awards attained by impressing one's fellow members of a guild or "academy." The Hugo alone is awarded by the audience toward which all these excellences are presumably aimed.)

But fandom, and a fannish way of life in which some would insist that the plural of fan is "fen," and some that Fandom Is Just A Goshdurn Hobby (usually neologized as "fijagh," opposed to "fiawol"), would be just another Goddamned social club if it weren't for its mailing lists.

The binding force in fandom—many of whose most active and influential members have never had eyes laid on them by more than a fraction of their peers—is the amateur publication, or fanzine (as distinguished from "prozine"—what you are reading now).

Only Sam Moskowitz knows how many fanzines there have been and not even Sam Moskowitz could tell you accurately how many are in the mail to how many readers at any given moment—just as any attempt at a fannish census would be the same as an attempt to paint all of the Golden Gate Bridge before the other end needed painting again. But there are fans of every stripe and coloration; the prozine and book collectors, something like those in the larger universe but not completely so; the conservative and radical political activists, who play out within the fannish universe those impulses toward establishmentarianism and feud which all flesh is heir to; the encyclopedists and historians; the sane and the insane, all in a jumble together—and yes, even those who are beyond the original interest which led them to discover somehow the names of a few other fannish types and to begin their entry into an arena in which they now discuss art films, sportscars, music, politics, drugs . . . almost anything but the concern which originally brought them here.

The main concern always holds the middle, however, and in that wide, undistributed place there exist spokesmen and advocates of astonishing persuasive power, sharpening the wits of all around them, pouring out an impressive succession of opinions from which some *pro tem* consensus is always emerging—perhaps to be recorded and perhaps not before the next determination submerges it but always there to be sensed.

It doesn't matter that you couldn't get two fans to agree what the fannish attitude is or that you couldn't write an accurate, thorough statement of your own. What counts is a perpetual ferment of ideas, many of them not overly related to SF at all, many of them clouded by personal motives, some destroyed—or enhanced—by the typographical accidents inherent in home-typed stencil duplication, many of them demonstrably juvenile, because their advocates are, in the median, below draft age chronologically and glandularly, though not always intellectually—what counts, as I was saying, is that there is this wealth of effective expression. From it the individual fan extracts a resultant attitude toward SF—among other things—which, though individual and dynamic, is nevertheless in rough agreement with other attitudes and which changes slowly enough so that there are such things as "*a* fannish attitude," and certain enduring institutions in the form of shibboleth.

What does this mean to Thee and Me? It means Somebody Cares—and has been caring long enough to establish a weight of tradition and a culture from which a given individual might emerge enroute toward other activities but which would remain inherent in his intellectual bones. Fandom may or may not be A conscious Way Of Life, but fanac leaves its mark. And thus it affects Thee and Me quite strongly, though thee mightn't know who 4sJ might be or the Futurians were and Me might be a decade or three beyond trotting all 26 copies of the latest issue of *Slantasy* down to the post office in Dorothy, N.J. Because they do grow up, you know, or at least get older—or did you think science fiction writers grow on trees?

RULES OF THE GAME

KATE WILHELM

I was watching a senator give a speech a few years ago: "They say it's not about money, it's about money. They say it's not about politics, it's about politics. They say it's not about sex— it's about sex."

Then Harry came in and said, "Hey, so the guy plays around a little. What's the big deal?"

Eleven months ago I kicked Harry out, after six years of being married. He talked me into calling it a trial separation, and agreeing to let him keep his office in our house because he had a year's supply of letterheads and cards with this address. He even had an ad in the yellow pages with this address and phone number: Computer Consultant, On Site. He hung out here, ate my food, drank my coffee, and was gone by the time I got home from work. Too late I realized that what he gained from our agreement was rent-free office space and freedom.

I left him a note in his pigsty of an office telling him I wanted a divorce. He never got around to answering. I left the divorce papers on his desk; they vanished. He was as elusive as a wet fish when I tried to reach him.

Two weeks ago I buried him.

Now I'm starting to clean up the messes he left behind, especially his office here in my house. There are dirty coffee mugs, glasses, half a sandwich with a thriving mold colony on it, papers everywhere, and three computers. I pick up two mugs and a glass and start to take them to the kitchen when suddenly he's there.

Harry Thurman, as big as life, if not as solid. I can see a lamp through him. He's like a full-color transparency.

I cry out and drop the mugs and the glass, and he yelps and disappears.

"And stay out!" I yell at the lamp.

I step over the mess on the floor, run from the office, and close the door behind me. I'm shaking. A hallucination, a figment of my imagination. A visitation? I've read that it's not uncommon to see the newly departed, a fleeting image, sometimes a comfort to the grief-stricken. I'm hardly that, not that I wanted him dead, just out of my life.

I admit I was shaken by the suddenness of the apparition, but I don't feel afraid. What I feel is anger. How dare he do that, show himself when I'm cleaning up after him again? My fury ignited when I opened his apartment to clean it out and found expensive suits, a huge flat-screen television, DVD system, Chivas Regal . . . He drove a two-year-old BMW. For a year I lived in near poverty, making our mortgage payments, insurance, his and mine, taxes . . . I cashed out my 401(k) to meet payments, since I couldn't sell the house without his cooperation. A small inheritance from my aunt made the down payment; I would have lost everything if I failed to pay up every month. My fury increased when I found two gift boxes in his bureau, one addressed to My Darling Marsha. That was a bracelet with semiprecious gems and pearls. The other was to Dearest Diane, a heavy gold chain. I also found four credit card bills totaling twenty-seven thousand dollars, for which I am responsible since I'm his widow and my name is on them along with his. And he had the nerve, the effrontery to show himself!

"Let it go," I tell myself, and head for the kitchen for a glass of water, and decide I really want more than just water. I take a gin and tonic into the living room where I sit and regard the bracelet and gold chain on the coffee table.

"Pretty, aren't they?" Harry says, and he's mostly there again, blinking on and off like a Christmas tree light.

Very carefully I put my glass down on the coffee table, then close my eyes hard. "Either come in all the way, or go out, but stop that blinking!"

"I'm doing the best I can."

When I look again, he's still there, no longer flickering, and I can still see through him.

"You're not hallucinating," he says. "I'm really here, or mostly here."

I take a long drink. "Why?" My voice is little more than a whisper.

"I don't know why. I just found myself here. You scared the shit out of me when you suddenly saw me, by the way."

"What do you mean? How long have you been here?"

"When did that real estate agent come?"

"This morning."

"I was here then. Two hundred seventy-five thousand for this place! Wow! You'll make out like a bandit. Didn't I tell you that mortgage insurance was a good idea? And double indemnity for my insurance, plus the BMW. Beautiful rich young widow. What are you going to do with all that dough?"

"Harry! Stop this. Why are you here? What do you want?"

"Aren't you scared?"

"No. I don't believe in ghosts."

After a moment, looking surprised, he says, "Neither do I."

"Isn't there someplace you should be? Report in or something?"

He shrugs expressively. He's very handsome, even if he is dead. Thick black hair just curly enough, wonderful dark blue eyes with makeup-ad lashes, cleft chin. He's wearing pale blue sweats, possibly the clothes he had on when a hit-and-run maniac clipped him and ran.

"You never used to drink alone," he says, eyeing the gin and tonic as if he's longing for one just like it.

"I never used to sit talking to my dead husband."

He nods. "There is that," he says. "You realize it's a first for me, too." He reaches for the gold chain. His fingers pass through it. "Ah well," he says. "Diane ran a credit check on me and said get lost. And Marsha wanted to get married and I said there was a little complication, namely you. She got sore. If you can find the receipts, you probably can return them. Be worth your while."

I need a therapist. It's one thing to hallucinate but quite another to hold a conversation with a hallucination. It could even be a serious disorder. I drink the rest of the gin and tonic.

"Did you find the pictures?" he asks.

"What pictures?"

"Oh. Well. What are you going to do with the furniture and things?"

"Garage sale, auction. I don't know."

"You might want to look in the desk drawer. Bottom lifts out, and there's a file folder . . . I'd get them myself, but . . ." He passes his hand through the bracelet and looks at me with what I used to think was an appealing expression, like a boy caught stealing a cookie.

I go back to his office, step over the broken mugs and glass on the floor, and head for his desk. There are pencils, pens, computer disks, miscellaneous office stuff in the drawer. I dump it out and there really is a fake bottom. The folder has Polaroid shots of seven different naked women, including me. Just one among many.

I take the folder, pick up a newspaper in the kitchen, and go out to the patio and the grill.

"Hey!" he says. "They're worth something, you know."

If he were not already dead, how satisfying it would be to hit him myself with a car, or a train, or a sledgehammer.

My lawyer said that when they find the guy who ran him down, and he seems confident that they will, we'll sue him for a million for wrongful death. Rightful death, I think, watching the Polaroid shots writhe, blacken, and curl up, emitting clouds of foul-smelling smoke.

He doesn't walk exactly, just drifts along, near me when I go out to the patio, near me when I go back inside.

"Why are you haunting me?" I demand in the kitchen. "I never did anything to you."

"I'm not haunting you," he says a bit indignantly.

"Then get out, go away, and don't come back."

"I can't," he says. "See, I'm doing my morning run down by the river, the way I always do, and whammo, just nothing. Then I'm here and you're talking to the real estate agent. And neither of you seems to see me or hear me even though I'm yelling my head off, making a hell of a racket."

"Who hit you? Do you know?"

"Nope. Came out of nowhere behind me."

"Have you even tried to find out what you're supposed to do now? Someone to ask what the rules are or something?"

"What rules?"

"I don't know. There must be a protocol, something you're supposed to do, someplace to check in. There are always rules."

"Maybe," he says. "I used to think there'd be a rosy-cheeked cherub waiting to take your hand and guide you, or maybe an old guy with a long white beard and a staff, maybe even a beautiful girl in a flowing white gown, something like that. But like I said, nothing, then here."

"A little guy in a red suit with a white-hot trident," I mutter. It's another bureaucratic snarl. I know something about bureaucracy, working for a law firm as I do, or did. I quit a week ago. There are always rules and procedures, routines to follow, and there are always some things that fall through the system and get lost. Like Harry.

"Look," I say, "I believe you're supposed to haunt the person or persons who did you in. You know, revenge, something like that. Or are you haunting the house? If I leave, do you stay with the house, like the refrigerator and stove?"

"I believe," he says, "the people who wrote those rules weren't the ones who knew much about it."

"Well, I'm going out now, and you stay here. Okay?" I pick up my purse, fish out the car keys and walk out, with him close enough to touch, if there were anything to touch besides a draft of cool air.

My neighbor Elinor Smallwood comes over to say hello, and it's apparent that she doesn't suspect that he is there; neither does her dachshund. "Lori, I hope you're bearing up. Was that a Realtor I saw leaving this morning? Oh, dear, I hope if a buyer turns up, it will be someone compatible who speaks English. You know what I mean?"

I nod and return to the house. He doesn't need doors; he flows inside while I'm still working with the key.

"It isn't fair!" I yell at him. "I don't deserve this! Get out of here! Let me get on with my life."

He flickers for a moment, then spreads his hands helplessly. "I'm as stuck as you are," he says.

I swallow hard as the realization hits me: he really won't, or can't, leave. No matter what I do, he'll be there watching, commenting. I haven't been to bed with a man in a year; I dated a few times but I never let things get out of hand. After all, I was still married. Now I'm not married; I'm thirty years old, and whatever I do, there will be my audience of one.

"Oh, God, what about Carl?" I say out loud. He's the attorney from the office who is helping with my legal affairs. He suggested a quiet dinner in a discreet restaurant, and I know he intended to seduce me afterward, and I intended to let him.

"Ah hah!" Harry says gleefully. "You have a boyfriend!"

I head for the telephone to break my date with Carl. Actually he never gave me a second glance until I became a fairly soon-to-be-rich widow.

After the call I sit on the bench by the wall phone, my gaze on Harry, who is trying to pick up a salt shaker on the table. He swoops like a striking snake and his hand goes through it without causing a tremor; then he sneaks up on it stealthily, with the same effect. Over and over. God help me. If he learns to materialize completely, what then?

I start down a list of friends and family, trying to decide if there is anyone I can confide in. There isn't. Who would believe me? Jo Farrell might, but she would find it exciting and want to hold a séance or something. I can imagine telling Super Iris; she thinks we mean like Superwoman, but it's really Superior Iris who always knows more than anyone else and is free with opinions and advice. I can hear her voice in my head: "Surely you understand that it isn't about ghosts . . ." Wherever she starts, it always ends the same: it's really your own fault.

It isn't my fault, but it certainly is my problem. I remember a little red phone book in the drawer with the false bottom. Why that when he had a Rolodex?

We go back to the office where I pick up the phone book. He tries to grab it, but the only effect is that of a cool breeze blowing across my hand.

In the kitchen I sit at the table and look over the names in the little red book. Twelve women! I even know one of them, Sheila Wayman.

Maybe, I tell myself, maybe one of those women still cares, maybe she'll want him back, or maybe I can just dump him on one of them. Transfer him. Turn over custodial care . . . I can feel hysteria mingling with fury now, and I draw in a deep breath. Twelve! I pick up the Portland phone book and look up Sheila and Roger Wayman. Southwest Spruce. A twenty-minute drive. Halfway to the door I stop. What will I say to her? I snatch up a paperback book from an end table, scrawl her name on the inside cover, and leave. He drifts along at my side.

"Where are we going?"

He just oozes between molecules or something and gets in the passenger seat as I get behind the wheel. For the first ten minutes or so he comments on the nice day, a beautiful June day in Portland, or the heavy traffic, or criticizes my driving, whistles in a low tone at a woman walking a dog . . . I ignore him. When I turn onto Spruce he leans forward, looking around, and now there's a note of uneasiness in his voice when he asks again, "Where are we going?"

A minute later when I slow down to examine house numbers, he says, "This is crazy. She might not even be home. She was a long time ago. She won't even remember me. What's the point? What are you going to do, make a scene, pick a fight with her?"

I continue to ignore him. At her house I pull into the driveway and get out holding the book. He is close behind me all the way. If she isn't home, I'll sit in the car and read and wait for her, I think grimly, but she answers the doorbell. A small boy on a tricycle is by her side, and she is fifteen pounds overweight.

"Sheila?"

She gasps, recognizing me, and her face pales. "What do you want?" she whispers.

"I'm cleaning out the house and I came across this. I was in the neighborhood and decided to drop it off." I hand the book to her.

"Wow! She's turned into a tub," Harry says at my side. Sheila doesn't even glance in his direction.

In the car again, I say, "One down, eleven to go." Harry lets out a ghostly type of moan, and tries to grasp my purse. He's in the passenger seat with my purse on the same seat, where his crotch would be if he had any substance; he is looking at the purse cross-eyed as he makes a quick snatching grab, draws his hand back and tries with the other one. I start to drive.

Back at home, I make myself an omelette and salad and he practices. "It's like having a muscle that you can't find exactly," he says. "Like wriggling your ears. I'll get it," he adds confidently. I'm very afraid that he will.

I plot out the following day, using a map, listing the women in the order of proximity, the closest ones on to the most distant. I had all day Saturday, when they might be home, and if not, then Sunday, on into the next week or however long it would take. I would track them down at their offices or schools or wherever they spent their time and see each one, give each one the opportunity to see Harry and, I hope, claim him.

And if none of them claims him? No answer follows the question.

I don't bother with an excuse again. When Hilary Winstead comes to the door, I say, "I'm Lori Thurman. I was cleaning out Harry's office and I came across your pictures. I burned them. I just wanted you to know."

Behind me Harry says, "She makes a mean martini."

Hilary Winstead stares at me, moistens her lips, and then slams the door.

Bette Hackman is tall and willowy, very beautiful. Harry sighs when she says, "What do you mean? I paid for those pictures. He swore that was all he had. That bastard!"

On southeast Burnside I detour a few blocks and park at the cemetery. A few people are around, none paying any attention to us as I walk to the new grave of Harry Thurman.

"That's where you planted me?"

"That's where you belong. Get in there and go back to sleep."

He shudders and drifts backward. "You're out of your mind."

I guess I am. What I was hoping was that a guy with a long beard and a staff, or a cherub, or even a beautiful woman would cry out, "Harry! We've been looking everywhere for you. Come along now." We return to the car and I drive on.

No one answers the doorbell at Wanda Sorenson's house.

Diane Shuster says, "I could care less."

"Shrewd, but nearly illiterate," Harry comments. "Great ass, though."

I am ready to give it up. No one sees him, or notices a cold breeze, or anything else out of the ordinary.

Then he says, "How it goes is they'd call for help with the

new computer, or new software, and I'd go in and find things screwed up royally. So I'd fool around and get things working, and accidentally log on to a porn site, something like that, and then . . . One thing leads to another."

I grit my teeth and look at the next name: Sonia Welch. He nods when I turn onto River Drive. "Ah, wait until you see that house! Gorgeous place! Sonia broke it off before I was ready, actually. Afraid her old man would find out."

He sounds regretful when he says, "That was part of it, of course, the fear of discovery, a mad husband with a gun, something like that. A little added spice."

My lips are clamped so hard they hurt. I am determined to ignore him until he is so bored he'll find a way to go somewhere else. He'll find someone who knows the rules.

"That's it," Harry says, pointing to a tall gray house nearly hidden behind shrubbery. It is beautiful, with bay windows, stained-glass panels, professional landscaping . . . A heavyset man in shorts, holding a can of varnish, is touching up a motorboat in the driveway.

"Hello," I say, getting out of the car. "I'm looking for Sonia. Is she home?"

The man looks me over as if I am up for auction.

"The husband. He's a shrink," Harry says. "Would you tell him your innermost secrets?"

I have to admit, although silently, that I would not. His eyes are as cold and fathomless as black ice.

"She's back on the terrace," Welch says. "Go on around." He motions toward a walkway and returns to his boat repair.

I walk under a lattice covered with roses in bloom. The fragrance is intoxicating. I see the woman before I step onto the terrace; she is dozing apparently, with a magazine over her face against the late afternoon sun.

"Sonia?" I say.

With a languid motion she moves the magazine and looks around over her shoulder. Then she jumps up and jams both hands over her mouth, staring wide-eyed, not at me, but at my side, at Harry.

"No," she cries then, and begins to back up, nearly falls over the chaise behind her, catches her balance, and continues to back up around a glass-topped table, staring, paler than death.

"I didn't mean to, Harry," she whispers. "It was an accident. Don't come closer. Stay back! Please, don't come closer!"

Harry is flickering wildly, moving toward her like a cloud fired with lightning. Then he goes out. Sonia keeps backing up.

"Harry, stay away! I had to do it. I told you he was suspicious! I told you to stay away! I had to do it! You should have stayed away! Don't touch me! Oh, God, don't touch me!"

I don't think she even saw me. I turn and retrace my steps under the roses and out to the car.

"Wasn't she there?" Welch asks, looking up.

"I think she's sleeping. I didn't want to disturb her. I just wanted to thank her for a favor she did me. It isn't important."

I knew there were rules, I tell myself, driving away. There are always rules.

A CHANCE REMARK

MARTIN H. GREENBERG

I t all started with a chance remark, one of those life-changing comments that you read about all the time, but don't ever think will happen to you.

It was January 1970, in the middle of my first year at the University of Wisconsin–Green Bay. I had been hired in 1969 fresh out of graduate school and taught my first class that summer. UWGB had just opened as the experimental and innovative campus of the University of Wisconsin and it featured a lot of team teaching and specialized courses.

One of those courses was on "Futurism," a movement given a great boost by the publication of Alvin and Heidi Toffler's *Future Shock* in 1968. It was a January interim four-week, team-taught course and one of the instructors was Professor Patricia Warrick, with whom I shared a small office. Pat later wrote what is still one of the best books on the work of Philip K. Dick, *Mind in Motion* (1987), and served as a president of the Science Fiction Research Association.

She asked me to give a lecture on "The Future of Politics," which I did. On the way out the door I noticed that the students had copies of Dick Allen's *Science Fiction: The Future* on their desks, one of the first, if not the first, science fiction anthology designed for classroom use. I immediately bragged that I had read everything ever written about science fiction and that I would be happy to come back the following week and talk about SF. I really didn't think it was bragging, because in January 1970, science fiction still hadn't really arrived as a reputable subject for study—I owned and had read books by Damon Knight, James Blish, Sam Moskowitz, and a few others—they were all I could find up until that time.

So I came back the next week with some favorite books, and talked to the class about what I knew of the history of then modern science fiction. And going out the door, Pat turns to me and asks, "Have you ever thought about combining your interest in political science with your interest in science fiction?" And a lightbulb went on that resulted in our putting together a proposal for what became *Political Science Fiction: An Introductory Reader*, which we eventually sold to Prentice-Hall. The idea was to assemble a book of stories that used science fiction to illustrate principles in political science and to parallel as closely as possible the structure of basic introduction to political science textbooks.

One of my responsibilities was to clear the permissions, a process I knew little about. I did know enough to understand that you had to pay people to reprint their stories and I set about finding addresses. This was a fateful endeavor. I wanted to use two stories by Isaac Asimov: "Evidence," in which one candidate for political office claims that his opponent is really a robot, and "Franchise," which examines voting in the future.

I found an address for Isaac and wrote him a letter asking his permission and offering him (I think) $150 per story for nonexclusive volume rights. Within what seemed like a few minutes he wrote back to me, and here I'm paraphrasing very closely:

Dear Martin Greenberg:

I have your letter of (whatever) asking to reprint "Evidence" and "Franchise." The terms you mention are acceptable except that I will not do any business with you whatsoever until you prove to me that you are not the Martin Greenberg of Gnome Press.

Sincerely yours,

Isaac Asimov

"Whatsoever" sounded pretty serious, but I had several anthologies edited by that Martin Greenberg and I knew that Gnome Press was one of the specialty publishers that started up after World War II to publish the stories and serialized novels that the "regular" publishing houses were not interested in.

I also knew that Gnome Press was the original publisher of Isaac's *Foundation Trilogy* and his *I, Robot* collection. What I didn't know at the time was that that Martin Greenberg was, shall we say, "financially challenged," and that Isaac did not see any income from the Gnome Press editions of his most famous works. Doubleday eventually retrieved the rights for him and published the books to enormous success.

I still don't understand what possessed me, but I wrote Dr. Asimov the following (again closely paraphrased) letter:

Dear Dr. Asimov
    I am Martin Harry Greenberg, son of Max and Mollie Cohen Greenberg. I was born on March 1, 1941, in St. Francis Hospital in Miami Beach, Florida.

After more silly but accurate detail, I signed the letter over my typed name

    Marty the Other

I quickly got a letter back from Isaac with the greeting, "Dear Marty the Other," and granting me permission to reprint the two stories.

Political Science Fiction didn't do all that well, but Pat and I, and then I with others, continued to do many more textbook anthologies, all of which contained stories by Isaac which involved permission requests from me to him that ended with "Marty the Other" and responses from him that started "Dear Marty the Other." The whole thing was a tremendous icebreaker and made what followed possible.

Later in 1978, it dawned on me to see if I could persuade Isaac to coedit an anthology, and I suggested what would become *100 Great Science Fiction Short Short Stories* to him because he had edited the excellent *Fifty Short Science Fiction Tales* with the late Groff Conklin, and because I knew he loved the short-short form, with its punch or pun endings. I said we could double the number and not repeat any stories and he loved the idea. We enjoyed working together so much that we edited other anthologies, and the next time I was in New York visiting family he invited me to dinner. Isaac, Janet, and I went to Shun Lee near his penthouse apartment and had a wonderful time.

This began a friendship that became so deep that we talked virtually every night for the last twelve years of his life.

Isaac opened doors for me that made my career in trade publishing possible, and was the best friend a man could have. At the urging of Lester del Rey, I used Martin Harry Greenberg on my books to differentiate myself from the other guy, whom I finally met at the Baltimore Worldcon in 1998.

These first two permission requests have led to our clearing over twenty-one thousand permissions for our books and novels—and I owe it all to a chance remark and to parents who named me Martin and not Marvin or Melvin.

WRITING SF IN THE SIXTIES

FREDERIK POHL AND
ELIZABETH ANNE HULL

The years of the decade of the 1960s were a good season for science fiction writers. The magazine markets for their work were not as numerous as they had been during the explosive growth of a couple of decades earlier, but there were enough of them to provide showcases for a lot of writers who were writing a lot of good science fiction in those years— yes, and sometimes taking in quite decent financial returns, too, because the giant slick magazines, too, had discovered science fiction, and magazines like *Collier's* and *The Saturday Evening Post* were publishing Ray Bradbury, Robert A. Heinlein, John Wyndham and others on slick paper for audiences of millions. And the long drowsing American book industry, which had failed to notice that such a publishing category as science fiction existed until a few threadbare fan groups began putting hardcover science fiction into the stores themselves, had finally caught on and half a dozen major publishing companies now had their own active lines.

Publishing people from other areas of the industry sometimes wonder, when the SF category enjoys one of its expansions, whether there are enough writers around to meet the demand. The answer to that is yes. There are. There always are, because SF has always generated its own major new writers, unceasingly. This happens regardless of the state of the market. What it is due to is the fact that some people with a good deal of talent discover that SF exists and that it gives its writers the otherwise scarce opportunity to think and write about all sorts of wonderful things.

They come because they want the scope of SF. Sadly, sometimes we lose them, even the most successful of them. But while they are with us we treasure them.

We would like to start by looking at a particular few of the writers whose careers began, or flowered (and sometimes also ended) in our period, especially four: Harlan Ellison, Walter Miller Jr., Larry Niven and Ursula K. Le Guin. (Though we will have things to say about others as well.)

Harlan Ellison, it is true, did not exactly appear from nowhere. He had been writing from an early age—had even had his work appear in *The New Yorker*, but had never really found his voice until the beginning of the period we're discussing when he began the astonishing series of pyrotechnical masterpieces sometimes referred to as the "Repent, Harlequin" stories.

More than for most writers, Harlan's stories and his life seemed both almost part of the same work of art. His home was in the hills overlooking Los Angeles—well, not exactly, in a technical sense, really overlooking it. To overlook the city from Harlan's front door you would have had to be able to see through some miles of solid rock, because he lived on the far side of the hills, but the house was worth the trip. The name on the door was Ellison Wonderland. His writing office would not have shamed a banker, though it centered on only a typewriter that was neither computer-based nor even electrified, powered only by the muscles of Harlan's fingers. His central sound system, he boasted, could deliver any music a visitor wanted at the press of a button; and the whole place, like any proper wonderland, had a secret chamber. And there, in those years of the 1960s, he wrote stories like "'Repent, Harlequin,' Said the Ticktockman," "I Have No Mouth and I Must Scream," "The Beast That Shouted Love at the Heart of the World," "A Boy and His Dog,"

"Pretty Maggie Moneyeyes" and "Shattered Like a Glass Goblin," racking up a considerable collection of Hugos and Nebulas in the process. (One writer said, "They ought to give him a Hugo every time he writes a story, just for the titles.") There was no doubt that Harlan was a major SF writer. The only jarring note was that Harlan was dissatisfied with that pigeonhole, and so his production of SF stories dwindled as he went on to the exploration of other pastures.

Harlan Ellison was not the only writer who tried to shake off the SF label. Kurt Vonnegut even went so far as to quietly ask some friends who were members of the SF writers' trade union, the Science Fiction Writers of America, not to vote for his novel *Slaughterhouse Five* for a Nebula. It wasn't that he thought it was a bad award. He just wasn't sure he could afford it. He had a good deal, and he knew it. His books were shelved in bookstores on tables of their own, up front and near the cash register, identified not by category but by his name. Sales were good. What they would be if the books were in the crowded shelves in the category areas he didn't know, and wasn't in any hurry to find out.

In a different category are the writers who make a great splash and then, with no apparent reason, disappear from the scene. By the sixties Walter Miller Jr. had become in a short period one of the most productive and esteemed SF writers around—John Campbell once remarked with a semi-embarrassed grin, "I just can't stop buying everything he sends in." People talked of him as the next Heinlein, sure to dominate the field for decades to come, especially after his 1961 novel, *A Canticle for Leibowitz*, won its Hugo. But then one of those invisible switches that people carry with them in their heads turned, and he stopped.

Then there's Larry Niven, one of science fiction's favorite writers for getting close to half a century now, but there was a time when that seemed unlikely to happen. Larry was born to money, was a millionaire as soon as the nurse began to clean him up to show to his mom. His parents were a nice young couple, related to the Dohenys of Doheny Drive and much other Los Angeles real estate. Mr. and Mrs. Niven loved their little boy, but as he began to become a bigger boy, then close to a man, there were worries. What interested him mostly, it seemed, wasn't anything to do with business or investments or any of the things wealthy people enjoyed; it was the possibility of nonhuman creatures from other planets and rocket ships. In short, young Larry was a faaan. There were friends and family members urging the Nivens to try to discourage the boy's aberration, some of them in terms of apocalyptic warning. They didn't want to interfere with their son's life, but they were getting concerned.

Then young Larry himself had a stroke of luck.

Like any true fan he had tried writing a story of his own. The SF magazine *If* had a policy of, in each issue, publishing one story by a brand-new writer, so Larry had sent his story there—and now the magazine had sent him a check. It wasn't much, $15. The story was very short and *If*'s rates were low.

But it had sold. Larry was now a published author.

How this first display of earning capacity impressed the Niven and Doheny families is not known, but that was not the end. Emboldened, Larry sent *If* another story and before long a check came back for that one, too. The word rate was the same but the story was longer so this time the amount was ninety dollars. And a little later Larry's third story sold, this one longer still and the rate better: $225. "And," Larry once said, "they thought the curve was going in an interesting way, so I didn't get much discouragement from my parents after that."

Although Robert A. Heinlein certainly did not begin his career in the 1960s, he came close to owning it, with three more Hugos (in addition to his earlier one for *The Puppet Masters*): *Starship Troopers* in 1960, *Stranger in a Strange Land* in 1962, and *The Moon Is a Harsh Mistress* in 1967. *The Moon Is a Harsh Mistress* in particular restored faith in Heinlein's almost magical storytelling gifts, for, just when his talents might be expected to be waning, up he came with what was arguably his very best novel ever. It may even have put the seal on a cult following such that his fans were apparently willing to read anything he wrote after that— and some of the later novels were not so great—in hopes of repeating the excitement they felt. Although Heinlein usually missed the mark when he tried to write explicitly feminist fiction, especially when his protagonist was female as in *Podkayne of Mars, I Will Fear No Evil*, and *Friday*, he did practice a kind of "quiet" feminism in that his women and girls were not simply wives, daughters, or sweethearts waiting to be rescued: they actually did things—that is they had jobs that were significant and they moved the action forward themselves rather than always waiting to be rescued.

But the end of the decade produced a novel that seemed to be a harbinger of the explosion of feminist novels and women writers that followed in the seventies, eighties and nineties and it's probably fair to say that this novel inspired both men and women writers to write differently and about subjects that especially interested the growing female readership. This was, of course, Ursula K. LeGuin's *The Left Hand of Darkness*, which won a Nebula in 1969. Especially remarkable is chapter 7, which can be excerpted as a short story on its own, and its challenging series of ideas beginning with the rhetorical opening, "Consider . . ." The fact that the protagonist is a black man is usually ignored by feminist critics who get caught up in the implications of LeGuin's gender comments, but it fit into the tradition of Heinlein's making Juan Rico Hispanic in *Starship Troopers* and Manuel black in *The Moon Is a Harsh Mistress*. Today even unadventurous writers will commonly make women and minorities be scientists and hold positions of responsibility (like mayor, governor, president, captain, commander, lieutenant, etc.) and women and girls do not need to rely on men and boys to figure out the clues to solve problems.

. . . So say the two of us.

However, one of us (Hull) is demanding that the other of us (Pohl) close this enterprise by saying a few words about himself as a writer in the decade of the 1960s. And so I therefore shall.

I should say that I wasn't a full-time writer in the 1960s. Horace Gold, the editor of *Galaxy* and *If*, was in poor health. For some time he had been increasingly unable to deal with the issues involved in getting the magazines out and had asked me for my assistance. At the last he had had to resign and Bob Guinn, the publisher, had asked me to take the job. I couldn't say no. Being given a magazine to edit, to me, is like being given the world's best set of electric trains when you are twelve years old. It's fun. Even dealing with the authors was pleasurable—well, more often than not, it was. Not surprisingly, SF writers have enough traits in common that it is easy for friendships to form. True, editing did interfere with writing in unexpected ways. There were sometimes stories I couldn't write because they were close to the kinds of stories some of my contributors were writing. Sometimes I suggested these to the contributor. There were even some I didn't want to write because I knew a contributor who could write that particular story far better than I. Neutron stars were hot news at the time and so I asked Larry Niven for a neutron-star story. It won him his first Hugo.

But such conflicts are rare. And one of the reasons why I've enjoyed doubling up as writer and editor so frequently is that editing has made me a better writer. Looking to see what another person has done wrong has definitely sharpened my perceptions of flaws of my own.

I think it may have been true for others, even including John Campbell. His work before he became an editor was pretty much derivative, particularly of Doc Smith's space-operas. He didn't do much to touch the heart and soul until after his experience with editing, when he became Don A. Stuart. (Sadly, he didn't keep the writing up as other interests came along.)

So, at the end, let's summarize: What was it like to be an SF writer in the 1960s?

Why, pretty much what it has been in every other decade since 1926. If you can be a good SF writer you probably could do somewhat better in terms of prosperity and social standing at something else. But if you can be a good SF writer why would you want to do anything else?

PRIDE AND PROMETHEUS

JOHN KESSEL

"**P**ride and Prometheus" is the second story for which John Kessel has won a Nebula Award, the first being "Another Orphan" in 1982. The story blends elements of *Frankenstein* and *Pride and Prejudice* with, of course, a unique twist. John is the director of the Master of Fine Arts Creative Writing program at North Carolina State University.

Had both her mother and her sister Kitty not insisted upon it, Miss Mary Bennet, whose interest in Nature did not extend to the Nature of Society, would not have attended the ball in Grosvenor Square. This was Kitty's season. Mrs. Bennet had despaired of Mary long ago, but still bore hopes for her younger sister, and so had set her determined mind on putting Kitty in the way of Robert Sidney of Detling Manor, who possessed a fortune of six thousand pounds a year, and was likely to be at that evening's festivities. Being obliged by her unmarried state to live with her parents, and the whims of Mrs. Bennet being what they were, although there was no earthly reason for Mary to be there, there was no good excuse for her absence.

So it was that Mary found herself in the ballroom of the great house, trussed up in a silk dress with her hair piled high, bedecked with her sister's jewels. She was neither a beauty, like her older and happily married sister Jane, nor witty, like her older and happily married sister Elizabeth, nor flirtatious, like her younger and less happily married sister Lydia. Awkward and nearsighted, she had never cut an attractive figure, and as she had aged she had come to see herself as others saw her. Every time Mrs. Bennet told her to stand up straight, she felt despair. Mary had seen how Jane and Elizabeth had made good lives for themselves by finding appropriate mates. But there was no air of grace or mystery about Mary, and no man ever looked upon her with admiration.

Kitty's card was full, and she had already contrived to dance once with the distinguished Mr. Sidney, whom Mary could not imagine being more tedious. Hectically glowing, Kitty was certain that this was the season she would get a husband. Mary, in contrast, sat with her mother and her Aunt Gardiner, whose good sense was Mary's only respite from her mother's silliness. After the third minuet Kitty came flying over.

"Catch your breath, Kitty!" Mrs. Bennet said. "Must you rush about like this? Who is that young man you danced with? Remember, we are here to smile on Mr. Sidney, not on some stranger. Did I see him arrive with the Lord Mayor?"

"How can I tell you what you saw, Mother?"

"Don't be impertinent."

"Yes. He is an acquaintance of the Mayor. He's from Switzerland! Mr. Clerval, on holiday."

The tall, fair-haired Clerval stood with a darker, brooding young man, both impeccably dressed in dove gray breeches, black jackets, and waistcoats, with white tie and gloves.

"Switzerland! I would not have you marry any Dutchman— though 'tis said their merchants are uncommonly wealthy. And who is that gentleman with whom he speaks?"

"I don't know, Mother—but I can find out."

Mrs. Bennet's curiosity was soon to be relieved, as the two men crossed the drawing room to the sisters and their chaperones.

"Henry Clerval, madame," the fair-haired man said. "And this is my good friend Mr. Victor Frankenstein."

Mr. Frankenstein bowed but said nothing. He had the darkest eyes that Mary had ever encountered, and an air of being there only on obligation. Whether this was because he was as uncomfortable in these social situations as she, Mary could not tell, but his diffident air intrigued her. She fancied his reserve might bespeak sadness rather than pride. His manners were faultless, as was his command of English, though he spoke with a slight French accent. When he asked Mary to dance she suspected he did so only at the urging of Mr. Clerval; on the floor, once the orchestra of pianoforte, violin, and cello struck up the quadrille, he moved with some grace but no trace of a smile.

At the end of the dance, Frankenstein asked whether Mary would like some refreshment, and they crossed from the crowded ballroom to the sitting room, where he procured for her a cup of negus. Mary felt obliged to make some conversation before she should retreat to the safety of her wallflower's chair.

"What brings you to England, Mr. Frankenstein?"

"I come to meet with certain natural philosophers here in London, and in Oxford—students of magnetism."

"Oh! Then have you met Professor Langdon, of the Royal Society?"

Frankenstein looked at her as if seeing her for the first time. "How is it that you are acquainted with Professor Langdon?"

"I am not personally acquainted with him, but I am, in my small way, an enthusiast of the sciences. You are a natural philosopher?"

"I confess that I can no longer countenance the subject. But yes, I did study with Mr. Krempe and Mr. Waldman in Ingolstadt."

"You no longer countenance the subject, yet you seek out Professor Langdon."

A shadow swept over Mr. Frankenstein's handsome face. "It is unsupportable to me, yet pursue it I must."

"A paradox."

"A paradox that I am unable to explain, Miss Bennet."

All this said in a voice heavy with despair. Mary watched his sober black eyes, and replied, "'The heart has its reasons of which reason knows nothing.'"

For the second time that evening he gave her a look that suggested an understanding. Frankenstein sipped from his cup, then spoke: "Avoid any pastime, Miss Bennet, that takes you out of the normal course of human contact. If the study to which you apply yourself has a tendency to weaken your affections, and to destroy your taste for simple pleasures, then that study is certainly unlawful."

The purport of this extraordinary speech Mary was unable to fathom. "Surely there is no harm in seeking knowledge."

Mr. Frankenstein smiled. "Henry has been urging me to go out into London society; had I known that I might meet such a thoughtful person as yourself I would have taken him up on it long 'ere now."

He took her hand. "But I spy your aunt at the door," he said. "No doubt she has been dispatched to protect you. If you will, please let me return you to your mother. I must thank you for the dance, and even more for your conversation, Miss Bennet. In the midst of a foreign land, you have brought me a moment of sympathy."

And again Mary sat beside her mother and aunt as she had half an hour before. She was nonplussed. It was not seemly for a stranger to speak so much from the heart to a woman he had never previously met, yet she could not find it in herself to condemn him. Rather, she felt her own failure in not keeping him longer.

A cold March rain was falling when, after midnight, they left the ball. They waited under the portico while the coachman brought round the carriage. Kitty began coughing. As they stood there in the chill night, Mary noticed a hooded man, of enormous size, standing in the shadows at the corner of the lane. Full in the downpour, unmoving, he watched the town house and its partiers without coming closer or going away, as if this observation were all his intention in life. Mary shivered.

In the carriage back to Aunt Gardiner's home near Belgravia, Mrs. Bennet insisted that Kitty take the lap robe against the chill. "Stop coughing, Kitty. Have a care for my poor nerves." She added, "They should never have put the supper at the end of that long hallway. The young ladies, flushed from the dance, had to walk all that cold way."

Kitty drew a ragged breath and leaned over to Mary. "I have never seen you so taken with a man, Mary. What did that Swiss gentleman say to you?"

"We spoke of natural philosophy."

"Did he say nothing of the reasons he came to England?" Aunt Gardiner asked.

"That was his reason."

"I should say not!" said Kitty. "He came to forget his grief! His little brother William was murdered, not six months ago, by the family maid!"

"How terrible!" said Aunt Gardiner.

Mrs. Bennet asked in open astonishment, "Could this be true?"

"I have it from Lucy Copeland, the Lord Mayor's daughter," Kitty replied. "Who heard it from Mr. Clerval himself. And there is more! He is engaged to be married—to his cousin. Yet he has abandoned her, left her in Switzerland and come here instead."

"Did he say anything to you about these matters?" Mrs. Bennet asked Mary.

Kitty interrupted. "Mother, he's not going to tell the family secrets to strangers, let alone reveal his betrothal at a dance."

Mary wondered at these revelations. Perhaps they explained Mr. Frankenstein's odd manner. But could they explain his interest in her? "A man should be what he seems," she said.

Kitty snorted, and it became a cough.

"Mark me, girls," said Mrs. Bennet, "that engagement is a

match that he does not want. I wonder what fortune he would bring to a marriage?"

In the days that followed, Kitty's cough became a full-blown catarrh, and it was decided against her protest that, the city air being unhealthy, they should cut short their season and return to Meryton. Mr. Sidney was undoubtedly unaware of his narrow escape. Mary could not honestly say that she regretted leaving, though the memory of her half hour with Mr. Frankenstein gave her as much regret at losing the chance of further commerce with him as she had ever felt from her acquaintance with a man.

Within a week Kitty was feeling better, and repining bitterly their remove from London. In truth, she was only two years younger than Mary and had made none of the mental accommodations to approaching spinsterhood that her older sister had attempted. Mr. Bennet retreated to his study, emerging only at mealtimes to cast sardonic comments about Mrs. Bennet and Kitty's marital campaigns. Perhaps, Mrs. Bennet said, they might invite Mr. Sidney to visit Longbourn when Parliament adjourned. Mary escaped these discussions by practicing the pianoforte and, as the advancing spring brought warm weather, taking walks in the countryside, where she would stop beneath an oak and read, indulging her passion for Goethe and German philosophy. When she tried to engage her father in speculation, he warned her, "I am afraid, my dear, that your understanding is too dependent on books and not enough on experience of the world. Beware, Mary. Too much learning makes a woman monstrous."

What experience of the world had they ever allowed her? Rebuffed, Mary wrote to Elizabeth about the abrupt end of Kitty's latest assault on marriage, and her subsequent ill temper, and Elizabeth wrote back inviting her two younger sisters to come visit Pemberley.

Mary was overjoyed to have the opportunity to escape her mother and see something more of Derbyshire, and Kitty seemed equally willing. Mrs. Bennet was not persuaded when Elizabeth suggested that nearby Matlock and its baths might be good for Kitty's health (no man would marry a sickly girl), but she was persuaded by Kitty's observation that, though it could in no way rival London, Matlock did attract a finer society than sleepy Meryton, and thus offered opportunities for meeting eligible young men of property. So in the second week of May, Mr. and Mrs. Bennet tearfully loaded their last unmarried daughters into a coach for the long drive to Derbyshire. Mrs. Bennet's tears were shed because their absence would deprive Kitty and Mary of her attentions, Mr. Bennet's for the fact that their absence would assure him of Mrs. Bennet's.

The two girls were as ever delighted by the grace and luxury of Pemberley, Mr. Darcy's ancestral estate. Darcy was kindness itself, and the servants attentive, if, at the instruction of Elizabeth, less indulgent of Kitty's whims and more careful of her health than the thoroughly cowed servants at home. Lizzy saw that Kitty got enough sleep, and the three sisters took long walks in the grounds of the estate. Kitty's health improved, and Mary's spirits rose. Mary enjoyed the company of Lizzy and Darcy's eight-year-old son William, who was attempting to teach her and Darcy's younger sister Georgiana to fish. Georgiana pined after her betrothed, Captain Broadbent, who was away on crown business in the Caribbean, but after they had been there a week, Jane and her husband Mr. Bingley came for an extended visit from their own estate thirty miles away, and so four of the five Bennet sisters were reunited. They spent many cordial afternoons and evenings. Both Mary and Georgiana were accomplished at the pianoforte, though Mary had come to realize that her sisters tolerated more than enjoyed her playing. The reunion of Lizzy and Jane meant even more time devoted to Kitty's improvement, with specific attention to her marital prospects, and left Mary feeling invisible. Still, on occasion she would join them and drive into Lambton or Matlock to shop and socialize, and every week during the summer a ball was held in the assembly room of the Old Bath Hotel, with its beeswax-polished floor and splendid chandeliers.

On one such excursion to Matlock, Georgiana stopped at the milliners while Kitty pursued some business at the butcher's shop—Mary wondered at her sudden interest in Pemberley's domestic affairs—and Mary took William to the museum and circulating library, which contained celebrated cabinets of natural history. William had told her of certain antiquities unearthed in the excavation for a new hotel and recently added to the collection.

The streets, hotels, and inns of Matlock bustled with travelers there to take the waters. Newly wedded couples leaned on one another's arms, whispering secrets that no doubt concerned the alpine scenery. A crew of workmen was breaking up the cobblestone street in front of the hall, swinging pickaxes in the bright sun. Inside she and Will retreated to the cool quiet of the public exhibition room.

Among the visitors to the museum Mary spied a slender, well-dressed man at one of the display cases, examining the artifacts contained there. As she drew near, Mary recognized him. "Mr. Frankenstein!"

The tall European looked up, startled. "Ah—Miss Bennet?"

She was pleased that he remembered. "Yes. How good to see you."

"And this young man is?"

"My nephew, William."

At the mention of this name, Frankenstein's expression darkened. He closed his eyes. "Are you not well?" Mary asked.

He looked at her again. "Forgive me. These antiquities call to mind sad associations. Give me a moment."

"Certainly," she said. William ran off to see the hall's steam clock. Mary turned and examined the contents of the neighboring cabinet.

Beneath the glass was a collection of bones that had been

unearthed in the local lead mines. The card lettered beside them read: *Bones, resembling those of a fish, made of limestone.*

Eventually Frankenstein came to stand beside her. "How is it that you are come to Matlock?" he inquired.

"My sister Elizabeth is married to Mr. Fitzwilliam Darcy, of Pemberley. Kitty and I are here on a visit. Have you come to take the waters?"

"Clerval and I are on our way to Scotland, where he will stay with friends, while I pursue—certain investigations. We rest here a week. The topography of the valley reminds me of my home in Switzerland."

"I have heard it said so," she replied. Frankenstein seemed to have regained his composure, but Mary wondered still at what had awakened his grief. "You have an interest in these relics?" she asked, indicating the cabinets.

"Some, perhaps. I find it remarkable to see a young lady take an interest in such arcana." Mary detected no trace of mockery in his voice.

"Indeed, I do," she said, indulging her enthusiasm. "Professor Erasmus Darwin has written of the source of these bones:

> *"Organic life beneath the shoreless waves*
> *Was born and nurs'd in ocean's pearly caves;*
> *First forms minute, unseen by spheric glass,*
> *Move on the mud, or pierce the watery mass;*
> *These, as successive generations bloom,*
> *New powers acquire and larger limbs assume;*
> *Whence countless groups of vegetation spring,*
> *And breathing realms of fin and feet and wing.*

"People say this offers proof of the Great Flood. Do you think, Mr. Frankenstein, that Matlock could once have been under the sea? They say these are creatures that have not existed since the time of Noah."

"Far older than the Flood, I'll warrant. I do not think that these bones were originally made of stone. Some process has transformed them. Anatomically, they are more like those of a lizard than a fish."

"You have studied anatomy?"

Mr. Frankenstein tapped his fingers upon the glass of the case. "Three years gone by it was one of my passions. I no longer pursue such matters."

"And yet, sir, you met with men of science in London."

"Ah—yes, I did. I am surprised that you remember a brief conversation, more than two months ago."

"I have a good memory."

"As evidenced by your quoting Professor Darwin. I might expect a woman such as yourself to take more interest in art than science."

"Oh, you may rest assured that I have read my share of novels. And even more, in my youth, of sermons. Elizabeth is wont to tease me for a great moralizer. 'Evil is easy,' I tell her, 'and has infinite forms.'"

Frankenstein did not answer. Finally he said, "Would that the world had no need of moralizers."

Mary recalled his warning against science from their London meeting. "Come, Mr. Frankenstein. There is no evil in studying God's handiwork."

"A God-fearing Christian might take exception to Professor Darwin's assertion that life began in the sea, no matter how poetically stated." His voice became distant. "Can a living soul be created without the hand of God?"

"It is my feeling that the hand of God is everywhere present." Mary gestured toward the cabinet. "Even in the bones of this stony fish."

"Then you have more faith than I, Miss Bennet—or more innocence."

Mary blushed. She was not used to bantering in this way with a gentleman. In her experience, handsome and accomplished men took no interest in her, and such conversations as she had engaged in offered little of substance other than the weather, clothes, and town gossip. Yet she saw that she had touched Frankenstein, and felt something akin to triumph.

They were interrupted by the appearance of Georgiana and Kitty, entering with Henry Clerval. "There you are!" said Kitty. "You see, Mr. Clerval, I told you we would find Mary poring over these heaps of bones!"

"And it is no surprise to find my friend here as well," said Clerval.

Mary felt quite deflated. The party moved out of the town hall and in splendid sunlight along the North Parade. Kitty proposed, and the visitors acceded to, a stroll on the so-called Lovers' Walk beside the river. As they walked along the gorge, vast ramparts of limestone rock, clothed with yew trees, elms, and limes, rose up on either side of the river. William ran ahead, and Kitty, Georgiana, and Clerval followed, leaving Frankenstein and Mary behind. Eventually they came in sight of the High Tor, a sheer cliff rearing its brow on the east bank of the Derwent. The lower part was covered with small trees and foliage. Massive boulders that had fallen from the cliff broke the riverbed below into foaming rapids. The noise of the waters left Mary and Frankenstein, apart from the others, as isolated as if they had been in a separate room. Frankenstein spent a long time gazing at the scenery. Mary's mind raced, seeking some way to recapture the mood of their conversation in the town hall.

"How this reminds me of my home," he said. "Henry and I would climb such cliffs as this, chase goats around the meadows, and play at pirates. Father would walk me though the woods and name every tree and flower. I once saw a lightning bolt shiver an old oak to splinters."

"Whenever I come here," Mary blurted out, "I realize how small I am, and how great time is. We are here for only seconds, and then we are gone, and these rocks, this river, will long survive us. And through it all we are alone."

Frankenstein turned toward her. "Surely you are not so lonely. You have your family, your sisters. Your mother and father."

"One can be alone in a room of people. Kitty mocks me for my 'heaps of bones.'"

"A person may marry."

"I am twenty-eight years old, sir. I am no man's vision of a lover or wife."

What had come over her, to say this aloud, for the first time in her life? Yet what did it matter what she said to this foreigner? There was no point in letting some hope for sympathy delude her into greater hopes. They had danced a single dance in London, and now they spent an afternoon together; soon he would leave England, marry his cousin, and Mary would never see him again. She deserved Kitty's mockery.

Frankenstein took some time before answering, during which Mary was acutely aware of the sound of the waters, and of the sight of Georgiana, William, and Clerval playing in the grass by the riverbank, while Kitty stood pensive some distance away.

"Miss Bennet, I am sorry if I have made light of your situation. But your fine qualities should be apparent to anyone who took the trouble truly to make your acquaintance. Your knowledge of matters of science only adds to my admiration."

"You needn't flatter me," said Mary. "I am unused to it."

"I do not flatter," Frankenstein replied. "I speak my own mind."

William came running up. "Aunt Mary! This would be an excellent place to fish! We should come here with Father!"

"That's a good idea, Will."

Frankenstein turned to the others. "We must return to the hotel, Henry," he told Clerval. "I need to see that new glassware properly packed before shipping it ahead."

"Very well."

"Glassware?" Georgiana asked.

Clerval chuckled. "Victor has been purchasing equipment at

every stop along our tour—glassware, bottles of chemicals, lead and copper disks. The coachmen threaten to leave us behind if he does not ship these things separately."

Kitty argued in vain, but the party walked back to Matlock. The women and William met the carriage to take them back to Pemberley. "I hope I see you again, Miss Bennet," Frankenstein said. Had she been more accustomed to reading the emotions of others she would have ventured that his expression held sincere interest—even longing.

On the way back to Pemberley William prattled with Georgiana. Kitty, subdued for once, leaned back with her eyes closed, while Mary puzzled over every moment of the afternoon. The fundamental sympathy she had felt with Frankenstein in their brief London encounter had been only reinforced. His sudden dark moods, his silences, bespoke some burden he carried. Mary was almost convinced that her mother was right—that Frankenstein did not love his cousin, and that he was here in England fleeing from her. How could this second meeting with him be chance? Fate had brought them together.

At dinner that evening, Kitty told Darcy and Elizabeth about their encounter with the handsome Swiss tourists. Later, Mary took Lizzy aside and asked her to invite Clerval and Frankenstein to dinner.

"This is new!" said Lizzy. "I expected this from Kitty, but not you. You have never before asked to have a young man come to Pemberley."

"I have never met someone quite like Mr. Frankenstein," Mary replied.

"Have you taken the Matlock waters?" Mary asked Clerval, who was seated opposite her at the dinner table. "People in the parish say that a dip in the hot springs could raise the dead."

"I confess that I have not," Clerval said. "Victor does not believe in their healing powers."

Mary turned to Frankenstein, hoping to draw him into discussion of the matter, but the startled expression on his face silenced her.

The table, covered with a blinding white damask tablecloth, glittered with silver and crystal. A large epergne, studded with lit beeswax candles, dominated its center. In addition to the family members, and in order to even the number of guests and balance female with male, Darcy and Elizabeth had invited the vicar, Mr. Chatsworth. Completing the dinner party were Bingley and Jane, Georgiana, and Kitty.

The footmen brought soup, followed by claret, turbot with lobster and Dutch sauce, oyster pâté, lamb cutlets with asparagus, peas, a fricandeau à l'oseille, venison, stewed beef à la jardinière, with various salads, beetroot, French and English mustard. Two ices, cherry water and pineapple cream, and a chocolate cream with strawberries. Champagne flowed throughout the dinner, and Madeira afterward.

Darcy inquired of Mr. Clerval's business in England, and Clerval told of his meetings with men of business in London, and his interest in India. He had even begun the study of the language, and for their entertainment spoke a few sentences in Hindi. Darcy told of his visit to Geneva a decade ago. Clerval spoke charmingly of the differences in manners between the Swiss and the English, with witty preference for English habits, except, he said, in the matter of boiled meats. Georgiana asked about women's dress on the continent. Elizabeth allowed as how, if they could keep him safe, it would be good for William's education to tour the continent. Kitty, who usually dominated the table with bright talk and jokes, was unusually quiet. The vicar spoke amusingly of his travels in Italy.

Through all of this, Frankenstein offered little in the way of response or comment. Mary had put such hopes on this dinner, and now she feared she had misread him. His voice warmed but once, when he spoke of his father, a counselor and syndic, renowned for his integrity. Only on inquiry would he speak of his years in Ingolstadt.

"And what did you study in the university?" Bingley asked.

"Matters of no interest," Frankenstein replied.

An uncomfortable silence followed. Clerval gently explained, "My friend devoted himself so single-mindedly to the study of natural philosophy that his health failed. I was fortunately able to bring him back to us, but it was a near thing."

"For which I will ever be grateful to you," Frankenstein mumbled.

Lizzy attempted to change the subject. "Reverend Chatsworth, what news is there of the parish?"

The vicar, unaccustomed to such volume and variety of drink, was in his cups, his face flushed and his voice rising to pulpit volume. "Well, I hope the ladies will not take it amiss," he boomed, "if I tell about a curious incident that occurred last night!"

"Pray do."

"So, then—last night I was troubled with sleeplessness—I think it was the trout I ate for supper, it was not right—Mrs. Croft vowed she had purchased it just that afternoon, but I wonder if perhaps it might have been from the previous day's catch. Be that as it may, lying awake some time after midnight, I thought I heard a scraping out my bedroom window—the weather has been so fine of late that I sleep with my window open. It is my opinion, Mr. Clerval, that nothing aids the lungs more than fresh air, and I believe that is the opinion of the best continental thinkers, is it not? The air is exceedingly fresh in the alpine meadows, I am told?"

"Only in those meadows where the cows have not been feeding."

"The cows? Oh, yes, the cows—ha, ha!—very good! The cows, indeed! So, where was I? Ah, yes. I rose from my bed and looked out the window, and what did I spy but a light in the churchyard. I threw on my robe and slippers and hurried out to see what might be the matter.

"As I approached the churchyard I saw a dark figure wielding a spade. His back was to me, silhouetted by a lamp which rested beside Nancy Brown's grave. Poor Nancy, dead not a week now, so young, only seventeen.'"

"A man?" said Kitty.

The vicar's round face grew serious. "You may imagine my shock. 'Halloo!' I shouted. At that the man dropped his spade, seized the lantern and dashed round the back of the church. By the time I had reached the corner he was out of sight. Back at the grave I saw that he had been on a fair way to unearthing poor Nancy's coffin!"

"My goodness!" said Jane.

"Defiling a grave?" asked Bingley. "I am astonished."

Darcy said nothing, but his look demonstrated that he was not pleased by the vicar bringing such an uncouth matter to his dinner table. Frankenstein, sitting next to Mary, put down his knife and took a long draught of Madeira.

The vicar lowered his voice. He was clearly enjoying himself. "I can only speculate on what motive this man might have had. Could it have been some lover of hers, overcome with grief?"

"No man is so faithful," Kitty said.

"My dear vicar," said Lizzy. "You have read too many of Mrs. Radcliffe's novels."

Darcy leaned back in his chair. "Gypsies have been seen in the woods about the quarry. It was no doubt their work. They were seeking jewelry."

"Jewelry?" the vicar said. "The Browns had barely enough money to see her decently buried."

"Which proves that whoever did this was not a local man."

Clerval spoke. "At home, fresh graves are sometimes defiled by men providing cadavers to doctors. Was there not a spate of such grave robbings in Ingolstadt, Victor?"

Frankenstein put down his glass. "Yes," he said. "Some anatomists, in seeking knowledge, will abandon all human scruple."

"I do not think that is likely to be the cause in this instance," Darcy observed. "Here there is no university, no medical school.

Doctor Phillips, in Lambton, is no transgressor of civilized rules."

"He is scarcely a transgressor of his own threshold," said Lizzy. "One must call him a day in advance to get him to leave his parlor."

"Rest assured, there are such men," said Frankenstein. "I have known them. My illness, as Henry has described to you, was in some way my spirit's rebellion against the understanding that the pursuit of knowledge will lead some men into mortal peril."

Here was Mary's chance to impress Frankenstein. "Surely there is a nobility in risking one's life to advance the claims of one's race. With how many things are we upon the brink of becoming acquainted, if cowardice or carelessness did not restrain our inquiries?"

"Then I thank God for cowardice and carelessness, Miss Bennet," Frankenstein said. "One's life, perhaps, is worth risking, but not one's soul."

"True enough. But I believe that science may demand our relaxing the strictures of common society."

"We have never heard this tone from you, Mary," Jane said.

Darcy interjected, "You are becoming quite modern, sister. What strictures are you prepared to abandon for us tonight?" His voice was full of the gentle condescension with which he treated Mary at all times.

How she wished to surprise them! How she longed to show Darcy and Lizzy, with their perfect marriage and perfect lives, that she was not the simple old maid they thought her. "Anatomists in London have obtained the court's permission to dissect the bodies of criminals after execution. Is it unjust to use the body of a murderer, who has already forfeited his own life, to save the lives of the innocent?"

"My uncle, who is on the bench, has spoken of such cases," Bingley said.

"Not only that," Mary added. "Have you heard of the experiments of the Italian scientist Aldini? Last summer in London at the Royal College of Surgeons he used a powerful battery to animate portions of the body of a hanged man. According to the *Times*, the spectators genuinely believed that the body was about to come to life!"

"Mary, please!" said Lizzy.

"You need to spend less time on your horrid books," Kitty laughed. "No suitor is going to want to talk with you about dead bodies."

And so Kitty was on their side, too. Her mockery only made Mary more determined to force Frankenstein to speak. "What do you say, sir? Will you come to my defense?"

Frankenstein carefully folded his napkin and set it beside his plate. "Such attempts are not motivated by bravery, or even curiosity, but by ambition. The pursuit of knowledge can become a vice deadly as any of the more common sins. Worse still, because even the most noble of natures are susceptible to such temptations. None but he who has experienced them can conceive of the enticements of science."

The vicar raised his glass. "Mr. Frankenstein, truer words have never been spoken. The man who defiled poor Nancy's grave has placed himself beyond the mercy of a forgiving God."

Mary felt charged with contradictory emotions. "You have experienced such enticements, Mr. Frankenstein?"

"Sadly, I have."

"But surely there is no sin that is beyond the reach of God's mercy? 'To know all is to forgive all.'"

The vicar turned to her. "My child, what know you of sin?"

"Very little, Mr. Chatsworth, except of idleness. Yet I feel that even a wicked person can have the veil lifted from his eyes."

Frankenstein looked at her. "Here I must agree with Miss Bennet. I have to believe that even the most corrupted nature is susceptible to grace. If I did not think this were possible, I could not live."

"Enough of this talk," insisted Darcy. "Vicar, I suggest you mind your parishioners, including those in the churchyard, more carefully. But now I, for one, am eager to hear Miss Georgiana play the pianoforte. And perhaps Miss Mary and Miss Catherine will join her. We must uphold the accomplishments of English maidenhood before our foreign guests."

On Kitty's insistence, the next morning, despite lowering clouds and a chill in the air that spoke more of March than late May, she and Mary took a walk along the river.

They walked along the stream that ran from the estate toward the Derwent. Kitty remained silent. Mary's thoughts turned to the wholly unsatisfying dinner of the previous night. The conversation in the parlor had gone no better than dinner. Mary had played the piano ill, showing herself to poor advantage next to the accomplished Georgiana. Under Jane and Lizzy's gaze she felt the folly of her intemperate speech at the table. Frankenstein said next to nothing to her for the rest of the evening; he almost seemed wary of being in her presence.

She was wondering how he was spending this morning when, suddenly turning her face from Mary, Kitty burst into tears.

Mary touched her arm. "Whatever is the matter, Kitty?"

"Do you believe what you said last night?"

"What did I say?"

"That there is no sin beyond the reach of God's mercy?"

"Of course I do! Why would you ask?"

"Because I have committed such a sin!" She covered her eyes with her hand. "Oh, no, I mustn't speak of it!"

Mary refrained from pointing out that, having made such a provocative admission, Kitty could hardly remain silent—and undoubtedly had no intention of doing so. But Kitty's intentions were not always transparent to Mary.

After some coaxing and a further walk along the stream, Kitty was prepared finally to unburden herself. It seemed that, from the previous summer she had maintained a secret admiration for a local man from Matlock, Robert Piggot, son of the butcher. Though his family was quite prosperous and he stood to inherit the family business, he was in no way a gentleman, and Kitty had vowed never to let her affections overwhelm her sense.

But, upon their recent return to Pemberley, she had encountered Robert on her first visit to town, and she had been secretly meeting with him when she went into Matlock on the pretext of shopping. Worse still, the couple had allowed their passion to get the better of them, and Kitty had given way to carnal love.

The two sisters sat on a fallen tree in the woods as Kitty poured out her tale. "I want so much to marry him." Her tears flowed readily. "I do not want to be alone, I don't want to die an old maid! And Lydia—Lydia told me about—about the act of love, how wonderful it was, how good Wickham makes her feel. She boasted of it! And I said, why should vain Lydia have this, and me have nothing, to waste my youth in conversation and embroidery, in listening to Mother prattle and Father throw heavy sighs. Father thinks me a fool, unlikely ever to find a husband. And now he's right!" Kitty burst into wailing again. "He's right! No man shall ever have me!" Her tears ended in a fit of coughing.

"Oh, Kitty," Mary said.

"When Darcy spoke of English maidenhood last night, it was all I could do to keep from bursting into tears. You must get Father to agree to let me marry Robert."

"Has he asked you to marry him?"

"He shall. He must. You don't know how fine a man he is. Despite the fact that he is in trade, he has the gentlest manners. I don't care if he is not well born."

Mary embraced Kitty. Kitty alternated between sobs and fits of coughing. Above them the thunder rumbled, and the wind rustled the trees. Mary felt Kitty's shivering body. She needed to calm her, to get her back to the house. How frail, how slender her sister was.

She did not know what to say. Once Mary would have

self-righteously condemned Kitty. But much that Kitty said was the content of her own mind, and Kitty's fear of dying alone was her own fear. As she searched for some answer, Mary heard the sound of a torrent of rain hitting the canopy of foliage above them. "You have been foolish," Mary said, holding her. "But it may not be so bad."

Kitty trembled in her arms, and spoke into Mary's shoulder. "But will you ever care for me again? What if Father should turn me out? What will I do then?"

The rain was falling through now, coming down hard. Mary felt her hair getting soaked. "Calm yourself. Father would do no such thing. I shall never forsake you. Jane would not, nor Lizzy."

"What if I should have a child!"

Mary pulled Kitty's shawl over her head. She looked past Kitty's shoulder to the dark woods. Something moved there. "You shan't have a child."

"You can't know! I may!"

The woods had become dark with the rain. Mary could not make out what lurked there. "Come, let us go back. You must compose yourself. We shall speak with Lizzy and Jane. They will know—"

Just then a flash of lightning lit the forest, and Mary saw, beneath the trees not ten feet from them, the giant figure of a man. The lightning illuminated a face of monstrous ugliness: Long, thick, tangled black hair. Yellow skin the texture of dried leather, black eyes sunken deep beneath heavy brows. Worst of all, an expression hideous in its cold, inexpressible hunger. All glimpsed in a split second; then the light fell to shadow.

Mary gasped, and pulled Kitty toward her. A great peal of thunder rolled across the sky.

Kitty stopped crying. "What is it?"

"We must go. Now." Mary seized Kitty by the arm. The rain pelted down on them, and the forest path was already turning to mud.

Mary pulled her toward the house, Kitty complaining. Mary could hear nothing over the drumming of the rain. But when she looked over her shoulder, she caught a glimpse of the brutish figure, keeping to the trees, but swiftly, silently moving along behind them.

"Why must we run?" Kitty gasped.

"Because we are being followed!"

"By whom?"

"I don't know!"

Behind them, Mary thought she heard the man croak out some words: "Halt! Bitter!"

They had not reached the edge of the woods when figures appeared ahead of them, coming from Pemberley. "Miss Bennet! Mary! Kitty!"

The figures resolved themselves into Darcy and Mr. Frankenstein. Darcy carried a cloak, which he threw over them. "Are you all right?" Frankenstein asked.

"Thank you!" Mary gasped. "A man. He's there," she pointed, "following us."

Frankenstein took a few steps beyond them down the path. "Who was it?" Darcy asked.

"Some brute. Hideously ugly," Mary said.

Frankenstein came back. "No one is there."

"We saw him!"

Another lightning flash, and crack of thunder. "It is very dark, and we are in a storm," Frankenstein said.

"Come, we must get you back to the house," Darcy said. "You are wet to the bone."

The men helped them back to Pemberley, trying their best to keep the rain off the sisters.

Darcy went off to find Bingley and Clerval, who had taken the opposite direction in their search. Lizzy saw that Mary and Kitty were made dry and warm. Kitty's cough worsened, and Lizzy insisted she must be put to bed. Mary sat with Kitty, whispered a promise to keep her secret, and waited until she slept. Then she went down to meet the others in the parlor.

"This chill shall do her no good," Jane said. She chided Mary for wandering off in such threatening weather. "I thought you had developed more sense, Mary. Mr. Frankenstein insisted he help to find you, when he realized you had gone out into the woods."

"I am sorry," Mary said. "You are right." She was distracted by Kitty's plight, wondering what she might do. If Kitty were indeed with child, there would be no helping her.

Mary recounted her story of the man in the woods. Darcy said he had seen no one, but allowed that someone might have been there. Frankenstein, rather than engage in the speculation, stood at the tall windows staring across the lawn through the rain toward the tree line.

"This intruder was some local poacher, or perhaps one of those gypsies," said Darcy. "When the rain ends I shall have Mr. Mowbray take some men to check the grounds. We shall also inform the constable."

"I hope this foul weather will induce you to stay with us a few more days, Mr. Frankenstein," Lizzy ventured. "You have no pressing business in Matlock, do you?"

"No. But we were to travel north by the end of this week."

"Surely we might stay a while longer, Victor," said Clerval. "Your research can wait for you in Scotland."

Frankenstein struggled with his answer. "I don't think we should prevail on these good people anymore."

"Nonsense," said Darcy. "We are fortunate for your company."

"Thank you," Frankenstein said uncertainly. But when the conversation moved elsewhere, Mary noticed him once again staring out the window. She moved to sit beside him. On an impulse, she said to him, sotto voce, "Did you know this man we came upon in the woods?"

"I saw no one. Even if someone was there, how should I know some English vagabond?"

"I do not think he was English. When he called after us, it was in German. Was this one of your countrymen?"

A look of impatience crossed Frankenstein's face, and he lowered his eyes. "Miss Bennet, I do not wish to contradict you, but you are mistaken. I saw no one in the woods."

Kitty developed a fever, and did not leave her bed for the rest of the day. Mary sat with her, trying, without bringing up the subject of Robert Piggot, to quiet her.

It was still raining when Mary retired, to a separate bedroom from the one she normally shared with Kitty. Late that night, Mary was wakened by the opening of her bedroom door. She thought it might be Lizzy to tell her something about Kitty. But it was not Lizzy.

Rather than call out, she watched silently as a dark figure entered and closed the door behind. The remains of her fire threw faint light on the man as he approached her. "Miss Bennet," he called softly.

Her heart was in her throat. "Yes, Mr. Frankenstein."

"Please do not take alarm. I must speak with you." He took two sudden steps toward her bed. His handsome face was agitated. No man, in any circumstances remotely resembling these, had ever broached her bedside. Yet the racing of her heart was not entirely a matter of fear.

"This, sir, is hardly the place for polite conversation," she said. "Following on your denial of what I saw this afternoon, you are fortunate that I do not wake the servants and have you thrown out of Pemberley."

"You are right to chide me. My conscience chides me more than you ever could, and should I be thrown from your family's gracious company it would be less than I deserve. And I am afraid that nothing I have to say to you tonight shall qualify as polite conversation." His manner was greatly changed; there was a sound of desperation in his whisper. He wanted something from her, and he wanted it a great deal.

Curious, despite herself, Mary drew on her robe and lit a candle. She made him sit in one of the chairs by the fire and poked the coals into life. When she had settled herself in the other, she said, "Go on."

"Miss Bennet, please do not toy with me. You know why I am here."

"Know, sir? What do I know?"

He leaned forward, earnestly, hands clasped and elbows on his knees. "I come to beg you to keep silent. The gravest consequences would follow your revealing my secret."

"Silent?"

"About—about the man you saw."

"You *do* know him!"

"Your mockery at dinner convinced me that, after hearing the vicar's story, you suspected. Raising the dead, you said to Clerval—and then your tale of Professor Aldini. Do not deny it."

"I don't pretend to know what you are talking about."

Frankenstein stood from his chair and began to pace the floor before the hearth. "Please! I saw the look of reproach in your eyes when we found you in the forest. I am trying to make right what I put wrong. But I will never be able to do so if you tell." To Mary's astonishment, she saw, in the firelight, that his eyes glistened with tears.

"Tell me what you did."

And with that the story burst out of him. He told her how, after his mother's death, he longed to conquer death itself, how he had studied chemistry at the university, how he had uncovered the secret of life. How, emboldened and driven on by his solitary obsession, he had created a man from the corpses he had stolen from graveyards and purchased from resurrection men. How he had succeeded, through his science, in bestowing it with life.

Mary did not know what to say to this astonishing tale. It was the raving of a lunatic—but there was the man she had seen in the woods. And the earnestness with which Frankenstein spoke, his tears and desperate whispers, gave every proof that, at least in his mind, he had done these things. He told of his revulsion at his accomplishment, how he had abandoned the creature, hoping it would die, and how the creature had, in revenge, killed his brother William and caused his family's ward Justine to be blamed for the crime.

"But why did you not intervene in Justine's trial?"

"No one should have believed me."

"Yet I am to believe you now?"

Frankenstein's voice was choked. "You have seen the brute. You know that these things are possible. Lives are at stake. I come to you in remorse and penitence, asking only that you keep this secret." He fell to his knees, threw his head into her lap, and clutched at the sides of her gown.

Frankenstein was wholly mistaken in what she knew; he was a man who did not see things clearly. Yet if his story were true, it was no wonder that his judgment was disordered. And here he lay, trembling against her, a boy seeking forgiveness. No man had ever come to her in such need.

She tried to keep her senses. "Certainly the creature I saw was frightening, but to my eyes he appeared more wretched than menacing."

Frankenstein lifted his head. "Here I must warn you—his wretchedness is mere mask. Do not let your sympathy for him cause you ever to trust his nature. He is the vilest creature that has ever walked this earth. He has no soul."

"Why then not invoke the authorities, catch him, and bring him to justice?"

"He cannot be so easily caught. He is inhumanly strong, resourceful, and intelligent. If you should ever be so unlucky as to speak with him, I warn you not to listen to what he says, for he is immensely articulate and satanically persuasive."

"All the more reason to see him apprehended!"

"I am convinced that he can be dealt with only by myself." Frankenstein's eyes pleaded with her. "Miss Bennet—Mary— you must understand. He is in some ways my son. I gave him life. His mind is fixed on me."

"And, it seems, yours on him."

Frankenstein looked surprised. "Do you wonder that is so?"

"Why does he follow you? Does he intend you harm?"

"He has vowed to glut the maw of death with my remaining loved ones, unless I make him happy." He rested his head again in her lap.

Mary was touched, scandalized, and in some obscure way aroused. She felt his trembling body, instinct with life. Tentatively, she rested her hand on his head. She stroked his hair. He was weeping. She realized that he was a physical being, a living animal, that would eventually, too soon, die. And all that was true of him was true of herself. How strange, frightening, and sad. Yet in this moment she felt herself wonderfully alive.

"I'll keep your secret," she said.

He hugged her skirts. In the candle's light, she noted the way his thick, dark hair curled away from his brow.

"I cannot tell you," he said softly, "what a relief it is to share my burden with another soul, and to have her accept me. I have been so completely alone. I cannot thank you enough."

He rose, kissed her forehead, and was gone.

Mary paced her room, trying to grasp what had just happened. A man who had conquered death? A monster created from corpses? Such things did not happen, certainly not in her world, not even in the world of the novels she read. She climbed into bed and tried to sleep, but could not. The creature had vowed to kill all whom Frankenstein loved. Mary remembered the weight of his head upon her lap.

The room felt stiflingly hot. She got up, stripped off her nightgown, and climbed back between the sheets, where she lay naked, listening to the rain on the window.

———

Kitty's fever worsened in the night, and before dawn Darcy sent to Lambton for the doctor. Lizzy dispatched an urgent letter to Mr. and Mrs. Bennet, and the sisters sat by Kitty's bedside through the morning, changing cold compresses from her brow while Kitty labored to breathe.

When Mary left the sickroom, Frankenstein approached her. His desperation of the previous night was gone. "How fares your sister?"

"I fear she is gravely ill."

"She is in some danger?"

Mary could only nod.

He touched her shoulder, lowered his voice. "I will pray for her, Miss Bennet. I cannot thank you enough for the sympathy you showed me last night. I have never told anyone—"

Just then Clerval approached them. He greeted Mary, inquired after Kitty's condition, then suggested to Frankenstein that they return to their hotel in Matlock rather than add any burden to the household and family. Frankenstein agreed. Before Mary could say another word to him in private, the visitors were gone.

Dr. Phillips arrived soon after Clerval and Frankenstein left. He measured Kitty's pulse, felt her forehead, examined her urine. He administered some medicines, and came away shaking his head. Should the fever continue, he said, they must bleed her.

Given how much thought she had spent on Frankenstein through the night, and how little she had devoted to Kitty, Mary's conscience tormented her. She spent the day in her sister's room. That night, after Jane had retired and Lizzy fallen asleep in her chair, she still sat up, holding Kitty's fevered hand. She had matters to consider. Was Kitty indeed with child, and if so, should she tell the doctor? Yet even as she sat by Kitty's bedside, Mary's mind cast back to the feeling of Frankenstein's lips on her forehead.

In the middle of the night, Kitty woke, bringing Mary from her doze. Kitty tried to lift her head from the pillow, but could not. "Mary," she whispered. "You must send for Robert. We must be married immediately."

Mary looked across the room at Lizzy. She was still asleep.

"Promise me," Kitty said. Her eyes were large and dark.

"I promise," Mary said.

"Prepare my wedding dress," Kitty said. "But don't tell Lizzy."

Lizzy awoke then. She came to the bedside and felt Kitty's forehead. "She's burning up. Get Dr. Phillips."

Mary sought out the doctor, and then, while he went to Kitty's room, pondered what to do. Kitty clearly was not in her right mind. Her request ran contrary to both sense and propriety. If Mary sent one of the footmen to Matlock for Robert, even if she swore her messenger to silence, the matter would soon be the talk of the servants, and probably the town.

It was the sort of dilemma that Mary would have had no trouble settling, to everyone's moral edification, when she was sixteen. She hurried to her room and took out paper and pen:

I write to inform you that one you love, residing at Pemberley House, is gravely ill. She urgently requests your presence. Simple human kindness, which from her description of you I do not doubt you possess, let alone the duty incumbent upon you owing to the compact that you have made with her through your actions, assure me that we shall see you here before the night is through.

Miss Mary Bennet

She sealed the letter and sought out one of the footmen, whom she dispatched immediately with the instruction to put the letter into the hand of Robert Piggot, son of the Matlock butcher.

Dr. Phillips bled Kitty, with no improvement. She did not regain consciousness through the night. Mary waited. The footman returned, alone, at six in the morning. He assured Mary that he had ridden to the Piggot home and given the letter directly to Robert. Mary thanked him.

Robert did not come. At eight in the morning Darcy sent for the priest. At nine-thirty Kitty died.

On the evening of the day of Kitty's passing, Mr. and Mrs. Bennet arrived, and a day later Lydia and Wickham—it was the first time Darcy had allowed Wickham to cross the threshold of Pemberley since they had become brothers by marriage. In the midst of her mourning family, Mary felt lost. Jane and Lizzy supported each other in their grief. Darcy and Bingley exchanged quiet, sober conversation. Wickham and Lydia, who had grown fat with her three children, could not pass a word between them without sniping, but in their folly they were completely united.

Mrs. Bennet was beyond consoling, and the volume and intensity of her mourning was exceeded only by the degree to which she sought to control every detail of Kitty's funeral. There ensued a long debate over where Kitty should be buried. When it was pointed out that their cousin Mr. Collins would eventually inherit the house back in Hertfordshire, Mrs. Bennet fell into despair: who, when she was gone, would tend to her poor Kitty's grave? Mr. Bennet suggested that Kitty be laid to rest in the churchyard at Lambton, a short distance from Pemberley, where she might also be visited by Jane and Bingley. But when Mr. Darcy offered the family vault at Pemberley, the matter was quickly settled to the satisfaction of both tender hearts and vanity.

Though it was no surprise to Mary, it was still a burden for her to witness that even in the gravest passage of their lives, her sisters and parents showed themselves to be exactly what they were. And yet, paradoxically, this did not harden her heart toward them. The family was together as they had not been for many years, and she realized that they should never be in the future except on the occasion of further losses. Her father was grayer and quieter than she had ever seen him, and on the day of the funeral even her mother put aside her sobbing and exclamations long enough to show a face of profound grief, and a burden of age that Mary had never before noticed.

The night after Kitty was laid to rest, Mary sat up late with Jane and Lizzy and Lydia. They drank Madeira and Lydia told many silly stories of the days she and Kitty had spent in flirtations with the regiment. Mary climbed into her bed late that night, her head swimming with wine, laughter, and tears. She lay awake, the moonlight shining on the counterpane through the opened window, air carrying the smell of fresh earth and the rustle of trees above the lake. She drifted into a dreamless sleep. At some point in the night she was half awakened by the barking of the dogs in the kennel. But consciousness soon faded and she fell away.

In the morning it was discovered that the vault had been broken into and Kitty's body stolen from her grave.

Mary told the stablemaster that Mrs. Bennet had asked her to go to the apothecary in Lambton, and had him prepare the gig for her. Then, while the house was in turmoil and Mrs. Bennet being attended by the rest of the family, she drove off to Matlock. The master had given her the best horse in Darcy's stable; the creature was equable and quick, and despite her inexperience driving, Mary was able to reach Matlock in an hour. All the time, despite the splendid summer morning and the picturesque prospects which the valley of the Derwent continually unfolded before her, she could not keep her mind from whirling through a series of distressing images—among them the sight of Frankenstein's creature as she had seen him in the woods.

When she reached Matlock she hurried to the Old Bath Hotel and inquired after Frankenstein. The concierge told her that he had not seen Mr. Frankenstein since dinner the previous evening, but that Mr. Clerval had told him that morning that the gentlemen would leave Matlock later that day. She left a note asking Frankenstein, should he return, to meet her at the inn, then went to the butcher shop.

Mary had been there once before, with Lizzy, some years earlier. The shop was busy with servants purchasing joints of mutton and ham for the evening meal. Behind the counter, Mr. Piggot senior was busy at his cutting board, but helping one of the women with a package was a tall young man with thick brown curls and green eyes. He flirted with the house servant as he shouldered her purchase, wrapped in brown paper, onto her cart.

On the way back into the shop, he spotted Mary standing unattended. He studied her for a moment before approaching. "May I help you, miss?"

"I believe you knew my sister."

His grin vanished. "You are Miss Mary Bennet."

"I am."

The young man studied his boots. "I am so sorry what happened to Miss Catherine."

Not so sorry as to bring you to her bedside before she died, Mary thought. She bit back a reproach and said, "We did not see you at the service. I thought perhaps the nature of your relationship might have encouraged you to grieve in private, at her graveside. Have you been there?"

He looked even more uncomfortable. "No. I had to work. My father—"

Mary had seen enough already to measure his depth. He was not a man to defile a grave, in grief or otherwise. The distance between this small-town lothario—handsome, careless, insensitive—and the hero Kitty had praised, only deepened Mary's compassion for her lost sister. How desperate she must have been. How pathetic.

As Robert Piggot continued to stumble through his explanation, Mary turned and departed.

She went back to the inn where she had left the gig. The barkeep led her into a small ladies' parlor separated from the taproom by a glass partition. She ordered tea, and through a latticed window watched the people come and go in the street and courtyard, the draymen with their percherons and carts, the passengers waiting for the next van to Manchester, and inside, the idlers sitting at tables with pints of ale. In the sunlit street a young bootblack accosted travelers, most of whom ignored him. All of these people alive, completely unaware of Mary or her lost sister. Mary ought to be back with their mother, though the thought turned her heart cold. How could Kitty have left her alone? She felt herself near despair.

She was watching through the window as two draymen struggled to load a large square trunk onto their cart when the man directing them came from around the team of horses, and she saw it was Frankenstein. She rose immediately and went out into the inn yard. She was at his shoulder before he noticed her. "Miss Bennet!"

"Mr. Frankenstein. I am so glad that I found you. I feared that you had already left Matlock. May we speak somewhere in private?"

He looked momentarily discommoded. "Yes, of course," he said. To the draymen he said, "When you've finished loading my equipment, wait here."

"This is not a good place to converse," Frankenstein told her. "I saw a churchyard nearby. Let us retire there."

He walked Mary down the street to the St. Giles Churchyard. They walked through the rectory garden. In the distance, beams of afternoon sunlight shone through a cathedral of clouds above the Heights of Abraham. "Do you know what has happened?" she asked.

"I have heard reports, quite awful, of the death of your sister.

I intended to write you, conveying my condolences, at my earliest opportunity. You have my deepest sympathies."

"Your creature! That monster you created—"

"I asked you to keep him a secret."

"I have kept my promise—so far. But it has stolen Kitty's body."

He stood there, hands behind his back, clear eyes fixed on her. "You find me astonished. What draws you to this extraordinary conclusion?"

She was hurt by his diffidence. Was this the same man who had wept in her bedroom? "Who else might do such a thing?"

"But why? This creature's enmity is reserved for me alone. Others feel its ire only to the extent that they are dear to me."

"You came to plead with me that night because you feared I knew he was responsible for defiling that town girl's grave. Why was he watching Kitty and me in the forest? Surely this is no coincidence."

"If, indeed, the creature has stolen your sister's body, it can be for no reason I can fathom, or that any God-fearing person ought to pursue. You know I am determined to see this monster banished from the world of men. You may rest assured that I will not cease until I have seen this accomplished. It is best for you and your family to turn your thoughts to other matters." He touched a strand of ivy growing up the side of the garden wall, and plucked off a green leaf, which he twirled in his fingers.

She could not understand him. She knew him to be a man of sensibility, to have a heart capable of feeling. His denials opened a possibility that she had tried to keep herself from considering. "Sir, I am not satisfied. It seems to me that you are keeping something from me. You told me of the great grief you felt at the loss of your mother, how it moved you to your researches. If, as you say, you have uncovered the secret of life, might you— have you taken it upon yourself to restore Kitty? Perhaps a fear of failure, or of the horror that many would feel at your trespassing against God's will, underlies your secrecy. If so, please do not keep the truth from me. I am not a girl."

He let the leaf fall from his fingers. He took her shoulders, and looked directly into her eyes. "I am sorry, Mary. To restore your sister is not in my power. The soulless creature I brought to life bears no relation to the man from whose body I fashioned him. Your sister has gone on to her reward. Nothing—nothing I can do would bring her back."

"So you know nothing about the theft of her corpse?"

"On that score, I can offer no consolation to you or your family."

"My mother, my father—they are inconsolable."

"Then they must content themselves with memories of your sister as she lived. As I must do with my dear, lost brother William, and the traduced and dishonored Justine. Come, let us go back to the inn."

Mary burst into tears. He held her to him and she wept on his breast. Eventually she gathered herself and allowed him to take her arm, and they slowly walked back down to the main street of Matlock and the inn. She knew that when they reached it, Frankenstein would go. The warmth of his hand on hers almost made her beg him to stay, or better still, to take her with him.

They came to the busy courtyard. The dray stood off to the side, and Mary saw the cartmen were in the taproom. Frankenstein, agitated, upbraided them. "I thought I told you to keep those trunks out of the sun."

The older of the two men put down his pint and stood. "Sorry, Gov'nor. We'll see to it directly."

"Do so now."

As Frankenstein spoke the evening coach drew up before the inn and prepared for departure. "You and Mr. Clerval leave today?" Mary asked.

"Yes. As soon as Henry arrives from the Old Bath, we take the coach to the Lake District. And thence to Scotland."

"They say it is very beautiful there."

"I am afraid that its beauty will be lost on me. I carry the burden of my great crime, not to be laid down until I have made things right."

She felt that she would burst if she did not speak her heart to him. "Victor. Will I ever see you again?"

He avoided her gaze. "I am afraid, Miss Bennet, that this is unlikely. My mind is set on banishing that vile creature from the world of men. Only then can I hope to return home and marry my betrothed Elizabeth."

Mary looked away from him. A young mother was adjusting her son's collar before putting him on the coach. "Ah, yes. You are affianced. I had almost forgotten."

Frankenstein pressed her hand. "Miss Bennet, you must forgive me the liberties I have taken with you. You have given me more of friendship than I deserve. I wish you to find the companion you seek, and to live your days in happiness. But now, I must go."

"God be with you, Mr. Frankenstein." She twisted her gloved fingers into a knot.

He bowed deeply, and hurried to have a few more words with the draymen. Henry Clerval arrived just as the men climbed to their cart and drove the baggage away. Clerval, surprised at seeing Mary, greeted her warmly. He expressed his great sorrow at the loss of her sister, and begged her to convey his condolences to the rest of her family. Ten minutes later the two men climbed aboard the coach and it left the inn, disappearing down the Matlock high street.

Mary stood in the inn yard. She did not feel she could bear to go back to Pemberley and face her family, the histrionics of her mother. Instead she reentered the inn and made the barkeep seat her in the ladies' parlor and bring her a bottle of port.

The sun declined and shadows stretched over the inn yard. The evening papers arrived from Nottingham. The yard boy lit the lamps. Still, Mary would not leave. Outside on the pavements, the bootblack sat in the growing darkness with his arms draped over his knees and head on his breast. She listened to the hoofs of the occasional horse striking the cobbles. The innkeeper was solicitous. When she asked for a second bottle, he hesitated, and wondered if he might send for someone from her family to take her home.

"You do not know my family," she said.

"Yes, miss. I only thought—"

"Another port. Then leave me alone."

"Yes, miss." He went away. She was determined to become intoxicated. How many times had she piously warned against young women behaving as she did now? *Virtue is its own reward.* She had an apothegm for every occasion, and had tediously produced them in place of thought. *Show me a liar, and I'll show thee a thief. Marry in haste, repent at leisure. Men should be what they seem.*

She did not fool herself into thinking that her current misbehavior would make any difference. Perhaps Bingley or Darcy had been dispatched to find her in Lambton. But within an hour or two she would return to Pemberley, where her mother would scold her for giving them an anxious evening, and Lizzy would caution her about the risk to her reputation. Lydia might even ask her, not believing it possible, if she had an assignation with some man. The loss of Kitty would overshadow Mary's indiscretion, pitiful as it had been. Soon all would be as it had been, except Mary would be alive and Kitty dead. But even that would fade. The shadow of Kitty's death would hang over the family for some time, but she doubted that anything of significance would change.

As she lingered over her glass, she looked up and noticed, in the now empty taproom, a man sitting at the table farthest from the lamps. A huge man, wearing rough clothes, his face hooded and in shadow. On the table in front of him was a tankard of ale and a few coppers. Mary rose, left the parlor for the taproom, and crossed toward him.

He looked up, and the faint light from the ceiling lamp caught his black eyes, sunken beneath heavy brows. He was hideously ugly. "May I sit with you?" she asked. She felt slightly dizzy.

"You may sit where you wish." The voice was deep, but swallowed, unable to project. It was almost a whisper.

Trembling only slightly, she sat. His wrists and hands, resting on the table, stuck out past the ragged sleeves of his coat. His skin was yellowish brown, and the fingernails livid white. He did not move. "You have some business with me?"

"I have the most appalling business." Mary tried to look him in the eyes, but her gaze kept slipping. "I want to know why you defiled my sister's grave, why you have stolen her body, and what you have done with her."

"Better you should ask Victor. Did he not explain all to you?"

"Mr. Frankenstein explained who—what—you are. He did not know what had become of my sister."

The thin lips twitched in a sardonic smile. "Poor Victor. He has got things all topsy-turvy. Victor does not know what I am. He is incapable of knowing, no matter the labors I have undertaken to school him. But he does know what became, and is to become, of your sister." The creature tucked the thick black hair behind his ear, a sudden unconscious gesture that made him seem completely human for the first time. He pulled the hood further forward to hide his face.

"So tell me."

"Which answer do you want? Who I am, or what happened to your sister?"

"First, tell me what happened to—to Kitty."

"Victor broke into the vault and stole her away. He took the utmost care not to damage her. He washed her fair body in diluted carbolic acid, and replaced her blood with a chemical admixture of his own devising. Folded up, she fit neatly within a cedar trunk sealed with pitch, and is at present being shipped to

Scotland. You witnessed her departure from this courtyard an hour ago."

Mary's senses rebelled. She covered her face with her hands. The creature sat silent. Finally, without raising her head, she managed, "Victor warned me that you were a liar. Why should I believe you?"

"You have no reason to believe me."

"*You* took her!"

"Though I would not have scrupled to do so, I did not. Miss Bennet, I do not deny I have an interest in this matter. Victor did as I have told you at my bidding."

"At your bidding? Why?"

"Kitty—or not so much Kitty, as her remains—is to become my wife."

"Your wife! This is insupportable! Monstrous!"

"Monstrous." Suddenly, with preternatural quickness, his hand flashed out and grabbed Mary's wrist.

Mary thought to call for help, but the bar was empty and she had driven the innkeeper away. Yet his grip was not harsh. His hand was warm, instinct with life. "Look at me," he said. With his other hand he pushed back his hood.

She took a deep breath. She looked.

His noble forehead, high cheekbones, strong chin, and wide-set eyes might have made him handsome, despite the scars and dry yellow skin, were it not for his expression. His ugliness was not a matter of lack of proportion—or rather, the lack of proportion was not in his features. Like his swallowed voice, his face was submerged, as if everything was hidden, revealed only in the eyes, the twitch of a cheek or lip. Every minute motion showed extraordinary animation. Hectic sickliness, but energy. This was a creature who had never learned to associate with civilized company, who had been thrust into adulthood with the passions of a wounded boy. Fear, self-disgust, anger. Desire.

The force of longing and rage in that face made her shrink. "Let me go," she whispered.

He let go her wrist. With bitter satisfaction, he said, "You see. If what I demand is insupportable, that is only because your kind has done nothing to support me. Once, I falsely hoped to meet with beings who, pardoning my outward form, would love me for the excellent qualities which I was capable of bringing forth. Now I am completely alone. More than any starving man on a deserted isle, I am cast away. I have no brother, sister, parents. I have only Victor, who, like so many fathers, recoiled from me the moment I first drew breath. And so, I have commanded him to make of your sister my wife, or he and all he loves will die at my hand."

"No. I cannot believe he would commit this abomination."

"He has no choice. He is my slave."

"His conscience could not support it, even at the cost of his life."

"You give him too much credit. You all do. He does not think. I have not seen him act other than according to impulse for the last three years. That is all I see in any of you."

Mary drew back, trying to make some sense of this horror. Her sister, to be brought to life, only to be given to this fiend. But would it be her sister, or another agitated, hungry thing like this?

She still retained some scraps of skepticism. The creature's manner did not bespeak the isolation which he claimed. "I am astonished at your grasp of language," Mary said. "You could not know so much without teachers."

"Oh, I have had many teachers." The creature's mutter was rueful. "You might say that, since first my eyes opened, mankind has been all my study. I have much yet to learn. There are certain words whose meaning has never been proved to me by experience. For example: *Happy.* Victor is to make me happy. Do you think he can do it?"

Mary thought of Frankenstein. Could he satisfy this creature? "I do not think it is in the power of any other person to make one happy."

"You jest with me. Every creature has its mate, save me. I have none."

She recoiled at his self-pity. Her fear faded. "You put too much upon having a mate."

"Why? You know nothing of what I have endured."

"You think that having a female of your own kind will ensure that she will accept you?" Mary laughed. "Wait until you are rejected, for the most trivial of reasons, by one you are sure has been made for you."

A shadow crossed the creature's face. "That will not happen."

"It happens more often than not."

"The female that Victor creates shall find no other mate than me."

"That has never prevented rejection. Or if you should be accepted, then you may truly begin to learn."

"Learn what?"

"You will learn to ask a new question: Which is worse, to be alone, or to be wretchedly mismatched?" Like Lydia and Wickham, Mary thought. Like Collins and his poor wife Charlotte. Like her parents.

The creature's face spasmed with conflicting emotions. His voice gained volume. "Do not sport with me. I am not your toy."

"No. You only seek a toy of your own."

The creature was not, apparently, accustomed to mockery. "You must not say these things!" He lurched upward, awkwardly, so suddenly that he upended the table. The tankard of beer skidded across the top and spilled on Mary, and she fell back.

At that moment the innkeeper entered the bar room with two other men. They saw the tableau and rushed forward. "Here! Let her be!" he shouted. One of the other men grabbed the creature by the arm. With a roar the creature flung him aside like an old coat. His hood fell back. The men stared in horror at his face. The creature's eyes met Mary's, and with inhuman speed he whirled and ran out the door.

The men gathered themselves together. The one whom the

creature had thrown aside had a broken arm. The innkeeper helped Mary to her feet. "Are you all right, miss?"

Mary felt dizzy. Was she all right? What did that mean?

"I believe so," she said.

When Mary returned to Pemberley, late that night, she found the house in an uproar over her absence. Bingley and Darcy both had been to Lambton, and had searched the road and the woods along it throughout the afternoon and evening. Mrs. Bennet had taken to bed with the conviction that she had lost two daughters in a single week. Wickham condemned Mary's poor judgment, Lydia sprang to Mary's defense, and this soon became a row over Wickham's lack of an income and Lydia's mismanagement of their children. Mr. Bennet closed himself up in the library.

Mary told them only that she had been to Matlock. She offered no explanation, no apology. Around the town the story of her conflict with the strange giant in the inn was spoken of for some time, along with rumors of Robert Piggot the butcher's son, and the mystery of Kitty's defiled grave—but as Mary was not a local, and nothing of consequence followed, the talk soon passed away.

That winter, Mary came upon the following story in the Nottingham newspaper.

GHASTLY EVENTS IN SCOTLAND

Our northern correspondent files the following report. In early November, the body of a young foreigner, Mr. Henry Clerval of Geneva, Switzerland, was found upon the beach near the far northern town of Thurso. The body, still warm, bore marks of strangulation. A second foreigner, Mr. Victor Frankstone, was taken into custody, charged with the murder, and held for two months. Upon investigation, the magistrate Mr. Kirwan determined that Mr. Frankstone was in the Orkney Islands at the time of the killing. The accused was released in the custody of his father, and is assumed to have returned to his home on the continent.

A month after the disposition of these matters, a basket, weighted with stones and containing the body of a young woman, washed up in the estuary of the River Thurso. The identity of the woman is unknown, and her murderer undiscovered, but it is speculated that the unfortunate may have died at the hands of the same person or persons who murdered Mr. Clerval. The woman was given Christian burial in the Thurso Presbyterian churchyard.

The village has been shaken by these events, and prays God to deliver it from evil.

Oh, Victor, Mary thought. She remembered the pressure of his hand, through her dressing gown, upon her thigh. Now he had returned to Switzerland, there, presumably, to marry his Elizabeth. She hoped that he would be more honest with his wife than he had been with her, but the fate of Clerval did not bode well. And the creature still had no mate.

She clipped the newspaper report and slipped it into the drawer of her writing table, where she kept her copy of Samuel Galton's *The Natural History of Birds, Intended for the Amusement and Instruction of Children*, and the *Juvenile Anecdotes* of Priscilla Wakefield, and a Dudley locust made of stone, and a paper fan from the first ball she had ever attended, and a dried wreath of flowers that had been thrown to her, when she was nine years old, from the top of a tree by one of the town boys playing near Meryton common.

After the death of her parents, Mary lived with Lizzy and Darcy at Pemberley for the remainder of her days. Under a pen name, she pursued a career as a writer of philosophical speculations, and sent many letters to the London newspapers. Aunt Mary, as she was called at home, was known for her kindness to William, and to his wife and children. The children teased Mary for her nearsightedness, her books, and her piano. But for a woman whose experience of the world was so slender, and whose soul it seemed had never been touched by any passion, she came at last to be respected for her understanding, her self-possession, and her wise counsel on matters of the heart.

SCIENCE FICTION IN THE 1970S: THE TALE OF THE NERDY DUCKLING

KEVIN J. ANDERSON

Just before the decade of the 1970s began, those of us with a science-fiction mind-set experienced our greatest moment of triumph and possibility: It was July 20, 1969. Neil Armstrong and Buzz Aldrin had set foot on the Moon— only six weeks after the very last episode of the original *Star Trek* was broadcast on TV.

I was seven years old, having grown up on a diet of SF books, movies, and comics.

Every TV station—on all three networks!—broadcast the suspenseful coverage. Excitement hung in the air, my parents and my neighbors were glued to their television sets, and I sat watching the grainy picture. Bleeps and static and time delays distorted the sound. Armstrong climbed down the ladder, then stepped onto the lunar surface. Where no man had gone before.

Though I was the only SF fan in the room, I felt less excited than my fellow observers. I was puzzled. "Haven't we done that already?" I'd been reading about space travel and setting foot on alien worlds for some time, and in this instance there were no underground cities, no Selenites, no secret alien bases. To a kid, it was something of a disappointment. But at least we made it. Science fiction had convinced us all that reaching the planets and stars was inevitable. Humanity's destiny.

Little did we know that on December 19, 1972, a mere two years into the new decade, the Apollo 17 moon mission would return to Earth, and mankind would never go back—at least not in the next forty years. What science fiction enthusiast would ever have believed that scenario? We came, we saw, we went home, we lost interest. Not a very good SF premise.

Also, one of the greatest and most influential editors in the genre, John W. Campbell, died on July 11, 1971.

Yes, indeed, it looked like dark times ahead for the future of science fiction.

Perhaps due to the fact that the highly anticipated future was stolen right out from under our imaginations, the genre itself was forced to shout louder and shine brighter. By the end of the 1970s, SF had caught its breath and surged forward to become one of the most powerful forces in entertainment. Science fiction stopped being a fringe genre read only by nerdy ducklings, socially maladjusted boys with thick glasses (yes, I was one of them), and the whole world had to pay attention.

How to summarize a decade of creativity in only a few pages? Exhaustive essays and analyses can be found elsewhere, written by people with far greater expertise in the period. I can only offer my subjective take, a view on the genre from a young and enthusiastic fan who had aspirations of becoming an author himself, and who by 1979 had just begun to receive his first rejection slips from Stanley Schmidt at *Analog* and Ed Ferman at *The Magazine of Fantasy & Science Fiction*.

As the decade opened, the New Wave movement in science fiction that began in the late 1960s reached its peak (and I was admittedly too young to grok it). New Wave works dominated the major SF awards ballots. Turning away from fast-paced tales set on imaginative worlds, a group of authors used highly experimental and artistic techniques—with nary a bug-eyed monster in sight—to gain literary respectability for our frowned-upon genre. Paramount among these architects of the New Wave were Samuel R. Delany, Michael Moorcock, J. G. Ballard,

Brian Aldiss, Thomas Disch, Ursula Le Guin, Barry N. Malzberg, and Harlan Ellison.

Though some works were more accessible than others (you know which ones I'm talking about), alas, for some readers like myself who grew up with traditional SF—Andre Norton, Edgar Rice Burroughs, Isaac Asimov, Arthur C. Clarke, and Frank Herbert's *Dune*—the New Wave achieved only incomprehensibility and a lot of head-scratching. But the critics liked those books, and they earned plenty of awards, so who am I to judge?

For those of us seeking vibrant and ambitious plots, exotic settings, and sense-of-wonder adventures, the 1970s saw truly great works of core science fiction, such as Larry Niven's *Ringworld*, Arthur C. Clarke's *Rendezvous with Rama*, Joe Haldeman's *The Forever War*, Niven & Pournelle's *The Mote in God's Eye* and *Lucifer's Hammer*, Frederik Pohl's *Gateway*, and many others. Poul Anderson did some of his best work in the 1970s, as did Robert Silverberg.

In 1972, Frank Herbert's *Dune Messiah*, the much-anticipated sequel to *Dune*, met with a mixed reaction because of its dramatic shift, turning hero Paul Atreides into a hated tyrant. Four years later, however, Herbert's *Children of Dune* (1976) became the first novel unabashedly marketed as science fiction to appear on the *New York Times* bestseller list, with a first hardcover printing of 100,000 copies. Only Michael Crichton's *The Andromeda Strain* (1972) had numbers that could match it, though Crichton's novel was marketed strictly as a "thriller," not SF.

Two years later, Anne McCaffrey's novel *The White Dragon* (with its seminal Michael Whelan cover) also hit the *NYT* list. McCaffrey, who began her *Dragonriders of Pern* series in 1967 with the novellas *Weyr Search* and *Dragonrider* (winners of the Hugo and Nebula, respectively), published the novel *Dragonflight* in 1968, then *Dragonquest* in 1970. Her young-adult Harper Hall trilogy (*Dragonsong, Dragonsinger, Dragondrums*) was published from 1976 through 1979. McCaffrey's imaginative and entertaining stories combined traditional dragon tropes with science fiction and captivated a wide audience. Her work both broadened and blurred the audience for science fiction and fantasy.

Stephen King appeared on the scene in 1974 with *Carrie* and produced some of his most influential work, developing a brand of fantasy/horror/sf that tapped into a significant mainstream readership. He followed his first novel with *Salem's Lot* (1975), *The Stand* (1978), and *The Dead Zone* (1979), all landmark bestsellers. (Interestingly, *The Dead Zone* was nominated for the World Fantasy Award, but King withdrew it because he considered precognition to be science fiction, not fantasy.)

Roger Zelazny's first *Amber* series spanned most of the decade, as did Katherine Kurtz's popular *Deryni* series; these books paved the way for a much larger fantasy audience. 1977 in particular was a very good year for the genre: Terry Brooks's *The Sword of Shannara* was the first fantasy novel ever to appear on the *New York Times* bestseller list. (*Shannara* was also the first novel published by Lester del Rey's new eponymous book line.) Stephen R. Donaldson's "Chronicles of Thomas Covenant the Unbeliever" debuted the same year with *Lord Foul's Bane*, as did J. R. R. Tolkien's posthumous *The Silmarillion* (which became a #1 bestseller with over a million copies sold in hardcover)— altogether launching a tremendous and unstoppable commercial fantasy boom.

Yes, the momentum was building.

Then a film was released that changed the perception of science fiction forever. As an unexpected follow-up to his Oscar-nominated nostalgia film *American Graffiti* (1973), George Lucas decided to do a big science fiction movie—and he wanted $11 million to do it right. Since it was common knowledge that science fiction films never made much money, and that the audience was small, the studios thought he was crazy to want such a large budget.

Lucas had already done a (rather dreary and slow) SF film in 1971, *THX-1138*, but now he was pitching something entirely different. *The Star Wars*. In order to get the movie made, he waived his up-front fee as a director (astonishing in light of the fact that *American Graffiti* had been nominated for an Academy Award) and in exchange Lucas negotiated to keep the merchandising rights for *Star Wars*, which the studio deemed to be without value anyway.

In its initial year alone, *Star Wars* took in over $270 million—the highest-grossing movie in history, up to that date. The same year, Steven Spielberg's SF entry, *Close Encounters of the Third Kind*, earned well over $80 million—a one-two punch that permanently convinced the world that there was a large audience for science fiction.

That same year, 1977, saw the first launch of the space shuttle. Ambitious fan Bjo Trimble—who had led a major write-in campaign to keep *Star Trek* on the air for one more season in the late 1960s and to resurrect it as an animated series (1973–1974)—organized a crusade among powerful *Star Trek* fans to get NASA to christen the first experimental orbiter *Enterprise*. Science fiction showed its newfound muscle, and the campaign succeeded.

After a long hiatus, just a few days before we turned our calendars over to 1980, *Star Trek* came to the big screen with *Star Trek: The Motion Picture*. I remember walking down a snowy State Street in Madison, Wisconsin, where I attended university; I had skipped classes so I could see the very first showing of the new movie. The credits rolled, and the Klingons appeared—with ridges on their foreheads? What? Yes indeed, more big changes were ahead for science fiction.

Who would have thought at the beginning of the 1970s that our relatively obscure and insular genre would become a juggernaut of entertainment, both on-screen and off? The nerdy duckling had transformed into a shining swan that was no longer teased or ridiculed. Science fiction had stepped out into the broad, vibrant relevance of the mainstream.

TROPHY WIVES

NINA KIRIKI HOFFMAN

Nina Kiriki Hoffman tends to write stories set in the Northwestern USA and has shown she is a master of horror, winning a Bram Stoker award for her first novel, *The Thread That Binds the Bones*. Her Nebula-winning short story is set on other worlds, but takes a look at relationships and marriage in a way only Nina would.

Alanna and I have been together most of our lives. She is the beautiful one, and I am the worker; at least, that's how it looks to people who see us now. It is not how we began. I was a princess in a tower, and she was a drudge who worked for my father, tending all the machinery that kept me imprisoned and alive, and trained me in my terrible purpose.

All that changed when we found and ate the bondfruit.

We live more than half our lives beneath the surface now. Inside, we are all sorts of different people, and outside, we have tried on many different roles, but we also meld into one another as we share eyes and thoughts and conversation. Still, I am the one who doesn't mind work and is driven mad by music, and she is the one who makes plans and minds details.

Alanna laughs and thinks, *Tell them your name, Ylva. You always forget the important things!*

Very well. My name is Ylva Sif.

Gwelf Kinnowar, currently married to Alanna, is the fourth husband we have had between us, and when we first met him, we thought he was the best. He didn't argue when Alanna told him that to marry her, he had to accept me into his household. He has plenty of money, and let us use it; and, though we live with him in various residences on planets where oppressive social conditions hold, he gives us freedom from the prevailing mores in the privacy of his house, so long as Alanna acts the perfect ornamental wife in public.

The first time Gwelf slept with another woman after the wedding, we lost faith in him. He didn't betray us in any other way, though, so we stayed, even though in his travels he often slept with other women. The benefits of the marriage still outweigh the troubles, so we adjusted our hopes and attitudes and went on with our real job, which is rescuing people, as we ourselves have been rescued.

Alanna was in the balcony room looking out over Haladion, the planet where Gwelf's main residence was. Alanna and I loved the balcony room. The mansion was built into the side of a cliff, among a cluster of others, and below the cliff lay all the world: at the base, the market town Risen, and beyond it, farmlands, with the spaceport to the west, ringed by businesses that catered to offworld travelers. Near the spaceport was the technomall for people who liked to shop for factory-made things in person.

Out beyond the farmlands lay the forest, with the Fang Mountains rising in the distance.

Alanna dialed controls on the focusing window and peered down at the central market square, where the servants of cliffside mansions bought fresh produce from the farmers. "Ripe sakal," she thought.

I was in the kitchen, a level below, checking our stores and making a list. I paused and styled sakal on my list. "Much?"

"Going fast," she thought. "Oh! Perberries! Only three pints left! At the SunGlo booth."

"On my way." I shut the list, grabbed a carrybag, and headed for the door. In the purification room, I dipped into the amber scent bowl and dabbed it at my wrists. I pulled on an outer robe and hooked my veil across my lower face, then coded through the privacy portal and entered the communal elevator bank. My pod opened a moment later onto the public access foyer to the outdoors at the base of the cliff. Others came and went in various pods.

Outdoors, the heat and scents and sounds were intense. Meat cooking, bread baking, the faint taint of scoot fuel, though no mechanized transport was allowed in the city core except float carts to carry home one's purchases. Voices called as people spoke to each other in person or at a distance.

I headed to the market. At the SunGlo booth, all the perberries the vendor had on display were gone, but she saw the sigil on my hood and smiled at me. As a farm worker, she wore no veil or head covering; she was outside the life lived in houses and only another farmer would look at her as a wife. So the people professed to believe, anyway. One heard stories.

"I knew you'd be by, Ser Sif," the vendor, Vigil, said, and reached under the table for a whole flat of perberries.

"Thank you, Vigil." I pressed my thumb to her pay pad without even discussing price. Sometimes it was worth paying extra.

"Oh, no! I wanted some of those," said a low voice to my left. I turned to see a stranger, her hood unmarked by house. Her eyes were large, dark, liquid, under narrow black brows, and she wore a very plain outer robe, dusty light blue with one line of white at the hem. Her veil was opaque, giving no hint of who she was beneath. "Someone at the clay booth said you had them," she said to Vigil, "and I so hoped."

"Maybe we can arrange something." I opened the compartment in the carrybag for fragile perishables and slid the flat in, activating the stasis field that would hold my berries safe.

Ask her who she works for, Alanna thought-whispered; she was present behind my eyes, as I was behind hers.

"Whose house are you affiliated with?" I asked.

The stranger's eyes looked frightened. "I can't say," she whispered.

"Come with me for coffee and I'll sell you some of my berries. Thanks again, Vigil."

"I have other shopping," said the stranger as I tugged her toward Kalenki's Tea House. They had rooms in the back where women could unveil.

"I'll help you with it when we've finished our talk. I can see you're a stranger here. I can show you all the best bargains." I raised my voice. "Kalenki!"

"Ser Sif." He smiled at me and twirled his waxed mustache. "The sandalwood room?"

"Please."

He gestured us toward the back, and I led the stranger to my favorite room, its walls fretted with carved wood, its scent warm and spicy. It had a heavy curtain that almost muffled outside sound and kept those within private enough to speak in low voices without fear. I took the bug zapper from the pouch at my waist and scanned the room for hidden ears. None today.

I settled onto the pile of cushions covered in white and red satin stripes, leaving the blue and green cushions for my guest, with the low inlaid-wood table between us. She looked at me, and then at the cushions, and then at her slippered feet.

She doesn't know how to sit! Alanna thought. *Who is she?*

"Sister, hold your skirts gently and sink down onto your rear," I said.

She grasped her outer robe in both hands and let herself sit, teetering. Then she straightened and looked at me with great intensity.

"If you are here stealthily," I said, or Alanna said, "what is it you intend? How did you even find a sigilless robe?"

"I escaped from a ship," she whispered. "I was sold into marriage, and the ship was carrying me to my husband in all luxury. I had a library. I knew Haladion was our only stop, and I studied everything in memory about it. I made this robe myself." She straightened, glanced around the room, fixed on me, as though realizing she was being too direct. "You aren't police?"

Just then, Kalenki whistled a warning and came in to take our order. "A big pot of spiced coffee, Ser, if you please," I said, "with all shades of color for it. Some of the lace biscuits as well."

"Your wish, Ser," he said, with a head bob, and dropped the curtain again.

I turned to the stranger.

"No, assuredly I am not police, just curious. I will not betray you."

"How can I know that? Have I given too much of myself away already?" She pressed the heels of her palms to the sides of her head and groaned. "I am so stupid."

Kalenki whistled again. His assistant brought the tray of purification, with its two basins of warm water, two cloths, a bowl of powdered soap, and a second basin for rinsing; also the censer with its fragrant smoke, redolent of roses, through which we could pass our hands before we drank. Kalenki himself carried in the coffee tray and set it on the table.

"Thank you. You are gracious," I said, and pressed my thumb into the pay pad he presented, tapped a tip into the options screen.

"Always a pleasure to have you visit, Ser," he said and followed his assistant out.

After he left, I tied the curtain closed, then settled on my cushions. "There, they have gone and we may unveil without fear of men's eyes on us." I unhooked my veil. The stranger stared at my face as though it were a lifesaving liquid she could drink with her eyes. I wondered why. I had been to many worlds, and on most of them, I was considered ordinary. "I am Ylva Sif," I said.

She did not drop her veil or offer a name. Rudeness, but perhaps she did not realize.

I showed her how to cleanse her hands, then poured coffee for both of us. "Have you tried our coffee before?" I asked. She shook her head. I handed her a cup with room left for colors. "Here is cream. This is cinnamon. This is pepper, and this, clarified butter. This is caramel syrup, and this holds serenity, and here is agitation. This—" I lifted a small spoonful of pale powder—"is clear-eye." I sprinkled it over my own drink, added a dollop of cream and two lumps of dark sugar, stirred with a cinnamon-flavored stick. "Here are chocolate shavings. These are sweeteners—sugar, rain sugar, invisible sugar, low-processed sugar, flowersweet. We consider coffee an art, one it takes time to master. You can start with something sweet and something white." I pushed the doctorments tray toward her and sat back to sip my own mixture.

Alanna was with me for the first sip. We both found that the best, and always shared. My mouth said, "Aah." I felt hers smiling too.

The stranger mixed cream and flowersweet into her coffee, lifted it toward her mouth, and encountered the dilemma I had presented her with. As a stranger, she did not know how to drop her hood over her face and drink below the veil, as one did in the presence of strange men. Finally she unhooked her veil and we saw her face. Alanna and I studied it closely. She was young, beautiful, tense. A small red flower hung on her left cheek beside her mouth, but whether birthmark, tattoo, or more temporary stain, I could not tell.

She had generous lips and a narrow nose, not at all native to Haladion, but we already knew that. Dark freckles sprinkled across her nose and upper cheeks. She took a cookie and gave us a chance to study her teeth; they were narrow and pointed. She wolfed the sweet, then took another and another. "Forgive me," she muttered. "I'm so hungry. I had only a few coins on me when I left the ship, and I dare not use my credit wand. I was about to buy food when I heard there were perberries here.

They come from my world, and I haven't tasted them since I was a child."

"My manners," I said. I opened the carrybag and drew out a pint of berries. "Please accept these as a gift."

Her skin paled, making her eyes look larger and darker than ever. Her freckles looked like fallen stars of night against a light sea. She nodded and reached for the berries, too anxious to be polite. "Thank you, thank you, thank you," she whispered and plunged both hands into the little veneer box, scooped up a double handful of dark berries and pressed her face into them.

When she lifted her face from the berries, some of the small seeds clung to her face. The stain they left was the same color as the flower on her cheek. She selected one squashed berry and put it on her tongue, then leaned back with eyes closed. Her smile started small and widened.

"Oh," she said, "it is the taste of the milk wind in the night sky on a hot summer night on Challis. My sister and I gathered these berries by starlight. They glow crimson in the dark to summon the night birds, and us. We said we were gathering for our mother. We ended up eating most of what we found. The thorns scratched us, but the berries were worth the pain." She ate another berry, then another. "How can I taste my child-planet on this faraway place? How can that taste translate to another world?"

"You carry your home planet in your head," Alanna said with my mouth. "The taste triggers memory; it is not the true place."

The stranger lowered her hands. She looked toward the wall. "Challis is gone," she said, "cindered in the Fractals War. My sister died in the attack."

"And now you're here, on Haladion," I said, "running away—from what?"

"We lived on a refugee satellite for the past several years. We only had access to terminals a couple hours a day; I practiced my music, and my brother studied for exams. He is gifted. My mother sold me into marriage to give my younger brother passage to university," she said. "She told me my intended was a Paki prince who would treat me like royalty, but I saw the ship's manifest. My husband is not even human. He is a toad, on Linkan, and he wants me to raise his status."

"Ah," I said. I had married a Linkan toad—my first and only marriage, which I contracted for so Alanna could get special training in cosmetology. "Those are hard to kill. Do you know his name?"

"I can't pronounce it," said the stranger. She tucked her hand into a fold in her robe, came up with a small mempad. A tap, and it displayed a word in Linkan script.

"Fimkim Ruggluff," I said. "Almost I remember that name."

"One of the ship's officers used to come talk to me. She said Linkans kept their wives in bubbles and invited other Linkans over to view them. She said I was cargo to live in a bubble."

"Yes," I said. "They stack up their wife bubbles for display and try to outbubble each other. Their status increases if they have varied wives from different species. Also, they feed you everything you most love. They like big women. The health plan is good. Electrocize, peak conditioning, key nutrients."

"What do the wives do all day?"

"Stare at stranger toads your husband brings to look at you. There's a bonus if you can look happy and excited. The occasional sexual congress, which is a bit cold and slimy but not actually painful. Not much conversation is necessary. You can listen to music and stories all day. It's not a hard life, and you will be let go the minute you get wrinkled. They give good parting gifts."

"How do you know so much about it?"

"Some of what I know is rumor, but I was a toad wife for a year."

"You don't look wrinkled."

I shrugged one shoulder. "My husband and I didn't suit. We

had a semi-amicable parting, though." After my fourth serious attempt to dispose of my husband, he and I had had a very intense discussion, and he had finally set me free. Sometimes we still messaged each other. Alanna and I had gone back to him twice to pretend we were his trophy wives; he had paid us well. All in all, a more satisfactory outcome for the three of us.

"The officer told me that with a Linkan, there was no possibility of divorce."

"Who is this officer? She sounds unpleasant."

"I don't know her rank, only that she wore a uniform. Was she right? Is there no way I can divorce my toad husband?"

"I'm afraid she was right about that. They lose face if their wives leave them. I made an arrangement with my ex-husband to return when he really needs to show me off; all other times, he tells his rivals I am too precious a treasure to exhibit often. There are ways to work around problems like this. But you are already in debt to this Fimkim, and he won't let you go yet. You should at least meet him."

"But then I'll be trapped!"

"You are trapped wherever you go," I said, though Alanna and I had not found this to be true. We had double vision, special training and talents, and twice the hands and feet other human people possessed, so we never felt as helpless as this stranger appeared to. We had been trapped, together and apart, but we always worked with or toward each other, and we always escaped.

I said, "You have chosen to be trapped on Haladion, unless you'd rather return to your ship. Do you know what you want to do next?"

She shook her head.

Ask for her name, Alanna thought. *You always forget the important things.*

"What is your name?" I asked.

"I won't tell you," she said.

"Is it such an important name I'll recognize it? Hmm," I said, "I know you're from Challis. Who could you be?" Alanna, in the house above, asked the homeputer questions about who had been lost on Challis. Unfortunately, the planet's death had been sudden, and many were missing and presumed dead. The list of living refugees was much shorter. Alanna scanned pix of survivors in a stream so fast I couldn't watch what she was doing and see what was in front of me.

"You can call me Lennox," said the stranger. Alanna put that into her search, even though we knew it was not the stranger's real name.

"All right, Lennox. What will you do if you are not a wife?"

Lennox sipped coffee and did not answer.

Alanna thought, "Hey. Lennox is a street name in the capital city of Ponder. I've got some views of the planet before it was burned. I'm mapping now. Beh. Lennox is a very long street. I'm viewing along it. Business districts. No, wait, now I'm watching houses." I could see as Alanna watched, but it was distracting; she was viewing a swoop down the street at the same time as survivors' shocked faces streamed past on the left margin. I aimed my ringcam at Lennox and snapped a shot, sent it to the homeputer. It could cross-reference much faster than Alanna, though Alanna was faster than most other people.

The stream of pix of planet-lorn people slowed, reversed, stopped as the computer matched Lennox's face with one of the people in the datafile. Alanna focused on that instead of the pix of houses. *Milla Lyan,* the caption read; *formerly of 455 South Lennox Street, relocated to orbital refugee camp, subsequently relocated to permanent resettlement on Linkan, attached to Fimkim Ruggluff; currently in transit.*

Alanna spoke the address, and the homeputer showed again the dizzying rush of Lennox Street. The view slowed, stopped on a small, decrepit black house with two cloudy front windows and a round door. We moved in closer, peered past wads of window drapery to see the back of a girl, who sat at a console with several extended keyboards. She worked her hands and music came out of small speakers inset in metal flowers on the wall. I sat back, my eyes closed, listening to music so inviting I couldn't resist it. One of my faults or gifts was to be susceptible to music, sensitive to its nuances and effects. On occasion this had saved our lives. Other times it had almost doomed us.

There were messages in this music. It had strange overtones, and it pulsed as though it breathed. Though there were no words in it, there was enticing information encoded in melody, repeating promises. Just listen, it murmured, and you will learn things to make your life better. Here's a mystery that will save you from grief—

Fingers gripped my shoulder. "Ser? Are you all right?"

I startled, looked up at Lennox's worried face.

Alanna paused the playback, ran it faster so the audio wasn't so compelling, found a spot where the musician turned toward the window. Lennox's face looked at us.

"I'm sorry," I said, as I stared up into a face I was also seeing a younger version of through Alanna's eyes. "Have you decided who to become now that your world and your place in it are gone?"

She shook her head.

"A musician," I said.

She drew back. "What makes you say that?" she whispered.

"I'll explain if you come home with me."

Her head was shaking before I finished my invitation. "No."

"Your choice," I said. "I had better finish my shopping before my mistress's husband gets home. He likes supper ready when he arrives." I drank the rest of my coffee; still divine, though cool now. Then I washed in the second bowl of water and passed my hands through rose-scented smoke, and she copied my motions. I said, "Please. Enjoy the berries. I hope you find safe haven." I collected my carrybag.

"Ser," she said. She climbed to her feet, struggling a little to free herself from the grip of the cushions. "Wait."

I paused in the posture of one trapped by a single thread of obligation, a good pose for getting people to open up.

"You have been nothing but kind to me. I am frightened, though, and don't know where to trust."

"I understand. You're not the only one who's run from danger. You are right to be suspicious of strangers."

"If you would help me . . ." She twisted one hand in the other, reached up to fasten her veil across her lower face, hiding the flower on her cheek. "Why would you help me?"

"That is one of my callings." I thought of the tapestry of my and Alanna's past, woven to include a number of people we had rescued. The tapestry of the one who had rescued us intersected with our early history. He had moved on, leaving us with the charge of helping others, which meant threads of his life were woven with ours as ours continued. "If I do it correctly, it becomes your calling, too. Will you accept my help?"

She looked toward the curtain, with the wide world outside that she was a stranger to. She looked at me. I kept my face still.

"I will," she said. "Thank you."

I closed my eyes to let Alanna tell me what she thought. She thought, *Good*.

"The first thing I must do is give you a sigil," I said.

"A sign on my hood?"

"An affiliation. Will you join my household?"

"What obligations does such a choice give me?"

I frowned. "At this point, it is nothing more than a mark on your clothing. You can choose Kinnowar, my mistress's husband's clan name, or you can join the houseless—that's a spiral sign and means you are without affiliation. Little protection in that, but recognized status. Or you can go unveiled and uncovered in public, and proclaim your status as a country worker. Not a comfortable existence."

"I will accept your mark," she said.

I took four of the berries from her basket and made the mark of Gwelf's house on her hood in juice. It would wash out if she changed her mind.

This was just a disguise, but after I lifted my hand, I felt a kinship shadow between us. She raised her head and stared into my eyes, and even though her face was veiled, I knew she, too, sensed that something had changed.

She tucked her berry basket into the sleeve of her robe and followed me out of the tea house. She walked a step behind me as I finished shopping for the evening and morning meals. Then she came with me in our pod up to the mansion. We paused in the purification room to let scented smoke wash away the accretion of pollution we had picked up in our encounter with the outside world, and then moved toward the arch into the house.

Alanna waited there.

Milla saw her and hid behind me, clutching a fold of my robe. "Who is that?" she whispered.

"This is my mistress, Alanna Brigid Kinnowar. She will help you, too."

"How do you know?"

"We are good friends," I said.

Ha! thought Alanna. She smiled wide and held out her hands. "Ser, how may I help you?"

Milla collected herself and stepped forward. She bowed to Alanna. "Ser," she said in a low voice. "Thank you for having me here."

"I welcome you, Ser," said Alanna.

"Thank you," Milla said again.

"Come into the kitchen," I said. "I've a meal to prepare." I led the way, Milla following, and Alanna after.

"I've put the name of your husband into search," Alanna said as the two of them sat in the breakfast cozy. I stored everything I had bought at the market in the proper places, cold, dry, damp, warm, what each thing needed, and assembled ingredients for the night's meal on the center table.

"You what?"

"Ylva and I have a link, so I know your story, Ser," Alanna said. "I apologize for this violation of your privacy." She put a projector on the cozy's table. "What I've discovered disturbs me. This husband of yours is an important person on Linkan. He has two hundred fifty-five wives already, and you are to make up the perfect four times four times four times four, two hundred fifty-six. This is the most wives anyone on the planet has. I think he's the king. I need to do some more checking. He has already started a massive search for you. His minions are in the market-place now, and people are telling them things." She tapped the projector on. It showed an overview of the marketplace, people moving among the stalls, those searching for Milla tagged with red. An impressive mobilization of diverse forces. "Did your parent get much money for your sale?"

"I—I—" Milla clutched her hooded head. "She didn't say. I thought not. Just enough to send my brother to university and keep my mother in food until she can find a career."

"She sold you cheap, then," said Alanna. "What's special about you? Ah, the music."

"The music?" she said faintly. "What do you know about that?"

"You left tracks on the net," said Alanna, "and we followed them back to your home on Challis."

"How could you? Challis is dead!"

"Everything gets recorded by someone. Your planet still exists in the netmem. So does your home. Your younger self, playing some keyboard on a wall. I prefer manufactured music, but Ylva was much moved by yours."

"What?" Milla whispered.

Alanna coded instructions on the projector, and it produced a 3-D image of that view through Milla's gold-gauze-shrouded window, Milla with her back to us, her fingers working over the stacked triple keyboards; black metal flower speakers sprouted from the pale gold wall. An older woman stood against the back wall, watching Milla play, her face blank.

Music spilled from the projector. I realized this was a different view than the one Alanna and I had studied earlier. This music was not about mysteries and promises. It was about being trapped in a box.

I stood by my worktable, my arms frozen at my sides, and tears flowed.

Alanna glanced at me. "Ticka!" she cursed, and tapped the pause button on the projector. "What happened, Ylva?"

I shuddered and broke loose of the residue of the music's spell. "That was a different piece," I said. Milla reached toward the image of herself, her eyes wide. She tapped the button to start the projection moving again, and I ran from the room, closing my link to Alanna so I wouldn't hear any more of the song.

"What's this?" Gwelf said from the entry. "I don't smell my supper, and you look distressed." He slipped off his shoes in the purification room, shed his outer robe, walked through sandalwood smoke on the men's side, pulled a fresh robe from the rack near the arch into the apartment, and slid it on over his undergarments.

"We have a visitor," I said.

"Another rescue?"

"In process. Alanna's showing her her own memories."

"And this distresses you?"

"I'm sorry, Ser. I expect you're hungry. I'll get you your supper."

He frowned, grunted, then said, "I'll be in my workroom."

I returned to the kitchen. The projector was off, and Milla was crying.

I worked to trim and peel vegetables I had just bought, set a pan over heat, added oil, and fried food quickly for Gwelf. He always appreciated a freshly made meal. No matter how well I programmed the homecooker, he could tell the difference. Besides, I liked to cook for him. He had given me a home.

"Gwelf?" Alanna said as the hot oil hissed and bubbled and engulfed everything I fed it.

"In his workroom." I added spices and flavors I knew Gwelf liked. He enjoyed things that burned the tongue, but only a little. "I'll fix supper for us when I'm finished with this."

"Milla said the song she was playing that froze you was her box song," Alanna said. She widened her eyes at me, and I opened my connection to her again. I always missed her when we separated, but sometimes we did it anyway, especially when she wanted to be private with her husbands.

Reconnecting with her was like sinking into the comfort of my favorite couch, something that supported and cushioned me. I smiled at her.

I stirred Gwelf's supper one last time through the singing oil, then spilled it onto a plate, set the plate with utensils and cleansing cloth and a bowl of hot, lemon-scented water on a tray. I poured a glass of cool tea for him as well.

"My box song was the song I wrote when my mother first mentioned selling me," said Milla. "Even before the planet died, she had that plan, and she wouldn't listen to no."

"I understand." Before Alanna and I shared bondfruit, I had been in a box, no hope in my future, little comfort in my present, and very few memories of light in my past. Alanna and our rescuer opened the door to my box, and nothing had been as bad afterward, not even living in a bubble and being gaped at by toads.

I didn't want to hear the box song again, ever.

"I'll be back." I took the meal to Gwelf. He cleared space for it on his workbench, moving aside tools and sculptures-in-progress. Sometimes Alanna said his hobby was his true love. He built small, fantastic dwellings, and carved the creatures that might live in them. Here, too, he disdained the use of instant manufacture, preferring to craft things by hand.

"Thank you, Sif," Gwelf said.

"You're welcome, Ser. Again, I apologize for my lateness."

"No matter. The rescue, why does it trouble you?"

He never asked questions about these things. We managed

them without troubling him with details; we needed to use his
funds for some of our arrangements, but he was generous that
way and never denied us. I wasn't sure what to tell him. "I am not.
troubled by her rescue, only by her talent. She's a musician—"

"Oh, no. Not the Ruggluff bride?"

"Ser?"

"There's a planetwide alert for her. I should have known."

"Why would a toad want a musician wife? How is she to
play inside a bubble?"

"He's an innovator, and wants to turn over the old order on
Linkan. To that effect, he's ordered a bubble big enough for the
bride and her instrument. No one else's wives perform for company, but he took the notion after watching too many netcasts
from other cultures. It was supposed to be a bold political move
and cement his popularity for the next election, but it falls flat
if the bride escapes. The Federation of Fair Traders was in favor
of the change, as perhaps it would lead toward more freedom for
the Linkan brides."

"But Ser, the girl—"

"Whoever aids the Ruggluff bride will have to pay a price."
He set down his food sticks and picked up a half-polished lump
of wood. He frowned.

"How high is the price, Ser?"

His gaze rose, and his brows lowered. "Such an act could
damage me politically," he said. For the first time I saw the power
of his actual profession, fair trader and financier, on his face, and
knew that the person he had always been toward me—a slightly
bumbling, pleasant, undemanding, often absent master—was
perhaps a construct, not his true character.

"Must we return her?" I asked/Alanna asked. He had never
interfered in a rescue before; but we had never rescued anyone
politically important before.

"Do they know you have her yet?" he asked.

In the kitchen, Alanna projected the marketplace over the
table again, with the searchers marked. They were spread wider

through the place, though most of the shops were closed for the evening. A concentration of red-tagged searchers had collected around Kalenki's Tea House.

Alanna zoomed the spy-eye closer and turned up audio. Kalenki himself stood at the door, talking to six of these men. He offered them tea. "A woman in an unmarked robe?" he said. "No one like that left here. Ask at Sook's, across the square. He caters more to the transient trade." He pointed.

"Sif?" Gwelf touched the back of my hand.

"Alanna is searching," I said. "So far, they don't know who has her, but they're getting closer."

In the kitchen, Alanna rose from the table, and gestured for Milla to follow her into the living room.

"I can't decide whether I should meet her or ignore her," Gwelf muttered.

Music sounded from the living room. Alanna had unlocked the keyboard that was in the house when we bought it. Neither of us played, so we usually hid it in the wall. Now Milla sat at it and ran her fingers over the keys, waking answering sounds.

Gwelf groaned and rose from his workbench. "I guess I'll have to meet her." He glanced toward his half-eaten supper. "Next time, call me when you're hosting one of these rescues, and I'll stay out until you've sent her on her way. I can deny knowledge."

"Alanna can hack the house records and make it so you were never here," I said.

"Of course she can," he said, and sighed. He snapped the code that dimmed the lights in the room and left, with me on his heels. We went to the living room, where Gwelf often entertained with Alanna at his side and me handling refreshments.

Milla was playing a third song now, an interleaving of hopes and fears. I wavered, afraid of the fears the song showed me, bonds and lashes, and the hopes that were hardly better, images of clawing through tearable sky to something Milla couldn't imagine but only hoped would be better. Ribbons of loneliness wove through the song.

"Come, Sif," said Gwelf; he stepped over the threshold into the living room, paused to look back at me. I was frozen, trapped in the living lace of the music. Alanna, inside my head, was intrigued by how I heard it, and able to resist its call.

At Gwelf's voice, Milla's hands stilled on the keys and she turned, her face panicked. She lifted a hand to raise her veil, fumbled it so it hung half across her mouth.

"Child, you're wearing my sign; you may as well be unveiled before me, at least until we straighten out the question of who you are."

"Gwelf," said Alanna, "why are you here?"

He glanced at me. Alanna and I had never known how aware of our bond Gwelf was; we had found it prudent not to ask. But now I knew he knew, had perhaps always known.

Perhaps that explained why he slept with other women. Alanna had betrayed him first, by our bond, even though it wasn't physical. My heart softened toward him.

"I heard music," he said.

"Ser Gwelf says there's a planetwide alert out for Ser Milla," I said. Planetwide did not mean very wide; all settlements on Haladion were new, with Risen the largest, when you combined its population with that of the spaceport. A few other small towns had sprung up, some of them with different social structures. This was a planet ripe for strange cults to take root in it, but so far they hadn't discovered it, despite the fact that it was a good stopover point on six major trade routes.

Alanna said, "There was a lot of activity about her being missing, but not right away. She wandered in the marketplace a while without attracting notice."

"I left a simulacrum with life signs in my cabin," said Milla. "But then I was so stupid with hunger and nostalgia . . ."

"It was not that so much as the unmarked robe," I said. "Everybody will have noticed. They're not always motivated to tell what they know to strangers, but it sounds like your husband-to-be has enough money to bribe everybody."

"If you return now, perhaps the penalty won't be steep," said Gwelf. "They can chalk it up to youthful spirits."

Tears seeped from her eyes as she stared at him. I heard again the box song, though she didn't touch the keyboard. It had moved into my head, ready to trap me whenever appropriate. Alanna came to my side and took my hand.

With a glance at our linked hands, Gwelf said, "Sif. Tell me what's so terrible about this fate."

"They'll lock her in with her gift," I said, and realized my own cheeks were wet. Inside, I was still trapped in my father's high-tech prison, pummeled every day by the sounds he chose— he knew I was sensitive to them, but he didn't understand what they did to me. He only saw the outward signs—that I was made pliant and would do what he wanted, not that I was broken in spirit, losing part of myself every day. He never heard what I heard in that pounding military music, the feet of soldiers walking over the hearts of children and the death of dreams.

Every day I was trained in the art of soundstrike, vocal skills that armed me; I carried no weapons but my voice. Every day he tried to teach me to look at people as targets. Every day I listened to other music in the archives and heard life stories, from lullabyes to dirges, jump rope rhymes to the songs of starships.

Alanna brought the bondfruit one day when I lay on my bed and wouldn't move, even to eat. "It's experimental, from the labs," she whispered as she massaged my arms. "There's a resonance component. Animals who eat from the same batch of bondfruits at the same moment synchronize their activities. The scientists haven't used it on humans yet. I got a matched set. If we each eat one at the same moment—" She slipped the small hard fruit into my mouth, positioned it between my teeth, used her palm under my chin to hold it steady. She put one between her teeth, too, a green thing the shape of an olive. "It could kill us," she whispered. "I could make you bite it by pushing your teeth together, but I want you to do it yourself. I'm going to count to three. Bite on three, and so will I. Maybe it'll work, and maybe it won't."

I don't know where she got the strength to do it. I hadn't responded to anything she said that day; I didn't even twitch when she worked my muscles too hard and it hurt. Yet she trusted.

She counted. We bit. We were both sick for a week afterward, but when the fever went down, we had our connection. Our lifeline.

Soon after that, they shut down the bondfruit experiments.

"What's so bad about being locked in with your talent?" asked Gwelf. "Doesn't that give you time to refine it?"

"Some kinds of talent are cold bedmates, unkind companions if you can't get away from them. It could kill her." I had cut out the talent my father had been force-training me in. I still had faint scars on my throat.

"I see," he said. "Well, then, I suppose we have to do something else."

Alanna released my hand and went to kiss Gwelf.

"Do you have a plan?" Gwelf asked us.

"No." I wondered why he kept asking me questions. It was all strange to me. Alanna made the plans.

"We could marry her ourselves and pay off Ruggluff," said Gwelf.

"Oh, Ser, I'm afraid it must be a lot of money," said Milla.

"Money is not the problem," said Gwelf. "It is maintaining face, and encouraging him to take the same steps with a different wife so that the proposed social reforms don't fall apart. We could manage that somehow, I suppose."

I turned to Milla. "I have asked you this question several times already, and gotten no answer. Who do you want to be, if you are not the Ruggluff bride?"

"I don't want to be a musician," she said. "That was always my mother's idea, since I was very young. She made me take the lessons and told me to write music. She entered my works in competitions. If I wrote songs that won, we ate good food for a couple of weeks. She made me get better at selling myself. That's not a part of myself I want to work with anymore. But I never had time to find out what I like."

"How musically knowledgeable are the toads?" Alanna asked me.

"I never noticed they had any particular taste, except for their own vocal stylings. In the bubble, I had access to music libraries imported from other cultures, but I didn't hear anything indigenous except mating songs," I said.

"So—any musician might do? The woman who plays evening music at Sook's, whose rescue we've been contemplating for a month?" asked Alanna.

She and I smiled at each other. Cassie, at Sook's, played for tips; Sook didn't pay her, but he let her use the keyboard. People who went to Sook's for the evening didn't care about music, so she didn't make much. She had run away from a worse place. Haladion was a good planet for runaways if you had a marketable talent and knew how to live off the land, but her skill wasn't very useful, and she had no woodcraft. She might like to disappear to a place of plenty using someone else's name, and she looked a bit like Milla.

Alanna says I always forget the important things. I remember what was important about this rescue. It woke many ghost wounds in me. When we succeeded in freeing Milla from the chains of her music, some of my wounds healed.

I washed the sigil from Milla's robe. Gwelf took it down to town, found Cassie in her secret roof home (Alanna liked watching the town through the focus window, and knew where most of the homeless lived), and consulted with her. Cassie was happy to get room, board, and a chance to entertain an uncritical audience. She didn't like sleeping out in the weather.

Milla shadows me through the mansion these days, trying

everything I do, waiting for a new trade to call her, one she'll choose for herself. The keyboard is locked back in the living room wall, but I remember the three songs I heard Milla play, whether I want to or not, and sometimes my ghost voice, the one that could kill, sings them. Only Alanna hears, and she doesn't let them hurt her.

INTO THE EIGHTIES

LYNN ABBEY

Nearing midnight on December 31, 1979, and Bob Asprin was holding court, as was his wont, amid a group of local fans at an Elks' Club–sponsored New Year's Eve party in Ypsilanti, Michigan. For the life of me, I can't remember why we'd chosen to gather there, but after the champagne, the balloons, and the ritual singing of "Auld Lang Syne," Bob mused that we were exactly halfway between the start of the sixties and a new century: if we were going to make our mark on the world, we'd make it now or miss it altogether. The Elks' Club wasn't the place for deep discussions and we swiftly moved on to other things, but the comment took root in my memory.

Unknown to us, Bob and I had already started making our mark. In 1978, Bob had come up with the idea for an anthology of original stories all set in the same seedy city he planned to call Sanctuary. He, Gordon Dickson, and I had converged for one of those over-the-top hotel dinners that are the true reason SF/F authors go to SF/F conventions. The convention was Boskone, so the chowder was heavier on clams than potatoes and they actually had bluefish on the menu.

As the unpublished author in attendance, I stayed focused on my bluefish as Bob complained about the fate of great worlds: Lieber's Lankhmar, Howard's Hyboria, Harrison's Deathworld, Morecock's Eternal Champions, Gordie's own Splinter Cultures. Why, by Gordie's own calculations, for every one word of story, the diligent author produced at least two and probably five words of world-building, all of which went to waste because not even the most prolific author could write all the stories implied by a well-built world. Gordie agreed and upped the ante, hinting that he'd always wanted to write a Lankhmar story but never would, since finishing the Childe Cycle would keep him busy until he was well past the century mark.

Gordie's admission required a toast and a refill of beverages *de nuit*, followed by existential questions: Where were our characters when we weren't writing about them? Did Fafhrd and the Gray Mouser prowl other towns when not on duty in Lankhmar? Suppose they went to an unfamiliar tavern to unwind . . . Suppose Conan was headed to the same place, for the same reason . . . Suppose Elric was already there, or Wagner's Kane . . . Imagine the banter, the boasts, the epic brawls in the tavern known as—

Bob leaned back, slim, brown cigarette in hand (because these were the days long before the restaurant-smoking ban), and conjured a name: The Vulgar Unicorn. If he'd come up with any other name, I think the whole enterprise would have died somewhere between dessert and brandy. Instead, the table talk shifted gears from small talk to manifest destiny: The tales of the Vulgar Unicorn must be written.

Foolishly, I suggested a "franchising" scheme: established authors licensing their creations to less-than-established authors (I was, after all, very much less-than-established at the time) and got a stereophonic lecture on the error of my ways. But the seed had been sown. Instead of licensing Lankhmar, we'd create a new setting, Sanctuary (the place where characters go to escape the demands of their creators), for an original anthology populated with new characters dreamed up by invitation-only authors, featuring the added gimmick that the authors could/would use each other's characters.

For Gordie and me, the hard work was done. It was up to Bob, our indefatigable huckster, to con some unsuspecting editor into buying the project. And over the course of the convention he did, seducing the available authors, one by one, and culminating with a cognac-fueled sales pitch to Jim Baen, of ACE books, at the Dead-Dog party. (Where were camera-equipped cell phones when we really needed them?)

The official title was simply *Thieves' World*, but the cover—with its quartet of outwardly staring medieval gangsters silently proclaiming, You just walked into the wrong bar, sucker—caught a surprising number of eyes and wallets. ACE had to go back for additional printings and *TW* earned out its advance, a rare occurrence for original anthologies. Even so, *TW* would have been a one-shot if Bob hadn't returned to our roots and suggested that volume two should bear the title *Tales From the Vulgar Unicorn*. Jim couldn't resist . . . and, back in Michigan, Bob and I began collecting some truly amazing (not to mention utterly unreproducible and anatomically impossible) tavern signage.

In retrospect, the eighties were pretty good times for our genre. Short-fiction markets were still plentiful and the New York publishers had stopped treating their SF/F editors as red-headed stepchildren. We hadn't quite repealed Sturgeon's law, but we'd "broken out," gone respectable, and successfully laid claim to a few slots on the major bestseller lists.

Collectively, we were making our marks. Individually . . .

Most change is gradual, but it took just one phone call in 1982 to change my life. I was talking to Beth Meacham at ACE about one of my own books when she let slip that ACE had just bought a book from Gordon Dickson, *Jamie the Red*, and they'd sweetened the deal by $5000 because Jamie was a *TW* character. They planned to use our *TW* artist for the cover and put a *Thieves' World* banner above the title.

I don't remember the rest of the conversation; it was as if a little bomb had gone off in the back of my mind. Granted, Gordie had been at the table when *Thieves' World* was conceived. He was the first author to commit to the project and Jim probably wouldn't have bought it if Bob hadn't been able to drop Gordie's name into the negotiation. Still, when push came to shove and Gordie's story arrived in the mail, Bob had done the unthinkable:

he'd rejected the story. Jim went apoplectic: newbie anthology editors didn't reject marquee stories. But Bob had stuck to his guns and in an epic conversation, notable mostly for its long silences, had prevailed.

Gordon R. Dickson remained very much a friend and mentor, but he had not become a *Thieves' World* author. *Jamie the Red*, however, was a *TW* character, because the *TW* character-sharing gimmick required that Bob circulate character information among the invited authors before they wrote their stories. Poul Anderson had featured Gordie's character prominently in his story, which Bob had accepted. ACE's new acquisition was an expansion of the story Bob had rejected and it was worth an extra $5000 because it could be associated with the anthology in which it hadn't appeared.

There's friendship, there's gratitude and respect; and then there's money. Bob didn't object to Gordie turning his rejected story into a saleable book—that was a stroke of genius. Bob objected to the $5000, and not because Gordie had gotten it—that was good fortune of the first water—but because ACE, having decided that a *Thieves' World* banner was worth $5000, was neither asking permission to use it nor sharing the wealth.

"By the author of _____" has been appearing on book covers since Gutenberg's day and by 1982 *Star Wars* and *Star Trek* had progressed from one-shot movie novelizations to steady streams of licensed original novels. But the idea that something one author had created could be worth $5000 to another author and his publisher . . . well, that struck a new and somewhat sour note.

Bob and his agent, who was also Gordie's agent, squared off with ACE. The *Thieves' World* association was pulled, but Gordie got to keep the extra $5000. And while that was happening, I asked a lawyer friend to come up with a paragraph or two we could add to our short-story contract that would clarify the conditions under which characters could be shared. Said lawyer pointed out that changing our contract wouldn't resolve the problem, because Bob had rejected Gordie's story. He said we'd need something different, something bound into the invitation to write for *TW*.

A formal invitation that spelled out the ground rules—I thought that sounded good. We were heading into our fifth volume by then and planning to send out a handful of new invitations. We could clarify the whole copyright situation—What copyright situation? my friend the lawyer asked. It was really very simple, I replied: the authors made free use of each other's characters, settings, etc., but *Thieves' World* wasn't work-for-hire and we'd been copyrighting the stories in their authors' names.

Most jaw-dropping moments are metaphors; not that one. My friend sat across the table, struck mute and frozen. When he finally did move, it was to toss his pencil at the ceiling. Apparently what I'd so glibly described had more legal implications than could be covered in a one-paragraph addition to the standard short-story contract. He suggested a weekend retreat, possibly two.

As an author, one would like to be remembered for one's stories; I fear that Bob and I are going to be remembered for a contract: the *Thieves' World* Master Agreement, the legalese novelette that unleashed the concept of "Shared Worlds" on a unsuspecting and not altogether welcoming industry. In effect, the Master Agreement solved the problem that had earned me a lecture in 1978. We'd turned the world of science fiction into marketable properties and preserved the intellectual property rights of both the creators and the participants.

Suddenly, Hollywood wasn't the only franchiser in town. Anyone who'd ever built a world could change the proper nouns in the Master Agreement and go into the exploitation business. And a good many did. The *Thieves' World* authors were among the first to exploit their worlds.

C. J. Cherryh wrote *The Angel with a Sword*. There were spaceships and aliens in the backstory, but the novel itself was pre-steampunk set in a city that reminded me of Venice . . . and

Sanctuary. I mentioned the similarities to her after reading the proofs. Sure enough, a shared world called Merovingen Nights was in the works. In addition to creating characters, Merovingen's authors would lay claim to their very own island. Did we want to play? Of course. After five years of editing *Thieves' World*, Bob and I were more than willing to be the pain in another editor's neck.

C.J. adopted the Master Agreement lock, stock, and pussycat. Janet Morris knew all about the hassles Bob and I endured and opted for something simpler: Hell. After all, you couldn't get more public domain than Hell. Her notion was that we'd write stories about the people who wound up there. Because our characters were to be based on real people, there wouldn't be a copyright problem; and because they were dead, Janet didn't think there'd be libel problems, either. Did we want to play? Bob said yes; I waffled until she suggested that I write a story about Brezhnev, Chernenko, and Andropov sharing a cold-water flat in the part of Hell that was indistinguishable from Siberia. How could I resist?

David Drake, who'd written for both *TW* and *Heroes in Hell*, and Bill Fawcett, came up with *The Fleet* in an attempt to inject some honest science fiction into what was becoming a fantasy-dominated sub-genre. They took the Master Agreement into intergalactic space where the writers sent their characters into a nasty, desperate war against an implacable enemy. They asked us to play, but by then we were learning how to say No.

Wendy and Richard Pini weren't part of the *Thieves' World* crew, but we'd been friends for years. They had a world, Elfquest, a sui generis tale of wolf-riding elves that Wendy told in a graphic novel format. They had a problem, too: A backstory that spanned ten generations of said elves. Even if she gave up sleeping and eating, Wendy couldn't draw it all. We gave Richard a copy of the Master Agreement, and the next thing we knew, he'd not only dreamed up *The Blood of Ten Chiefs* project, he'd convinced us to sign on as coeditors until he got up to speed as a prose, rather than graphic, editor.

There were others. Beth Meacham (who'd really gotten the ball rolling when she told me about *Jamie the Red*) shepherded Emma Bull and Will Shetterley's *Liavek* series into existence. George R.R. Martin questioned me about the Master Agreement when he was putting *Wild Cards* together. I waited and hoped for a call from Spider Robinson. Even more than the *Vulgar Unicorn*, Callahan's *Crosstime Saloon* seemed a natural shared-world setting, but Spider, wise man that he is, proved immune to our infection.

Throughout the eighties, we described *Thieves' World* as the "*Hill Street Blues* of sword-and-sorcery" or "*Dungeons and Dragons* for authors." It was the decade of using one brand name to describe another, the era of subrights and exploitation. ACE published their final *TW* anthology in 1989, after which it was time for the eighties and all they had spawned to fade into history. For better or worse, we'd made our mark: we don't just write books anymore, we create properties, and if we're careful, we're the ones who control and profit from them.

TALKING ABOUT FANGS

M.J. ENGH

The Author Emerita award this year went to M.J. Engh. Mary Jane Engh has written such notable books as *Arsian* and *Wheel of the Winds*. She has been publishing science fiction since 1964. While being honored as writer emerita, she plans to continue crafting amazing novels. Here is a short story she wrote in 1995.

'll get back to the subject in a minute, but first let's talk about fangs. You've seen these vampire movies? With the vampires dislocating their jaws to show their pointy canines? I think the great American public would like vampires to have fangs like rattlesnakes, except equipped for suction instead of injection. But what humans have to work with are these little dull canine teeth way out toward the sides of our mouths.

Even if they were bigger and sharper they'd be more like railroad spikes than a rattlesnake's hypodermics. Look at a dog's canines. They're for hanging on to a struggling victim and doing as much damage as possible, not sliding in and out and leaving a cute little hole. But people are hung up on the fang idea. It's the word *fang*, I think. Sounds all sinister and thrilling.

So you see these movie vampires with their artificially lengthened and sharpened canines, twisting their heads around and trying to make cute little holes in somebody's neck. It's not easy; no matter how long and pointy you make them, they're still in the wrong place for that kind of bite—too far back in the mouth and too far apart.

Okay, we're supposed to be talking legal business. But imagine if you decided to lean over your desk right now and bite my neck. You can't drop your lower jaw out of the way like a rattlesnake, and you can't just go *whack* with your upper jaw and there's a hole wherever a tooth hits. No, you'd have to get a piece of me between your uppers and lowers and chew.

And how about these stories where a pair of vampires simultaneously chomp each other's neck? Picture the contortions required, and ask yourself if it wouldn't be easier to get at a wrist. The main reason fictional vampires have this throat fetish is the public thinks it's sexy.

Which is another thing. Something snuffling and masticating and slurping under your chin is *not* necessarily sexy. And except for mosquitoes, sucking is a separate operation from biting, so the process can get messy. Yes, I did say "something," not "somebody." A vampire is not a person, and it's not male or female. It's a monster. You can say getting sucked by a vampire is a sensual experience, but so is being swallowed by an anaconda. A vampire is an animated corpse, and what animates it isn't something you'd invite for dinner. It's an infection, a parasite, and it's about as romantic as diarrhea.

Personally, I think this sexy-vampire stuff is a legacy of good old American puritanism. We've been so uptight about sex and how ooh yikes *physical* it is, a couple of generations have grown up convinced that anything physical has got to be, really, deep down, sexy.

Let me tell you, I'm tired of this sinister-but-thrilling bullshit. Getting vampirized isn't a sinister but thrilling step to immortality. It's a dreary, yucky death, a lot like AIDS, only faster. And what stands up out of that grave isn't you. There may be some traces of your personality left—the thing's using your body, and a lot of personality is physical. But it doesn't have your memories. The brain is the first thing to go. After that, the digestive system gets reorganized.

Talking about graves reminds me of another thing. Yes, the will, we'll get back to that, but first, coffins. Vampires are supposed to sleep in their coffins, or the soil they were buried in, or maybe both, and if they don't they go all to pieces. Not what you'd call a mobile lifestyle. Think about taking your own bed with you every time you make an overnight trip.

Only it doesn't work that way. Real vampires are drifters. They can't afford to stay put. Look at it ecologically. The more they eat, the more competitors they create, not to mention the chances of a vampire scare in the neighborhood. It makes sense just to browse a little and move on. And they don't need any special box or dirt to get a good day's sleep.

They're very physical beings, vampires. They don't have a religion, no more than a tapeworm does, and they don't give a damn about yours. So all the crosses and crucifixes and communion wafers in Christendom don't bother them as much as one good whiff of garlic. Garlic and sunlight are unhealthy for vampires, that much is true. But it's like wood alcohol and radioactivity are unhealthy for humans. A big enough dose can be fatal, but a little isn't going to knock you off your chair.

Vampires are like fish; they're not immortal, they just don't die until something kills them. You might think modern embalming techniques would be as good as a stake through the heart, but think again. The crap the funeral home puts into you isn't toxic enough to disinfect against vampirism, and what they take out isn't all that essential. The ancient Egyptians did it better. The only vampires in ancient Egypt were the poor working stiffs who couldn't afford to get mummified.

I've done a lot of research on this, you see. Figured some of it out on my own, learned some of it from books. Not the bestsellers, you can bet on that! The rest of it you might say I got from the horse's mouth.

And speaking of animals reminds me of the bat business. That's one of the silliest pieces in the whole package. You know how big a bat is? About one ounce and five inches, that's how big. Can you figure any way to condense a human body into that size? We're not talking fantasy here, we're talking vampires. Sometimes the stories try to get around that with *giant* bats. But think about the wingspan on a two-hundred-pound vampire. Or even a hundred pounds; you do tend to lose a lot of weight. Anyway, it's a lot less conspicuous to buy a ticket and take the plane.

You want to know why I'm telling you all this? Okay, let's get to it. I've already said embalming isn't good enough. There's a way, though, and it's legal, and perfectly sane people do it. Cremation. You burn a body, you kill whatever's in it. Killed. Dead. Finished. Now you understand why I wanted to make a new will?

Get this: I'm dying. Dying a dreary, yucky death, and there's nothing anybody can do to stop it, though the transfusions slow it down. Most of my friends and ex-friends think I've got AIDS. That's what you thought yourself, wasn't it? My doctor doesn't know what the hell to make of it. I'm past the stage where garlic could have helped. I'm infected. I'm digesting myself, like a caterpillar turning into a butterfly. Only what I'm turning into won't be pretty. No, more like a caterpillar one of those parasitic wasps has laid eggs in—something eating me from inside, turning me into it. Using my blood is the least of it. I can feel the brain going. Part of my doctor's final diagnosis is going to be Alzheimer's.

That's why I'm here now, getting the new will finalized, setting up the trusts and all of that, before anybody can say I'm too far gone. Been talking to the family too, letting everybody know what to expect. The good news is, nobody objects to the trust for you. You're not just my lawyer, you're an old friend.

The trouble is, nobody in my family has ever been cremated. We've got that family plot in Oakdale cemetery, right across the street from here. Look, you can see it from your office window. My mother put a lot of store on all of us being buried close together. Some of the family just think cremation is silly, but for others it's like sacrilege. I might as well ask for voodoo rites at my funeral.

That's where you come in. You've got to make it very clear to all my loving relatives that unless my corpse is cremated, nobody gets anything. The trusts are dissolved, the legacies annulled, and everything goes to AIDS research. Well, hell, there isn't any vampire research. That includes the trust for you. Essentially, you don't get paid if I don't get burned. You know that carrot and stick approach? That's the carrot.

It's not selfishness. I'll be dead, whatever happens. I'm not trying to save myself from turning into a monster. Well, maybe some of that. It's not a sweet picture, my dead body creeping around in the dark like an animated vacuum cleaner, looking for veins to suck. But mostly it's the one favor I can do for the world, and this world needs all the favors it can get.

I hope it hasn't been a mistake, talking to you like this. If I tried it with any of my family, they'd be sure I'd gone over the edge. But I feel a little better now. I've done what I can; from here on it's in your hands. So don't take this personally, old friend, just hear it as a statement of fact: if you let them bury me uncremated, you'll be sorry. That's the stick.

SCIENCE FICTION IN THE 1990S: WAITING FOR GODOT . . . OR MAYBE NOSFERATU

MIKE RESNICK

The science fiction field seemed to have no boundaries in the 1990s. Six-figure advances no longer made headlines; seven-figure advances were not unheard of; there were even some eight-figure advances, this in a field where more than half the acknowledged classics had been written for two cents a word or less.

There was a time when science fiction movies were solely for the true believers. They were made up of guys in robot suits, scientists' beautiful daughters who couldn't get work in "A" movies, and painfully clumsy and obvious special effects. No more. By the end of the decade, more than a dozen of the top twenty all-time box office grossers were science fiction or related films, and mighty few A-list directors and stars didn't take a shot at one (or more).

There was a time—a lot of people don't remember it, and the younger ones usually don't believe it—when *Star Trek* was a dismal flop, when it hung out near the bottom of the Nielsen ratings for the entire three years of its existence before the network, which had given in to Bjo Trimble's Save Trek campaign once, elected not to do so again. Move the calendar ahead, and counting animation there were over one hundred science fiction shows on television in the 1990s.

Things looked pretty rosy. The Old Wave/New Wave wars were over, the general public was discovering that we weren't all just writing that crazy Buck Rogers stuff, there were viable publishers everywhere you looked, and there was a constant influx of new, talented writers.

If you looked closely enough, there were some problems too. At the three-quarter mark of the century, there were something like seventeen New York houses with science fiction lines. We published more books in 1999 than 1975, far more . . . but there were only eight houses with science fiction lines (and in another decade there would be only six—that's not a lot of editorial taste to spread around). The anthology market was incredibly healthy at the beginning of the decade, less so at the end. The magazines had been selling very well in 1990; by 1999 each had lost more than half its circulation, and a new title, *Science Fiction Age*, which was actually the bestselling of them all a year or two into its existence, was gone by the end of the decade.

There were a number of truly fine novels in the 1990s, but I don't believe any had the immediate classic status of predecessors such as *The Forever War*, *Dune*, *The Left Hand of Darkness*, *Neuromancer*, or *Ender's Game*. Still, there were some wonderful and popular novels, among them Lois McMaster Bujold's *Barrayar* and *The Vor Game*, Connie Willis's *Doomsday Book*, Nancy Kress's *Beggars in Spain* (an expansion of a now-classic novella), and the truly unique and important trilogy of *Red Mars*, *Green Mars*, and *Blue Mars* by Kim Stanley Robinson, each of which won a Hugo or a Nebula.

Speaking of awards, the decade was dominated by Connie Willis, who won seven Nebulas and Hugos, and by 1999 was the all-time leader in both categories. Others to win three or more Hugos and Nebulas combined during the decade include Lois McMaster Bujold (4), Kim Stanley Robinson (3), Nancy Kress (3), Joe Haldeman (5), and your humble undersigned (4). Major work was also done by Robert J. Sawyer, Michael Swanwick, Greg Bear, Vernor Vinge, David Brin, Kristine Kathryn Rusch, James Morrow, Allen Steele, Ursula K. Le Guin, Harry Turtledove, Maureen McHugh, William Gibson, Neal Stephenson, and many others.

Among the editors, Gardner Dozois won nine of the ten Hugos given during the decade (there is no Nebula for editing), and Kristine Kathryn Rusch won the other. Among artists (where there is also no Nebula), Bob Eggleton walked away with five Hugos, while Michael Whelan and Don Maitz won two apiece, and Jim Burns picked up the remaining one.

We also had our share of very talented newcomers break into science fiction during the 1990s, including Kage Baker, Ted Chiang, Tobias S. Buckell, Michael Burstein, Nalo Hopkinson, Cory Doctorow, Kay Kenyon, Susan R. Matthews, Laura Resnick, Ellen Klages, Mary Doria Russell, Nicholas A. DiChario, Michelle Sagara West, Julie Czerneda, and many more.

We also lost our share of writers: gone were Isaac Asimov, Fritz Leiber, Roger Zelazny, Lester del Rey, Marion Zimmer Bradley, James White, Walter M. Miller Jr., Avram Davidson, John Brunner (who became the first writer or fan to die at a Worldcon), Bob Shaw, Judith Merril, Jo Clayton, Frank Belknap Long, Ed Emshwiller, Jack Finney, and more.

A number of our authors appeared regularly on the various bestseller lists: Robert Jordan, Anne McCaffrey, Terry Goodkind, Stephen Donaldson, Sir Arthur C. Clarke, Sir Terry Pratchett, Kevin J. Anderson (alone and in collaboration with Brian Herbert), Timothy Zahn, David Weber, and more. Dean Koontz, who used to write halves of Ace Doubles for $1,500 a shot, joined Stephen King as the two writers of the fantastic who belong to that tiny community of authors whose manuscripts command eight-figure advances.

It was no longer difficult to get funding, or stars, or star directors, for science fiction movies. CGI has made it possible to put anything you can imagine on the screen, which we all thought would be a boon to the cinema . . . but I have come to the conclusion that it may be the very worst thing to happen to science fiction movies, because they can now throw so many mind-blowing images at you that more and more often the images are taking the place of plot and characterization.

This is not to say the audiences weren't pleased, and weren't willing to shell out multiples of $100 million at the box office. 1990's *Jurassic Park* took in a billion dollars by the time the DVDs were through selling. (It also asked you to believe that a hungry T. rex cannot spot you from six inches away if you don't move.) The sequel, *The Lost World*, another megahit, suggests that a tyrannosaur can catch an elevated train, but cannot catch a bunch of panicky tourists fleeing on foot in a straight line. *Armageddon*, which became Disney's top live-action grosser until Johnny Depp visited the Caribbean, asked you to believe that some not-very-bright wildcatters could become astronauts easier than highly-trained physically-fit astronauts could be taught to find and extract oil. *Starship Troopers* poured money into the production, but would have been better titled "Ken and Barbie Go to War." The long-awaited fourth *Star Wars* movie (or first, if you're into fictional chronology) was in profit before a single foot of film was shot, which was all for the best. *Terminator 2* and *The Matrix* had their moments, and the latter sported a stunning cyberpunk look, but I think at decade's end the two most artistically successful science fiction films were two of the least demanding and ambitious (which may well explain why): *Men in Black* and *Galaxy Quest,* a pair of delightful comedies.

(I have been discussing theatrical releases here. Actually, the best fantastic film of the decade was *The Wonderful Ice Cream Suit*, scripted by Ray Bradbury from his own story. It had charm, grace, poignancy, and beauty in abundance—so of course it was released directly to video.)

I gave up on television in the early 1980s, and have not watched a single network series since then, so I asked a number of fans from my Listserv to suggest the best of the 1990s television shows, and it is their consensus that the following were the best of the lot: *Babylon 5, The X-Files, Highlander, Star Trek: Deep Space Nine, Star Trek: Voyager, Buffy the Vampire Slayer, Lois and Clark, Sliders, Xena, Third Rock from the Sun*, and *Stargate SG1.*

As the decade drew to a close, no one was quite sure what

was coming next. But with the advantage of hindsight, it's not too difficult to see that there were two major innovations between the end of the New Wave as a movement, and the beginning of the new millennium: William Gibson became the creator and the finest exemplar of cyberpunk; and Anne Rice decided that vampires, which had hitherto been unclean dead things that sucked away your lifeblood, were sexy.

The critics loved cyberpunk and snickered at vampire romances. Which is one more reason why we don't pay much attention to the critics. I doubt that there are three cyberpunk novels a year these days; I also doubt that there are fewer than ten vampire romances a week, and a lot of them live on the bestseller list. It's a billion-dollar industry, and more and more science fiction publishers are starting to yield to the pressure.

I don't think anybody in the 1990s saw it coming. So much for science fiction's vaunted talent for prognostication.

THE RHYSLING AND DWARF STAR AWARD-WINNING POETRY

Since 1978, when Suzette Haden Elgin founded the Science Fiction Poetry Association, its members have recognized achievement in the field of speculative poetry by presenting the Rhysling Awards, named after the blind bard protagonist of Robert A. Heinlein's "The Green Hills of Earth."

Every year, each SFPA member is allowed to nominate two poems from the previous year for the Rhysling Awards: one in the "long" category (50+ lines) and one in the "short" category (1–49 lines). Because it's practically impossible for each member to have read every nominated poem in the various publications where they originally appeared, the nominees are all collected into one volume, called *The Rhysling Anthology*. Past winners have included Michael Bishop, Bruce Boston, Tom Disch, Joe Haldeman, Alan P. Lightman, Ursula K. Le Guin, Susan Palwick, Lucius Shepard, Jeff VanderMeer, Gene Wolfe and Jane Yolen.

In 2006, the SFPA created a new award, the Dwarf Star Award, to honor poems of 10 lines or fewer.

PLACE MAT BY MOEBIUS

GREG BEATTY

Greg Beatty lives with his wife in Bellingham, Washington, where he tries, unsuccessfully, to stay dry. He writes everything from children's books to essays about his cooking debacles. Greg won the 2005 Rhysling Award (short-poem category) and recently published his first poetry chapbook, *Phrases of the Moon*. Here is his Dwarf Star winner:

> Place mat by Moebius;
> wine bottled by Klein. You sigh.
> This dinner never ends.

EATING LIGHT

F. J. BERGMANN

F. J. Bergmann frequents Wisconsin and fibitz.com. She has no academic literary qualifications, but hangs out a lot with people who do. Publications where her work has appeared include *Asimov's, Doorways, Mythic Delirium, Strange Horizons, Weird Tales,* and a bunch of regular literary journals that should have known better. She attended Viable Paradise in 2008 and is the author of three chapbooks: *Constellation of the Dragonfly* (Plan B Press, 2008), *Aqua Regia* (Parallel Press, 2007), and *Sauce Robert* (Pavement Saw Press, 2003).

It all started when I was sent to bed
without supper. I was playing with my flashlight
under the covers and tried shining it in my mouth.
Light flooded my throat like golden syrup.

Soon I was tasting light everywhere,
the icy bitterness of fluorescents, a burst
of intensely spiced flavors from an arc welder,
the dripping red meat of sunsets.

Natural light was most easily digestible,
but at night I was limited to the sparse glow
of fireflies and phosphorescent rotting logs,

and inevitably succumbed to the artificial flavors
of a strip mall's jittering neon rainbow.

Sodium lamps always had a nasty, putrid aftertaste,
like rotting oranges, which is why I so frequently
vomited in nighttime parking garages,
but mercury-vapor emissions foamed on my tongue,
aromatic, green. Have you ever had key lime mousse,
or lemon-mint custard? It's nothing like that at *all*.

Each Hallowe'en I followed trick-or-treaters
from door to door, gorging myself
on jack-o'-lanterns' sweet candlelight.
Autumn bonfires burnt my lips
with the pungent heat of five-alarm chili,
smoky with the ghost of molé sauce. I hid
strings of holiday lights in my underwear drawer,
in case of a sudden craving.

On a high school field trip to a nuclear facility,
I was finally overcome with an insatiable hunger
for the indigo twilight of a reactor pool, glowing
with the underwater gradient of Cherenkov radiation,
a blue light luscious as chocolate, hypnotic as a liqueur,
decadent as dissolved gemstones.

I am no terrorist—merely an addict.

THE SEVEN DEVILS
OF CENTRAL CALIFORNIA

CATHERYNNE M. VALENTE

Born in the Pacific Northwest in 1979, Catherynne M. Valente is the author of *Palimpsest* and the *Orphan's Tales* series, as well as *The Labyrinth*, *Yume no Hon: The Book of Dreams, The Grass-Cutting Sword*, and five books of poetry. She is a winner of the Tiptree Award, the Mytho-poeic Award, the Rhysling Award, and the Million Writers Award and has been nominated for the Pushcart Prize, short-listed for the Spectrum Award and was a World Fantasy Award finalist in 2007. She currently lives on an island off the coast of Maine with her partner and two dogs.

I. THE DEVIL OF DIVERTED RIVERS

Put out your tongue:
I taste of salt. Salt and sage
and silt—
dry am I, dry as delving.

My fingers come up
through the dead sacrament-dirt;
my spine humps along the San Joaquin—
remember me here, where water was
before Los Angeles scowled through,
hills blasted black
by the electric hairs of my forearms.

319

Pull the skin from my back and there is gold there,
a second skeleton,
carapace smeared to glitter in the skull-white sun.
There is a girl sitting there,
between the nugget-vertebrae,
who came all the way from Boston
when her daddy hollered Archimedes' old refrain—
Eureka, baby, eureka, little lamb,
I'll have you a golden horse
and a golden brother
and golden ribbons for your golden hair,
just you pack up your mama and come on over Colorado,
not so far, not so.

They flooded out her daddy's valley
when she was seventeen
and skinny as a fork.
Crouched down she was,
rooting potatoes out of the ground,
brushing beetles from her apron,
and the wind sounded like an old Boston train.

I am waiting for you to stop in your thrum,
for you to pause and look towards Nevada:
I am holding back the waters
with the blue muscles of my calves,
waiting for you.

All the way down to the sea,
one of these mornings bright as windows,
I'll come running like a girl
chasing golden apples.

I deny you, says the city below.
I deny you, says the dry riverbed, full of bones.
I deny you, say the mute, fed fields far off from the sea.

II. THE DEVIL OF IMPORTED BRIDES

Look here: my fingernails show through
the lace and dried orange blossoms of a dress
I never wore.

You can see them up on the ridgeline like a fence
severed by earthquake:
yellow and ridged, screw-spiraled, broken,
brown moons muddy and dim.

The roots of the Sierras are blue and white:
the colors of stamped letters, posted,
flapping over the desert like rag-winged vultures,
gluey nose pointed east. All around the peaks
the clack of telegraphs echo
like woodpeckers:

Would like a blonde, but not particular.
Must be Norwegian or Swede, no Germans.
Intact Irish wanted,
must cook better than the ranch-hands.
Don't care if she's ugly enough
to scare the chickens
out of their feathers,
but if she ain't brood-ready,
she goes right back to Connecticut
or the second circle of hell
or wherever it is
spit her out.

Look here: my horns spike up sulfurous through
a veil like mist on the fence-posts. My tail rips the lace;
thumps black on the floor of an empty silver mine.
Never was a canary in the dark

with a yellow like my eyes. Sitting
in the cat-slit pupil with her bill of sale
stuffed in her mouth—

Why, hullo, Molly! Doesn't your hair look nice!
If you glisten it up enough
he'll be sure to love you real and true,
not for the silver nuggets you pull out of the rock
like balls from the Christmas box,
not for the crease-eyed boys he pulls from you
like silver nuggets, but for the mole on your little calf,
and the last lingering tilt to your voice,
that remembers Galway.

It was the seventh babe killed her,
and I sat up in her bloody bed,
orange blossoms dead on the pillow,
the clacking of brass-knockered codes
so loud in my ears
I flew down to the mine,
deeper than delving,
just for silence.

It is cold down here,
what silver is left
gnarls and jangles.
I put my hands up through the mountains
like old gloves with their fingers torn,
and wait.

I deny you, says the father of seven, bundled against the stove.
I deny you, says the silver, hanging in the earth
like a great chandelier.
I deny you, say the mountain towns, minding their own.

III. THE DEVIL OF FRUIT PICKERS

Strawberries and nickels
and the sun high as God's hat.
My old callused feet stamp down
the green vines and leaves of Fresno,
my throat of bone whistling still
for water.

My wings are tangled in grapevine
and orange-bark,
pearwood and raw almonds,
green skin prickles my shoulder blades,
lime-flesh and rice-reeds,
soybean pods and oh,
the dead-leaved corn. I can hardly fly
these days.

But I burrow, and stamp,
and how the radishes go up in my path.

Between the wings rides Maria,
born in Guadalajara with strong flat feet,
fishy little mouth scooped clean
by her father with fingers like St. Stephen.
This was before the war, of course.
Her black hair flies coarse as broom-bramble,
bags of oranges belted at her waist,
singing while I dance, riding me like her own
sweat-flanked horse.

She saved her nickels, and picked her berries,
bent over,
bent over,

bent over in the fields till her back was bowed
into the shape of an apple-sack,
and nothing in her but white seeds and sunburn.
She curled up into me,
dry as an old peapod,
and how we ride now,
biding our time,
over the dust and cows,
over all her nickels in a neat bank-row.

Watch our furrows, how we draw them,
careful as surveyors,
careful as corn-rows.

I deny you, say the strawberries, tucked tight into green.
I deny you, say the irrigation ditches, glimmering gold.
I deny you, say the nickels, spent into air.

IV. THE DEVIL OF GOLD FLAKE

My hair runs underneath the rivers,
gold peeling from my scalp. I remember
the taste of a thousand rusted pans
pulling out ore like fingernails at the quick.

I lie everywhere;
I point at the sea.

All along my torso are broken mines,
like buttons on a dress. The state built
a highway through them,
a gray rod to straighten my back. The driller-shacks
shudder dusty and brown,
slung with wind-axes and bone-bowls:
my stomach dreams of the ghosts of gold.

They suck at my skin,
hoping for a last gurgle of metal,
tipping in for the final bracelet and brick—
there must be something left in me,
there must be something—why do I not give it to them,
selfish creature, wretched mossy beast?

Underneath the deepest drill
hunches Annabella, the miner's wife,
who sifted more gold
than her coarse-coated man,
so deft and delicate were her fingers
round that old, beaten pan. He brought her
from St. Louis, already pregnant—and manners
make no comment there—already heavy with gold.
She smelled of the Mississippi
and steam-fat oatmeal cakes,
even after the oxen died, and with blood in her hair,
she crossed half of Wyoming on foot.

But the boulders loved her,
watched her every day from a high blue perch.
They wriggled at her, her yellow dress
gone brown with creek-silt, her bustle
and wire hoops collapsed on the grass.
While she knelt with gold in her knuckles,
they snapped to attention,
slid laughing to the creek-bed—she doesn't blame
the poor things, even now.
Her babies left cabbages and peppermints
at the creek for years after.

I felt the highway roll smooth and hot
over my ox-drenched head,
and the only gold I allowed to ooze up from my scalp

were the broken dashes marking lanes
like borders on an old map
showing a river like a great hand flattening the page.

But I confess:
I am an old wretched beast, and my tail,
waiting in the spangled dust,
is made of quartz-shot boulders
clapped in moss.

I deny you, say the desiccated lodes.
I deny you, say our great-grandchildren, with such clean hands.
I deny you, says the highway, blithe and black.

V. THE DEVIL OF MINE CANARIES

Watch the sun peek out over the Siskiyous
with their lavish snow like ladies' bonnets—
see my feathers, how bright, how brave!
I open my wings over the thin green
boyish arms of the Russian River,
yellow as sulphur, yellow as gas,
wide as any Italian angel.

What is a devil
but death and wind?
I come golden as a mineshaft,
and how black, how ever black,
come my eyes!

Who remembers where they got the songbirds?
Bought from Mexico, from Baja with shores
like sighs? They got the cages
out of their wives' bustles, wrangled

to hand and wing. *Pretty bird, pretty bird!*
Don't be afraid of the dark.

Yella-Girl loved her miner, thought
her black demon,
white eyes showing clam-shy through the dust,
was the greatest raven born since Eden.
She pecked corn-meal from his palm,
stood guard at his bedknob,
little golden sentinel. She'd draw the gold
for him, she thought, like to like.

For birds, the angry gases
have a strange color:
pink, almost pretty (Pretty bird, pretty bird!)
curling up from the dark like beckoning.
Yella-Girl seized up in midstroke,
falling onto a carpet of jaundiced feathers
half a leg deep. She fell thinking
of her miner, of corn in his black hand,
and I stood up
out of the canary-grave,
body crawling with pretty, pretty birds,
beaks turned out
like knives.

I deny you, says the buried mine, long stopped up.
I deny you, say the crows, too big to tame.
I deny you, says the miner, a new bird swinging at his side like a
    lunchbox.

VI. THE DEVIL OF ACORN MASH

I am hard to see.
You will have to look carefully.

Carefully down,
at your well-shod feet
to see the shallows in the rock,
where she and her son,
light beating their black hair like blankets,
worked rough-husked black oak acorns
into mash and meal,
bread and pancakes.
Like horse-hooves driven into
the granite, the hollows still breathe.

These are my footprints.
I have already passed this way
and gone.

I deny you, says the forest, full again.
I deny you, say endless feet.
I deny you, says the treeless plain, flat and brown.

VII. THE DEVIL OF THE RAILROAD

If I just try, I can taste bitter tang
of the golden tie bent over my toe
somewhere in Kansas,
like the memory of licking clean a copper plate.

But here at my head,
between the Santa Lucias and two crescent bays,
ribboned and raw-boned, bonneted in iron,
coal-shod and steam-breathed, I taste
corn-freight and cattle, pallets of tomatoes
and stainless steel screwdrivers, and there, behind my
    tongue,
the phosphorescent traces

of silver forks and weak tea shaking on linen,
burning the air where they no longer
drink themselves down to calm nerves like baling wire,
to spear Pacific salmon before the conductor ever sighted
     blue.

Out of the slat-cars come thousands of horns,
honest black and brown,
bull-thick, tossing in the heat.

In the slick, wet turn of my silver-steel against the rail
Li-Qin sings a little song, full of round golden vowels.
She wore gray shapeless things, hammering ties,
taking her tooth-shattering turn at the drill,
laying rail with bloody, sun-smashed hands
while the pin against wood sounded her name over and
     over
like a command to attention:
Li-*Qin*, Li-*Qin*, Li-*Qin*!
She had tea from thrice-used bags
and a half bowl of rice at the end of the day,
one grain of sugar dissolving in her cup
like snow.

With her hair bound back she plied the drill
until it slipped like splashed water,
hammered into her heart,
laying track for the train to bellow through her,
blood red as cinnabar on the wooden stays.

There is a car swinging back and forth
between a shipment of umbrellas to San Francisco
and swordfish packed in ice for Santa Barbara.
I have such a tail, you know, enough to bring them all

from the mountains and the sea.
With silver forks and weak tea
they sit at a long table with a cloth of cobwebs,
clinking their cups as I rattle them through the desert:

a Boston goblin with drowned lips violet,
a bridal imp, her veil torn and burning,
a gnomish grandmother,
sucking tea through slices of strawberries,
an old, wretched, bustleless beast, smug as a river,
a yellow bird, brimstone-wings folded around
a little urchin in deerskin, her hands full of acorns,
and a demon in gray with a huge flayed heart
hanging in her breast like a pendant.

I brought them on my tail,
my endless black tail,
like a dragon out of books older than any of us,
I brought them like freight,
like wagons,
like horses,

and we are coming to dance on the shore
by the great golden bridge,
we are coming to remember ourselves
to the tide,
to sing at the moon until it cracks,
to stamp our hooves under so many crinoline
    dresses,
to stamp our hooves under so many rags,
to stamp our hooves on the earth like pickaxes,
and sunder California along every wrinkle,
send her gleaming
into the sea.

I deny you, shudders the sky, whole and inviolate.
I deny you, whispers the unwilling sea.
I deny you, trembles the fault line.

The sun dips deep into salt and foam,
and a long engine-whistle
breaks the blue
into seven pieces.

THE ANDRE NORTON AWARD

First presented in 2006, the Norton Award, chosen by a vote of SFWA members, is given yearly to outstanding works of science fiction and fantasy intended for young adults. Its name honors the late Andre Norton, a SFWA Grand Master who influenced generations of young readers and writers. While not part of the Nebula Award voting, it is given each year at the Nebula Awards banquet. This year's winner, Ysabeau Wilce, began writing in 2007. The complete name for her award-winning novel is *Flora's Dare: How a Girl of Spirit Gambles All to Expand Her Vocabulary, Confront a Bouncing Boy Terror, and Try to Save Califa from a Shaky Doom (Despite Being Confined to Her Room)*

FLORA'S DARE

YSABEAU S. WILCE

Flora Fyrdraaca wants nothing more than to become a ranger, but first she must master the magickal—and dangerous—language of Gramatica. In her search to find a teacher, Flora discovers that Firemonkey, a notorious magician, and someone who owes her a favor, is playing with his band at the Poodle Dog. She persuades her best friend Udo to accompany her to the show. Her plan: confront Firemonkey and ask him to cancel his debt by taking her as his student. But Flora and Udo turn out not to be the only ones at the Poodle Dog on serious magickal business. They'll be lucky if they get out of the Poodle Dog alive—and home before their curfew.

THREE
UDO'S BANK ACCOUNT.
SOLD OUT. UDO DROOLS.

Mamma had to return to the Presidio for an evening inspection, so she dropped me off at Case Tigger on her way. This ride lessened my lateness a bit and saved me the horsecar fare. At Case Tigger I ran the gauntlet of parents (one mamma, two daddies), siblings (six—all absolute horrors), and various pets before finding Udo in the loo, primping.

Udo is sickeningly good-looking: his jaw perfectly square, his hair perfectly gold, and his eyes perfectly blue. He is also sickeningly vain and spends much of his time trying to improve upon perfection. I pried him away from his mirror, where he was taking forever to decide between red lip rouge or blue, and if his hair looked better on the top of his head in the shape of a rolled doughnut, or braided into five plaits and dangling free. After I told him that the red lip rouge made his face look too thin and the doughnut hairstyle made his face look fat, he quickly decided on braids and blue and we were able to make our exit.

We caught the N horsecar just as it was pulling up, and managed to get the last two seats. Udo fished a silver case out of his greatcoat and lit up a foul clove cigarillo.

"Don't you think you have enough nasty habits, Udo?" I waved my hand ineffectually through the blue smoke. "You'll ruin your lungs."

"Ha," he said. "Ayah, but I can blow a smoke ring."

"That'll be some consolation when you die of black lung," I said. "We'll put that on your memorial stone: Ayah, but he could blow a smoke ring."

"You are an old crab, Flora." Udo added insult to injury with a nip from his flask—another bad habit I did not intend to acquire. "And you get precious little fun out of life."

"I'd get even less if Poppy had his way. I have to be back by midnight," I said morosely. "Can you believe it? On the first night of vacation."

Udo hooted. "Midnight! That's outrageous. The Horses of Instruction won't even have gone on by then, probably. You're going to miss the show."

"*We're* going to miss the show."

"*I* don't have a curfew."

"If you plan on coming back to Crackpot with me, then you're on the same curfew I am."

"The whole point of going home with you, Flora, is, that way, the Daddies don't know what time I get home. If you've got a curfew, then that defeats the whole purpose."

"Sorry," I said, not in the least bit sorry. Before I could tell Udo about my plan to approach Firemonkey, he started up on his favorite topic.

"Look, Flora, I've been thinking about the Letter of Marque."

Oh no! Here we went again. Udo's pirate ambitions had not abated, not even after the Dainty Pirate incident. If anything, they'd grown even stronger, and now he was even more obsessed about obtaining a Letter of Marque. A Letter of Marque is a document issued by the Warlord authorizing the bearer to seize and confiscate property. It makes piracy legal, as long as you are willing to give the Warlord a cut of your prize.

If the Dainty Pirate had had a Letter of Marque, Mamma would not have been able to sentence him to hang. And of course since Udo didn't want to end up dangling from a rope, he was determined to get a Letter of Marque, but they cost a lot of money. Udo is cheap and pinches every diva until it squeaks, but he was still a long way away from the purchase price. And all his money-making ideas were harebrained and ignored the most obvious solution: Get a job. I was sick of the subject, and anyway, I had other things to worry about, like Firemonkey.

"Can't you leave it alone for one night, Udo?"

"Ha! The Fyrdraacas are one of the most wealthy families in the City. Easy for you to say to forget all about money."

"Maybe so, but I'm not the Heir to my House, so I get zippo, zilch, nada, nothing. Idden gets all the swag and the House, and I'm a pauper."

Udo waved dismissively. "You've got your allowance from Buck, but I must make my way through life on my wits, and ships don't grow on trees. Neither do Letters of Marque. Do you have any idea how much one costs?"

The exact amount was seared on my brain by Udo's constant whining. "A hundred and fifty thousand divas. But the Warlord doesn't issue Letters of Marque anymore. The Dainty Pirate didn't have one."

"Only because he refused to recognize the Warlord's authority, not because the Warlord wouldn't give him one. If Florian sees enough of my gold, he'll write me one up, I promise. That's why I need cash!"

"You could get a job, Udo."

Udo rolled his eyes dismissively. "I have a better idea." He took off his hat and fished a crumpled piece of paper out of its crown. I knew what was coming: another crazy scheme. Earlier crazy schemes: chicken-farming in Case Tigger's backyard (nixed by city zoning), organizing the siblings into a street-sweeping brigade (nixed by the Daddies), renting his little brother Gesilher out for medical experiments (nixed by Gesilher's demand for 20 percent). Now what?

Udo continued. "Look, I have a cunning idea of how to get some cash, and it'll be easy, too. I happened to be walking by the post office on the way home this afternoon, and look what I noticed on the wall!"

I smoothed the crumples out of the paper and angled it toward the overhead light. "'Dead or alive,'" I read. "'Ringtail Peg, the Masher Queen. Wanted for grand larceny, gambling, fixing, mashing, arson, and murder. Five thousand divas in gold payable upon delivery of prisoner or corpse. By command of the Attorney General of Califa, under the Warlord's Sigil and Sign.'"

"See?" Udo waved more papers. "There are tons of them. Droolie Bee, wanted for larceny, fifteen hundred divas in gold. Firefly Andrews, tax evasion, two thousand divas in gold. Springheel Jack, fifty thousand divas in gold. It would be easy money! Just like taking candy from a baby. We'd be rich and we'd be doing the City a favor. What? Why are you giving me that evil eye?"

"You want to take up bounty hunting?" I said. "You have got to be kidding me!"

"Think on it! Five thousand divas in gold. And keep your voice down—I don't want anyone to steal my idea."

"Udo, you don't like to get your hands dirty and now you are suggesting that we go out and track down criminals and bring them in? How are we going to do that?"

"Well, I figure we'd need some capital, but I'm willing to put out a little to get a little back. We go South of the Slot and—"

"And get ourselves robbed. Remember what happened last time we went South of the Slot? We were jacked by a ten-year-old kid!"

Udo ignored my cold hard truth. "And check out some of those dives."

"Remember the last dive we checked out? Pete's Clown Diner? We got caught in a riot!"

Again, with the ignoring: "Grease a few palms—"

"We'll be killed, or worse."

Udo said huffily, "Would you let me finish! Grease a few palms and then track them down, tie them up, and bring them in. It will be easy. I mean, they don't even have to be alive, so if they give us any trouble, we just peg 'em and we still get the cash. And even though it was my idea, Flora, I'll be happy to cut you in for 10 percent."

"Oh how kind," I said sarcastically. "Ten percent of being robbed, killed, or worse. You are so generous."

"It's a good idea, Flora. Didn't Nini Mo go into bounty hunting for a while?"

"Ayah, but she was Nini Mo, the Coyote Queen. She had her reputation behind her. They just took one look at her and folded. I don't think the people you have mentioned are going to let you walk right up, introduce yourself, and say, 'Oh by the way, I'm taking you in, dead or alive; would you please come with me.'"

Udo said, exasperated, "Well, of course they will not. I'm not an idiot, Flora. I thought of that, too. See?" This time he fished in the inner pocket of his greatcoat, then displayed a small red enamel case. "This is going to make all the difference in the world."

"It's a compact. Are you going to powder their noses if they refuse to come with you?"

"Well, in a manner of speaking, yes, I am. This is no ordinary powder—no, don't open it! If you spill it, we'll be in super-big trouble. It's Sonoran Zombie Powder. One whiff of this stuff and you are no more willful than a piece of cheese. They use it in Huitzil to control sacrifices and wanton wives. Makes the most obnoxious hellion as smooth and easy as glass."

"Where'd you get it?" I took the compact from him and inspected it more closely. The red enamel top was embossed with a sigil shaped like a spiky wheel, and the clasp was cunningly fashioned like two hands holding each other at the wrist. The label pasted on the bottom read: MADAMA TWANKY'S SONORAN ZOMBIE POWDER.

"Oh, I have my sources," Udo said mysteriously.

"You got it from an advertisement in the back of the *Califa Police Gazette,* didn't you? Those adverts are all cheats, Udo. Remember when you ordered that lotion that was supposed to turn your skin the color of bronze, and it turned you green instead? You've wasted your money."

"Ha! Fool me once, shame on you; fool me twice, shame on you. Do you think I'm a baby, new-dipped in milk? Of course, I tested it out already, and it worked perfectly. On the way home from Sanctuary, I stopped at the Park and zombified a duck. It followed me right home and we ate it for dinner."

"Udo!" That poor duck. Before I could ask him how he could be so mean, the horsecar jolted to a halt.

"Back door! Back door!" Udo pounded on the handrail. The door popped open and we scrambled out into the drizzly night.

The street in front of the Poodle Dog was packed with people; I'd had no idea that the Horses of Instruction were so popular. It looked like every wolfgirl, b-boy, gawker, masher, glitterette, and gothick in Califa were loitering outside the Poodle

Dog, hoping to throw themselves at the band's feet. A knot of City militia stood to one side, watching the crowd suspiciously.

I grabbed at Udo's sleeve, trying to keep up with his push through the crowd. "Did you get tickets already?"

"We'll get them at the door!"

"I thought you said you were going to get tickets!" My heart sank. If we didn't have tickets already, we were out of luck.

"There's a line!" a b-boy protested as Udo tried to push his way past. "And the end of it is back there."

A chorus of angry voices joined the b-boy's protests, and in the face of clear-cut menace, we fell back to find the end of the line. When we finally found it, my heart sank further. It was two blocks away from the club and there was no way we were going to get in.

"Pigface Psychopomp," Udo swore. "I never thought the show would be this packed."

"What are we going to do now?" I demanded. "My whole evening is blown, Udo."

"We'll go around back and see if we can get in that way. After all, we know Firemonkey. We ought to be able to get through the Bruisers that way."

Udo's suggestion seemed like a long shot, but it was our only shot, and it would get me closer to Firemonkey, anyway. We tried to make our way to the alley that led to the backstage entrance; the throng was thick. We were pushy, but it was still hard going, and at the rate of our progress, we weren't going to get around back before my curfew was up. Blast Udo!

Then, before us, a Chickie materialized out of the crowd like cold air bursts out of an icebox. The crowd fell back for her and she pointed a gloved finger at Udo. "Come with me."

In the fluttering streetlights, the Chickie looked like congealed darkness: hair black as coal, eyes black as coal, lips black as coal. Her skin was corpse white, and just in case the moonlight was too strong for her fragile coloring, she was sheltering under a large black parasol. A gloom of Boy Toys stood behind her, each dressed somberly in black sack-suits, black ties, black shirts, and each with some variation of a bored snarl on his face.

"Me?" Udo croaked.

"Ayah, you," the Chickie said impatiently. "Come on. The show's about to start."

Udo stood mesmerized, staring slack-jawed at the Chickie, though whether he was drooling over the Chickie herself or her fabulous leather trenchcoat with the huge ruffy black wolf fur collar was unclear. She turned and the crowd continued to melt out of her way, as ice melts before salt, and Udo, hypnotized, followed. Well, I wasn't going to wait outside—alone—nor was I going to let Udo go forward—alone—so I, too, sailed, falling in behind the Boy Toys, who didn't even give me a glance.

Past the rest of the line we went, and not a quibble came from the queue. The Chickie's powers to strike dumb were not confined to Udo. The doorman said not a word as we approached, just unclipped the red velvet rope and waved us in.

FOUR
THE POODLE DOG. A BRUISER.
A DISGUSTING POTTY.

Inside, the Poodle Dog was a mob scene: wall-to-wall, floor-to-ceiling hipsters, packed tighter than pickles in a jar. The air was heavy with the smell of Madama Twanky's Bear Oil hair pomade and a gauzy haze of cigarillo smoke. Outside, the night had been chilly; inside, it was so hot that I immediately regretted wearing my redingote. Not two steps and I was bathed in sweat.

The Inside Mob parted for the Chickie, just as the Outside Mob had, with Udo, the Boy Toys, and me coasting along in her wake. Up the stone staircase we marched, to where it widened into a landing and split into two sweeping curves. Then around the right-hand curve and out onto the dance floor.

The Poodle Dog's grand hall is designed to look like the courtyard of a small village. Fake stucco covers the walls, creating a facade of small stone houses, each with doors that don't open and windows that look into darkness. High above, fake rooftops support the balcony. Higher above, the rounded ceiling is painted a vivid nighttime blue, pricked with ignis stars, and swirling with lights that simulate clouds. A huge red velvet tent takes up the far end of the hall; when the show starts, the front of the tent rises, revealing the stage behind.

Ahead, the Chickie, Udo, and the Boy Toys were swallowed whole by the crowd, and I was abandoned. I had meant to enlist Udo's help in getting to Firemonkey, but clearly he now had no time for me. Well, let them go. I would have more success without Udo hanging on my neck, anyway.

One of the many annoyances of shortness is that you are invariably crushed in a crowd. And you can't see anything. And people spill their drinks on you and ash their cigarettes in your hair. It seemed as though everyone at the club was taller than me. Thus, my view was mostly of people's chests, even when I hopped. But even if I had been in the front row, once the show started I still would not have been able to see the stage because Weatherhead, the opening act, is notorious for their pyrotechnics. Their music is great, but best not to stand too close or you might find yourself on fire.

In anticipation of a crowd, I had left my spurs on; it's amazing how a few good jabs will get people out of your way. By this action, I was able to make my way through the throng. One small benefit of being short is that you can slide out of the way before people realize it was you who just put a rent in their red velvet knickers. *Hurry, before they notice,* said Nini Mo.

In front of the stage, a mosh pit had already formed. Bully-boys in lacy black kilts and wolfgirls with electric-blue hair were kicking and shoving and flinging themselves against each other, smacking heads and fists—this despite the only music being the dull roar of anticipatory chatter. In the flickering footlights, the red gape of the still-curtained proscenium arch looked very much like a hungrily gaping mouth.

I skirted the mosh pit and kicked my way toward a small wooden door set in one of the towers that flanked the stage. Halfway there, I saw a flash of moldering green and, by bouncing up on my tippy-toes and craning my neck, spotted the back of a familiar tricorn hat: Firemonkey. Behind him filed a chubby man in a gauzy white robe, carrying two drumsticks, and a tall figure in a wide-brimmed hat, pulled low, and a black leather duster, with a banjo slung over one shoulder.

I put some muscle into my push, adding elbow to spurs, but the crowd had thickened and I couldn't seem to catch up to him—Firemonkey was always just out of reach. And then suddenly my way was barred by a wide expanse of purple-and-yellow-checked weskit, a noxious color combination that no doubt would have had Udo salivating.

"Where are you going, girlie?" A huge round face floated above the floppy black tie that emerged from the weskit: a Bruiser set to guard backstage access. I pretended I didn't hear and tried to dodge around him, but I was blocked on one side by a sweaty bully-boy and on the other by a rum-bubbler, so the only way in was through the Bruiser, who was as solid as a brick wall.

"You got a backstage pass?" the Bruiser growled, and though he didn't raise his voice, I could hear him easily. There was something strange about his face. It seemed oddly flat and one-dimensional, as though it was a flesh-colored mask. His lips moved stiffly, and his eyes were two points of emptiness sunk into hollow sockets.

"A what?" I pretended ignorance. The longer I stared up at the Bruiser, the more papery flat his face seemed, and I realized why: He wore a Glamour. I blinked, and for a brief flashy second saw what was behind the Glamour. Small tusks punctuated a large flappy mouth, and tiny pink eyes glared under tufty mouselike eyebrows. I recognized him from the Entity Spotter appendix in the back of *The Eschata*: an obstructionist dæmon; extremely bad juice and almost impossible to get through. If Firemonkey had brought him in for muscle, he really did not want to be disturbed.

The Bruiser growled, "Backstage. You ain't allowed backstage if you ain't got a backstage pass. You got no pass, you skedaddle."

"Look, I have to speak to Firemonkey. It's important. You are impeding my way." I tried bluster and made to push by, but he was as solid as a rock. "Let me pass."

"Firemonkey don't talk to no one before the show. They all wanna talk to him. He gotta have quiet to banish and invoke. He don't talk to no one."

If blustering fails, said Nini Mo, *try flustering.* I remembered also from the Entity Spotter that flattery was an obstructionist dæmon's weakness.

I looked up at the Bruiser through fluttering eyelashes. "Oh sieur, I do so adore your weskit. It's supercool. Where did you get it?"

The Bruiser looked down at himself, and a tiny smile floated over his pudgy lips. He tucked bananalike thumbs into the edges of the weskit and preened. "I designed it myself. And made it, too." He was puffing up, literally. If I slitted my eyes, I could see through the Glamour, see his head actually inflating like a balloon. His forehead distended upward, and his eyes began to bug out like little red marbles. Yuck.

"You are so clever," I wheedled, thinking, *I can't believe I sound so soppy.* But it was working. "Do you design professionally?"

"I gotta shop down in LoHa; make suits, too. Fine tailoring, no fusing for me, all hand-stitched. I give you me card, you come down, lolly, and I make you over, better than that slop jacket you got on." The Bruiser fished in the pocket of the awful weskit and pulled out a damp piece of cardboard, which I had no choice but to take. "I make you pretty."

"Thank you, sieur, but please . . ." I grinned sweetly at him and turned the flutter up to hurricane level.

The Bruiser hesitated. I almost had him; I could feel it. He was going to let me through. Then, just as he was about, I was sure, to give in to my sweet flattery, there was a roaring cheer, and the club plunged into darkness. Red and white sparks arced into the air, and a drum pounded like thunder. In the spitting, sparking light, I saw that the Bruiser was gone, and the stage-access door firmly closed.

Pigface Psychopomp, I had been so close!

Well, there was still the outside backstage door. Firemonkey had to leave the club somehow, at some time, right? And maybe I would have better luck with the Bruiser stationed there, or maybe the door was left unguarded and was merely locked. Without an audience, I was confident that I could pop the lock pretty quickly. Lock-picking is an elementary skill I mastered when I was just a tot.

I pushed through the crowd, which was now bouncing up and down to the heartbeat rhythm of Weatherhead's music. The drone was so loud, it made my ears ring, vibrated my legs, and made the back of my throat hum and buzz. Spicy black fog rolled down off the stage, parting long enough to give a quick glance at a yellow mackintosh spastically jerking across the stage. Something wet and spongy hit my head, bounced off my shoulder; my hand came away wet and red, smelling of liver. Weatherhead were throwing organ meat.

I had just washed my hair that morning; time to take cover. And I had to potty. Better get that done before I started on lock-picking. I kicked my way down the stairs toward the pisser, looking out hopefully for Udo, but not seeing him anywhere.

The pisser was full of jostling girls trying to adjust cleavage and maquillage in front of a cracked wall mirror. After the darkness of the club, the bright gaslights made my eyes water. In the mirror, my reflection was raccoon-eyed with smudged black eyeliner. My hair looked like I had been hit by a bolt of lightning; it stuck straight out from my head in a frizzy red halo. I wetted my hands and tried to smooth it back down, though I knew that would only make the frizz worse.

A wolfgirl exited a stall and I nipped in before the door slammed shut behind her. The walls of the stall were scrawled with graffiti, and what wasn't illegible was obscene enough that I wished it *were* illegible. The floor was slick—I hoped it was water, but maybe it wasn't. Greenish water gurgled in the toilet, which was missing its seat. Even before Poppy started cleaning, the potty at Crackpot had never been half this bad. Our outside bog, which we have to resort to if the inside pipes get plugged, is dark and spidery and the seat has splinters, but it is never this horrible. But I really had to go. *Don't stand on ceremony when you gotta squat,* said Nini Mo.

I tucked my kilts up as high as I could and was glad that I had remembered my hankie; of course there was no potty paper. I was about to cautiously squat, when there was a loud gurgle behind me and a splash of cold wetness on my hinder. I jerked up and around. The water in the toilet was bubbling, and these bubbles were popping into an awful smell. I buried my nose in the crook of my arm, trying to drown out the stench with the smell of lavender laundry soap.

"Hey!" The stall door behind me thumped. "I gotta go! Hurry up!"

Nasty water began to rise up and over the toilet's rim, and I danced back. Something was starting to slither up out of the water. This something was shaped like a long wiggly parsnip: a pallid white tentacle. Long and pointy, its tip was covered with suckers, just like the little squiddies that Mamma loves so much, marinated in soy sauce and grilled. Only this tentacle was much, much bigger. Bigger around than my arm, in fact, with suckers as large as tea cakes.

"I GOTTA GO!" The door banged again. The tentacle wiggled in the air, bending this way and that, as though it was searching for something. I stood like a rock, motionless, hoping that the tentacle wouldn't notice me. I couldn't open the stall door without moving toward the tentacle, and this seemed like a very bad idea. It paused for a second; I held my breath. The tip pulsated bright red, and the rest of it blushed a deep pink; and then, with a lashlike motion, the tentacle snapped toward me.

I jerked back, banging against the stall door—not far enough. The tentacle had grabbed a wad of my kilt. I twisted and turned, trying to get free without ripping my kilt too badly, but the tentacle had a hard grip.

I grabbed my kilt hem and yanked. The fabric tore and I was free. I pressed against the door and tried to flatten myself down as though I were a piece of paper. The tentacle jabbed in my direction, but it seemed to be at the end of its reach, and I was now out of range. Out of range, but trapped.

Carry the important stuff on you, Nini Mo said, and there are few things more important than fire. I fumbled in the inside pocket of my redingote and found the trigger case I had *borrowed* from Poppy (who didn't need his smoking encouraged with easy access to matches). The tentacle was straining and stretching; it knew I was just out of reach, and was trying to close the gap. With fumbly fingers I managed to open the silver case, withdraw a match, and strike it against the wall. The triggers were supposed to strike anywhere. The match head sputtered and did not light.

"Pigface!" I swore, and shook out another trigger. My hands were shaking in a most unrangery way. I didn't look in the direction of the tentacle, but I knew by the sloshing sound that it was still there. I flicked the second match head with my finger; the trigger snapped and blossomed into a happy orange flame, small but hot.

I flicked this match onto the tentacle, which writhed and withdrew, but then shot forward like a striking rattlesnake and grabbed my waist, almost yanking me off my feet. I dug my heels in and grabbed onto the purse-ledge, but the metal shelf was slick and my hands slid right off it. The tentacle squeezed tightly; my lungs sucked together and for a moment the world went spotty black. Only the steel bones of my stays were keeping me from being snapped in two; putrid water sloshed over my toes. My knife was in my boot; I couldn't reach it.

Then I remembered the fan hanging at my waist, tucked into one of Mamma's old sabre slings. Paimon had given it to me as a part of my Catorcena outfit, and though it looked fragile and delicate, the tips of its ribs were razor sharp. Now I fumbled for it, wincing at the slimy slick warmth of the tentacle—luckily the fan case itself was hidden in the folds of my kilt. Gasping for breath, I managed to hook a finger into the ring at the end of the fan and pull hard. The fan flew up in the air, and I caught it, ripped it open with a flick of my wrist, and slashed it downward.

The razor barbs of the fan sliced the tentacle like it was butter. Spurting slime, the tentacle let go of my waist, wiggling and writhing. I slashed again. The tentacle slithered back toward the potty, and I pursued it, hacking at it. With a giant slurp it sucked back into the water and was gone.

The stall tilted up—I fell against the door heavily, banging hard against the purse-ledge. Plaster showered down, and outside the stall door, people began to squeal. The trembler stopped abruptly. I yanked the door and stumbled out, running into a pissy-looking dollymop.

"Took enough time! Pigface, what the hell were you doing in there? Contemplating infinity?" She started to push by me. "I almost peed my drawers."

"You'd better be careful," I said breathlessly. "Something grabbed me."

"What?" The girl paused.

"Something crawled out of the toilet and tried to grab me."

The girl peered into the stall, then said scornfully, "There's nothing in there, snapperhead. You've had too much jake."

I peered around her, and indeed there was no tentacle, no bubbly water, no slime. The toilet stood serenely in the middle of the stall. The floor wasn't even wet. The trigger case lay where I had dropped it, and I leaned over to scoop it up.

Had I imagined the whole thing? I held up the fan; glowing green slime dripped off the barbs.

I had not.

FIVE
FIREMONKEY INCITES.
A MOB SCENE. CRUSHED.

I staggered out of the pisser into a roar that practically propelled me backward. Most of this roar was music: the high-pitched, whiny grind of a hurdy-gurdy; the dull, headachy throb of a bass propelled by staccato drumming. But some of it was shouting, a persistent chant I couldn't understand. I recognized the tune, though: "Nonny O!," the Horses of Instruction's most popular song.

The tentacle had really unnerved me, and my desire to get far, far away from that toilet was really strong. All I wanted now was to go home. *Rangers don't retreat,* said Nini Mo, *but they know when to regroup.* The Horses of Instruction might just be starting, but I was done.

I fought my way through the noise, which was like trying to stand against a high wind, elbowing through the crowd, trying to find Udo, so together we could make our escape. The hall was dark, lit only by intermittent flashes, and when these split the gloom like bolts of lightning, I saw a hazy, gyrating mass of people, thickly packed. The figures were indistinct, shadowy, and none of them seemed to be Udo. Where had he gone, the snapperhead, just when I needed him most? I slid between a woman in a heavy leather jacket, well festooned with chains, and a bald man coated in silvery paint, and found myself at the stage.

Above my head, the stage lights flickered with a garish blue glow, illuminating Firemonkey, blackish-green hair straggling out from under a soggy tricorn, pumping at the handle of a hurdy-gurdy as though he were possessed. To his left, a cadaver flogged an upright bass; on his right, the duster twanged on a banjo that hung down around black leather knees. This close to the band, the noise made my ears ring and my stomach heave; Firemonkey must have invoked the biggest amplification dæmon ever to get such loudness. Forget Udo, I had to get out of the Poodle Dog before I puked. He'd have to make it home on his own. But before I could turn around and try to push my way to open air, the music stopped. The audience continued to chant. Suddenly I understood what they were shouting.

"*Azota! Azota! Azota!*"

The Butcher Brakespeare's nickname.

Firemonkey raised up his hand and, when the crowd quieted, cried, "She died so that we might live!"

At first I thought he meant the Goddess Califa, but when the crowd resumed its chanting, I realized he was referring to the Butcher. Firemonkey raised his hand again, and again waited a few seconds for the chanting to die down.

"But despite her sacrifice, we live like slaves! Should Florian not die so that we may live free? So that Azota shall not have sacrificed in vain?"

The crowd howled its agreement.

The queasy feeling in my stomach suddenly had nothing whatsoever to do with the music and everything to do with the fact that Firemonkey was preaching treason. I remembered the militia outside; nothing riles them faster than someone stirring up a crowd to sedition. I had no desire to end the night in the City Gaol; I would miss my curfew for sure, then. My urge to get out of the Poodle Dog became overwhelming. But despite my kicking and prodding, I was stuck. The people around me were staring raptly upward, immobile.

"*Cierra Califa!*" Firemonkey cried, and threw his arms wide. A huge curl of coldfire roiled out of his greatcoat. The coldfire flowed upward, twisting and turning until it formed an insignia that glowed in the darkness like a rope of fire: the sinuous twist of an azota, a riding whip, the source of the Butcher's nickname.

"Azota and Cierra Califa!" Firemonkey roared, and the crowd roared back while the band launched into "Califa Strong and Mighty." The crowd began to gyrate and bounce again in time to the music, their chanting frenzied. But then abruptly the overhead lights flipped on, and the coldfire insignia was suddenly invisible in the bright glare. The roars of excitement were pinpricked with screams.

"In the name of the Warlord, you are all under arrest!" someone shouted from the back of the hall. The crowd erupted into screaming and pushing. *The best place to be in a stampede,* said Nini Mo, *is not in a stampede.* But I was still stuck, pressed hard up against the stage. The crush was suffocating; I could barely breathe, and what air I was able to gasp was tainted with smoke and perfume. If I went down, I'd be trampled underfoot in no time, and there'd be nothing left of Flora but goo on the soles of a lot of supertrendy shoes.

Then an iron grip grabbed my shoulders and hauled me up over the edge of the stage. I stumbled upright, wheezing. The Horses of Instruction's banjo player had me by the arm and was now dragging me across the stage. Firemonkey and the cadaver had disappeared; the chubby drummer was still drumming, his head flinging back and forth like a pendulum, heedless of the pandemonium. The banjo player and I ran into the wings, past the amplification dæmon still caught in his protection circle. He snapped his crocodile-long jaws at us as we passed, but the charged circle held and his gnashing teeth snapped empty air.

Backstage was a melee of frantic roadies and screaming groupies. The banjo player was taller than me and used that height and bulk to clear a path. Shoving people out of our way, we ran down a corridor, and then flung ourselves through a doorway. I fell against a row of costumes, coughing and wheezing, my lungs burning. A bright girdle of pain now encircled my waist where the tentacle had squeezed me. I coughed until it felt as though my lungs had been torn into fragments, but when I was done, despite the pain, I felt better. At least I could breathe again. The banjo player had slammed the door shut behind us and now leaned against it, regarding me.

"You all right?"

"Ayah. Thanks for grabbing me."

"My pleasure, Tinks."

The banjo player pulled off the wide-brimmed hat. And there was my sister Idden, grinning at me, looking exactly the same as the last time I had seen her. Except that now she was as bald as an egg.

SIX
SURPRISE! REVOLUTIONARY FERVOR.
A HASTY EXIT.

I gaped at Idden like a greenhorn at her first sight of snow. Of all the questions that ran through my head—*What are you doing here? How did you get here? When did you learn to play the banjo?*—what came out of my mouth was, "What happened to your hair?" Idden has always looked a lot like Mamma: same blue eyes, same high cheekbones, same yellow hair. Even without hair, the resemblance was still strong.

Idden laughed, her gold lip-plug (also new) winking in the sputtering light. "I got tired of washing it. Cool, eh? Give me a hug, tiny sis."

We squeezed each other so tightly that the buttons of Idden's duster ground into me painfully. She smelled like cigarillo smoke and lemon verbena, and she felt thin and bony.

I asked, "What are you doing here? I thought you were at Fort Jones."

"I was, baby, but obviously I'm not anymore."

"Are you on leave?"

Idden laughed. "You could say that. Toothache-leave."

Toothache-leave—that's Army slang for deserting. I yanked out of Idden's embrace and stared at her. Idden had deserted? Never in the history of the Fyrdraaca family had anyone ever deserted! I could not imagine it. Deserted! And though enlisted soldiers desert sometimes, officers hardly ever. Enlisted soldiers have to serve out their term, but officers can resign at will and therefore have no reason to scrarper. I had never heard of an officer deserting.

Idden grinned. "Got nothing to say to that, Tinks?"

"Mamma is going to kill you!" I said, ignoring the provocative use of my despised kiddie nickname.

"She'll have to catch me first," Idden said, "and I'm guessing from your reaction that she doesn't even know."

"We all thought you were at Fort Jones. Poppy just got a letter from you. But, Idden, how could you desert? What were you thinking? They'll shoot you if they catch you."

"Let them try," Idden answered. "You don't look any taller, Tinks. I think you've stunted."

Again, I ignored the slur. That's one of Idden's tricks, to deflect you from topics she doesn't want to discuss—try to rile you with unflattering personal observations and stupid nicknames. I refused to be deflected.

"You never answered me."

Idden gave me a superior little smile that I knew only too well. "Because I'd had it, Flora. I've been pushed around long enough. I'm sick of Buck, sick of the Army."

"Why didn't you just resign? That would be better than running away."

She snorted. "Ha! Do you think for one minute that Mamma would let me resign? She'd never accept my resignation—I had to get out without her knowing. And anyway, I don't recognize the Warlord's authority anymore, so I consider my oath to him null. He's a Birdie puppet, Flora. Obeying him is like obeying the Virreina of Huitzil. He has got to go, and all his lackeys, too. Collaborators all, even Buck."

"Mamma is not a collaborator! She's just trying to keep Califa safe."

Idden looked scornful. "Safe for what? Safe for whom? Safe for the rich and the powerful? What about everyone else? Slaves—one and all. First slaves to the Warlord, who sold them to the Birdies, now slaves to them, too. Safety in slavery isn't worth having."

I'd never heard Idden this worked up about anything before. She'd always been mild as milk toast and done exactly as Mamma had said. Not only done it, but acted as though Mamma's Will was hers as well, that their desires were exactly the same. Maybe Idden had gone mad. Maybe she had Army Green Sickness—it happens to people who spend too much time in too isolated a post. They start imagining things, and become paranoid, and then nostalgic, and eventually have to be taken away to the Califa Asylum for the Unfortunate and Lost. Mamma could hardly be mad at Idden for being insane, could she?

Idden continued. "My duty to Califa is higher than my duty to the Birdies' puppet. I am loyal to Califa and those who died for her—like Azota Brakespeare!"

"But she was a murderer and a war criminal," I protested. "And she almost got Poppy killed."

Something flared in Idden's eyes and she pinched me hard. "Birdie lies! They made her out to be a criminal so they could get rid of her. I knew her, Flora, and she was nothing as they say. She loved Califa, and she died trying to keep Califa free. Mark me, Flora. Change is coming. The tree of liberty must be watered with the blood of tyrants."

"What does that mean?" I asked, almost afraid of the answer.

"It means, Flora, that there comes a time when we have to decide either to risk death for freedom, or to live as slaves. I have made my decision; that's why I joined Firemonkey's band. Califa must be free."

"But, Idden—"

The shouting and screaming outside had gotten louder, and

now people were pounding on the door, demanding to be let in. It did not seem a good idea to open the door, but the only other exit was a small window high on the back wall.

Idden cut me off. "Look, I don't have time to argue with you now. We have got to get out of here. The militia will be here any minute, and neither of us wants to end up in gaol. Come on."

"But we're trapped!"

"You'll see—come on." Idden unbuttoned her duster and drew her service revolver. "Fire in the hole, Tinks."

I covered my ears just in time; she fired twice, the shots echoing explosively. I ducked my head, barely avoiding a face full of flying debris, and when I looked back up, the small window gaped open, and my ears rang. The acrid smell of black powder was choking.

"Ayah, Tinks, this is where you get off. But first, Flora, swear you will not tell Buck that you saw me."

I saw the grab coming and tried to dodge, but Idden was quick, and she's much taller than me. Despite my kicks, Idden got me into a headlock from which I could do nothing but spit ineffectually.

"Swear it, Flora!"

Nini Mo says an oath sworn under duress is not binding. I couldn't cross my toes in my boots, and Idden had my hands pinned, so I crossed my eyes and said, "Ayah, so, I promise."

"I think only of your best interests, Flora," Idden said, releasing me. "You don't want to be there when Buck finds out I'm gone. And you sure don't want to be the messenger."

I glared at her. "Ayah, so you say, but you know what—you sound just like Mamma when you say that!"

"You can't rile me, Flora, so don't even try. Come on, boost up."

Idden crouched by the window, linking her hands together into a cradle. I stepped and she boosted me up to the window, grunting. "Pigface, you've grown."

"Thanks to Poppy's food." I puffed, grabbing at the window

frame. The edge of the sill was ragged and some glass remained, but Idden's propulsion gave me no choice but to go through. The window opened into an alley; below me was a six-foot drop, but, lucky for me, about half of that drop was taken up by a giant trash bin. Before I could protest, Idden heaved me the rest of the way through the window. I hit the closed top of the bin with a painful thump, scrabbling for a handhold, and just barely managed to keep myself from rolling off the side. A horde of hipsters were roaring down the alley, pushing, shouting, and screaming, and it would have been bad news for me if I had landed in their path.

Idden's head poked through the window. "I'm sorry I missed your Catorcena. If I could have gotten leave, I would have."

I glared at her. "You talk pretty big, Idden. But you are going to get yourself killed. You aren't being fair to Mamma, or Poppy, either. Think of all they have gone through."

"My country comes first."

"Now you sound just like Mamma," I jeered.

Idden glared back at me. "You'd better get going. Toss me a kiss, Tinks."

"Aren't you coming?"

"I got another way to go—better get yourself out of this alley before you are blocked in. Fine, keep your kiss. If I'm dead next time you see me, you'll be sorry you were such a stick, Flora."

And then Idden pulled her head back inside and was gone.

I jumped off the trash bin and squeezed between its side and the wall: A tiny bit of shelter but better than nothing. That window hadn't been such a good exit after all; at the far end of the alley, the militia had already thrown up a barricade. At the other end, the rioters had pulled another bin in front of the club's fire door, and from behind this barricade they were shouting and screaming at the militia. Me, the monkey in the middle.

How was I going to get out of here? *If you get in,* said Nini Mo, *you can get back out again.*

Something much larger than a brick hit the wall above me, which sent a roar of noise through my ears and practically knocked me down. Now everything sounded distant; my ears were ringing. Cautiously, I again peered around the edge of the trash bin. The militia were firmly entrenched at the far end of the alley; behind their stacked riot shields, cavalry had formed up. The riot line broke open to allow a caisson to pull forward. Behind it came another carriage, upon which sat a gleaming fieldpiece: a gas gun.

Gas guns shoot canisters containing a burning acid smoke. One breath of that and you are coughing up the bloody shreds of your lungs. Get the stinging smoke in your eyes and you will be lucky if you ever see anything again. Despite my best efforts, panic began to bubble up my throat. I was no longer the monkey in the middle. Now I was a sitting duck.

If you need a light, said Nini Mo, *look up for the stars.*

Above my head, a fire ladder dangled, its bottom rung just about out of reach. Jumping didn't close the gap, and if I tried to heave the trash bin into range, I'd expose myself to the firing. The cannoneers had unlimbered the gun and swiveled it around until its barrel pointed down the alley. The barricaded hipsters began to jeer loudly. The battery ignored their cries, and the gunner began to sight the gas gun.

Not for the first time did I bemoan getting the short end of the Fyrdraaca stick, height-wise. Even with my highest hop, I could not reach the bottom rung of the ladder. I pulled off my sash and began to scrabble in my dispatch bag for something weighty to tie onto the end, with the intent of making a grapple that I could use to pull the ladder down. A brick hit the wall above me and shattered into dust.

"Pigface Psychopomp!" Nini Mo says you should always remain graceful under pressure, but it was hard to be graceful with death whizzing over my head. My long wooden pencil case was pretty heavy; maybe that would work. I was tying the sash around it when the lid of the trash bin swung open and a tousled head grinned down at me.

"Hey, Flora, talking to yourself?"

"It's about time you showed up, Udo." The sudden relief at seeing him almost made me feel faint. "Get out here and pull that ladder down before we are snorting our lungs out our noses."

Udo jumped out of the trash bin and reached a hand back to haul the Chickie out after him. She was wearing his greatcoat and both of them had mussed hair and smeared lip rouge. Udo didn't need to climb on top of the trash bin to snag the ladder down; he just reached up one long arm and pulled.

A gas canister whizzed by us, trailing sparks and smoke. This put a hustle into our scramble; it's amazing how fast you can move when the threat of scorched lungs is literally hot on your heels. The Chickie went up the ladder first, in a flurry of black skirts; I was next. At the top, the Chickie paused, blocking my way.

I started to give her a good shove, and then saw, beyond her, flickering red light.

The roof of the Poodle Dog was on fire.

SEVEN
FIRE. TO THE HORSECAR.
A SHOOT-OUT.

The fire had not yet fully engulfed the roof, so we were able to weave a path around the little licks of hot flame. But the thought of all the flammable alcohol and hair products that might still be in the club below, coupled with the wafting gas behind us, made me very eager to get off the roof as fast as possible.

We were not the only ones who had thought of this escape route; on the far side of the roof, other clever shadows were creeping out of the stairwell and dashing past the flames to leap the gap between the Poodle Dog and the warehouse next door. We rushed to follow their example. The buildings were packed so tightly together that the distance was not too great; but still, it wasn't a short jump. Udo went first, his half-undone braids flapping, then turned to offer a hand to the Chickie, who ignored the gallant gesture. She made a graceful ballet leap and a graceful ballet landing on the other side.

At the edge, I hesitated. The gap was large and my legs are short. But the heat behind me was hot, and Udo was shouting, and Nina Mo once leaped fifteen feet over a chasm sixty feet deep—without a running start. But surely her legs were longer than mine, and stronger, too. And she wasn't wearing pinchy stays that kept her from sucking in a good deep breath.

"Come on, Flora!" Udeo shouted. The Chickie was tugging on his arm impatiently. That gesture steeled my resolve; I was not going to let her leave me behind.

Dare, win, or disappear, I thought grimly. For luck. I clutched at Poppy's ranger badge hanging from my neck, and as a whiff of smoke wafted over me, I ran forward and hurtled myself across the gap, gasping like a teakettle. There was a dizzy roar in my ears, swooping blackness, and then I was in Udo's arms, and Udo was staggering backward, moaning theatrically.

"You weigh a ton, Flora."

"Come on," said the Chickie impatiently. "I'm getting smoke in my hair."

I jerked away from Udo, annoyed. We tore across the roof, weaving past chimney pots, around piles of broken beer bottles and soiled mattresses, and then slid down the fire ladder onto Kautz Street, which was thick with people. Some of these people, like us, were trying to scarper. Others were running toward the ruckus, confusing those of us trying to advance in the opposite direction, as Nini Mo once defined *retreat*. Cries of *"Azota and Cierra Califa!"* mixed with the sound of sirens, the rhythmic rat-a-tat of the gas gun, the howls of pain. Something very fast whizzed by my head, so close that I could almost feel it parting my hair.

We pelted around the corner onto Geary where, up ahead, the welcoming lights of the J horsecar were gliding out of the darkness toward us. Waving our arms frantically, we got to the stop just as the car pulled up.

Udo, the Chickie, and I flashed our car passes at the driver and headed for the back. We plopped down in the last row; I peered out of the window. The sirens were getting louder and the streams of people thicker; in a minute the J horsecar was going to be stuck in the crowd. But the car didn't leave the stop.

"Come on!" Udo shouted. "Get going!"

The driver was yelling at a man who was standing in the car doorway. "You gotta pay the fare!"

The man didn't answer, just tried to move past the driver, who threw out a barricading arm.

"Fare!" the driver said again. He had closed the door, but through the glass, I could see several angry-looking people with large guns converging on the trolley. The stranger did not answer. "I ain't going anywhere without your fare, bud."

"Pig face!" Udo was searching his pockets. "I don't have any change. Do you have some change, Zu?"

The Chickie ignored the request. I dug in my pocket, rushed back down the aisle, and threw a lisby in the fare basket. The driver, satisfied, dropped his arm, and the man went past me without a word of gratitude. The car clanged forward, just as large sweaty hands pounded against the door.

"Thanks, Flora!" Udo said when I lurched back to my seat. He and the Chickie were now snuggling. Most of Udo's lip rouge had transferred to the Chickie's lips, which now gleamed blackly blue. The stranger plopped himself down in the second to last seat, next to me.

I peered out the back window to see if we were still being

pursued. We had already passed the last streetlight at Fluery and the Slot, and the darkness behind appeared empty of angry running guns. I breathed as much a sigh of relief as my pinchy stays would allow.

"What the hell happened back there?" Udo asked. "The Zu-Zu and I went outside for a few minutes and the next thing we knew we were in the middle of mayhem. We had to take cover in that trash bin." It was a testament to his bedazzlement that he didn't complain about crawling into a trash bin; normally, Udo would rather be shot than get dirty. He gave the Zu-Zu—what a stupid name—a moony look.

Udo was hardly even breathing hard. Neither was the Zu-Zu; other than the smeared lip rouge, she looked as composed as though she had just been for a stroll in the park. She snapped open a black beaded purse, removed a small black compact, and began to repair. I, on the other hand, thanks to my too tight stays, was wheezing like a hurdy-gurdy, and a bright spike of pain was trying to cleave my brain in two.

I glared at Udo. "If you'd been in the club, where I was looking for you, you'd have known what happened. You missed the big rally," I said, when I could do so without too much wheeze.

Udo grinned at me, and I felt like smacking him. "I was busy."

"Well, then, I guess you didn't miss much."

Weatherhead's drummer exploded," the Zu-Zu said. I'll bet she had spent hours practicing her husky voice, so perfectly bored-yet-cool. "It's the fourth drummer they've lost this year. They shouldn't use percussive dæmons. They are too unstable."

"The Zu-Zu is in a band," he said admiringly.

"Huzzah," I answered. "Anyway, that's not what happened. Firemonkey got up onstage and incited the crowd into a mob." I decided to wait until Udo and I were alone before telling him I had seen Idden; Fyrdraaca family business was none of the

Zu-Zu's affair. Nor was the tentacle attack, which I recalled with a shiver.

The Zu-Zu pursed her blackened lips in a pout at my correction, then tossed back a lank black lock of hair from her paper-white forehead. Udo gave me a dirty look.

"What time is it?" I asked him.

He hauled his watch out of his pocket. "Eleven forty-two."

"Pigface, I'm going to get canned if I'm not back by midnight."

"Flora," Udo told the Zu-Zu, "has a curfew."

"Pity." The Zu-Zu looked unsympathetically at me. She smiled slightly. I had the sudden urge to smack her.

Instead I said maliciously, "'You have a curfew too, Udo."

"Oh no—I just have to make sure Flora gets home safely, and then I'm free." Udo smiled at the Zu-Zu. "I haven't had a curfew since I was a sprout."

Now, this was a big fat lie. Udo's *always* had a curfew, even back in the days when I did not. The Daddies are pretty strict—with the six kids, they have to be. Otherwise the nuts would take over the nuthouse.

Before I could point this out to him, something hit the back window, not hard enough to break it, but hard enough to make me jump. I looked back.

"There are people with guns chasing the horsecar, Udo," I said. "And I don't think they are militia."

Udo and the Zu-Zu turned around and peered out the back window.

"I was afraid this might happen," Udo said. "Though I was hoping we could lose them in the mob scene."

"Lose who? What are you talking about?" I asked. "Why would men be chasing us?"

"Oh, probably because of him." Udo pointed toward the man whose fare I had paid. He had been sitting so quietly that I had forgotten all about him. The man was staring straight ahead, his hands neatly folded on his lap, his face slack and stupid. He looked asleep, almost, but his eyes were open. A thin string of drool dangled from his lips.

Udo chortled, and my stomach twisted up. He was grinning too much like a fool not to actually have done something incredibly foolish. "Don't you recognize him, Flora?"

"It's too late to play games, Udo. Just tell me."

Udo scrunched his face in disappointment. "It's Springheel Jack, of course! Pigface, Flora, he's just been all over the *CPG* for the last two weeks and you don't even recognize him?"

Springheel Jack! The cutthroat bunco artist and cat burglar! The leader of the infamous Red Heels gang, which practically controlled the South of the Slot. Only last week the *CPG's* front page had trumpeted Springheel Jack's latest exploit: He'd gotten into a bar fight with the equally infamous Gallus-Meg and gnawed off her ear. Later, when sober, he had returned it to her in a silver locket, accompanied by a gallant note saying that it was not normally his habit to gnaw upon ladies and she must blame his ill manners on too many Pisco Punches. The press had swooned over his gentility, but it didn't seem to me that a note of apology was much return for having your ear chewed off.

At the moment, however, Springheel Jack didn't look particularly aggressive. In fact, he was dribbling like a fountain.

"Why is he following us?" I asked. "And why is he drooling?"

"It's a pretty story; see, the Zu-Zu and I had nipped outside to get some air, you know," Udo said, "and who should we see but Springheel Jack pissing against the wall. Even though it was dark, I recognized him by his boots instantly."

I peered at the floor. Springheel Jack's footwear was indeed somewhat noticeable—great big sparkly red boots with five-inch heels. Little snake heads spouted from the toes, but they, too, were droopy and half asleep. In the thin light of the horsecar, the boots glittered like rubies.

Udo continued. "I played it cool. I just sidled up to him and asked him for a light, and when he leaned over to light my cigarette, *aqui!*" He brandished the red enamel compact. My heart sunk so low that I swear it fell through the bottom of the car and right onto the road below.

"You snapperhead!" I added a few choice adjectives to the noun. "What were you thinking?"

Udo glared at me, puffing. "I was thinking about the bounty on his head, fifty thousand divas, that's what I was thinking."

"Udo told me his plan," the Zu-Zu interjected. "I thought it an excellent idea and it showed a lot of initiative."

I ignored her, because obviously she was a snapperhead, too, and, anyway, who cared what she thought? I said to Udo, "Plan? There was no plan! We discussed the bounty hunting and decided it was a stupid idea—"

"No, you decided it was a stupid idea," Udo said hotly. "I thought it was a brilliant idea. And I was right! Look at him, fifty thousand divas on his head, and as easy as pie. If we hadn't had to run, we wouldn't even have broken a sweat!"

"I think it was a brilliant idea, Udo," the Zu-Zu said. "Never mind her."

"With his gang after us, trying to kill us, or worse!" I said, still ignoring her. "What are we going to do now, Sieur Brilliant Plan?"

Behind Udo, through the glass, I saw the dim shadow of a man, waving something that was much too long and shiny to be his hand. Good rangers know when to act on instinct. I rolled to the floor, flailing at Udo to do the same, just as the window next to me exploded into a slivery halo of glass.

EIGHT
ANGRY OUTLAWS. AN OMINOUS
APPEARANCE. UDO MAKES A CHOICE.

crouched on the floor and felt the glass pelt down upon me like little nuggets of razor-sharp rain. The window on the other side of the car cracked, thus leading me to the brilliant conclusion that we were flanked on both sides. That was bad, superbad, but surely it couldn't get any worse—until I realized that the *pop-pop-pop* coming from above my head was Udo firing back with the little revolver that he had gotten for his Catorcena, and which I hadn't realized he was carrying. *It can always be worse,* said Nini Mo, *and usually will be if you wait long enough.*

"Udo!" I yelled, crawling under the seat and grabbing at his twitching feet. The floor of the horsecar was disgusting, sticky with spilled liquids and awash in torn paper. Why couldn't people take their trash with them?

"I got one! I think I got one!" Udo dropped back down and broke open the frame of the revolver, spraying empty shells in the air. "Zu—reach in my left breast pocket and hand me some more cartridges."

The Zu-Zu had dropped down onto the seat when the shooting started, thus keeping her pristine self above the trash. Now she rolled onto her side, fumbling in the pocket of Udo's greatcoat, as unperturbed as though she got caught in a firefight every day.

"What the hell are you doing, Udo?" I hissed.

"What the hell does it look like? Defending our lives!" He dropped the last cartridge into the cylinder and snapped it closed. Before I could stop him, he bobbed back to his feet, firing wildly. Udo's desire to impress the Zu-Zu was going to get us killed.

The horsecar, which somehow had kept moving during all the implosions and explosions, suddenly jolted to a halt. The driver's yelling was punctuated with another shot, then ominous silence.

I gingerly poked my head up next to Udo's, expecting any minute to feel the horrible bite of a bullet blowing my head off, but the firing didn't start up again. Two men in long white trench coats were hauling something thumpy down the front steps: the poor driver. The windshield was liberally sprayed with blood.

It was time, yet again, to advance in the opposite direction.

In other words, to retreat. I looked wildly around to see how to accomplish that action and noticed the emergency door. Reaching up, I twisted the door handle, trying very quietly to jiggle it open. Someone from the front of the car hollered: "Hey! You, in the back! Let Jack go and no one will get hurt."

Udo fired again, but this time my whacking arm ruined his aim and the shot disappeared through the roof.

"FLORA!" Udo shouted, pushing me away and dropping back down. I fell against the emergency door, adding a bruising pain on my side. The Zu-Zu smiled at me. I did not smile back.

"Come on, kiddies, the game is up!" the outlaw yelled.

"My game has just started!" Udo shouted back, the snapper-head. I gave up being stealthy and pushed the emergency door hard. It popped open, and the Zu-Zu peered around outside, then nodded encouragingly to me. I motioned with my chin, and she rolled off the seat and slid down into the darkness.

"Come on, Udo! Hurry!" I hissed.

Udo gestured toward Springheel Jack, who sat stock-still, oblivious to the ruckus. "I'm not going without him."

Something had to be done to give us enough cover to grab Springheel Jack and run. We needed a diversion. Maybe if I could lob a ball of coldfire at the outlaws, that would distract them enough to let us escape. A coldfire ball is easy—I've done it many times and never gotten it wrong.

"⚡🐚 ᴵᵖ ✦═ 'ⱬ⁹" I whispered, holding out my palm. A bead of coldfire bloomed above my open hand, smaller than I would have liked.

"⚡🐚 ᴵᵖ ✦═'ⱬ⁹ᴹ!" The coldfire light increased in size until it was about the size of a grapefruit. Cradling it in my hands, I popped up and threw the ball as hard as I could toward the outlaw—who neatly caught it and said, with an evil laugh, "I'll return this to you, missy." And then he suggested something that didn't sound very pleasant.

Clearly I needed something bigger. Much bigger. But I didn't know any bigger sigils—well, I knew some bigger sigils in principle, but not in action. What would Nini Mo do? She'd dazzle them with a Scintilla Sigil, or confuse them with an Ambiguity Sigil, or turn them into goats with a Transubstantiation Sigil. But while I knew *of* these sigils, I did not know their Gramatica.

The outlaw was advancing down the aisle. My mind had gone blank with terror—surely not a problem Nini Mo ever faced—and a funny taste was growing in the back of my throat, a rotten meaty taste. I swallowed hard, but that just made me gag, and when I opened my mouth to spit, a low ominous noise came out instead, a noise that vibrated my teeth and made the hair on the back of my neck tingle. A pale sickly glow began to seep through the car, the kind of light that makes the living look dead and the dead look decomposed. With detached horror, I realized that the glow was coming from me. I stood up and stepped out into the aisle, coldfire writhing like galvanic green ribbons from my outstretched fingertips. The outlaw dropped his gun and screeched.

"Flora—what are you doing?" Udo asked from somewhere behind me, his voice breaking.

"⌇⊟≡◐ ⇊◣ ⌿ ⚏⤳ ⊐⤶ρ ⚏⚏◔!" The Word exploded from my mouth, its glittering coldfire letters whirling in a haze of furious fuliginous blackness, its edges as sharp and black as a Birdie obsidian sacrificial knife. The Word flung down the aisle, making *whomp-whomp* noises, and caught the outlaw square in the kisser. He screamed, a horrible sound that plunged into my brain like an ice pick in the ear. For a moment his head was separated from his body by a thick line of blackness, and then his head flew upward, buoyant on a spray of blood. He was still screaming, or maybe that was air howling as it escaped from his neck. Whatever the noise, it was horrific.

A sharp poke pushed me out of my daze. Udo was shoving me toward the emergency door. I crawled over to the door and rolled out, catching myself just before I hit the pavement, where the Zu-Zu waited. Udo prodded at Jack, who staggered out after me. We broke into a tearing run, eager to leave the howling shrieks and screams and the pallid glow of the horsecar as far behind as possible. No one followed.

Somehow, somewhere, we stopped running. Or rather, Udo and the Zu-Zu stopped, and then I couldn't run anymore and had to stop, too. In fact, not just stop, but sit down, not just sit down, but collapse, which I did. The curb was dirty and wet, but I didn't care. I had to get new stays; I was squeezed so tightly into the old ones that my lungs were sucking against each other, and all the blood was bouncing around inside my skull, so that I felt as though I was going to upchuck.

Udo leaned over, folding his arms around his stomach, gasping. "What . . . hell . . . Flora . . . hell? Your hair . . . on fire . . ." His braids flopped over his bright red face.

"An Ominous Apparition, followed by an Active Protective Sigil," the Zu-Zu said. She was barely winded, but her hair, I noticed happily, had become even more disarranged. "Where did you learn all that, Flora?"

"I didn't," I gurgled. "I dunno—"

"Whatever. I want a coffee," the Zu-Zu said. "Let's go to el Mono Real, Udo, and you can get me a coffee."

I straightened up and tried to look refreshed and relaxed, as though I invoked Ominous Apparitions, flung forth Active Protective Sigils, and ran pell-mell from killers all the time, no big. What I really wanted to do was expel the contents of my tum and then collapse on the ground in a little pile of goo. "What about Springheel Jack?"

The outlaw had kept pace with our flight and had stopped with our stop; he didn't look winded at all, or concerned, or worried. Just blank and drooly.

"Oh, he can have coffee, too, if he wants," the Zu-Zu answered. "Come on, Udo. We're only a block from el Mono Real. I'm perishing."

"Ayah, so," Udo agreed, as though he was actually going to go with the Zu-Zu for coffee, thus leaving me to wait and see if the outlaws caught up with us.

"Hey! What about Jack's gang?" I demanded.

"Are you kidding, Flora? I think at this point they probably know better than to mess with us," Udo said. "Come on, let's get coffee."

"And what are you going to do about Jack?"

The Zu-Zu was already drifting down the street, a blot of imperious spookiness who didn't seem to care if we followed her or not. Udo glanced at her and then back at me, and took two steps in her direction. "Turn him in tomorrow, Flora. Come on."

"I have to get home, Udo. I've got a curfew, remember, and so do you."

"Don't be a stick—"

The Zu-Zu had stopped and turned. "Udo!"

"Come on, Flora," Udo said, half-pleadingly.

"I have to go home, Udo. You can go get coffee, if you want—with your pallid girl and your zombie pard. But I have to go home."

Udo stood up straight and said loftily, "Then go. No one is stopping you."

And with that, Udo trotted after the Zu-Zu, Springheel Jack close on his heels, leaving me standing alone in the middle of the empty street.

MEDIUM WITH A MESSAGE

JODY LYNN NYE

Since mass entertainment began, in the theaters of ancient Greece, or perhaps just as likely around a Neanderthal's campfire, stories often came with a maxim, a warning, or a moral intended for the public welfare that the storyteller wanted to get across to his listeners. "The gods would be angry if we are disobedient to their will." "Obey the king, the senate, your master, your father." "Do not waste the bounty of the earth." "Have compassion for the weak and the poor." "Do not fear the stranger, for he may have gifts to give you." An effective and compelling script, well acted, and set perhaps just a little outside their own sphere of existence, would amuse the members of the audience and give them something to think about later. Sneak an idea into their subconscious, and you can change the world for the better. Some playwrights were more subtle in their approach than others, but their intention was the same: to change the world's mind for the better by presenting a new idea in a way that was palatable to the audience.

For over a hundred years, science fiction films have provided an excellent medium for the promotion of new or important ideas. Tolerance, new technology, ecology, warnings against nuclear war, pollution, communism or the dehumanization of mankind have all been tucked into—or plastered across—feature films.

The trend began early in cinema. George Melies's ground-breaking film *From the Earth to the Moon* (1902) was not even plausibly scientific, but it introduced a visual representation of rockets and space travel. Audiences could now aspire to land on the moon. The idea was planted; though it took nearly seventy years to come to fruition, it excited the imagination of audiences throughout that time.

Much more a warning than an idea to which to aspire was Fritz Lang's 1927 silent blockbuster, *Metropolis*. The epic black-and-white film was based partly upon a novel by the director's wife, Thea von Harbou, as well as other science fiction novels and stories of the day and Lang's observation of society in postwar Europe. Future society became divided between the haves and the far larger population of have-nots to the point where there is little to no contact between them. The latter live only to supply the wants and whims of the former. Their misery goes unobserved by the privileged class until the son of the dictator falls under the influence of Maria, a mysterious and eloquent woman, sees the broken half of society for himself and vows to put an end to slavery and poverty.

A similar warning that mankind could become dehumanized by dividing itself into the social elite and the working drones came in the George Pal version of *The Time Machine*, based on the novel by H.G. Wells. Those remaining dregs who had a purpose, however base, would retain intelligence, while those who existed only to enjoy life would lose their potential. As the Morlocks had become cannibals who preyed upon the ethereal Eloi, Wells's story was an extreme example of the divergence of the two halves of humanity's potential. Filmmakers have rarely claimed to be social architects, but a visual representation of horror is a powerful inducement to an audience to retain all of its faculties.

The original film of *The Thing* (1951), directed by Howard Hawks (listed as producer, but reportedly also its director), was based upon *Who Goes There?* by John W. Campbell. Its subtext reflects the public fears of the time about atomic weapons and invasion by dangerous enemies that can masquerade as friends. The substitution of creatures for human beings was a frequent theme, including such movies as *The Invasion of the Body Snatchers* (1956, remade in 1978). At the time, paranoia over communism and other movements to destroy society was widespread. *Invasion* made the hidden monster real instead of philosophical—you could not tell by looking who was the enemy who would destroy you until it was too late.

Fear of nuclear weapons was a pervasive theme, usually characterized as causing the uprising of ordinary creatures mutated into giants by radiation, such as *Them*, about giant ants, and *The Beginning of the End*, featuring enormous grasshoppers wreaking havoc upon Chicago. The most popular in this vein has to be the Japanese cult film, *Gojira*, or as it was renamed in the United States, *Godzilla*. The original film saw the giant lizard awakened as a result of atomic explosions. Along the way, Godzilla became beloved, even a hero, when fear of bombs gave way to fear of environmental pollution, and he defeated the eponymous enemy in *Godzilla vs. the Smog Monster*. (The closing song, translated from the Japanese, begins, "Savior! Savior!") A more heavy-handed production was *The War of the Worlds* (1953), an adaptation of H. G. Wells's novel. Its special effects evoked the horror of the bombs dropped on Hiroshima and Nagasaki in the silhouettes made of soot that were all that was left of victims of the invaders.

Directed by Robert Wise, *The Day the Earth Stood Still* (1951) offered the opposite thesis, in which humankind itself was the enemy of nature, by introducing an intelligent alien who brings a warning that Earth must be destroyed if it did not embrace peace. The way in which the characters treated the messenger, Klaatu, suggested that humankind wasn't ready for interstellar peace, but perhaps one day it could be.

Science fiction had its first A-list picture in 1957 with *Forbidden Planet*, starring Walter Pigeon and Leslie Nielsen. The plot was based upon William Shakespeare's *The Tempest* in a futuristic setting. Like *The Tempest*, it showed humanity's greed and folly, but held out hope it could become wise in time.

Disney joined the SF legions with a big-budget picture, *20,000 Leagues Under the Sea*, Jules Verne's story of a disaffected sea captain whose unique submarine, the *Nautilus*, predated modern nuclear submarines. Sick of humankind, Captain Nemo had turned his back upon the land in favor of the ocean. Beings who dwelled in its depths took only what they needed from nature.

One of the most haunting films with a theme of preservation of the environment was *Silent Running* (1972), a Douglas Trumbull picture that starred Bruce Dern as Freeman Lowell. The ship carrying the last of Earth's precious forests is ordered destroyed by the powers that be. Lowell cannot in conscience carry out the order, and goes on the run. His only helpers on board are three small worker robots—drones—who were the precursors to *Star Wars*'s R2D2: Huey, Dewey and Louie. The story is a tragedy because the freighters are ordered to jettison their irreplaceable cargo in the interests of immediate profit. Lowell sacrifices himself rather than allow the last of Earth's forests to die.

This year's winner of the Nebula for best script, *WALL-E*, offers the gentle story of a lonely robot who finds romance among the trash left behind after humanity departed for the stars. The stark landscape of rotting discards and rusted machinery throws into sharp relief the single living plant that WALL-E discovers. There could be no more poignant reminder that our ecology is fragile, but Pixar did not shove it down the audience's collective throat—instead, we are drawn to care more about the feelings of a mechanical trash collector, cheer on the heroics of a complaisant human starship captain who learns to fight bureaucracy and his own indolence, and rejoice in not one, but two love stories. We can't help but notice the desolation of Earth, and should go away resolving to live greener lives.

Still, you can ignore all that and just sit back and enjoy the movie.

WALL-E

WALL-E is an exceptional movie on many levels. It not only used animation to tell a strong story with a message, but managed to bring emotion and pathos to animated robots. Writing a script for a movie that had so little dialogue had to be a challenge and the two excerpts that follow show how this was done for the Nebula Award–winning movie.

EXCERPT 1

An air of enchantment.
Eve is taken aback.

> WALLY
> (beeps)
> [Come on in.]

She drifts through the sea of knickknacks.
Becomes spooked by a SINGING BILLY BASS FISH.
Threatens to shoot it, but Wally calms her down.
He is compelled to show her everything.

Hands her an eggbeater . . .

. . . bubble wrap (so infectious to pop) . . .

. . . a lightbulb (lights when she holds it) . . .

. . . the Rubik's Cube (she solves it immediately) . . .

. . . his *Hello Dolly* tape.

Curious, she begins unspooling the tape.

> WALLY
>
> (loud beeps)
> [My tape!!]

He grabs it back. Protective.

Inserts it carefully into the VCR. Please still work.

The movie eventually appears on the TV.

Plays a clip of *POYSC*.

Wally is relieved.

> WALLY
>
> (beeps)
> [What do you think?]

Mimics the dancing for Eve.

Encourages her to try.

She clumsily hops up and down.

Makes dents in the floor. Rattles everything.

Wally politely stops her.

> WALLY
>
> (beeps)
> [How 'bout we try a different move?]

Spins in a circle. Arms out.

Eve copies.

Spins faster, and faster . . .

Too fast.

Accidentally strikes Wally. He flies into the shelves.

Eve helps him up from the mess.

Wally's LEFT BINOCULAR EYE falls off.

Dangles from two wires.

Eve GASPS with concern.

Wally placates her.

S/Legal/Mktg/Licensing/Science Fiction Fantasy Writers of America (Wall E)
(Disney to SFFWA 07 09 09).doc License Agreement—Science Fiction
Fantasy Writers of America

EXCERPT 2

EXT. TRUCK—NIGHT

Wally motors outside.

Turns over his Igloo cooler to clean it out.

Pauses to take in the night sky.

STARS struggle to be seen through the polluted haze.

Wally presses the PLAY button on his chest.

The newly sampled *It Only Takes A Moment (IOTAM)*
    plays.

The wind picks up.

A WARNING LIGHT sounds on Wally's chest.

He looks out into the night.

A RAGING SANDSTORM approaches off
    the bay . . .

Unfazed, Wally heads back in the truck.

IOTAM still gently playing.

. . . The massive wave of sand roars closer . . .

Wally raises the door.

Pauses.

WHISTLES for his cockroach to come inside.

The door shuts just as the storm hits.

Obliterates everything in view.

INT. TRUCK—SAME
> Wally alone in the center of his shelter.
> Unwraps a BNL SPONGECAKE (think Twinkie).
> Lays it out for the cockroach to sleep in.
> It happily dives in.
> Wally collapses himself into a storable cube.
> Backs into an empty shelf space.
> Rocks it like a cradle . . .
> . . . and shuts down for the night.
> Outside the wind howls like the Hounds of Hell.

INT. WALLY'S TRUCK—NEXT MORNING
> Wally's CHARGE METER flashes "WARNING."
> He wakes. Unboxes.
> Groggy and lifeless.
> Stumbles outside.

EXT. ROOF OF WALLY'S TRUCK
> The morning sun.
> Wally fully exposed in its light.
> His front panel splayed out like a tanning shield.
> A solar collector.

EXCERPT 3

> His CHARGE METER chimes full.
> Solar panels fold away into hiding.
> Wally, now awake, collects his lunch cooler.
> Heads off to work.
> . . . and accidentally runs over the cockroach.

Horrified, Wally reverses.
Reveals the FLATTENED INSECT under his tread.
The cockroach simply pops back to life.
No biggie. Ready to go.
Relieved, Wally resumes their commute.

EXT. WALLY'S WORK SITE—THAT MORNING
A SERIES OF "WALLY AT WORK" MOMENTS:
    CU of Wally's hands digging into garbage.
CU of trash being scooped into his chest
    compactor.
A cube lands by the cockroach.

    Wally discovers a BRA in the garbage.
Unsure what it's for.
Tries placing it over his eyes, like glasses.
Tosses it in his cooler.

    Wally finds a set of CAR KEYS.
Presses the remote lock.
Somewhere in the distance a CAR ALARM CHIRPS.

    Plays with a paddle ball.
The ball keeps smacking him in the face.
He doesn't like it.

    Wally discovers a DIAMOND RING in a JEWEL
        CASE.
Throws out the ring. Keeps the case.
The jewel case drops into the cooler, then . . .
. . . A RUBBER DUCKY . . .
. . . A BOBBLE HEAD DOLL . . .
. . . AN OLD BOOT . . .
. . . A TROPHY . . .

Wally finds a FIRE EXTINGUISHER.
Activates it.
FOAM blasts in his face.
It's tossed far, far away from his cooler.

Wally's shovel hand strikes something solid.
Faces a REFRIGERATOR much larger than himself.
Now what?

CU on fridge door.
A WELDING BEAM moves down its center.
It emits from between Wally's SPLIT BINOCULAR
    EYES.

THE ACCEPTANCE SPEECH OF BRADBURY AWARD WINNER, JOSS WHEDON

First given by Ben Bova in 1992, the Bradbury Award is for excellence in screenwriting. It was named in acknowledgment of Ray Bradbury's contributions to the fields of science fiction and screenwriting. While it is not a Nebula Award®, it is awarded as part of the Nebula Awards Banquet. This award is given only when a work or body of work is exceptional. Past winners include James Cameron for *Terminator 2*, J. Michael Strazinski for *Babylon 5*, and Yuri Rasovsky and Harlan Ellison for *2000X—Tales of the Next Millennia.*

Joss Whedon was in Canada working on a movie at the time of the banquet. Anyone who has watched *Serenity*, *Dollhouse*, *Buffy*, or any of Joss Whedon's creations is familiar with his sense of humor. When his name was announced for the award, a screen lit up and he made the following acceptance speech.

What's this? How do I come to be in this room full of luminaries? When mere moments ago I was in Canada, filming a film?

Aha, I have fooled you. My image is being beamed to you through a waveavatronic electron machine that causes you to see me although I am not here. That's right: this is the future. This is one of the many future gadgets you will soon learn to enjoy.

Future is my business, because I write fictionalized scientific, or as the kids call it nowadays, fi sci. And right now, I'm very honored to be, not physically but spectrally, among so many people that I admire, especially you, and you . . . and that hot chick over there—why are you even here? I would like to be with you physically, but I can't, because I'm filming a movie that I feel certain will cause you to take this award back away from me.

But, if I could be there, I would probably say something exactly like what I am saying now. Which is simply that there is no bigger influence on my writing, really, than Ray Bradbury. He is the forefather of us in so many ways. Nobody made fi sci more human, more exciting, the horror, the engagement. It's stayed with me my whole life, before Stephen King, before Frank Herbert, before so many people I admire, Bradbury was the first. This award is something that I will genuinely treasure when I actually get to be near it physically.

Thank you all. And now . . . I disappear.

AN APPRECIATION OF THE GRAND MASTER: HARRY HARRISON

TOM DOHERTY

Harry Harrison—Grand Master, writer, critic, illustrator, friend. He has entertained us for over half a century. He's been published in twenty-five languages. And he's a creator of worlds and characters that will be long remembered.

In *Make Room! Make Room!* he made us consider the consequences of overpopulation and of our consumption of the world's resources. The novel was the basis for the movie *Soylent Green*. I never thought the movie did justice to the book, but it was still good enough to win the 1974 Nebula Award for Best Dramatic Presentation.

Over the years, Harry has excited us with the hardest of hard science fiction—and spoofed the same genre with his *Bill, The Galactic Hero* series. He's combined adventure with humor in the tales of Slippery Jim diGriz, *The Stainless Steel Rat*, the first of which he sold to John W. Campbell for *Astounding* in 1957, thereby initiating a long and productive relationship. It's his longest-running and probably his most famous series, and he's currently polishing the first draft of its latest installment, the novel *The Stainless Steel Rat Returns*, which we plan to publish at Tor next year. Among his many other memorable works are the disaster novel *Skyfall*, the Deathworld series with its endless and harrowing struggle for human survival, and the marvelous parallel worlds of the Eden series and *The Transatlantic Tunnel, Hurrah!* Few have produced such quality at such range over such an extended period of time.

When I met my wife in Leningrad, back in the days of the old Soviet Union, he was one of the few American science fiction writers well known to her and her friends. Truly a man of the world, he had traveled in Russia and been published there when there was still an Iron Curtain. He's been the honorary president of the Esperanto Association of Ireland. In our long friendship I've visited with him and with his lovely wife Joan in Mexico, in Ireland, in England, and at my own home on Long Island. They have also lived and worked in Italy, Denmark and, of course, in the United States. Wherever he's lived, he's always had stories to tell of his travels, his work, and the great people he's worked with.

He started out in comics in the 1940s, working both as an illustrator and as a writer. In the 1950s and '60s I loved his internationally syndicated *Flash Gordon* newspaper comic strips and those wonderful stories in *Astounding*. At the same time he did magazine illustrations and some covers. He edited magazines— the first issue of *Rocket Stories*, and for a short time *Amazing* and *Fantastic*. He edited books, including a number of distinguished anthologies alone and with Brian Aldiss. Along with Brian he raised the level of science fiction criticism. Most of all he wrote *wonderful stories.* To be proclaimed a Grand Master is a very special thing and I am delighted it has come to so special a man.

THE STREETS OF ASHKELON

HARRY HARRISON

Somewhere above, hidden by the eternal clouds of Wesker's World, a thunder rumbled and grew. Trader Garth stopped suddenly when he heard it, his boots sinking slowly into the muck, and cupped his good ear to catch the sound. It swelled and waned in the thick atmosphere, growing louder.

"That noise is the same as the noise of your sky-ship," Itin said, with stolid Wesker logicality, slowly pulverising the idea in his mind and turning over the bits one by one for closer examination. "But your ship is still sitting where you landed it. It must be, even though we cannot see it, because you are the only one who can operate it. And even if anyone else could operate it we would have heard it rising into the sky. Since we did not, and if this sound is a sky-ship sound, then it must mean . . ."

"Yes, another ship," Garth said, too absorbed in his own thoughts to wait for the laborious Weskerian chains of logic to clank their way through to the end. Of course it was another spacer, it had been only a matter of time before one appeared, and undoubtedly this one was homing on the S.S. radar reflector as he had done. His own ship would show up clearly on the newcomer's screen and they would probably set down as close to it as they could.

"You better go ahead, Itin," he said. "Use the water so you can get to the village quickly. Tell everyone to get back into the swamps, well clear of the hard ground. That ship is landing on instruments and anyone underneath at touchdown is going to be cooked."

This immediate threat was clear enough to the little Wesker amphibian. Before Garth had finished speaking Itin's ribbed ears had folded like a bat's wings and he slipped silently into the nearby canal. Garth squelched on through the mud, making as good time as he could over the clinging surface. He had just reached the fringes of the village clearing when the rumbling grew to a head-splitting roar and the spacer broke through the low-hanging layer of clouds above. Garth shielded his eyes from the down-reaching tongue of flame and examined the growing form of the gray-black ship with mixed feelings.

After almost a standard year on Wesker's World he had to fight down a longing for human companionship of any kind. While this buried fragment of herd-spirit chattered for the rest of the monkey tribe, his trader's mind was busily drawing a line under a column of figures and adding up the total. This could very well be another trader's ship, and if it was his monopoly of the Wesker's trade was at an end. Then again, this might not be a trader at all, which was the reason he stayed in the shelter of the giant fern and loosened his gun in its holster. The ship baked dry a hundred square meters of mud, the roaring blast died, and the landing feet crunched down through the crackling crust. Metal creaked and settled into place while the cloud of smoke and steam slowly drifted lower in the humid air.

"Garth—you native-cheating extortionist—where are you?" the ship's speaker boomed.

The lines of the spacer had looked only slightly familiar, but there was no mistaking the rasping tones of that voice. Garth had a twisted smile when he stepped out into the open and whistled shrilly through two fingers. A directional microphone ground out of its casing on the ship's fin and turned in his direction.

"What are you doing here, Singh?" he shouted towards the mike. "Too crooked to find a planet of your own and have to come here to steal an honest trader's profits?"

"Honest!" the amplified voice roared. "This from the man who has been in more jails than cathouses—and that a goodly number in itself, I do declare. Sorry, friend of my youth, but I cannot join you in exploiting this aboriginal pesthole. I am on course to a more fairly atmosphered world where a fortune is waiting to be made. I only stopped here since an opportunity presented, to turn an honest credit by running a taxi service. I bring you friendship, the perfect companionship, a man in a different line of business who might help you in yours. I'd come out and say hello myself, except I would have to decon for biologicals. I'm cycling the passenger through the lock so I hope you won't mind helping with his luggage."

At least there would be no other trader on the planet now, that worry was gone. But Garth still wondered what sort of passenger would be taking one-way passage to an undeveloped world. And what was behind that concealed hint of merriment in Singh's voice? He walked around to the far side of the spacer where the ramp had dropped, and looked up at the man in the cargo lock who was wrestling ineffectually with a large crate. The man turned towards him and Garth saw the clerical dog-collar and knew just what it was Singh had been chuckling about.

"What are you doing here?" Garth asked, and in spite of his attempt at self-control he snapped the words. If the man noticed this he ignored it, because he was still smiling and putting out his hand as he came down the ramp.

"Father Mark," he said, "of the Missionary Society of Brothers. I'm very pleased to meet . . ."

"I said what are you doing here." Garth's voice was under control now, quiet and cold. He knew what had to be done, and it must be done quickly or not at all.

"That should be obvious," Father Mark said, his good nature still unruffled. "Our missionary society has raised funds to send spiritual emissaries to alien worlds for the first time. I was lucky enough . . ."

"Take your luggage and get back into the ship. You're not wanted here—and have no permission to land. You'll be a liability and there is no one on Wesker to take care of you. Get back into the ship."

"I don't know who you are, sir, or why you are lying to me," the priest said. He was still calm but the smile was gone. "But I have studied galactic law and the history of this planet very well. There are no diseases or beasts here that I should have any particular fear of. It is also an open planet, and until the Space Survey changes that status I have as much right to be here as you do."

The man was of course right, but Garth couldn't let him know that. He had been bluffing, hoping the priest didn't know his rights. But he did. There was only one distasteful course left for him, and he had better do it while there was still time.

"Get back in that ship," he shouted, not hiding his anger now. With a smooth motion his gun was out of the holster and the pitted black muzzle only inches from the priest's stomach. The man's face turned white, but he did not move.

"What the hell are you doing, Garth?!" Singh's shocked voice grated from the speaker. "The guy paid his fare and you have no rights at all to throw him off the planet."

"I have this right," Garth said, raising his gun and sighting between the priest's eyes. "I give him thirty seconds to get back aboard the ship or I pull the trigger."

"Well I think you are either off your head or playing a joke," Singh's exasperated voice rasped down at them. "If it is a joke, it is in bad taste. But either way you're not getting away with it. Two can play at that game—only I can play it better."

There was the rumble of heavy bearings and the remote-controlled four-gun turret on the ship's side rotated and pointed at Garth. "Now—down gun and give Father Mark a hand with the luggage," the speaker commanded, a trace of humor back in the voice now. "As much as I would like to help, Old Friend, I cannot. I feel it is time you had a chance to talk to the father;

after all, I have had the opportunity of speaking with him all the way from Earth."

Garth jammed the gun back into the holster with an acute feeling of loss. Father Mark stepped forward, the winning smile back now and a Bible taken from a pocket of his robe, in his raised hand. "My son—" he said.

"I'm not your son," was all Garth could choke out as the bitterness and defeat welled up within him. His fist drew back as the anger rose, and the best he could do was open the fist so he struck only with the flat of his hand. Still the blow sent the priest crashing to the ground and hurled the white pages of the book splattering into the thick mud.

Itin and the other Weskers had watched everything with seemingly emotionless interest. Garth made no attempt to answer their unspoken questions. He started towards his house, but turned back when he saw they were still unmoving.

"A new man has come," he told them. "He will need help with the things he has brought. If he doesn't have any place for them, you can put them in the big warehouse until he has a place of his own."

He watched them waddle across the clearing towards the ship, then went inside and gained a certain satisfaction from slamming the door hard enough to crack one of the panes. There was an equal amount of painful pleasure in breaking out one of the remaining bottles of Irish whiskey that he had been saving for a special occasion. Well this was special enough, though not really what he had had in mind. The whiskey was good and burned away some of the bad taste in his mouth, but not all of it. If his tactics had worked, success would have justified everything. But he had failed and in addition to the pain of failure there was the acute feeling that he had made a horse's ass out of himself. Singh had blasted off without any good-byes. There was no telling what sense he had made of the whole matter, though he would surely carry some strange stories back to the trader's lodge. Well, that could be worried about the next time Garth signed in. Right now he had to go about setting things right with the missionary. Squinting out through the rain he saw the man struggling to erect a collapsible tent while the entire population of the village stood in ordered ranks and watched. Naturally none of them offered to help.

By the time the tent was up and the crates and boxes stowed inside it the rain had stopped. The level of fluid in the bottle was a good bit lower and Garth felt more like facing up to the unavoidable meeting. In truth, he was looking forward to talking to the man. This whole nasty business aside, after an entire solitary year any human companionship looked good. *Will you join me now for dinner? John Garth*, he wrote on the back of an old invoice. But maybe the guy was too frightened to come? Which was no way to start any kind of relationship. Rummaging under the bunk, he found a box that was big enough and put his pistol inside. Itin was of course waiting outside the door when he opened it, since this was his tour as Knowledge Collector. He handed him the note and box.

"Would you take these to the new man," he said.

"Is the new man's name New Man?" Itin asked.

"No, it's not!" Garth snapped. "His name is Mark. But I'm only asking you to deliver this, not get involved in conversation."

As always when he lost his temper, the literal-minded Weskers won the round. "You are not asking for conversation," Itin said slowly, "but Mark may ask for conversation. And others will ask me his name, if I do not know his na—" The voice cut off as Garth slammed the door. This didn't work in the long run either because next time he saw Itin—a day, a week, or even a month later—the monologue would be picked up on the very word it had ended and the thought rambled out to its last frayed end. Garth cursed under his breath and poured water over a pair of the tastier concentrates that he had left.

"Come in," he said when there was a quiet knock on the door. The priest entered and held out the box with the gun.

"Thank you for the loan, Mr. Garth, I appreciate the spirit that made you send it. I have no idea of what caused the unhappy affair when I landed, but I think it would be best forgotten if we are going to be on this planet together for any length of time."

"Drink?" Garth asked, taking the box and pointing to the bottle on the table. He poured two glasses full and handed one to the priest. "That's about what I had in mind, but I still owe you an explanation of what happened out there." He scowled into his glass for a second, then raised it to the other man. "It's a big universe and I guess we have to make out as best we can. Here's to Sanity."

"God be with you," Father Mark said, and raised his glass as well.

"Not with me or with this planet," Garth said firmly. "And that's the crux of the matter." He half-drained the glass and sighed.

"Do you say that to shock me?" the priest asked with a smile. "I assure you that it doesn't."

"Not intended to shock. I meant it quite literally. I suppose I'm what you would call an atheist, so revealed religion is no concern of mine. While these natives, simple and unlettered Stone Age types that they are, have managed to come this far with no superstitions or traces of deism whatsoever. I had hoped that they might continue that way."

"What are you saying?" The priest frowned. "Do you mean they have no gods, no belief in the hereafter? They must die . . . ?"

"Die they do, and to dust returneth. Like the rest of the animals. They have thunder, trees and water without having thunder-gods, tree sprites, or water nymphs. They have no ugly little gods, taboos, or spells to hag-ride and limit their lives. They are the only primitive people I have ever encountered that are completely free of superstition and appear to be much happier and sane because of it. I just wanted to keep them that way."

"You wanted to keep them from God—from salvation?" The priest's eyes widened and he recoiled slightly.

"No," Garth said. "I wanted to keep them from superstition until they knew more and could think about it realistically without being absorbed and perhaps destroyed by it."

"You're being insulting to the Church, sir, to equate it with superstition . . ."

"Please," Garth said, raising his hand. "No theological arguments. I don't think your society footed the bill for this trip just to attempt to convert me. Just accept the fact that my beliefs have been arrived at through careful thought over a period of years, and no amount of undergraduate metaphysics will change them. I'll promise not to try and convert you—if you will do the same for me."

"Agreed, Mr. Garth. As you have reminded me, my mission here is to save these souls, and that is what I must do. But why should my work disturb you so much that you try and keep me from landing? Even threaten me with your gun, and . . ." The priest broke off and looked into his glass.

"And even slug you?" Garth asked, suddenly frowning. "There was no excuse for that, and I would like to say that I'm sorry. Plain bad manners and an even worse temper. Live alone long enough and you find yourself doing that kind of thing." He brooded down at his big hands where they lay on the table, reading memories into the scars and calluses patterned there. "Let's just call it frustration, for lack of a better word. In your business you must have had a lot of chances to peep into the darker places in men's minds and you should know a bit about motives and happiness. I have had too busy a life to ever consider settling down and raising a family, and right up until recently I never missed it. Maybe leakage radiation is softening up my brain, but I had begun to think of these furry and fishy Weskers as being a little like my own children, that I was somehow responsible to them."

"We are all His children," Father Mark said quietly.

"Well, here are some of His children that can't even imagine His existence," Garth said, suddenly angry at himself for allowing gentler emotions to show through. Yet he forgot himself at once, leaning forward with the intensity of his feelings. "Can't you realise the importance of this? Live with these Weskers a while and you will discover a simple and happy life that matches the state of grace you people are always talking about. They get pleasure from their lives—and cause no one pain. By circumstances they have evolved on an almost barren world, so have never had a chance to grow out of a physical Stone Age culture. But mentally they are our match—or perhaps better. They have all learned my language so I can easily explain the many things they want to know. Knowledge and the gaining of knowledge gives them real satisfaction. They tend to be exasperating at times because every new fact must be related to the structure of all other things, but the more they learn the faster this process becomes. Someday they are going to be man's equal in every way, perhaps surpass us. If—would you do me a favor?"

"Whatever I can."

"Leave them alone. Or teach them if you must—history and science, philosophy, law, anything that will help them face the realities of the greater universe they never even knew existed before. But don't confuse them with your hatreds and pain, guilt, sin, and punishment. Who knows the harm . . ."

"You are being insulting, sir!" the priest said, jumping to his feet. The top of his gray head barely came to the massive spaceman's chin, yet he showed no fear in defending what he believed. Garth, standing now himself, was no longer the penitent. They faced each other in anger, as men have always stood, unbending in the defense of that which they think right.

"Yours is the insult," Garth shouted. "The incredible egotism to feel that your derivative little mythology, differing only slightly from the thousands of others that still burden men, can do anything but confuse their still fresh minds. Don't you realise that they believe in truth—and have never heard of such a thing as a lie. They have not been trained yet to understand that other kinds of minds can think differently from theirs. Will you spare them this . . . ?"

"I will do my duty which is His will, Mr. Garth. These are God's creatures here, and they have souls. I cannot shirk my duty, which is to bring them His word so that they may be saved and enter into the kingdom of heaven."

When the priest opened the door the wind caught it and blew it wide. He vanished into the storm-swept darkness and the door swung back and forth and a splatter of raindrops blew in. Garth's boots left muddy footprints when he closed the door, shutting out the sight of Itin sitting patiently and uncomplaining in the storm, hoping only that Garth might stop for a moment and leave with him some of the wonderful knowledge of which he had so much.

By unspoken consent that first night was never mentioned again. After a few days of loneliness, made worse because each knew of the other's proximity, they found themselves talking on carefully neutral grounds. Garth slowly packed and stowed away his stock and never admitted that his work was finished and he could leave at any time.

He had a fair amount of interesting drugs and botanicals that would fetch a good price. And the Wesker artefacts were sure to create a sensation in the sophisticated galactic market. Crafts on the planet here had been limited before his arrival, mostly pieces of carving painfully chipped into the hard wood with fragments of stone. He had supplied tools and a stock of raw metal from his own supplies, nothing more than that. In a few months the Weskers had not only learned to work with the new materials, but had translated their own designs and forms into the most alien—but most beautiful—artefacts that he had ever seen. All he had to do was release these on the market to create a primary demand, then return for a new supply. The Weskers wanted only books and tools and knowledge in return, and through their own efforts he knew they would pull themselves into the galactic union.

This is what Garth had hoped. But a wind of change was blowing through the settlement that had grown up around his ship. No longer was he the center of attention and focal point of the village life. He had to grin when he thought of his fall from power; yet there was very little humor in the smile. Serious and attentive Weskers still took turns of duty as Knowledge Collectors, but their recording of dry facts was in sharp contrast to the intellectual hurricane that surrounded the priest.

Where Garth had made them work for each book and machine, the priest gave freely. Garth had tried to be progressive in his supply of knowledge, treating them as bright but unlettered children. He had wanted them to walk before they could run, to master one step before going on to the next.

Father Mark simply brought them the benefits of Christianity. The only physical work he required was the construction of a church, a place of worship and learning. More Weskers had appeared out of the limitless planetary swamps and within days the roof was up, supported on a framework of poles. Each morning the congregation worked a little while on the walls, then hurried inside to learn the all–promising, all–encompassing, all–important facts about the universe.

Garth never told the Weskers what he thought about their new interest, and this was mainly because they had never asked him. Pride or honor stood in the way of his grabbing a willing listener and pouring out his grievances. Perhaps it would have been different if Itin was on Collecting duty; he was the brightest of the lot, but Itin had been rotated the day after the priest had arrived and Garth had not talked to him since.

It was a surprise then when after seventeen of the trebly-long Wesker days, he found a delegation at his doorstep when he emerged after breakfast. Itin was their spokesman, and his mouth was open slightly. Many of the other Weskers had their mouths open as well, one even appearing to be yawning, clearly revealing the double row of sharp teeth and the purple-black throat. The mouths impressed Garth as to the seriousness of the meeting: this was the one Wesker expression he had learned to recognise. An open mouth indicated some strong emotion; happiness, sadness, anger, he could never be really sure which. The Weskers were normally placid and he had never seen enough open mouths to tell what was causing them. But he was surrounded by them now.

"Will you help us, Garth," Itin said. "We have a question."

"I'll answer any questions you ask," Garth said, with more than a hint of misgiving. "What is it?"

"Is there a God?"

"What do you mean by 'God'?" Garth asked in turn. What should he tell them? What had been going on in their minds that they should come to him with this question?

"God is our Father in Heaven, who made us all and protects us. Whom we pray to for aid, and if we are Saved will find a place . . ."

"That's enough," Garth said. "There is no God."

All of them had their mouths open now, even Itin, as they looked at Garth and thought about his answer. The rows of pink teeth would have been frightening if he hadn't known these creatures so well. For one instant he wondered if perhaps they had been already indoctrinated and looked upon him as a heretic, but he brushed the thought away.

"Thank you," Itin said, and they turned and left.

Though the morning was still cool, Garth noticed that he was sweating and wondered why.

The reaction was not long in coming. Itin returned that same afternoon. "Will you come to the church?" he asked. "Many of the things that we study are difficult to learn, but none as difficult as this. We need your help because we must hear you and Father Mark talk together. This is because he says one thing is true and you say another is true and both cannot be true at the same time. We must find out what is true."

"I'll come, of course," Garth said, trying to hide the sudden feeling of elation. He had done nothing, but the Weskers had come to him anyway. There could still be grounds for hope that they might yet be free.

It was hot inside the church, and Garth was surprised at the number of Weskers who were there, more than he had seen gathered at any one time before. There were many open mouths. Father Mark sat at a table covered with books. He looked unhappy but didn't say anything when Garth came in. Garth spoke first.

"I hope you realise this is their idea—that they came to me of their own free will and asked me to come here?"

"I know that," the priest said resignedly. "At times they can be very difficult. But they are learning and want to believe, and that is what is important."

"Father Mark, Trader Garth, we need your help," Itin said. "You both know many things that we do not know. You must help us come to religion, which is not an easy thing to do." Garth started to say something, then changed his mind. Itin went on. "We have read the Bibles and all the books that Father Mark gave us, and one thing is clear. We have discussed this and we are all agreed. These books are very different from the ones that Trader Garth gave us. In Trader Garth's books there is the universe, which we have not seen, and it goes on without God, for He is mentioned nowhere, we have searched very carefully. In Father Mark's books He is everywhere and nothing can go without Him. One of these must be right and the other must be wrong. We do not know how this can be, but after we find out which is right then perhaps we will know. If God does not exist . . ."

"Of course He exists, my children," Father Mark said in a voice of heartfelt intensity. "He is our Father in Heaven who has created us all . . ."

"Who created God?" Itin asked and the murmur ceased and every one of the Weskers watched Father Mark intensely. He recoiled a bit under the impact of their eyes, then smiled.

"Nothing created God, since He is the Creator. He always was . . ."

"If He always was in existence—why cannot the universe have always been in existence? Without having had a creator?" Itin broke in with a rush of words. The importance of the question was obvious. The priest answered slowly, with infinite patience.

"Would that the answers were that simple, my children. But even the scientists do not agree about the creation of the universe. While they doubt—we who have seen the light *know*. We can see the miracle of creation all about us. And how can there be a creation without a Creator? That is He, Our Father, Our God in Heaven. I know you have doubts and that is because you have souls and free will. Still the answer is simple. Have faith, that is all you need. Just believe."

"How can we believe without proof?"

"If you cannot see that this world itself is proof of His existence, then I say to you that belief needs no proof—if you have faith!"

A babble of voices arose in the room and more of the Wesker mouths were open now as they tried to force their thoughts through the tangled skein of words and separate the thread of truth.

"Can you tell us, Garth?" Itin asked, and the sound of his voice quieted the hubbub.

"I can tell you to use the scientific method, which can examine all things—including itself—and give you answers that can prove the truth or falsity of any statement."

"That is what we must do," Itin said. "We had reached the same conclusion." He held a thick book before him and a ripple of nods ran across the watchers. "We have been studying the Bible as Father Mark told us to do, and we have found the answer. God will make a miracle for us, thereby proving that He is watching us. And by this sign we will know Him and go to Him."

"This is a sign of false pride," Father Mark said. "God needs no miracles to prove His existence."

"But *we* need a miracle!" Itin shouted, and though he wasn't human there was still the cry of need in his voice. "We have read here of many smaller miracles, loaves, fishes, wine, snakes—many of them, for much smaller reasons. Now all He need do is make a miracle and He will bring us all to Him—the wonder of an entire new world worshipping at His throne, as you have told us, Father Mark. And you have told us how important this is. We have discussed this and find that there is only one miracle that is best for this kind of thing."

His boredom and amused interest in the incessant theological wrangling drained from Garth in an instant. He had not been really thinking or he would have realised where all this was leading. By turning slightly he could see the illustration in the Bible where Itin held it open, and knew in advance what picture it was. He rose slowly from his chair, as if stretching, and turned to the priest behind him.

"Get ready!" he whispered. "Get out the back and get to the ship, I'll keep them busy here. I don't think they'll harm—"

"What do you mean . . . ?" Father Mark asked, blinking in surprise.

"Get out, you fool!" Garth hissed. "What miracle do you think they mean? What miracle is supposed to have converted the world to Christianity?"

"No!" Father Mark said. "It cannot be. It just cannot—"

"GET MOVING!" Garth shouted, dragging the priest from the chair and hurling him towards the rear wall. Father Mark stumbled to a halt, turned back. Garth leaped for him, but it was already too late. The amphibians were small, but there were so many of them. Garth lashed out and his fist struck Itin, hurling him back into the crowd. The others came on as he fought his way towards the priest. He beat at them but it was like struggling against the waves. The furry, musky bodies washed over and engulfed him. He struggled until they tied him, and he still struggled until they beat on his head until he stopped. Then they pulled him outside, where he could only lie in the rain and curse and watch.

Of course the Weskers were marvellous craftsmen, and everything had been constructed down to the last detail, following the illustration in the Bible. There was the cross, planted firmly on the top of a small hill, the gleaming metal spikes, the hammer. Father Mark was stripped and draped in a carefully pleated loincloth. They led him out of the church and at the sight of the cross he almost fainted. After that he held his head high and determined to die as he had lived, with faith.

Yet this was hard. It was unbearable even for Garth who only watched. It is one thing to talk of crucifixion and look at the gentle carved bodies in the dim light of prayer. It is another to see a man naked, ropes cutting into his skin where he hangs from a bar of wood. And to see the needle-tipped spike raised and placed against the soft flesh of his palm, to see the hammer come back with the calm deliberation of an artisan's measured stroke. To hear the thick sound of metal penetrating flesh.

Then to hear the screams.

Few are born to be martyrs and Father Mark was not one of them. With the first blows, the blood ran from his lips where his clenched teeth met. Then his mouth was wide and his head strained back and the awful guttural horror of his screams sliced through the susurration of the falling rain. It resounded as a silent echo from the masses of watching Weskers, for whatever emotion opened their mouths was now tearing at their bodies with all its force, and row after row of gaping jaws reflected the crucified priest's agony.

Mercifully he fainted as the last nail was driven home. Blood ran from the raw wounds, mixing with the rain to drip faintly pink from his feet as the life ran out of him. At this time, somewhere at this time, sobbing and tearing at his own bonds, numbed from the blows on the head, Garth lost consciousness.

He awoke in his own warehouse and it was dark. Someone was cutting away the woven ropes they had bound him with. The rain still dripped and splashed outside.

"Itin," he said. It could be no one else.

"Yes," the alien voice whispered back. "The others are all talking in the church. Lin died after you struck his head, and Inon is very sick. There are some that say you should be crucified too, and I think that is what will happen. Or perhaps killed by stoning on the head. They have found in the Bible where it says . . ."

"I know." With infinite weariness. "An eye for an eye. You'll find lots of things like that once you start looking."

"You must go, you can get to your ship without anyone seeing you. There has been enough killing." Itin as well spoke with a newfound weariness.

Garth experimented, pulling himself to his feet. He pressed his head to the rough wall until the nausea stopped.

"He's dead." He said it as a statement, not a question.

"Yes, some time ago. Or I could not have come away to see you."

"And buried of course, or they wouldn't be thinking about starting on me next."

"And buried!" There was almost a ring of emotion in the alien's voice, an echo of the dead priest's. "He is buried and he will rise on High. It is written and that is the way it will happen. Father Mark will be so happy that it has happened like this." The voice ended in a sound like a human sob, but of course it couldn't have been that since Itin was alien, and not human at all. Garth painfully worked his way towards the door, leaning against the wall so he wouldn't fall.

"We did the right thing, didn't we?" Itin asked. There was no answer. "He will rise up, Garth, won't he rise?"

Garth was at the door and enough light came from the brightly lit church to show his torn and bloody hands clutching at the frame. Itin's face swam into sight close to his, and Garth felt the delicate, many-fingered hands with the sharp nails catch at his clothes.

"He will rise, won't he, Garth?"

"No," Garth said, "he is going to stay buried right where you put him. Nothing is going to happen because he is dead and he is going to stay dead."

The rain runnelled through Itin's fur and his mouth was opened so wide that he seemed to be screaming into the night. Only with effort could he talk, squeezing out the alien thoughts in an alien language.

"Then we will not be saved? We will not become pure?"

"You were pure," Garth said, in a voice somewhere between a sob and a laugh. "That's the horrible ugly dirty part of it. You were pure. Now you are . . ."

"Murderers," Itin said, and the water ran down from his lowered head and streamed away into the darkness.

THE SFWA AUTHOR EMERITUS

SFWA inaugurated the Author Emeritus program in 1995 to recognize and appreciate senior writers in the genres of science fiction and fantasy who have made significant contributions to our field but who are no longer active or whose excellent work is no longer as well known as it once was. Fiction by the first five authors emeriti is collected in *Architects of Dreams*. The 2009 Author Emerita is M. J. Engh.

2008 NEBULA AWARDS

Best Novel: *Powers* by Ursula K. Le Guin

Best Novella: *The Spacetime Pool* by Catherine Asaro

Best Novelette: "Pride and Prometheus" by John Kessel

Best Short Story: "Trophy Wives" by Nina Kiriki Hoffman

Best Script: *WALL-E* Screenplay by Andrew Stanton, Jim Reardon, Original story by Andrew Stanton, Pete Docter

Andre Norton Award: *Flora's Dare: How a Girl of Spirit Gambles All to Expand Her Vocabulary, Confront a Bouncing Boy Terror, and Try to Save Califa from a Shaky Doom (Despite Being Confined to Her Room)* by Ysabeau S. Wilce

Solstice Award: Kate Wilhelm, Algis Budrys, and Martin H. Greenberg

SFWA Service Award: Victoria Strauss

Bradbury Award: Joss Whedon

Grand Master Award: Harry Harrison

Author Emerita: M. J. Engh

2007 NEBULA AWARDS

Best Novel: *The Yiddish Policeman's Union* by Michael Chabon

Best Novella: *Fountain of Age* by Nancy Kress

Best Novelette: "The Merchant and the Alchemist's Gate" by Ted Chiang

Best Short Story: "Always" by Karen Joy Fowler

Best Script: *Pan's Labyrinth* by Guillermo del Toro

Andre Norton Award: *Harry Potter & the Deathly Hallows* by J. K. Rowling

Grand Master: Michael Moorcock

Author Emeritus: Ardath Mayhar

SFWA Service Award: Melisa Michaels and Graham P. Collins

2006 NEBULA AWARDS

Best Novel: *Seeker* by Jack McDevitt

Best Novella: *Burn* by James Patrick Kelly

Best Novelette: "Two Hearts" by Peter S. Beagle

Best Short Story: "Echo" by Elizabeth Hand

Best Script: *Howl's Moving Castle* by Hayao Miyazaki, Cindy Davis Hewitt, and Donald H. Hewitt

Andre Norton Award: *Magic or Madness* by Justine Larbalestier

Grand Master: James Gunn

Author Emeritus: D. G. Compton

SFWA Service Award: Brook West and Julia West jointly

2005 NEBULA AWARDS

Best Novel: *Camouflage* by Joe Haldeman

Best Novella: *Magic for Beginners* by Kelly Link

Best Novelette: "The Faery Handbag" by Kelly Link

Best Short Story: "I Live with You" by Carol Emshwiller

Best Script: *Serenity* by Joss Whedon

Andre Norton Award: *Valiant: A Modern Tale of Faerie*, by Holly Black

Grand Master: Harlan Ellison

Author Emeritus: William F. Nolan

2004 NEBULA AWARDS

Best Novel: *Paladin of Souls*, by Lois McMaster Bujold

Best Novella: *The Green Leopard Plague* by Walter Jon Williams

Best Novelette: "Basement Magic" by Ellen Klages

Best Short Story: "Coming to Terms" by Eileen Gunn

Best Script: *The Lord of the Rings—The Return of the King* by Fran Walsh and Philippa Boyens and Peter Jackson; based on *The Lord of the Rings* by J. R. R. Tolkien

Grand Master: Anne McCaffrey

Service to SFWA Award: Kevin O'Donnell Jr.

2003 NEBULA AWARDS

Best Novel: *The Speed of Dark* by Elizabeth Moon

Best Novella: *Coraline* by Neil Gaiman

Best Novelette: "The Empire of Ice Cream" by Jeffrey Ford

Best Short Story: "What I Didn't See" by Karen Joy Fowler

Best Script: *The Lord of the Rings—The Two Towers* by Fran Walsh and Philippa Boyens and Stephen Sinclair and Peter Jackson; based on *The Lord of the Rings* by J. R. R. Tolkien

Grand Master: Robert Silverberg

Author of Distinction: Charles Harness

Service to SFWA Award: Michael Capobianco and Ann Crispin jointly

2002 NEBULA AWARDS

Best Novel: *American Gods: A Novel* by Neil Gaiman

Best Novella: *Bronte's Egg* by Richard Chwedyk

Best Novelette: "Hell Is the Absence of God" by Ted Chiang

Best Short Story: "Creature" by Carol Emshwiller

Best Script: *The Lord of the Rings—The Fellowship of the Ring* by Fran Walsh and Philippa Boyens and Peter Jackson; based on *The Lord of the Rings* by J. R. R. Tolkien

Grand Master: Ursula K. Le Guin

Author Emeritus: Katherine MacLean

2001 NEBULA AWARDS

Best Novel: *The Quantum Rose* by Catherine Asaro

Best Novella: *The Ultimate Earth* by Jack Williamson

Best Novelette: "Louise's Ghost" by Kelly Link

Best Short Story: "The Cure for Everything" by Severna Park

Best Script: *Crouching Tiger, Hidden Dragon* by James Schamus, Kuo Jung Tsai, and Hui-Ling Wang; from the book by Du Lu Wang

President's Award: Betty Ballantine

2000 NEBULA AWARDS

Best Novel: *Darwin's Radio* by Greg Bear

Best Novella: *Goddesses* by Linda Nagata

Best Novelette: "Daddy's World" by Walter Jon Williams

Best Short Story: "macs" by Terry Bisson

Best Script: *Galaxy Quest* by Robert Gordon and David Howard

Grand Master: Philip José Farmer

Bradbury Award: Yuri Rasovsky and Harlan Ellison, *2000X—Tales of the Next Millennia*

Author Emeritus: Robert Sheckley

1999 NEBULA AWARDS

Best Novel: *Parable of the Talents* by Octavia E. Butler

Best Novella: *Story of Your Life* by Ted Chiang

Best Novelette: "Mars Is No Place for Children" by Mary A. Turzillo

Best Short Story: "The Cost of Doing Business" by Leslie What

Best Script: *The Sixth Sense* by M. Night Shyamalan

Grand Master: Brian W. Aldiss

Author Emeritus: Daniel Keyes

Service to SFWA Award: George Zebrowski and Pamela Sargent jointly

1998 NEBULA AWARDS

Best Novel: *Forever Peace* by Joe Haldeman

Best Novella: *Reading the Bones* by Sheila Finch

Best Novelette: "Lost Girls" by Jane Yolen

Best Short Story: "Thirteen Ways to Water" by Bruce Holland Rogers

Grand Master: Hal Clement (Harry Stubbs)

Bradbury Award: J. Michael Straczynski, *Babylon 5*

Author Emeritus: William Tenn (Phil Klass)

1997 NEBULA AWARDS

Best Novel: *The Moon and the Sun* by Vonda N. McIntyre

Best Novella: *Abandon in Place* by Jerry Oltion

Best Novelette: "The Flowers of Aulit Prison" by Nancy Kress

Best Short Story: "Sister Emily's Lightship" by Jane Yolen

Grand Master: Poul Anderson

Author Emeritus: Nelson Slade Bond

Service to SFWA Award: Robin Wayne Bailey

1996 NEBULA AWARDS

Best Novel: *Slow River* by Nicola Griffith

Best Novella: *Da Vinci Rising* by Jack Dann

Best Novelette: "Lifeboat on a Burning Sea" by Bruce Holland Rogers

Best Short Story: "A Birthday" by Esther M. Friesner

Grand Master: Jack Vance

Author Emeritus: Judith Merril

Service to SFWA Award: Sheila Finch

1995 NEBULA AWARDS

Best Novel: *The Terminal Experiment* by Robert J. Sawyer

Best Novella: *Last Summer at Mars Hill* by Elizabeth Hand

Best Novelette: "Solitude" by Ursula K. Le Guin

Best Short Story: "Death and the Librarian" by Esther Friesner

Grand Master: A. E. van Vogt

Author Emeritus: Wilson "Bob" Tucker

Service to SFWA Award: Chuq Von Rospach

1994 NEBULA AWARDS

Best Novel: *Moving Mars: A Novel* by Greg Bear

Best Novella: *Seven Views of Olduvai Gorge* by Mike Resnick

Best Novelette: "The Martian Child" by David Gerrold

Best Short Story: "A Defense of the Social Contracts" by Martha Soukup

Grand Master: Damon Knight

Author Emeritus: Emil Petaja

1993 NEBULA AWARDS

Best Novel: *Red Mars* by Kim Stanley Robinson

Best Novella: *The Night We Buried Road Dog* by Jack Cady

Best Novelette: "Georgia on My Mind" by Charles
Sheffield

Best Short Story: "Graves" by Joe Haldeman

1992 NEBULA AWARDS

Best Novel: *Doomsday Book* by Connie Willis

Best Novella: *City of Truth* by James Morrow

Best Novelette: "Danny Goes to Mars" by Pamela
Sargent

Best Short Story: "Even the Queen" by Connie Willis

Grand Master: Frederik Pohl

1991 NEBULA AWARDS

Best Novel: *Stations of the Tide* by Michael Swanwick

Best Novella: *Beggars in Spain* by Nancy Kress

Best Novelette: "Guide Dog" by Mike Conner

Best Short Story: "Ma Qui" by Alan Brennert

Bradbury Award: James Cameron, *Terminator 2—-
Judgment Day*

1990 NEBULA AWARDS

Best Novel: *Tehanu: The Last Book of Earthsea* by Ursula
K. Le Guin

Best Novella: *The Hemingway Hoax* by Joe Haldeman

Best Novelette: "Tower of Babylon" by Ted Chiang

Best Short Story: "Bears Discover Fire" by Terry Bisson

Grand Master: Lester del Rey

1989 NEBULA AWARDS

Best Novel: *Healer's War* by Elizabeth Ann Scarborough

Best Novella: *The Mountains of Mourning* by Lois Mc-
Master Bujold

Best Novelette: "At the Rialto" by Connie Willis

Best Short Story: "Ripples in the Dirac Sea" by Geoffrey
Landis

1988 NEBULA AWARDS

Best Novel: *Falling Free* by Lois McMaster Bujold

Best Novella: *The Last of the Winnebagos* by Connie Willis

Best Novelette: "Schrodinger's Kitten" by George Alec Effinger

Best Short Story: "Bible Stories for Adults, No. 17: The Deluge" by James Morrow

Grand Master: Ray Bradbury

1987 NEBULA AWARDS

Best Novel: *The Falling Woman* by Pat Murphy

Best Novella: *The Blind Geometer* by Kim Stanley Robinson

Best Novelette: "Rachel in Love" by Pat Murphy

Best Short Story: "Forever Yours, Anna" by Kate Wilhelm

Grand Master: Alfred Bester

1986 NEBULA AWARDS

Best Novel: *Speaker for the Dead* by Orson Scott Card

Best Novella: *R&R* by Lucius Shepard

Best Novelette: "The Girl Who Fell Into the Sky" by Kate Wilhelm

Best Short Story: "Tangents" by Greg Bear

Grand Master: Isaac Asimov

1985 NEBULA AWARDS

Best Novel: *Ender's Game* by Orson Scott Card

Best Novella: *Sailing to Byzantium* by Robert Silverberg

Best Novelette: "Portraits of His Children" by George R.R. Martin

Best Short Story: "Out of All Them Bright Stars" by Nancy Kress

Grand Master: Arthur C. Clarke

1984 NEBULA AWARDS

Best Novel: *Neuromancer* by William Gibson
Best Novella: *Press Enter* by John Varley
Best Novelette: "Bloodchild" by Octavia Butler
Best Short Story: "Morning Child" by Gardner Dozois

1983 NEBULA AWARDS

Best Novel: *Startide Rising* by David Brin
Best Novella: *Hardfought* by Greg Bear
Best Novelette: "Blood Music" by Greg Bear
Best Short Story: "The Peacemaker" by Gardner
Dozois
Grand Master: Andre Norton

1982 NEBULA AWARDS

Best Novel: *No Enemy But Time* by Michael Bishop
Best Novella: *Another Orphan* by John Kessel
Best Novelette: "Fire Watch" by Connie Willis
Best Short Story: "A Letter from the Clearys" by
Connie Willis

1981 NEBULA AWARDS

Best Novel: *Claw of the Conciliator* by Gene Wolfe
Best Novella: *The Saturn Game* by Poul Anderson
Best Novelette: "The Quickening" by Michael Bishop
Best Short Story: "The Bone Flute" by Lisa Tuttle
(Ms. Tuttle declined the Award)

1980 NEBULA AWARDS

Best Novel: *Timescape* by Gregory Benford
Best Novella: *The Unicorn Tapestry* by Suzy McKee
Charnas
Best Novelette: "The Ugly Chickens" by Howard
Waldrop

Best Short Story: "Grotto of the Dancing Bear" by
   Clifford D. Simak
Grand Master: Fritz Leiber

1979 NEBULA AWARDS

Best Novel: *The Fountains of Paradise* by Arthur C. Clarke
Best Novella: *Enemy Mine* by Barry Longyear
Best Novelette: "Sandkings" by George R. R. Martin
Best Short Story: "giAnts" by Edward Bryant

1978 NEBULA AWARDS

Best Novel: *Dreamsnake* by Vonda N. McIntyre
Best Novella: *The Persistence of Vision* by John Varley
Best Novelette: "A Glow of Candles, a Unicorn's Eye"
   by Charles L. Grant
Best Short Story: "Stone" by Edward Bryant
Grand Master: L. Sprague de Camp

1977 NEBULA AWARDS

Best Novel: *Gateway* by Frederik Pohl
Best Novella: *Stardance* by Spider and Jeanne Robinson
Best Novelette: "The Screwfly Solution" by Raccoona
   Sheldon
Best Short Story: "Jeffty Is Five" by Harlan Ellison
Special Award: *Star Wars*

1976 NEBULA AWARDS

Best Novel: *Man Plus* by Frederik Pohl
Best Novella: *Houston, Houston, Do You Read?* by James
   Tiptree, Jr.
Best Novelette: "The Bicentennial Man" by Isaac
   Asimov
Best Short Story: "A Crowd of Shadows" by Charles L.
   Grant
Grand Master: Clifford D. Simak

1975 NEBULA AWARDS

Best Novel: *The Forever War* by Joe Haldeman

Best Novella: *Home Is the Hangman* by Roger Zelazny

Best Novelette: "San Diego Lightfoot Sue" by Tom Reamy

Best Short Story: "Catch that Zeppelin!" by Fritz Leiber

Best Dramatic Writing: Mel Brooks and Gene Wilder for *Young Frankenstein*

Grand Master: Jack Williamson

1974 NEBULA AWARDS

Best Novel: *The Dispossessed* by Ursula K. Le Guin

Best Novella: *Born with the Dead* by Robert Silverberg

Best Novelette: "If the Stars Are Gods" by Gordon R. Eklund and Gregory Benford

Best Short Story: "The Day Before the Revolution" by Ursula K. Le Guin

Best Dramatic Presentation: *Sleeper* by Woody Allen

Grand Master: Robert A. Heinlein

1973 NEBULA AWARDS

Best Novel: *Rendezvous with Rama* by Arthur C. Clarke

Best Novella: *The Death of Doctor Island* by Gene Wolfe

Best Novelette: "Of Mist, and Grass, and Sand" by Vonda N. McIntyre

Best Short Story: "Love Is the Plan, the Plan Is Death" by James Tiptree, Jr.

Best Dramatic Presentation: *Soylent Green*

Stanley R. Greenberg for Screenplay (based on the novel *Make Room! Make Room!*)

Harry Harrison for *Make Room! Make Room!*

1972 NEBULA AWARDS

Best Novel: *The Gods Themselves* by Isaac Asimov

Best Novella: *A Meeting with Medusa* by Arthur C. Clarke

Best Novelette: "Goat Song" by Poul Anderson

Best Short Story: "When It Changed" by Joanna Russ

1971 NEBULA AWARDS

Best Novel: *A Time of Changes (Berkley Book: Science Fiction)* by Robert Silverberg

Best Novella: *The Missing Man* by Katherine MacLean

Best Novelette: "The Queen of Air and Darkness" by Poul Anderson

Best Short Story: "Good News from the Vatican" by Robert Silverberg

1970 NEBULA AWARDS

Best Novel: *Ringworld* by Larry Niven

Best Novella: *Ill Met in Lankhmar* by Fritz Leiber

Best Novelette: "Slow Sculpture" by Theodore Sturgeon

Best Short Story: None

1969 NEBULA AWARDS

Best Novel: *The Left Hand of Darkness* by Ursula K. Le Guin

Best Novella: *A Boy and His Dog* by Harlan Ellison

Best Novelette: "Time Considered as a Helix of Semi-Precious Stones" by Samuel R. Delany

Best Short Story: "Passengers" by Robert Silverberg

1968 NEBULA AWARDS

Best Novel: *Rite of Passage* by Alexei Panshin

Best Novella: *Dragonrider* by Anne McCaffrey

Best Novelette: "Mother to the World" by Richard Wilson

Best Short Story: "The Planners" by Kate Wilhelm

1967 NEBULA AWARDS

Best Novel: *The Einstein Intersection* by Samuel R. Delany

Best Novella: *Behold the Man* by Michael Moorcock

Best Novelette: "Gonna Roll the Bones" by Fritz Leiber
Best Short Story: "Aye, and Gomorrah" by Samuel R. Delany

1966 NEBULA AWARDS
Best Novel:
Flowers for Algernon by Daniel Keyes
Babel-17 by Samuel Delany
Best Novella: *The Last Castle* by Jack Vance
Best Novelette: "Call Him Lord" by Gordon R. Dickson
Best Short Story: "The Secret Place" by Richard McKenna

1965 NEBULA AWARDS
Best Novel: *Dune* by Frank Herbert
Best Novella: *The Saliva Tree* by Brain W. Aldiss
Best Novelette: "The Doors of His Face, the Lamps of His Mouth" by Roger Zelazny
Best Short Story: "'Repent, Harlequin!' Said the Ticktockman" by Harlan Ellison